PRAISE FOR J'NELL CIESIELSKI

"*To Free the Stars* is a fast-paced, thrill ride of a spy novel, tempered by moments of profound tenderness and emotion. J'nell Ciesielski writes with energy and passion, bringing brilliant life to two dynamic characters battling extremes on every front. A star-bright story of perseverance, devotion, and above all, love."

—MIMI MATTHEWS, *USA TODAY* BESTSELLING AUTHOR OF *THE BELLE OF BELGRAVE SQUARE*

"*To Free the Stars* is a perfect conclusion to Ciesielski's epic duology. Full of action, drama, and romance, Ciesielski offers a masterfully detailed roller coaster of a ride that leaves the reader—after a long-held breath—releasing a satisfying sigh. Fantastic from start to finish!"

—KATHERINE REAY, BESTSELLING AUTHOR OF *A SHADOW IN MOSCOW*

"*To Free the Stars* is Captain America meets *The Alice Network* in this final unforgettable installment in the Jack & Ivy series. A sweeping romance comes alongside an intense adrenaline-inducing mission around the world to create a story that will steal your heart from the first page. As Jack and Ivy fight for peace and each other, a most important truth emerges clearly—that war may wrap its evil tentacles around our necks, and peril may meet us at every breath, and memory may fail. Even so, love WILL remain."

—JOY CALLAWAY, INTERNATIONAL BESTSELLING AUTHOR OF *ALL THE PRETTY PLACES*

"I love a heroine who can beat the men in hand-to-hand combat, and Ivy is the best! This is a fast-paced, unputdownable adventure story with a strong emotional core."

—GILL PAUL, *USA TODAY* BESTSELLING AUTHOR OF *THE MANHATTAN GIRLS*

D0180350

"From thrilling fight scenes to tender romance, *To Free the Stars* races off the page, dropping readers into the middle of a desperate fight between good and evil set against the glamor and danger of the Roaring Twenties. You won't be able to put this one down!"

—Julia Kelly, international bestselling author of *The Last Garden in England* and *The Lost English Girl*

"Ciesielski starts off her new series with a kiss and a bang, and neither the romance nor action slows down from there."

—*Library Journal*, starred review, for *The Brilliance of Stars*

"Ciesielski launches her Jack and Ivy duology with this captivating and immersive tale of espionage and romance amid the dangers of World War I."

—*Publishers Weekly* for *The Brilliance of Stars*

"An epic, Bond-style tale set during the First World War, *The Brilliance of Stars* grips the reader from the first page. With mesmeric settings, nonstop action, and witty dialogue, Ciesielski crafts a thrilling love story of powerful equals working tirelessly to save the world from darkness."

—Erika Robuck, national bestselling author of *Sisters of Night and Fog*

"Action! Romance! Spies! Secrets! *The Brilliance of Stars* has it all. This electrifying read from J'nell Ciesielski comes to life with historical details and sparkling descriptions that will leave the reader begging for book two!"

—Amy E. Reichert, author of *Once Upon a December*

"Excuse me while I go read *The Brilliance of Stars* by J'nell Ciesielski a second time. The intrigue of master assassins, a secret society, a cat-and-mouse game, all while the world is teeming with tension from the Russian Revolution and the First World War. Not to mention while Jack and Ivy are falling in love. Who knew a grenade pin could be so romantic? This thrilling historical novel has it all, and I look forward to more 'Jack and Ivy.'"

—Jenni L. Walsh, author of *Becoming Bonnie* and *The Call of the Wrens*

"[*The Ice Swan*] is well written, with superb similes and metaphors. Highly recommended."

—Historical Novel Society

"Ciesielski delivers an intense love story set during World War I. Fans of historical romance should snap this up."

—Publishers Weekly for The Ice Swan

"A Scottish lord and an American socialite discover love during World War I in this gorgeous historical romance from Ciesielski . . . The undercurrent of mystery and Ciesielski's unflinching approach to the harsh realities of wartime only enhance the love story. Readers are sure to be impressed."

—Publishers Weekly, starred review, for Beauty Among Ruins

"Beauty Among Ruins is an atmospheric, engrossing romance for fans of Downton Abbey and Somewhere in France. A real gem!"

—Aimie K. Runyan, internationally bestselling author

"Ciesielski has created a fresh and original tale in this inspiring World War I romance about a dour Scottish laird and an American socialite."

—Tea Cooper, author of The Fossil Hunter, for Beauty Among Ruins

"With sweeping romance and evocative prose, Ciesielski transports readers to World War II–era Paris, where a British aristocrat loses her heart to a Scottish spy . . . Ciesielski's vivid characterizations and lush historical detail quickly draw readers into this expertly plotted tale. Readers looking for an immersive, high-stakes historical romance will be wowed."

—Publishers Weekly, starred review, for The Socialite

"Smart, savvy, and seductive, The Socialite shines bright as the City of Light and then some!"

—Kristy Cambron, bestselling author of The Italian Ballerina

"In the tradition of Ariel Lawhon and Kate Quinn, The Socialite immerses readers in the glamour and destruction of Nazi-occupied Paris. This impeccably researched love story stands out in a sea of World War II–era fiction with its distinctive crystalline voice and unforgettable hero and heroine."

—Rachel McMillan, author of The Mozart Code

"Readers will devour each moment leading up to the satisfying ending."

—Publishers Weekly, starred review, for The Songbird and the Spy

"The Songbird and the Spy is a must-read!"

—Kate Breslin, bestselling author

TO FREE
THE STARS

ALSO BY J'NELL CIESIELSKI

TO FREE THE STARS

A Jack and Ivy Novel

J'NELL CIESIELSKI

THOMAS NELSON
Since 1798

To Free the Stars

Copyright © 2023 J'nell Ciesielski

Published in Nashville, Tennessee, by Thomas Nelson. Thomas Nelson is a registered trademark of HarperCollins Christian Publishing, Inc.

Interior design by Phoebe Wetherbee

Map by Matthew Covington

Amil, Segovia. "Warrior." Pinterest image, January 19, 2023, https://www.pinterest.com/pin/561964859747835488/. Printed by permission.

Selden, Edgar and Herbert Ingraham. "All That I Ask of You Is Love." New York: Shapiro Music Publisher, 1910. Song lyrics. Public Domain.

Thomas Nelson titles may be purchased in bulk for educational, business, fundraising, or sales promotional use. For information, please email SpecialMarkets@ThomasNelson.com.

Library of Congress Cataloging-in-Publication Data

Names: Ciesielski, J'nell, author.
Title: To free the stars / J'nell Ciesielski.
Description: Nashville, Tennessee : Thomas Nelson, [2023] | Series: A Jack and Ivy Novel ; 2 | Summary: "Completing the epic duology from bestselling author J'nell Ciesielski, To Free the Stars incorporates her signature blend of thrilling adventure, glamorous espionage, and sweeping romance"-- Provided by publisher.
Identifiers: LCCN 2023003924 (print) | LCCN 2023003925 (ebook) | ISBN 9780785248484 (paperback) | ISBN 9780785248491 (epub) | ISBN 9780785248507 (audio download)
Subjects: LCGFT: Romance fiction. | Action and adventure fiction. | Novels.
Classification: LCC PS3603.I33 F74 2023 (print) | LCC PS3603.I33 (ebook) | DDC 813/.6--dc23/eng/20230206
LC record available at https://lccn.loc.gov/2023003924
LC ebook record available at https://lccn.loc.gov/2023003925

Printed in the United States of America

23 24 25 26 27 LBC 6 5 4 3 2

To the romantics, the adventure seekers,
and the book nerds. I salute you.

Show me a hero and I will write you a tragedy.

—F. Scott Fitzgerald

THE FALL

THE EARTH WAS COLD, FROZEN, AND SLICK. SNOW BILLOWED FROM THE mountains, drowning the early morning light to dull lead. Ivy struggled to her feet after a restless night on the unforgiving ground sheltered by the fortress's ominous stone walls. Her body ached in places she hadn't known existed, not to mention her broken ribs thanks to that brute. She got her own, though, when she stabbed him in the neck with her pearl hairpin.

It had been a fight to the death on the cliffside, yet the three of them resembled anything but victors. Her, broken and bruised. Jack, scratched and mangled. And Philip . . .

"Where's Philip?"

Jack looked up from cleaning his knife. "He hasn't returned since last night."

"He said he was going to look for firewood." Icy fear grabbed her by the throat. "What if something happened? Wolves—or he slipped. It was pitch dark last night and this mountainside is treacherous. We need to go look for him."

The bushes rustled. Ivy and Jack pulled their guns.

1

Philip walked out, glassy-eyed and pale.

"Where have you been? You had me worried sick." Ivy slid her gun into her belt and rushed to him, her side stitched with pain. "Are you all right?"

"Well enough." His voice was void of emotion as he pushed past her.

"You don't look so good, mate." Jack frowned and tucked Undertaker back into its holster.

Philip stared at him before blinking and casting his eyes up at the fortress walls. "It's this place. The sooner we leave the better."

"I won't argue with that," Ivy said. The place was evil. The stones seething with hate and the air spiked with poison.

Each step they took away allowed a fresh breath of relief into her lungs, yet her heart remained weighed down at the sight of Philip trudging ahead on the mountain trail, his ragged frame thin and hunched, his limbs twitching. Yet it was his eyes that worried her most. Clouded and unfocused, they seemed to trap his spirit behind a lostness.

What he'd suffered at the hands of Balaur Tsar she could not begin to imagine, but she would do everything in her power to see her dearest friend, her brother really, healed from the hell he endured while imprisoned.

Their progress was slow going down the mountain as snow continued falling. Trees curved up around them now like stalking giants. Jagged rocks poked up from the frozen ground to snag careless footsteps. And always the icy river rushed below.

Philip disappeared around a bend ahead.

"Philip, wait! We can't see you." Snow pelted Ivy's face.

"Not much farther," came his muffled reply through the trees.

"Don't rush, love." Jack's arm tightened gently around her waist. "We don't need to slip and break anything else."

She winced as his fingers grazed her side. "There is nothing left to break."

A twig snapped in the forest behind them. Then a roar split the air as a man wearing all black charged them. After knocking Ivy into a bush, he slammed into Jack and they tumbled to the ground. Jack's gun skittered across the trail.

The shiny silver of a knife flashed between them as they grappled toward the edge of the cliff. Jack rolled to his feet, but the attacker was quick and fresh, slashing his knife as Jack dodged.

"Philip!" Ivy's body screamed in agony as she struggled to her feet. Her gun—Where was her gun? Her frozen fingers fumbled for a weapon, but the dark slush made it difficult to see anything. "Philip!"

Philip rushed through the trees as Jack and the attacker skirted the edge of the cliff. He grabbed Jack's gun, raised it, and fired.

Bam! The attacker jolted, crashing into Jack.

Bam!

The man's body pitched over the ledge, his hand gripping Jack's arm.

Jack hung suspended for a moment, surprise scrawled across his face. His gaze latched onto Ivy's, and a strange numbness of déjà vu passed over her as time slowed.

One second, there he stood and her feet moved toward him, her arms outstretched.

The next, he tipped backward into open space.

Her mouth opened on a scream. And then he was gone.

She rushed forward and flung herself to the ground at the edge of the cliff. The rushing river far below flung up icy daggers, stinging the cuts on her face.

"Jack!" Her hands clawed empty air. "Jack!"

A savage cry tore through her chest, splintering her insides. She tilted forward into the yawning blackness.

"Ivy, no!" Philip clamped onto her shoulders and yanked her back. "He's gone."

THE RISER

The frozen air is black as it scratches the night. He stands on a mountain ledge that cleaves away to sheer nothingness below. Nothingness, dark and brutal, to conceal the deeds that must be done.

His eyes cut up to the inked sky pierced with thousands of tiny bright lights. The only light in this nothingness. And the light calls to him.

He reaches out a hand, splaying his cut and scarred fingers as if to grasp the bullets of light, but stops. Blood and death are carved into the grooves of his skin. One touch would stain the light, and that he cannot do. Her voice fills the silence.

My name is Death. Ancient and trembling on the tongue.

My weapon is Death. Cold and silent as the eternal tomb.

My purpose is Death. It is deliverance and torment.

Night after countless night he searches this nothingness, and for reasons he cannot understand, the call slices through skin, scar tissue, and bone to a cracked place inside him. A place where something might exist beyond the nothingness, but that something is trapped. If only he could rend it open to spill out its meaning, but the something is not like blood that spills all too easily. This something, this meaning, is a target too far out of range.

Slowly he lowers his hand, curling the hardened fingers together. He will never strike the secret hidden in the shining lights. Never know why they call to him, and yet he will continue to seek them. This he knows without doubt.

Footsteps break the quiet. "You're not supposed to be out here."

He turns toward the harsh voice, which comes from nothing more than a man wearing black with a silver crescent moon and gold star emblazoned on his chest. He takes a step toward the uniformed man, impervious to the bitter cold slashing across his face. He has learned to endure far worse.

The man reaches for the gun strapped to his side and stumbles a step back. As if this could save him. As if this gives the man a standing chance.

He stops to stare at the man, hardened fingers tense at his side. If he meant to kill, the man would be hanging from a broken neck by now. But those are not his orders. So he waits.

The man knows this and stops stumbling, though his hand remains on the gun. He, like the other men stamped with the moon and star, is trained to shoot at the first sign of insubordination, but such defiance never comes. It is against orders.

"You've a new assignment, Riser. Pack your bags. You're off to London."

Bags are for those in need of comfort. He is not allowed such things. All he requires is a target. All he is capable of is death.

The man knows this, too, and smirks despite the fear in his eyes. There is always fear.

"Get inside. She's waiting for you."

He follows the man, leaving the mountain ledge and its vale of nothingness. He casts not a parting look at the bullets of light. He looks only to what lies before him.

I am Death and I am coming.

PART 1

But now my soul hath too much room—
Gone are the glory and the gloom—
The black hath mellow'd into grey,
And all the fires are fading away.
—EDGAR ALLAN POE

ONE

FROM HER ROOFTOP PERCH HIGH ABOVE MOONLIT WHITEHALL, IVY shucked off her blood-crusted blouse and skirt and dropped them into a pile to be incinerated. The garments were beyond saving, covered in muck and grime from another successful mission.

Spain and its colonial war with northern Morocco, which the Order of the Rising Moon was using to their advantage, had been a hot, bloody affair that earned her a new scar across her shoulder from a knife. So much for wearing her new sleeveless fringed gown anytime soon. Most people were too far under the giggle water these days to notice the sun in the sky, but a jagged scar branded on a woman's skin was bound to provoke a few questions, and she'd rather not answer.

She held up her long coat and searched for more evidence. Her fellow ship passengers had stared at her for wearing such a heavy covering in the July heat, but what she wore underneath would have brought even more unwanted attention. Her travel case had been blown up when she crossed the Spanish border four days ago, and she was left with nothing but the bloody tatters on her back. The coat was mostly clean except for a few smears on the lining. Nothing a bit of

9

cold water and white vinegar couldn't clean up—a combination that had saved countless clothes from utter ruination.

She slipped into a drop-waist red-and-cream dress she'd hastily bought on her way from the docks, then bent over to roll on her stockings. A small weight gently swung from her neck.

Without need of persuasion, her fingers moved to the interlocking circles on the chain that hung around her neck. After ten years the thin metal pieces felt as natural as her own skin. Ten years and she was still filled with as much love as the day she'd made a vow with them. Ten years and she had not once taken them off. Her gaze lifted skyward to the spangle of stars glittering across the heavens. They whispered to her like a bittersweet chime of bells.

Let's fly to the stars where they'll never find us.

Pain stabbed her heart like a hot knife. The blistering heat had scalded the edges to numbness long ago, but the blade's tip still found its tender mark. Her assassin of grief never missed.

The door behind her banged open.

"Are you insane?" Philip yelled. "Of course you are. Otherwise you wouldn't be standing here instead of traveling on a ship back to America."

Ivy stuffed the necklace under the collar of her dress and shuttered her gaze from the stars.

"Hello, Philip. Nice to see you too."

"I didn't want to believe you'd be reckless enough to disobey orders. I thought it was a joke when I got your message telling me to come up here." He pulled a wadded slip of paper from his pocket and waved it in the air like a flag to incite a bull. "Washington is going to string you upside down with feet cuffs when he finds out you defied him. Again."

"Impossible. Washington doesn't have feet cuffs. Hamilton does."

"Ives! You cannot gallivant around doing as you please. It's bad enough you've gained a reputation of such thorough ruthlessness while on missions that you've earned yourself a title. Maiden. There are rules, you know."

The title, given by her enemies, rankled her. Its very definition mocked her status as a once married woman turned widow. "Talon is fully aware of my methods just as they are painfully aware that they cannot bench me for long. I track down Order members and dispatch them as ordered. It's all I ever do. Root them out. Wipe them from the face of existence. I'm good at what I do."

"Too good, some might say. If there was anything left of them to speak."

"I complete my missions as I see fit and as the targets deserve. After my last assignment I thought to take a more leisurely route home, stopping to see my dear friend, who is clearly not pleased to see me." She flipped away her ruined skirt with her toe and nudged a small dented box in his direction. "I brought you *turrón*. Crunchy, just the way you like it."

He eyed the Spanish candy with a flicker of interest before rounding on her once more. "You might be able to sweet-talk your way back into Washington's good graces like you always do—"

"I bought him a new book. The Spanish translation of *The Metaphorical Revolution of Alhambra*."

"—but Britannia is on the warpath, and seeing you is going to set him to self-destruct."

"I have apologized repeatedly for shooting an arrow through the candles on his dining table. How was I to know the centerpiece was a gift from His Majesty?" She buckled her T-strap shoes. "What's the old battle-ax going on about now?"

Philip's expression stonewalled. "Nothing. Forget I said anything."

She grabbed her bundle of ruined clothes and brushed past him, her heels sounding a staccato *pock-pock* across the cement roof. "If it's nothing, you wouldn't be so irritated."

His moods were often like grenades-in-a-box. One day peacefully aligned, the next tossed into exploding chaos by a simple jostle. Franklin said the mood swings could be attributed to the mental trauma Philip endured at the torturous hands of Balaur Tsar. Philip did his best to control the lingering strain on his mind, but some days were a true struggle.

"They've got agents already on it, so there's no need to get involved. You're only just back from assignment."

"It must be important if we've been summoned to London." She pulled open the roof door. "How much spittle was Britannia flinging?"

"*I* was summoned." Philip hesitated, but he couldn't resist the disgusting observation. "Buckets full of spittle."

"Bound to be a real sockdolager of an assignment then."

The more spittle, the more excited the British head of office was, and woe to the agent who got too close. Ivy made that mistake three years ago when Lenin was extinguished under a bout of failing blood vessels. Or so the official records stated. That bit of excitement produced only one bucket of spittle. Whatever this new mission was, Ivy wasn't about to miss it.

She bounded down the rickety flight of stairs to the spare second level of Dover House and then descended a more refined set of marble steps to the unusual, rotunda-shaped entrance hall on the ground floor. Stepping behind a marble column that flanked the round space, she pressed a tiny button with the seal of an eagle set into the stone base. A door swung open, and she and Philip squeezed inside the column.

"Why did they choose this cramped space for a lift?" Philip fumbled the door closed, sealing them inside the column. A light flickered and buzzed inches over their heads.

"It's inconspicuous. Who would think to look in marble for the entrance to a secret lair? Did you know this was the first lift installed in London? When the infamous Lady Caroline Lamb lived here in private residence, she would use it to slip away and meet her lover, Lord Byron."

Ivy pressed a black button, the only button, on a panel screwed into the wall. The metal grate shifted beneath their feet and the lift eased down. Down, down, down underground until it jerked to a halt.

Philip unlatched the metal gate that served as a door and swung it open. He snorted with annoyance. "Useless thing. Can't even stop where it's supposed to."

As usual, the finicky invention had stopped a good three feet above the floor. Philip jumped out and reached up his hand to Ivy.

She accepted the assistance and leaped down behind him, the hem of her pleated skirt flaring out to flash the garters above her knees. No rolled-down stockings or rouged knees to draw attention to *her* bared legs despite society's thirst for scandal.

"Wouldn't be Talon if everything went according to plan."

For Talon was indeed where they were, despite the London address. After the Great War the world shrank in on itself with happenings no longer untouched by foreign shores. Talon's covert skills were a necessity; old threats lingered in the bloody loss and new threats scrambled for power as lines and allies were reconfigured. For two centuries Talon stood alone in its shadowed fight against evil, but the war to end all wars was only the beginning. Talon was forced to armor itself as needed, starting with its own allies.

An office in Paris was established before the ink was dry on the Treaty of Versailles. Next came an office in Amsterdam, then one in Munich. Leningrad was taking much longer to establish, but that was to be expected. Here in London they had built their greatest stronghold across the Atlantic—an amusing upending of expectations considering Talon was founded among the ashes of a war with Britain. Nevertheless, everyone had put aside ancient history to forge ahead with like-mindedness.

Taking a smidge of inspiration from its American counterpart, Talon's London headquarters burrowed itself deep belowground in what was designed as an underground railway station. A high ceiling of green tiles arched over the wide central platform with two tracks running on either side. A series of abandoned wooden carriages sat on each track and served as offices, weapons storage, and training facilities. Demolitions and shooting ranges were quartered off down the long tunnels that led nowhere as the tracks were abandoned before being connected to other lines.

The doors pushed open on the carriage parked at the right center of the platform, and out stormed an enormous belly. Attached to the belly was a towering walrus of a man with a drooping mustache and a salted black mane of hair that waved ferociously atop his head. Britannia, head of Talon's London operations.

"I called a meeting ten minutes ago. Why is everyone milling about the platform? Hurry along. Pip-pip."

Agents in various states of going about their tasks scattered away from him like quail flushed from a covey.

Whipping out a solid gold watch from a pocket in his yellow-and-red tartan waistcoat, Britannia popped it open and peered at the numbers, then snapped the lid shut before scouring the platform for agents daring to linger. His sharp eyes caught Philip.

"You there, chap."

"Philip, sir."

Britannia cocked his head as if hearing a fish splash in the distance. "What was that?"

"My name, sir. It's Philip."

"The American chap." If Britannia had one weakness, it was remembering names. He'd known Philip for five years.

Philip smiled with polite deference. "Yes, sir."

"What are you standing about for? This is not a queue for

tomatoes." Britannia pronounced the word *toh-ma-tohs* as did all good citizens of the king's language.

"I'm on my way to the meeting, sir. I only had to fetch Ivy first."

Ivy had the misfortune of falling under Britannia's unrelenting gaze. "The American bird. You're supposed to be in Spain causing *them* trouble. Not me." He eyed the bundle of foul clothes tucked under her arm.

"I completed my mission and arrived in London this afternoon, sir," Ivy said.

"If it's completed, why have you not reported back to Washington?"

Because Washington would have her chained to a desk filling out reports on Spain and Morocco as she slowly spiraled into death by boredom. The only action happening on American soil at present was the nightly raids on speakeasies that hosted illegal champagne parties, which she had no desire to help break up. She craved the thrill of the chase, the solidity of her Beretta in hand, the blood singing in her veins as she closed in on a target. Anything less and the blackness would creep to the edge of her mind, drawing out precious moments of memory like knotted thread from a spool that snagged the pitiful measure of sanity she had cobbled together. Left alone without purpose, she would pull at those threads and hang herself with their unraveled pain.

Balling up her agony, she shaped it into a more appropriate response. "I thought to offer my help here, sir."

"That's against protocol. Agents do not offer. They are assigned." Prying open his watch again, he examined the time and snapped it shut. "Get a move on, chap. Washington didn't send you here to stand on your ear, what." With that he turned on his heel and strode to the train car.

"Stay behind me and keep quiet," Philip whispered before jogging after Britannia.

Ivy waited a full four seconds after they disappeared into the carriage at the end of the platform before dumping her soiled clothes into a garbage bin and following. She slipped in and sat behind Philip and the six British agents at the back of the car.

"Tomorrow is Trooping the Colour," Britannia intoned from where he stood at the front. A map of London sprawled on the wall behind him while the windows were covered with various maps of Britain and Europe.

"I need not remind you of this most momentous date on our country's calendar to mark our sovereign's birthday as it has for the past two hundred years. Precautions are being taken as always, but this year we have evidence of a new threat." He paused, mustache bristling. "Though I suppose this is what one might call an ancient threat, having been around for some time making mischief on the world's stage. Tell us more, eh, chap?"

The British agents looked from one to the other, clearly confused about which "chap" their leader referred to. The solitary female agent would have no issue discerning herself when "bird" was called upon.

Britannia waved an agitated hand. "Yank chap. Up you go. Don't hold us in suspense."

Philip stood and cleared his throat, the arrow tips of his collar rippling with the movement. "Yes, sir. We have reason to believe the king is in danger of an assassination attempt during his ceremonial ride from Buckingham Palace to Horse Guards Parade."

"Plenty of communists out to get him," one of the younger agents piped up. Tallyho, was that his name? "Even hear rumblings from the German *Sturmabteilung*."

"It's not the Reds or the Brownshirts." Philip paused and cleared his throat again. His fingers knotted together behind his back. "It's the Order of the Rising Moon. We have reason . . ."

A bomb may as well have detonated overhead and caved the roof in for all Ivy could decipher beyond those hated words. They strung together to carve into her darkest nightmares. *Order of the Rising Moon. Balaur Tsar. Vlad Dracul. Poenari Castle. Frozen rushing river. J—*

All these years of tracking the Order she'd held out hope of finding him alive, but no more than dead ends of soot and ash crusted around the gaping hole where her heart had once been.

Balaur Tsar had made it no secret that the Order of the Rising Moon stretched worldwide, but its members were as elusive as smoke, burrowing into places of power and waiting for the opportune moment to strike. Perhaps the shadows biding their time in England had decided to step into the light. And Philip hadn't told her.

She leaned forward and snatched at his hand, but he shook her off and continued. "They are fanatics founded by none other than Vlad the Impaler during the fifteenth century when he wiped out an entire Wallachian village to begin purging the corrupt of the world. He spared two survivors, two worthy of his vision, who became the initial members of the Order, and left them to expand and fester with his ideals. Over the centuries their ranks have swelled as they've remained hidden in the cracks of history, biding their time for the opportune moment to purge the entire world of corruption and begin again with only the Order."

Boiling blood pummeled through Ivy's veins and thrummed in her ears. She dug her nails into Philip's wrist. He wrapped his fingers around hers and squeezed in warning. Or understanding. Either way it made no difference. She had long ago given up the subtle instinct of caring for others' suggestions about how she should feel and behave.

"The Great War was to be their deliverance into power, but that plan was foiled," Philip said. "Talon gave orders to wipe out their remaining strongholds after the war, but like rats buried deep underground, they manage to survive. We believe the Order is behind the recent assassinations of world leaders."

Of course they were. They were the rotted root of misery that had turned her life into a shell of itself. Ivy's hand dropped like a deadweight to her lap. Voices buzzed all around, but not a single word was comprehensible except *Order of the Rising Moon.*

Those words trampled across her overwrought mind with the clatter of a devilish horde, blackened hooves stamping out the scraps of humanity she had fumbled together for the past ten years. The hooves bore down. She wanted to scream, to cry, to lash out. But most of all she wanted vengeance. And vengeance she would have.

The voices cobbled together word by word into sense and dragged her out from under the crushing black hooves.

Britannia's commanding tone rose above the rest. "The Yank chap has been summoned because he remains the only agent who has experience with this Order. He shall inform us of everything we need to know about our adversary now that they've brought the fight to British soil."

Ivy shot out of her seat. "I volunteer. Besides Philip I'm the only one who has dealt directly with them." Not entirely true, but Beatrix, Victor, and Fielding—her fellow agents from the Russia mission—had been reassigned to monitor rumblings in Germany. Only she and Philip remained from the original team of agents who knew what to expect from the Order.

Philip spun around, tugged her arm, and hissed, "Sit down!"

She ignored him. "The Order is not to be underestimated. We'll need all the experience we can gather if we're to defeat them. For good." Pulling her arm free, she stared at Philip with full intent. "Not a trace left this time."

Philip's lips compressed into a thin line, but he didn't argue. He was biding his time until they were alone and he could give her another ear blister on why she didn't belong here. He could blister all he wanted. She deserved this kill and no one would take it from her.

Britannia stared at her as if his eyelids had forgotten their purpose. "Be that as it may, Agent Vale, you've only just completed your last assignment and have yet to report to Washington. It is against protocol to send an agent out again with little to no turnaround. Request denied."

"But, sir, the king's life may be in danger. It would behoove Talon as well as all of Britain to have as many agents as possible working to terminate this threat."

As she predicted he would react to talk of the crown and its empire being under duress, Britannia wavered. "You may offer what details you have, but first thing in the morning you will be bound for America to report to Washington, which you should have done instead of coming here. There are rules to be followed. Do I make myself clear?"

Ivy bit back a rising argument and nodded in respect. Her real quarrel was with Philip for not telling her sooner. "Yes, sir."

When they were dismissed, Philip dragged her down one of the empty tracks where the rails ran into a solid wall of concrete that had been chipped by bullet holes during target practice.

He rounded on her. "What happened to being quiet?"

"You cannot deny me this." Her hands clenched. "Why didn't you tell me?"

"Because I knew you would show up, and so you have! You're not even supposed to be in London. You were to take a ship directly from Spain to America as Washington ordered."

"Washington would have me withering away at a desk filling out paperwork. I can't do that. You know that, Philip. If I stop for one second . . ." Her nails bit into her palms as the unraveling threads within began to fray.

Bare light bulbs sagged on wires strung the length of the tunnel. A few were no more than bits of broken glass thanks to stray bullets, while the others sputtered with little interest in fulfilling their purpose.

A yellowish hue flickered across Philip's face, wedging smudges into the creases around his eyes—eyes that once twinkled with mischief and now sadly shunned such youthful antics. "He was a long time ago, Ives. It's past time to move on."

"Those bastards took him from me. I cannot move on." She pressed a fist to her stomach to keep the threads from knotting into a tangle of emotion. "I need to finish this once and for all. How can they still crawl the earth when we tracked down every known and rumored stronghold the Order had and obliterated them? Not one stone was left unscorched, yet here they are, foul revenants refusing annihilation."

After the fall of Balaur Tsar, Talon had thrown all its power into hunting down every last trace of the Order and destroying it. The hunt had satiated her hunger for revenge for a time, but anger seethed close to the surface constantly, burning just below her skin. Clawing for release. Soon after recovering from Poenari Castle, she started tracking down members of the Order, unleashing her rage bullet by bullet, and earning her savage reputation as the Maiden. But there were never enough bullets. Could never be enough to reseal the hole of bitterness that consumed her night and day.

"You won't find peace in these rabid executions."

"Peace no longer exists for me, not after J—" Her mouth worked back and forth, but the word refused to form. Saying his name aloud would open the wound so deep that it may never close again. "I should have died with him that day."

The shadows digging into his face hardened. "Don't you dare go morbid on me. Not after everything we've been through. The grief. The revenge killing. You wanting to die."

"I tire of the weight of mortality. I want to tear it from my veins until I bleed the bleakness from my body, until I feel nothing."

He grabbed her shoulders and shook her. "Step back from the ledge, Ivy. I mean it."

That ledge. She closed her eyes. High above the river. Her bare toes blue on the snow-crusted edge. Icy mist stinging her face. Sweet relief beckoning her.

Philip shook her again. "Don't let go!"

A familiar scrawl inked the inside of her eyelids. *You must go on, love.* She squeezed her eyes against the gentle plea, the last one she ever received from him, written before they knew it was to be the end. Written in case he was forced to break his promise of being there for her always. The words thumped in her heart, forcing it to beat alone day after day.

Opening her eyes, she blinked away the gray lead sky and the ledge above the frozen river. With the image drained away all trace of the vulnerability that had taken her years to shave off and refashion into a hardened shield. It chafed against her raw soul, but behind it she was better protected than she was by a bleeding heart.

She took Philip's hand, squeezing it tight as she used to when they were children huddling under the shelter of a fire escape when the night was stormy and lonely all around them. They'd always had each other for comfort.

"I miss him so much. Do you miss him, Philip?"

He held her hand for a moment, then dropped it. "He's gone, Ives. Constant grieving won't bring him back. Life has to go on."

Philip had never been overly sentimental, preferring anger to tears or avoidance to consolation. She had accepted his mercurial moods when they were children, but there were times when she simply needed him to hold her hand in the rain.

"But do you miss him?"

"He was my best friend." His low words scuffed the ground as if he could not force them upright. "Though you know my memories of him are spotty. Many things are."

Dust. That vicious liquid killer had eaten away parts of his mind, leaving blackened holes in its wake. He rarely spoke about their lives since coming to Talon, lingering mostly on their time together as orphans when it was just the two of them.

Perhaps it wasn't only the Dust crippling his ability to remember anything good. Perhaps her grief had crippled him as well. So lost in herself that she had never considered what her behavior was doing to him. She couldn't change her past actions, but she could offer him a temporary reprieve from worry.

"I'll go."

His head came up. "Just like that? No counterargument or side attack?"

"Perhaps you're right. I've tottered too close to the ledge, and J—well, he'd want me to tread carefully. If anyone else has a right to vengeance against these devils, it's you, and I know you'll serve justice in my stead."

Philip's expression shuttered as it did anytime his ordeal at the hands of Balaur Tsar was referenced. He'd told Washington and Jefferson about it after returning from Romania in 1917 but refused to speak of it since. She understood. Memories were often worse than death.

He removed his hand from her grip and shoved both of his hands in his pockets before starting back down the tracks.

"There's a ship leaving Portsmouth tomorrow afternoon. I'll see you to the train at Charing Cross, but now I need to brief the agents for tomorrow." He paused and looked back when she didn't follow. "You coming?"

"No, you go ahead. There's nothing more I can relate that you don't already know." She patted her hand over a yawn. "Think I'll go rest for tomorrow."

"We'll finish it, Ives. I'll see it done. Trust me." His footsteps echoed away, solitary clips that shivered off the broken tiles and metal rails.

Ivy reached into the pocket she had sewn inside her brassiere, which thankfully was still wearable after her mission, and pulled out a worn piece of paper. Time had aged the crisp white to a soft yellow and blurred the stamped letterhead of the Trans-Siberian Railroad, where the note had been written during that first week of wedded bliss. The once precise creases had thinned from repeated folding. There was no need to open it, really, for the words had been carved on her heart long ago.

You must go on, love. For me. For us.

She tucked the letter away, the interlocking bands on her necklace hanging softly over it like guardians.

It was time to pack.

Back down the tracks, the platform was empty as all the agents had gathered back into the meeting carriage. Philip's muted voice filtered out through the glass windowpanes. She ducked into the weapons carriage on the opposite track and smiled at the rows of pistols, rifles, grenades, and knives.

"Hello, lovelies. Care for a little outing tomorrow?"

TWO

CROUCHED BEHIND THE LOW RAIL ON TOP OF THE HORSE GUARDS building, Ivy slid her knife into the top of her boot—careful not to cut the
bit of her trouser leg stuffed down there—and readjusted its twin in
the hidden sheath tied up her sleeve. With any luck she wouldn't be
close enough to use them, but best to be prepared. All she planned
to require was the Springfield rifle with its extended scope, precise
enough to pick a flea off a dog or, considering the event, remove an
assassin from the crowd.

She lifted her head a few inches above the rail and brushed a
bobbed curl from her eyes, then scanned the surrounding rooftops
and ground area of Horse Guards Parade. It was a large space surrounded on three sides by towering government buildings stuffed to
the gills with state secrets and open on the west side to St. James's
Park, where crowds were gathering for the spectacle. Within the
raked-gravel rectangle itself, horses stamped their feet and snorted
with impatience as their riders sat erect in spiffy uniforms gleaming
with gold braid and medals. British flags of blue, red, and white waved
gaily despite the clouds rolling in. Hopefully any rain would hold off.
Terribly inconvenient, sighting through a water-speckled scope.

Three Talon agents were in the crowd. Two rode in the proces-
sional behind the king. Britannia was stationed on the balcony below;

Tallyho and Philip were positioned on other rooftops. She had yet to be spotted, and if all went according to plan, she wouldn't be.

A cheer from the crowd rolled down the Mall—the broad avenue leading from the gates of Buckingham Palace to the parade ground—swelling until it came to a head of drums and horns announcing the grand arrival. Dozens of horses trooped in soldierly fashion. Red uniforms and gold helmets splashed color against the beige gravel and weathered buildings, while flags waved and feet marched. If there was one thing the Brits did well, it was grand pageantry.

Separating himself from the head of a column of soldiers was none other than King George V wearing a splendid scarlet tunic and tall bear-fur hat. He rode a magnificent glossy black horse that trotted past the other columns and rows one by one. All eyes were riveted on the royal as he inspected his troops, but Ivy trained her gaze through the scope and slowly swept the crowd.

More flags. Fluttering trumpet banners. A woman in a beautifully trimmed silver frock—had she purchased it on Bond Street? Guards marching. Ivy turned her scope to the rooftops. Treasury Building. Soot-stained chimneys. Dover House. Pigeons sleeping on a waterspout. Admiralty Building—apparently the place where cryptographers cracked the Zimmermann Telegram and changed the course of the Great War.

"Should've cracked it sooner and saved us all a load of muddy grief," Ivy muttered, rotating the rifle.

A glint flashed in her scope.

She trained on it, finger hovering near the trigger. Waiting.

It flashed again.

There. From a top window in the Admiralty Building. The glass was cracked open with a rifle muzzle sticking out. The figure holding the gun stood in shadow. Was he with Talon? No. Britannia had assigned no agents inside buildings. It limited range.

Her finger moved to the trigger as she calculated the length of the mystery rifle to its intended target. All eyes were on the king in the center of the parade ground, but this shooter aimed at the . . . viewing stand? A few colonels, standard bearers, and the secretary of state for war.

The king wasn't the target!

She never heard the blast of the bullet leaving the silenced gun.

She pulled her trigger. A sharp whizz was all her rifle offered through the silencer, but when she looked up the window was empty.

In a matter of seconds screams rose from below. The honored guests scrambled from the viewing stand. Guards rushed to surround the king. The crowd jostled and panicked, shouting as they stampeded away from what had been a celebration but now dissolved into deadly chaos. The secretary of state for war slumped in his chair with blood trickling from a dead-center shot to his forehead.

She dropped the rifle as a hindrance in favor of her Beretta and raced across the connecting rooftops with her eye ever on the shooter's window. If he was an assassin worth his weight in gunpowder, he would make his escape as quickly as possible with discretion. Although considering the roar of confusion on the parade ground, the assassin could light himself on fire and hurl himself from the roof and no one would notice. He'd better not pull such a stunt. If he was part of the Order, she had a few questions to ask before she herself pitched him over the rail.

After leaping onto the Admiralty Building rooftop, she shot the lock off an access door, then raced inside, down a set of metal stairs, and out to the top floor. Her footsteps pounded over the tile as she whizzed along the corridor, counting the dark oak doors. Sixth from the end she burst into the chamber.

The yellow flocked wallpaper, dripping chandelier, and antique chairs were more conducive to stately talks than the staging of a murder, but then, she'd had her own fair share of unusual venues—an

Alpine ski slope, Arlington Cemetery at night, a junk sailing on the Yellow Sea, which she would *not* recommend.

The window remained open with a soft breeze tickling the brocade drapes. The bullet from her rifle was lodged in the back of a gold pin-striped chair a mere six feet from where the assassin had knelt. If only she hadn't hesitated.

A series of doors leading from one chamber to the next opened to the right. Through there. Alert to any movement or sound, she crept to one room, then the next, until she reached a small antechamber with no door but the one she'd come through.

The noise was soft enough to be a mouse's footstep, but it was enough. Ivy whirled into a crouch as a knife sliced the air her head had just occupied.

She fired. Her mistake for aiming in the direction the knife had come from. A shadow cut from the left and then the killer was on her.

He was as fast as a snake striking and covered head to toe in relentless black, including a hooded mask with chain mail hanging from nose to throat like those the tank crews wore during the Great War.

Faceless, expressionless, with black reflecting glass for eyeholes. An obstruction of humanity. If given a moment to consider, she might have been terrified out of her mind, but as matters stood, she was too occupied fending off a series of knife stabs aimed at her heart.

She returned the favor with a blade to his thigh, but he dodged and her knife slid harmlessly off the leather belts strapped around his waist. Attacking to keep him on the defense, she stabbed, punched, and kicked.

He blocked every single attack, each move quicker than the last as if he anticipated her hits. She knocked the knife from his hand and he snatched another from his belt. When that one was kicked away, he pulled another and another.

The adrenaline racing through Ivy's veins, the drug that stopped all thought and time beyond immediate survival, screamed in her bones and muscles as she fended off each attack.

Their feet moved together, leading and following like the silent intimacy of a dance with each partner attuned to the other's steps. She roundhouse-kicked. He caught her foot and flipped her. She hit the floor on her stomach, rolling at the last second as his knees slammed down on either side of her, crushing her with his weight.

He was too strong and heavy to throw off.

"Use what you have."

She jammed two fingers into his windpipe—well, tried to, but the chain mail served as the perfect foil. His head reared back as his hand reached for her throat.

Jerking sideways, she yanked the knife from the top of her boot and slashed upward. It sliced through the chain links and tore the metal away, exposing the lower half of his face.

She whipped the blade back in the opposite direction to cut off the lower half of that face, but he caught her wrist and twisted.

The knife tumbled to the floor.

She swung her legs up, locking her feet around his neck, and yanked him backward, then sprang to her feet and grabbed the nearest object, a rectangular serving tray.

He came at her again, and she swung the tray, hitting him upside the head where the tray's corner tore through his hood. A lock of long, dark brown hair spilled from the crack as the corner of a blue eye, void of emotion, stared back at her.

Human after all.

One punch with his gloved fist and the tray splintered to pieces. The fist kept coming, collided with her stomach, and sent her flying over a settee.

He sailed after her, but she slammed her boot into his face, knocking off his hood and mask and forcing him backward into a window.

Glass snapped.

The impact dropped him to the floor in a ball, revealing a web of leather belts and buckles with holsters for weapons and bullets strapped around him like a restraint jacket.

In one swift motion he leaped to his feet and faced her. Unkempt, shoulder-length hair gave way to pale skin, dark stubble, and muscles straining against his neck. Eyes deep and blue and empty.

Ivy's knees buckled as the world slid out from beneath her.

Her heart went into a free fall, down, down, and down at the impossibility.

"Jack?"

Not a whisper of recognition crossed his face. Not a flicker of history or love appeared in those cold blue eyes. Only death.

Voices rang through the corridor. "In here!"

He pulled a pistol from his leather vest and aimed. Straight at her.

Britannia and Tallyho crashed into the room.

Bam!

Ivy ducked as the bullet soared over her shoulder. The cracked glass shattered. In the instant it took her to lift her head, Jack was gone.

She sprang to her feet. "Where is he?"

"Out the window, of course. Bloody bugger." Britannia lowered his gun and stared at her with suspicion bordering on contempt. "What are you doing here? I ordered you back to America."

"What's all this?" Philip rushed in and skidded to a stop, brow wrinkling at Ivy, though he had the courtesy not to look surprised. "I should've known you'd be here."

The world was tilting again, shifting light and movement into slow motion. "Did you see him?"

"See who?"

"Jack."

The wrinkles on Philip's brow sharpened to daggers of disbelief. "Ives—"

She ran to the window and leaned over the jagged shards still hanging from the frame. They bit into her skin, but she gave them no mind for they could cut no deeper than the shock lancing her heart.

Philip's hand settled heavily on her shoulder. "Jack isn't here. He's been dead for ten years."

"It was him."

"I know you think that, but—"

She threw off his hand and looked down with sickening trepidation. A straight four-story drop.

"He was right . . ." No body. No splatter of blood. The sickening trepidation turned to something equally dangerous.

Hope.

He was right . . . here.

THREE

KEROSENE LANTERNS SEEPED THEIR OILY LIGHT OVER THE CAVE'S WALLS, slick with rust and slime. He tilted his head back against the chair and stared at the stalactites ringed overhead. Sharpened fangs pinioned him in their dead center. Water drops slipped off the points and *splat* on the rocky floor around his chair.

Splat. Splat. Splat.

Like blood dripping from slashed fingertips.

A man in a long white coat leaned over him and thumped his bare chest, a chest riddled with old and new scars like a patchwork of skin pieced and pulled together over the years. Unlike the smooth skin of the doctors gathered around him, free of pain and tally marks for missions completed. Three of them were poking and prodding and sketching notes, but he didn't watch them.

Splat. Splat. Splat.

Tiny vestiges of the rushing water far above, beyond layers of dirt and rock, where a mighty river cut through the earth and crashed over a ledge into a rocky pool.

Ledge. River. Rocks. Images flashed across his mind.

Ledge. He grapples with a man. A woman is there. She is screaming, but there is no sound.

River. He plunges far below the surface. So cold. It carries him far away.

Rocks. They dig into his back as he lies staring up at a lead sky. A woman, horrible and dead-eyed, is leaning over him.

Splat. Splat. Splat.

No. He wanted the other woman. The woman from the ledge. He squeezed his eyes shut and conjured her face, but it melded into a different image. It was still her, but she wasn't on the ledge. She was in a room and staring at him. Why was she staring at him? Her mouth moved with one simple word. He heard it this time.

"Jack."

Why did she call him that? Was it a key to the black splotches in his mind? Splotches corroded until bullets, blades, blood, and destruction were all that remained. If ever a part had existed wholly unto himself, it had long since been wiped away. His only agency now was of death.

Splat. Splat. Splat.

"Jack."

The black splotches curled at the edges of his mind. If he could peel them back and discover—

A hand clenched his chin and yanked down. His eyes flew open. On instinct he grabbed the doctor by the throat and squeezed. The doctor's eyes rolled back to whites as air gasped from his lungs. A pathetic noise that escaped all victims. A guard armed with a club rushed forward. Another pathetic attempt to save one of their own. The club swung toward his arm. He hurled the doctor at the guard. They flew backward, slamming into the wall, and crumpled in a heap.

Rifle safeties clicked off. Muzzles aimed straight at him. Let them shoot. Let them riddle him with holes. Inside they would find nothing, for he was a hollow vessel filled, emptied, and filled with the monster they had created.

A sound scraped down the tunnel. A catching of rough mate-rial over uneven ground like scales slithering on stone. His attention sharpened to the point of a knife, focused and alert. His muscles tight-ened, readying themselves.

The scratching material drew into the cave, filling the chamber with its dark intent. He raised his gaze to meet it.

She was hideous. Bloated and crude and flaking at the edges. All flesh and sagging bones and deadness, like the gore he scraped from his vest after a mission. Yet they dared to call her the Silver One. With one flutter of her puffy hands, the rifles dropped and the guards stepped back. There was no need for violent threats, not now that she was here. Her will was absolute, and to oppose her was to receive a sentence greater than death.

"Riser." Her voice scratched his ears with its soft harshness. The hem of her skirt dragged like deadweight across the floor, collect-ing pebbles and rusty water in its threadbare folds. "Riser. You will answer me."

Her hand cracked across the side of his face. His head whipped to the side. The black corrosion of his mind crackled. The ledge, a woman, a river. The room, a woman, *Jack*.

"The woman. Who is she?"

The Silver One had the mindless stare of a toad, her eyelids seeming to have been skinned back away from her bulbous eyes. "Collateral damage to your true target. Nothing more."

"She knew me."

"*Da*. She is part of the terror organization hunting us down. She was sent to kill you."

But she didn't. She'd had the shot. She could have taken him, but she didn't.

"Talon wishes to tie the world in bondage with the same fervent passion as we wish to set it free. For so long we have kept to shadow and crevice, and you have been the one to deliver us to the light."

The Silver One stepped closer. Pungent earth soaked in decay wafted from her. "Your work of Fate ensures only the righteous chosen will remain to see the world arise on a new moon of our Order. The old leaders must be put down by your hand so that our brothers and sisters may rise to claim their positions and lead our Order to greatness, but the work is not done. Your work is not complete. Not as long as there are those to oppose us."

"But she knew me."

"*Jack*." He clutched the word like a wound likely to spill open. If she discovered it, the Silver One would gouge her claws in and strip his possession of it, twisting it with foulness.

But it was his, even if nothing else was. This one word could be his own.

"And you will be the one to kill her for your next mission. You will kill her and destroy Talon." Her flat lips pressed into a long line that drooped into the flesh of her chin. Still she didn't blink. She never blinked. "Dust him."

A doctor hunched behind her. "But, madam, Dust lingers in his bloodstream from the last dose. If we inject him too soon, he's at risk of instability." He glanced at his motionless colleague still crumpled across the chamber. "Again."

The Silver One turned colorless eyes on the doctor. "He is at risk of thinking. Risers do not think. They do what they are told. Dust him." Her voice was like nails dragged through gunpowder. The tunnel echoed with her dragging skirts as she retreated. There was no need for her to remain or look back. Her command would be followed.

Two doctors rushed forward and clamped his arms to the chair with metal braces. They had been chains once, then leather cuffs, both of which he had torn through in a rage. That was before the black splotches and corrosion, before, when he had more to cling to than a single word. What more was, he could no longer recall. She had made sure of that.

"No. Wait." She stopped and turned, a gleam in her eyes as the doctor stepped forward with the Dust-filled syringe. "Let him do it."

The men restraining his arms let go and handed him a leather strap. He took it and wrapped it around his upper arm, then squeezed his hand into a fist until the veins in his arm bulged near the surface of his skin.

A muzzle slipped over his mouth to stifle the screams that would later inhabit his body as the Dust choked his blood. The syringe was placed in his hand. It was cold and heavy. He hated it, yet the blood in his veins began to jitter with anticipation. The craving. The need. And for that, he loathed himself all the more.

He held up the syringe to the oily light. A thick white substance clotted the metal body. Knowing what must be done and unable to stop himself, he pressed the tip of the needle to his arm and plunged it through the skin. The white glob swelled in his veins, swallowing his blood and pushing itself along the tracts of his body like a bullet.

Everywhere it went, hot lead poured through him. The syringe fell from his hand as his skin strained white and red where the Dust coursed until endless ridges stretched across every surface of his body. This was the pain of hellfire. This was his undoing. It slogged into his brain, scorching the ledge, the river, the room, the woman, until at last it formed a fiery ring around the one thing he clung to.

This piece the fire would not take. This piece of him he would not forget, not this time.

"Jack."

FOUR

Ivy held the only photograph she had of Jack and her, taken before they left for Russia in 1916. They were so young with bright-eyed excitement that not even the sepia tones could diminish.

The photographer had told them not to smile, no movement at all lest it blur the image, but she'd been unable to stop herself when Jack slipped his arm around her. His fingers could be seen peeking around the curve of her waist, but the most extraordinary thing was that he was gazing down at her with a look of pure adoration.

She had never imagined that look would change. But she'd been wrong. So very wrong.

Ivy replaced the photograph next to the jars of cold cream and rouge on her vanity, then reached for the heated tongs and got to work setting marcel waves in her bobbed hair. It was all the craze, this short hairstyle that reportedly set women free from stuffy Edwardian constraints and beckoned them into a new era of liberation, but Ivy's shorn locks were not inspired by the dazzling Zelda.

Her gaze slid to the photograph. Her reasons were much more personal. Jack had loved her long hair. He'd spent hours of wedded bliss combing his fingers through it as they talked about their dreams for the future. Dreams that ended on the ledge of a cliff ten years ago.

She didn't want the reminder of what could have been, so she'd found a pair of rusty scissors and hacked it all off.

Smoke wafted under her nose.

"Drat!" She yanked the tongs away from her head. Several strawberry-blonde hairs stuck to the heated metal. Peering in the mirror, she frowned at the frizzy S wave compared to the sleek ones on the other side of her head. "Nothing an accessory can't mend."

She plucked a bejeweled peacock-feather comb from the top drawer and angled it into place. Perfect. Now for the finishing touch, a swipe of vamp-red lipstick to her Cupid's bow lips that would make Miss Clara Bow proud.

Knock, knock.

Ivy blotted her lips on a hankie. "Enter."

Philip stepped into her room dressed in gleaming black-and-white evening wear. "Are you ready yet? I've been waiting for twenty—" He stopped midstride and sniffed the air. "Are you burning something?"

"No." Resisting the urge to pat her hair, she stood and did a little twirl. Her waist-length beaded necklace swung dramatically. "Well?"

He flopped down on her pink chaise, careful to keep his oil-slicked hair from touching her cushions, and picked up the copy of *Photoplay* resting on the tufted arm. "Well, what?"

"How do I look?"

"You'll do." He flipped through the magazine. "Huh. Hollywood is trying to put sound in motion pictures. It'll work about as well as banana oil."

"I spent all the earnings from that job we pulled in Rio on this dress, and that's all you can muster? 'You'll do'?"

He flicked a brief glance over the top of the magazine. Dorothy Mackaill and her drawn eyebrows proved more interesting.

"You look berries."

Pleased with having twisted his arm for the compliment, she ran a hand over the supple velvet material. The dress was emerald green at the top and then darkened to deepest forest at the bottom with gold designs swirling over it. Her shoulders were bare, save for thin gold straps that perfectly matched her T-strap heels.

As quickly as the pleasure came, it evaporated. "I don't feel berries. I feel like one that's rotted through." She walked to the window overlooking Talon's back garden where gardenias, azaleas, and hydrangeas burst into riots of color that silvered under the moon's gaze. Beauty and life that mocked the bleakness churning inside her.

"Why are we even doing this tonight? Why are we back in DC as if nothing happened in London?"

"Our orders were to return to headquarters because whether we like it or not, we still have a job to do, and tonight that involves taking down a crime lord in a speakeasy."

"A job the feds can handle. We should be in London or somewhere in Europe looking for Jack."

"Washington has ordered you to stay put. And don't even think of trying to slip off, because the Eastern Seaboard ports have all been alerted not to let you on a ship."

It had taken Philip and two London agents to carry her aboard the ship to America. They'd locked her in the room after a very public rant of refusal all the way from Horse Guards Parade to the dock, which drew more than one curious eye and caused more than a dozen mothers to cover their children's ears. The dockworkers, on the other hand, were more than helpful in suggesting new additions to her vocabulary, which she used liberally to assault the ears she intended to box on Philip's head. He'd even threatened her with sedation when she tried to shimmy through the porthole.

She couldn't understand why he wasn't the first person to believe her. Even Washington and Jefferson had exchanged skeptical glances when she told them. "Hysterical with grief," Philip had called her, just as he had when she returned to that ledge with her bare feet in the snow, the sound of rushing water calling to her from below. He'd forced her away then too. This was nothing like then.

None of them would admit it, but their true reason for grounding her was fear of her going off the deep end. Again. But she wouldn't be an agent worth her salt if she didn't know how to work around Washington's order or find a captain willing to turn a blind eye for a well-greased palm. She eyed her top dresser drawer where a single passenger ticket bound for Calais was stamped for departure on the morrow. She didn't know whose gasket would blow hotter when they found her gone, Philip's or Washington's.

Could no one else feel the brightness of hope that Jack was alive?

Philip sighed, likely intending to blow out her flickering brightness. "I know you think it was him—"

"It *was* him!"

"We need to face facts. Jack fell off a ledge into a river. There is no possible way he survived that fall, and even if he did, the freezing water would have finished him off. I'm sorry to be so blunt, but it's been ten years, Ives. You have to stop looking for him in every face passing by."

It was true. She did search for him in crowds, in empty fields, on city sidewalks, and in shooting stars. For years she hadn't said his name out loud because the pain of it was a bullet to her heart. For years they'd told her she would learn to live without him, but her life was nothing close to living. It was scratching out the will to live each and every day while grief drowned her from within. Most days it was all she could do not to give in to the crushing depths if only to take away the pain.

She smoothed her hand down the front of her dress and stopped just below the flat of her belly. Every hope had been snatched from her that day, so she'd hollowed herself against ever finding it again. Within the emptiness she forced a hardness, a callousness to fend off any softness remaining to torment her, and thus became the most feared agent in Talon. Yes, she could outrun, outshoot, and out-track any target they placed before her, but in the end, what did it matter? She lived counting down the days until she could finally be reunited with Jack in the peaceful beyond.

Except the man she had reunited with mere days ago was anything but peaceful. He was cold, inhuman, merciless. What she had seen in him was death as a habit and ruthlessness honed by years of numbness.

She was not the only one robbed of life that day. Clenching her hand briefly over her flat stomach, she dropped it to her side and turned to face Philip.

"He's not the Jack I knew, nor did he seem to recognize me. It was as if his entire mind had been wiped clean and filled with metal. What if . . ." The truth had been gnawing at her heart, but she didn't have the courage to voice it out loud for what it would mean. Courage or not, the time had come.

"What if the experiments didn't stop after Balaur Tsar's death? What if the Order of the Rising Moon found him and turned him into a Riser?"

A sharp bark of laughter escaped Philip, the kind cut by the blade of a knife. He tossed the magazine aside and swung his feet off the chaise. "Preposterous! We destroyed all of their facilities including the batches of Moondust."

"Moondust?"

"What they call—*called*—the serum they used to create Risers."

"You've never mentioned that before—a specific name for the serum."

He pushed off the chaise and paced over the thick rug in quick, jerky steps. "It's all this resurgence of the Order business. Somehow the memories they took from me are starting to piece themselves back together."

"We may have destroyed all of their facilities and equipment, but clearly that hasn't stopped them from regenerating. Who's to say they haven't been rebuilding their experiments all these years? That would explain Jack's appearance. He's become their assassin."

Assassin. A word she'd long since grown, if not comfortable with, at least accustomed to because there was honor in what Talon did to keep the world safe from evil. The Order had twisted Jack into something else entirely.

She walked to the vanity and slipped the gold compact into her beaded handbag next to the pearl-handled derringer, her mind firm in its course. "We have to stop him. We must bring him back from the torment."

Philip whirled, bunching the rug beneath his shiny shoes. Red splotched his neck as fire blazed in his eyes. "There is no bringing him back! He's gone. Leave it be."

Ivy's mouth dropped open in disbelief. There was that raging anger burning out his sorrow. "I thought you would be delirious with joy that your best friend lives, but you refuse to believe me. Can you stop dismissing me like all the others and just be my friend?"

"I know you want me to share your hurt, but I can't do that. I'm not you."

"You did once."

"Yes, when we were children." He took several deep breaths. The red spidering up his neck slowly receded. "I don't want to see you disappointed when it turns out not to be him."

Ivy flicked the handbag's clasp. *Snap.* Sharp and metallic. A sting to the tension strung in the air. "You think I don't know my own husband?"

He came to her and gently placed his hands on her shoulders. His eyes softened to the familiar brown she'd known since childhood, but she could not make out the familiar friend.

"I think the mind can play tricks, making us see what we want to see. You've been hurt too many times, and I'm afraid one day I won't be able to pull you back from it."

"It was him. Before I even saw his face there was a familiarity. I could anticipate his moves, the way he held his knife, the style of his punch because I've sparred with him a thousand times before. It was almost as if we were . . . dancing."

"I swear by all the stars, I'll be forever true."

A hundred times and more she and Jack had danced to the song that still beat in her bones like a drum. "I never imagined I would see him again, but here he is very much alive. I don't care what it takes—I'm getting him back."

"Be careful what you wish for. You may get more than you intend."

She shrugged him off and took a step back. "What does that mean?"

Shoving his hands in his pockets, Philip shuffled to the door. He turned back and watched her quietly for a moment, all manner of emotions darting across his face until only sadness lingered, then he tipped his head.

"Come on. The band goes onstage in half an hour."

★★★

Emptiness crowded Sixteenth Street NW by eleven o'clock with all the hardworking businessmen and upright citizens of the nation's capital tucked peacefully in their modest homes that quiet Tuesday night. Only two types of characters existed at this late hour. The graveyard shift workers and those up to no good.

Ivy couldn't decide which they were as she stared up at the unassuming three-story facade of number 1020. Odd hours were expected of Talon agents and their work generally consisted of the nefarious kind, so perhaps they were of both ilk.

After using a special key gifted only to those in the know, she and Philip entered the front door and made their way up the narrow stairs to the top floor where a few marked doors indicated offices and water closets.

"Where to now?" Ivy's voice sounded too loud in the cramped space, particularly so since they hadn't spoken in the past hour. The cab ride had been tense, to say the least.

Rather than reply, Philip strode to the men's room and walked in without a backward glance. She deliberated a moment before following.

Philip stood at the sink. "Didn't think you'd come in."

Keeping her eyes strictly forward, Ivy held her arms and hands close. She did not want to brush up against anything in this room. "As long as we don't have to stay in here for long."

"Not long at all." He twisted the faucet's handle, and the hutch containing hand towels, aftershave, and lotions swung away from the wall to reveal a hidden door. "Ladies first."

Ivy stepped through into a smaller chamber with a single flickering gaslight overhead. Philip joined her and clicked the hidden door back into place before turning to the enormous oil painting of former president and US Army general Ulysses S. Grant, whose grandson once resided within these premises. Given his history with the bottle, he might have found it amusing that his family's home now sold giggle water under the government's very nose.

It was right on Grant's nose where Philip rapped his knuckles.

Grant's dark gray eyes peeled back to reveal two leery green ones. "Password."

"Jelly Roll Morton."

The portrait swung in, and out blared the sounds of clinking glasses, laughter, trumpet, and saxophone in a sin-worthy haven they called a speakeasy. Ivy and Philip stepped through the hole and beyond a curtain of heavy velvet into a world of illegal liquor, frothy champagne, rouge-kneed women, and men with wads of cash, all cavorting to the bright notes of swinging jazz.

Philip swept a hand toward the ecstasy. "Welcome to the Gaslight Club."

Ivy smoothed her expression into one of a woman who frequented unlawful clubs, yet inside she hummed with awe. This was by far the swankiest joint she'd seen, in cool tones of black, white, and silver. Gaslights burned between panels of mirrors circling the room that threw the light around like confetti. A sleek ebony bar stocked high with glittering bottles of all shapes and colors took up the entire right wall, while a stage packed with wailing musicians sat opposite. Dozens of small round tables and chairs filled the space between, while a bank of dimly lit booths cozied together at the far back.

They found a table near the bar that offered a somewhat unrestricted view of the entire room and gave their order to a harried waiter in a starched apron and black tie. A gin rickey for Ivy and a sidecar for Philip.

"Spot him yet?" Philip asked once their drinks had been delivered.

"Center back booth." Ivy pretended to sip her concoction as she scanned the scene, implying she had all the time in the world. "A girl next to him and two guards posted."

Without skipping a beat, the band swung into "The Charleston" and sent all the Bright Young Things into a frenzy. They jumped to their feet and made a dash to the dance floor, cramming together as their feet flew to the dance inspired by the song itself. Garters flashed on bare thighs, sweaty hands waved high in the air, bow ties loosened, and gin coursed all around like a liquid ribbon, flowing and smooth.

Ivy tapped her toe, following the steps she knew so well. Perhaps on a night that didn't require her undivided attention she might put on her own dancing shoes.

Philip leaned close to be heard over the ruckus. "Your nose is shiny."

Ivy's toe stopped tapping. She pushed away her unfinished drink and picked up her handbag. "I'd better go powder it then."

She left the table and asked a waiter for directions to the ladies' room, which was conveniently cordoned off by the velvet curtain at the entrance. Pausing behind the curtain, she gave a little pat of powder to her nose, which was indeed shiny thanks to the windowless room and numerous bodies.

The band hopped into "Dippermouth Blues." Drat. She adored this song.

After slipping her compact into her handbag, she gathered all the air she could into her lungs, then tore through the curtain screaming, "Raid!"

FIVE

As one might expect when police burst into an illegal joint sell-ing illegal booze, pandemonium ensued. Women screamed, men shouted, and tables toppled as the crowd scrambled for the exits. No one noticed there were no policemen to be seen.

Ivy slipped calmly through the chaos to the back booths and scooted into a recently vacated one. She pulled the derringer from her handbag, then stood on the seat and leaned over the partition to where the rotund Russian crime lord was attempting to propel himself out from behind the table.

"*Privyet.*" She pulled the hammer back with a satisfying *click*.

The crime lord's eyes swiveled up and widened in horror at the dainty gun pointed at his head. His splutter of outrage drew the atten-tion of the two bodyguards who had been blocking the table lest any mayhem approach their boss. Their meaty hands went to the guns strapped to their belts.

"Tsk-tsk," Ivy drawled. "No sudden moves, boys," she ordered in Russian.

"Move your hands where I can see them." Two more hammers clicked as Philip appeared behind the guards with pistols pointed at each of their backs. Scowling, the guards raised their hands in the air. "Am I late for the party?"

"Not in the least." Ivy eyed the girl cowering in the seat next to the crime lord. "Get out."

The girl didn't have to be told twice as she grabbed her handbag and climbed from the table, her silver shoes disappearing into the crush of fleeing patrons.

Ivy propped her elbow atop the partition, steadying her shooting hand. "Now that we're alone, perhaps we can have ourselves a little tête-à-tête about the narcotics ring you're hustling into the city."

The crime lord's dark eyes narrowed to slits of insolence. Here was a man accustomed to giving orders and laying out threats like morning headlines. Having questions aimed at him was beyond the limits of his patience. "Who are you? The police?"

"Of course not. If this were a simple case of chasing down the mad dragon, the police would be more than competent. However, you're using the profits to purchase arms not only for Russia but also in a few lucrative deals for Germany, Serbia, and Turkey, which happens to violate half a dozen peace treaties. Not trying to start another war, are you?"

His lip curled, revealing a gold tooth stamped with a tiny ruby. "What if I am?"

"I was afraid you'd say that." Ivy sighed dramatically. "I've heard through the grapevine that you're also supplying a mangy group here in Washington. Order of the Rising Moon. Sound familiar?"

One of the guards inched his hand toward his gun.

Philip tapped him on the back of his head with his pistol muzzle. "Don't even think about it unless you want a hole right here. Keep your hands raised where I can see them."

The crime lord sneered and spat at the partition. "I tell you nothing." He then proceeded to tell her about the only thing she was good for.

Ivy maintained her expression of bored indulgence. Slugging him in the face would only force her to touch his sweaty skin.

"I can tolerate a great many of men's shortcomings, but rudeness isn't one of them, and that, you horrendous pig, was rude. Now listen closely because this is what's about to happen. I have a few questions, and if you think to answer incorrectly, my companion here will put a bullet into your men, one for each wrong or evasive answer. Once they're tenderized to swiss cheese, it'll be your turn. *Ponimayu?*"

"*Idi k chertu.*" A suggestion of where she could burn once her previously suggested nighttime services were rendered.

She'd slug him with the butt of her gun, that was what she'd do.

The two guards jerked forward and crashed to the floor. Penny-size black holes oozed blood from the dead-center marks on the backs of their heads.

Ivy shot Philip a look of annoyance. "I hadn't asked the question yet."

He shook his head in bewilderment. "It wasn't me."

Before true alarm could settle in, the crime lord gasped, stiffened, then crumpled facedown on the table. Blood poured from the hole in his head to mingle with the spilled gin.

Time did a funny dance where everything happened within a split second yet stilled to allow for a striking clarity of detail. The dark stain spreading across the table, Philip's widening eyes, the shatter of glass bottles on the floor, and a lone figure in solid black with dark hair matted around his face as he stood in the receding sea of people, his pistol trained on her. Ivy's heart lurched.

Jack.

Time snapped back into place.

"Get down!" She dove to the seat. The bullet razed her feather headpiece, sending bits of iridescent blue and green puffing into the air.

She peeked under the table. Two legs clad in black with weapons strapped to the thighs strode toward her. Her husband had come to kill her.

We'll see about that.

Taking careful aim, she shot the table directly in his path.

He didn't stop. Nor did the menacing deadness in his eyes flicker. It would be useless to look for mercy from this unrecognizable killer.

She fired again, this time splintering a chair mere inches from his leg. His stride never broke pace and he'd be on her any second. Doubtful it would be for an affectionate reunion.

Tossing her spent gun, she reached for the table leg. Tipping the top over might spare her enough seconds—

"There you are, you great big bastard. Back from the dead." Philip launched himself at Jack. Jack pulled the trigger without hesitation. Philip twisted sideways and the bullet ripped through his bow tie.

After that there was a flurry of arms and legs striking quick as lightning while Ivy crawled out of the booth.

He was fast, impossibly so. Each move stripped of finesse and shaved to the bare-bones necessity of killing. Like fighting Death itself. But Death could not be allowed to win, no matter what she had to do to bring Jack back from its pit.

She slipped off her necklace and lassoed it around Jack's neck. He caught the stringed beads and yanked. Ivy went flying into a stack of chairs.

"That's not how we treat ladies, mate." Philip swung a trombone, whacking Jack across the back. "Especially that one."

Jack spun, backhanding Philip. Philip caught the blow on the cheek, then kicked out. Jack blocked and punched. Back and forth they traded blow for blow. Spitting blood, muscles pummeling muscles.

Ramming his shoulder into Philip's stomach, Jack flipped Philip through the air. Philip hit the ground hard with a grunt of pain. Jack was on him, punching again and again. Blood spurted from Philip's mouth and nose as his head knocked back and forth from the blows he feebly tried blocking.

Pain shot down Ivy's side as she righted herself from the tangle of broken chair legs. She'd have a walloping bruise come morning. If they lived that long.

She clambered on top of a table, then threw herself on Jack's back, latching on tight as she hooked her arm around his throat and squeezed. The thick muscles in his neck constricted and pulsed as he grabbed at her, tearing her dress and stockings in his frenzy.

"You just cost me a three-month paycheck, love." Ivy grunted and held on tighter. If her brand-new outfit was destroyed, she'd make certain it was for a purpose.

Philip kicked Jack's knees and Jack buckled to the floor. He went down hard, taking Ivy with him, but she didn't lessen her grip. Not until the pulse slowed and the straining muscles relinquished their fight. Her husband dropped unconscious.

She'd succeeded with the move she failed at when they first met under the bridge all those years ago.

Slowly uncurling her arm from his warm skin—skin she'd so longed to touch again—she pushed what remained of her drooping feather from her eyes and blew out a breath.

"Told you he was alive."

SIX

Every muscle in his body screamed for relief as the Dust with-ered from his blood. He clawed at his skin as it stretched tighter over his bones like knives scraping rock.

They'd caged him in like a beast. Four walls, a bare cot, and a door with a slit that opened for faces to peer in at him. None he knew—except one. The woman. The woman from the ledge, from London, and from the club. Her face came to the door more than any other. Her face haunted him with each perishing drop of Dust. Why was she everywhere? Why did she remain when all else was ripped from his memory?

The last fumes of Dust whispered to him, enforcing their power. *Death, that is who you are.* Pain ravaged his insides as his body strained to hear the fading words. Only more Dust could end this torment.

He struck a wall, again and again, fists denting the fortification until there was barely a smooth space intact. Dust did this. Dust soothed the rage and focused it on a target—always a target of the Silver One's choosing. But the Silver One wasn't here.

The other woman was. The woman who chipped away at his mind's blackness. The woman he had been ordered to kill. He beat a hand against his head. Dust did this too. It scrubbed his memory, tearing away the past and defying the future until he existed only for the now. Without it filling his veins, his body rioted out of control. Without Dust there was no control. Only fury burning in his blood and a woman who would not ease his torment.

He wanted to die, but who would claim Death?

★★★

Ivy quietly shut the view box and slid down the wall in despair. The man in that cell was unrecognizable as the one she'd pledged her heart and life to. He was an animal beating his fists against the wall until his knuckles split apart and blood flowed.

Long greasy hair, cheeks and jaw that hadn't seen a razor in weeks, sallow skin, and always that deadness in his eyes. Eyes she once claimed were as blue and fathomless as the ocean. Now all she saw was ice.

Dropping her head to her bent knees, she squeezed her eyes closed, but it did little to stop the tears from seeping through the cracks in her heart and falling down her face. All those years ago she'd returned to that ledge wanting nothing more than to die so she could be with him, but cruel fate had rooted her to this lonely existence where the sun rose every morning and the stars brightened every night sky as if her entire world had not been ripped away from her. Now to have Jack returned to her not as the man she knew, but rather as a mindless weapon bent on destruction, absolutely gutted her.

"It's the drug."

Ivy jerked her head up to find Jefferson standing near the cell door. A cell far below Talon's floors where they used to hold criminals, terrorists, anarchists, and individuals of all other manner of ill repute. For the past two days it had held Jack.

Jefferson leaned one shoulder against the wall. "It will take time for whatever drugs they pumped him with to leave his system. Right now his body is going through severe withdrawals. The next few days are critical to his recovery."

"Recovery from what? What did they do to him?"

"We don't know. Yet." His tall frame sagged as if the fight had left his bones. Gray saturated the hair around his face, fading the once brilliant red to a mere afterthought of color. Lines creased the corners of his eyes with the expression of a wearied soul. Still the most fearsome fencing instructor at Talon and never an opponent she wished to go up against in hand-to-hand combat, he had aged beyond his years, and with age came a broken bitterness that had once been tempered by youth's calculating restraint. More often she was on the receiving end of his sullenness and called out for correction during training.

Quicker feet.

Quicker hands.

Quicker mind.

She saw now that Jefferson's judgments weren't for discipline. Rather, they were accusations for an irretrievable loss. Quicker feet could have gotten her to Jack in time on that ledge. Quicker hands could have reached for him as he tumbled over. A quicker mind could have conjured a plan to save him.

Was it not enough that her failure flayed her day and night? Was it not enough that the last sight of Jack's wide blue eyes locked onto her before he disappeared over that cliff haunted her every breath? Her fingers clenched over her stomach. Was it not enough that they were not the only ones lost to each other that day?

Jefferson knew none of that. No one did. Oh, they surely surmised the grief of a wife for her husband, but the core truth of it she never spoke aloud. She carried it deep within her like a sharp-bladed talisman that cut her again and again, and it was from that bottomless well of pain that she fastened around herself a hardened shell for Talon's use. She could offer the world nothing more than her skills as she had fashioned herself into a weapon Talon had a great many uses for. In that, she and Jack were now alike. Two blades forged into a double-edged sword.

Inside the cell Jack punched the wall. Again and again. Ivy wanted to shut her ears to the thuds reverberating down the hall, a drumming that matched the tormented beat of her heart. The pain of each hit was enough to crack her apart.

"Is there nothing we can do to ease his suffering? Franklin must have a sedative."

Jefferson shook his head. "Franklin has no way of knowing what chemicals are flooding Jack's blood. Adding a sedative could make them worse. I'm afraid we'll have to wait this one out the old-fashioned way. I'm not sure what more can be done."

"I'll wait months, years, if there's the slightest chance he'll come back. There must be hope."

Emotions were a lethal cocktail of highs and lows, taking a person from one feeling to the next in such sharp thrusts that the heart strained at its seams, fearing its own continuity. Happiness was fleeting. Peace came at a cost. Contentment was seldom found and was then lost quickly.

Then there was fear. A strange beast. It settled into one's chest and seeped through layers of defense until all that remained was the nakedness of the human spirit, a spirit that could either perish under the pressure or cast off fear in the struggle to overcome.

Hope was the most dangerous of all. Hope told a person what might be. It whispered sweetness in the ear, encouraged one to take a chance. Hope bloomed in rebellion against fear. Hope would be their savior.

Ivy stood, gathering what strength she could from her own resolution. Even if it meant standing alone.

"I will never give up on Jack. Never."

"Jack was the best of us. Efficient, quick, strong, and intelligent.

Talon placed great pride in him." A sheen slicked over Jefferson's eyes, but he blinked it away. "He has been taken into darkness, and there he resides. I wonder if light shall ever pierce him again."

"I will follow him into the dark and bring him back to the light."

The corner of Jefferson's mouth ticked. Not quite a smile but not disappointment either. It was a start.

"A noble sentiment. Time will tell if it is misplaced."

Ivy dusted the grime from her hands. She didn't want to think about the hours she'd spent on this filthy floor instead of slipping up to her chamber for cleaning or rest. If Jack was here, so was she. They'd been apart too long.

"In the meantime, what is to be done about the Order of the Rising Moon? You remember them, don't you? An evil threat seeking world domination. We thought we obliterated them years ago only to discover they're back from the dead, and wouldn't you know it? They've been torturing my husband for the past ten years. I'm certain information as crucial as this somehow slipped the instructors' minds."

"You were on a mission in Spain. Bringing the Order to heel is not a task bestowed solely on you. It will take many hands and clear minds."

And mine was too greatly filled with wifely sorrow to provide sound judgment. It didn't bear repeating. The result only came with quiet looks of *See? I told you she was distraught.*

"Now that hands and minds have been gathered, what is Talon's next step?"

"That will depend greatly on Jack. He can offer insight on how they've managed to survive and resurge onto the playing field. From there we'll make our plan." Jefferson pushed off the wall, then turned toward the stairs leading up to the light, aboveground and away from the despair festering along this corridor.

"Why did you not believe me when I told you and the other

instructors Jack was alive?" she called after him. "Why can you not see the extraordinary chance we've been given?"

Foot paused on the first step, he turned back to her. The customary disdain of his brow dipped under sorrow. "Because I am a doubting Thomas. Facts and logic do not breed with sentiment." He spread his hands, palms up. Shame twisted his proud mouth.

"I didn't dare to hope."

★★★

She hated to do it, but by the fourth day Ivy was worried a pack of rats might mistake her hair for a nest. She gave over her charge of Jack to Philip while she ran upstairs for a hot meal, a bath, and clothes that didn't smell like another inducement for the creeping vermin. A white laced blouse, tan knickerbockers that buttoned at the knees, thick argyle socks, and low-heeled oxfords. Much warmer for this belowground corridor than a flippy skirt and stockings. With no overnight time to set her hair in pin curls, she brushed her freshly washed locks and pinned them back with two small combs.

The air grew cooler and heavier with moisture as she descended the stairs to the holding area. It was constructed after the Civil War with enough cells to hold troublemakers from both sides of the Mason-Dixon. Many of the bricks were etched with signatures and declarations of allegiance, much like the prisoner holdings in the Tower of London. Thankfully, Talon didn't behead its prisoners on the back lawn.

Philip stood at Jack's door staring through the viewing box. Fingers tapping an agitated beat against the reinforced metal, he was talking, but the low tones did little more than bounce down the corridor in distortion.

She hurried forward. "Has something happened?"

Philip startled. "What? No, nothing."

Elbowing him out of the way, she stood on tiptoe and peered into the cell. Jack sat unmoving on the bare cot staring at the opposite wall. Hanks of greasy hair hung over his face as his back hunched like that of a dog beaten low. Dried blood still clung to his tenderized knuckles.

Relief and sorrow formed wet pools in her eyes. His demon frenzy had calmed, but his body paid the ravaging toll even now in silence.

"How long has he been like this?"

"About an hour. He took one last whack at the wall, then sat down and hasn't moved since."

"You were talking to him. Did he respond?"

Philip looked sharply at her with the same beat of hesitant expectation as when one of his explosives accidentally rolled off the table. Muscle by muscle his expression relaxed.

"Only staring with the occasional blink."

Perhaps it was lingering withdrawal. Franklin had said despondency often came after the mad rush as the body groped for ways to deal with the phantoms of dependency.

"Do you suppose he's all right to eat now? He must be starving. I'll go get him a tray." She whirled away. Medium-rare steak, hot potatoes with butter, peppered green beans, steaming hot biscuits, and a thick wedge of chocolate cake. A feast after such deprivation. Then again, deprivation often called for plainer foods as one worked one's way back to richness. Cook would know the right balance after spending forty years whipping up meals for Talon agents in various states of injury.

Philip snared her arm before she had a chance to link elbows with the dream steak. "Washington gave orders that Jack is not to be fed until Franklin has a chance to examine him, which he's been unable to do. That animal in there is likely to bite him."

Ivy reared back. Of all the callous, unfeeling, monstrous things to say. Her anger flared hot and scorching as she wrenched from his grasp.

"Do not ever call Jack that again. How different would you be—or any of us—if we were forced to endure torture at the hands of those vampire followers?"

Philip shoved up his sleeve and jabbed at faded brown spots on the inside of his arm. "He isn't the only one who's been tortured by them. My arms still bear the marks where their needles stabbed me again and again, thickening my blood with their poison."

With every thought over the past week pinioned to Jack, she'd barely taken note of Philip. In fact, she'd gone out of her way to avoid him since their recent tiff. From the look of things, he had not been faring well. Purple blotched under his eyes, his hair was roughly combed, and the skin around his mouth was pinched.

"No one has forgotten your experience at the hands of Balaur Tsar, which makes you the best person to understand Jack and what he's going through."

"Do you know what Dust is? What it does to you?"

"Yes, you told us be—"

"It's a drug injected into you that turns your mind into a hollow metal casing that they fill with missions of death and obedience to the Order alone. Only the Silver One can give commands. The ability to speak and think for yourself is wiped away. You exist as that metal casing filled with their gunpowder and charged to explode at her will. Rational thought, morals, memories, right and wrong, your identity—none of that exists anymore once Dust fills your veins, and with each injection you crave more because the body builds a tolerance to it. You are the most elite killer but lower than a dog and completely submissive to your master, the Silver One. Or in my case, Balaur Tsar."

He paused, working his jaw back and forth as if grinding out the words. "Sometimes they forget to administer the next dose of Dust on schedule, and it weakens in your veins. Your mind tries to gather fragments of understanding, but injection after injection has eaten away at your memories. Some you may recall in pieces, but others are lost forever. Jack has been on Dust for *ten years*. The damage is irrevocably done."

"You cannot write him off as a mindless killer. That man in there is not the Jack we know."

"Precisely! The one you would take a bullet for is now the one behind the trigger. The Order killed Jack, emptied his mind, and filled the leftover carcass with their poison." He yanked his sleeve down, covering his scars. "He is no longer a man. He is a killing machine with guns for arms and knives for fingers. Humanity was driven from his bones long ago, leaving nothing but cold ruthless-ness. You know this! You just won't admit it, least of all to yourself."

Anger boiled to her fingertips, curling them in rage. "That is your best friend in there, yet you talk about him as if he is not the man most willing to lay down his life for you."

Philip's lip curled. "An ironic choice of words."

"What do you mean by that?"

"Only that perhaps Jack hasn't always been the hero."

Who was this person standing before her? Surely not the same boy who had shared bread scraps with her when they were street orphans or the friend who carried her all the way to a Romanian hospital when she was frozen and bleeding and half out of her mind with hysteria. Nor could this be the same man who sat at her bedside mourning the greatest loss they had ever experienced. This person before her was unrecognizable.

"Why are you being so cruel? We should be rejoicing and you've nothing but sourness to spill. This is Jack we're talking about. The man who plucked us off the streets. Who carried you to bed when you feel asleep at the dining table after a long training day. Who taught you to box and had your back in any fight. Do you not remember at all?"

"Those may be your golden memories, but they're not mine." He pressed the heel of his hand to his forehead, grinding against the bone as if in pain, then dropped his hand. "I see the outcome of all this when none of the rest of you do. I know what he's become, what they've made him, and there is no going back. You think me cruel, but you've yet to see what he's truly capable of. Stay away from him, Ives. For your own safety."

"No."

"My whole life I've tried to protect you. I won't stop now just because you haven't the sense to see to it yourself."

With that he stormed off, leaving Ivy to seethe in her own irate juices. Philip above all others should be standing here shoulder to shoulder with her ready to fight the demons on Jack's behalf, but instead of reaching out a hand to pull his friend from the pit, he cried the distance was too great and Jack a lost cause.

Not once had Jack betrayed Philip as a lost cause when Balaur Tsar abducted him from Lake Baikal. For months they had searched as Jack was eaten alive by guilt at not having rescued his best mate that fateful night. Jack would prefer that the torment had fallen on him than have anyone he cared about go through such horror. Fate, in all her cruelty, had granted his wish, yet Philip could not rouse himself to save Jack.

Nightmares of his captivity at Balaur Tsar's hands still haunted him. She often heard him shouting during the night, though he never spoke of it. The memories lingered like a burn scar. Time had healed the wound, but the knotted web of damaged skin remained forever a reminder of the pain inflicted.

Seeing Jack again had no doubt brought it all crashing back, and for that she might forgive him. In time. At the moment she wanted nothing more than to slug him in his insolent mouth.

Taking several deep breaths, she rolled away the anger and summoned calm. She peered through the viewing box. Jack sat unmoving on the cot. No doubt he'd heard every stinging word, though he gave no notice to the strife his presence created.

"Humanity was driven from his bones long ago."

Philip's words wriggled in her mind like worms of doubt, snuffling about for grains of hope to devour. What if he was right? What if Jack's humanity could not be excavated?

No. Her love for him, her faith in him, could not be buried so easily.

She curled her fingers over the rim of the box.

"Jack?" His shoulders rose and fell with his breaths. Even and steady, as he'd always been. Longing swelled within her. Ten years she'd been without him and aching to the hollowness of her core. At night she would dream of him but wake to hold only the cold air of loneliness. She mourned him, grieved for the losses stolen from them and all that might have been. Now he was here, yet he'd never seemed so far away.

For all the oceans, countries, and time itself that had separated them, the door between them now proved too great a barrier.

Against Washington's orders, she slipped the key from the hook and fit it into the lock. She turned the key and the locking mechanism unhitched like the bang of a shotgun. With a shaking hand, she opened the door.

"Jack?" He didn't so much as lift his head. The worms of doubt wriggled their damning blasphemy. *He is a Riser. A killer. He could snap your neck before you think to blink.* A chill of fear prickled over her and was immediately battled by a scorch of shame at her weakening resolve.

Bending her legs into motion, she took a step inside the cell, keeping near the door as a precaution.

"Do you not recognize me?"

A twitch, a blink, a nod, a tick of the mouth, anything to acknowledge her would have sufficed, but he offered her no relief.

She longed to kneel before him, circle her arms around him, and lay her head on his chest so she might feel his beating heart and breathe the same air once more. With no welcomed purpose, her arms hung useless at her sides as she tried to satiate her desperation for him by taking in the familiar lines of his face and body. They were the same, yet he had changed much.

His legs were as ever long but his thighs were thickened with muscle. His back and shoulders had grown wider, and a new scar ran ragged down the side of his neck. The long hair could not hide the crimp in his left ear—won in a boxing match from his youth—nor the stubble of reddish-brown growing over his cheeks and scaling down his throat. She could almost feel the hairs bristling softly beneath her palm as they had on lazy mornings when she shaved him. Those mornings had been too few for her liking. Would they ever know them again?

Clearing the nostalgia from her vision, she stepped closer.

"It's Ivy." The proximity threatened to undo her, but not nearly so much as his lack of response to it. It was the drugs. It had to be, for she would allow nothing else to have wiped his memory clean of her.

"Ten years ago we hunted a man by the name of Balaur Tsar in Romania. He was killed. We were later attacked coming down the mountain and you fell from a cliff. I thought you were dead, but somehow you survived and were taken by the Order of the Rising Moon. They gave you a drug to control you and turned you into an assassin called a Riser. Does any of this sound familiar? I thought you were dead and my heart could not take the loss. I died on that ledge with you. God knows I tried to, at least."

Tears clogged her throat, but she pushed on. "Then London. It was as if the sun burst forth over winter and breathed life into its barren plains. Yet my joy was stunted by witnessing what they'd done to you. You can no longer see me for the ice those monsters have frozen in your veins."

She squatted, tilting her head to see past the strands of dirty hair curtaining his face. "Assassin. Murderer. Riser. They speak these names as if they know you. They speak in fear, cowering in the shadows, as if saying the word in the open might summon you and all the terror carried in your name. But you are not Death. You are the man I love. You are Jack Vale."

Why would those blue eyes not look at her, even for a moment? A crack in the ice was all she needed. "I don't know what will happen to us. Fate is fickle and the stars are silent, but I do know this: no matter how difficult the circumstances or how savagely the world tries to tear us apart, I am here with you."

She stood and backed through the door, desperate to string out her last seconds in the same room with him. To her utter wretchedness, he didn't seem to notice when she came or went. She softly closed the barrier between them and locked the door while her heart remained on the other side.

"Surprise, surprise. Agent Vale violating my express order that no one step foot in that cell. Quite frankly, I wonder how you managed the patience this long."

Ivy jumped at Washington's accusing drawl. The key tumbled from her hand. He swooped down to retrieve it and hung it back on the hook. Only then did she notice the gun in his hand.

Seeing her focused point of interest, he held it up. The dim light did little to brighten the silver's dullness. "A tranquilizer gun. Should he have attacked you." Spearing her with one of his infamous stares, he tucked the gun into the back of his belt.

"I'm sorry, sir. I didn't mean to go against your orders."

"Yes, you did. As you frequently do." He settled into the corridor's lone chair and crossed his legs as if he were upstairs in his library and not three levels belowground watching over a mind-controlled killer. "Did he tell you anything?"

Ivy shook her head, rebuked but not remorseful. "He gave no

recognition of anything. Names, the Order, his supposed death . . . me. He merely stares at the wall."

"Give him time. Brainwashing takes a lot out of a man." He reached into his breast pocket and pulled out a pipe and pouch of tobacco. He pressed a pinch of the dried leaves into the bowl and held a lit match until it caught to a fragrant burn. "Do not grow disheartened. Jack has been lost to darkness for so long that it will take a great deal of courage to draw him back. You must stay the course and forgive others when they stumble from doubt."

Of all the instructors, Washington had seemed most eager to believe her report from London, but his brilliant mind hesitated without solid facts to observe. She had known this about her mentor yet could not hide her disappointment. Now that she had returned with her ghost for all to see, no one doubted her sanity, but new questions had arisen. Ones she was afraid would leave her fighting alone.

"Then you do not believe him lost and irretrievable?"

"No one can be truly lost as long as there remains one searching for him, but a word of caution. The path forward will not be easy, and the shadows of what once was may rise up to devour you in despair. You may find it difficult to escape."

She'd had a dream once that Jack had returned to her alive. He'd swept her into his arms and kissed her. His words were sweet and low in her ear as he promised never to leave her again. That their love could never be destroyed. She'd awoken with tears of happiness that quickly turned to sadness as she realized that would never be their fate. Their reunion now, so real it took her breath away, was anything but a tender dream. It was dark and twisted with demons, but it was theirs, and for now that was enough.

"If I can't run from the shadows, then I'll invite them to dance."

Washington's gaze drifted off as smoke puffed around his bald head. Unlike Jefferson, he had not allowed time to hold him down long enough to stamp him.

"The pair of you have always been attuned to a melody all your own. If I were a man given to romantics, I'd say it's rare to find notes to make up such a composition."

"Sir, you do yourself a discredit to think you lack in romance when you quote Ethel Waters at the drop of a—" Music. That was it! The sentimental key to unlocking the depth of emotions where other memories hadn't the profundity to tread.

"Washington, you're a genius! Purely, utterly brilliant." She whirled toward the stairs after planting an impulsive kiss on his cheek, a dozen album titles skipping through her head. But there was only one she needed to play.

"To the greatest heights or lowest depths, I'd go to be with you."

Washington called after her. "Before you set about an impromptu concert, inform Franklin that Jack might be up for a health examination, then have Cook make up a tray of barley broth, soda crackers, and green tea from the stash Hamilton brought back from China last month. He hides it in his study behind the Waterloo painting. There'll be time enough for questions and answers once we've got him good and fed. A man can become more himself on a full belly."

"Yes, sir."

"Oh, and Mrs. Vale." Ivy paused on the step and looked back. Smoke curled from Washington's mouth. "I've called an all-hands meeting for eighteen hundred to discuss the dispatches I've already sent to Talon headquarters in London, Paris, and Berlin about the Order. We're going after those bastards until not one vile speck of Dust remains."

★★★

He listened as her steps faded away. A trace of perfume lingered in the cell, flowers—which kind he could not recall—that beckoned him from the bitterness of gunpowder and metal to a place just beyond the darkness mottling his mind.

He pushed at the darkness, straining against its boundaries, but the border was thick and entrenched. He had tried scaling it, but his fingers couldn't gain purchase on the slick walls that hurled him back into the darkness. Somehow her perfume weaved its way over the edge to offer a glimpse of what lay beyond, a softness that was not reinforced with bullets and knife tips. A softness that knew him.

She knew him. Knew what had happened to him. Knew who he was before—he stared down at his cut and bruised knuckles that stung with pain since there was no more Dust to stop it—before he'd become this.

Like a hunter, he'd become attuned to his prey. She was small and quick, her reactions instinctual as she used skillful offense to disarm rather than brute strength. Like a dance she'd done many times before. Ducking around him, jumping on his back, locking her arm around his neck. She had not pinned him to the floor. He'd done that. Green eyes staring up at him, her voice pleading with sorrow as she'd done here in the cell.

"I am here with you."

He dropped his head into his hands, squeezing his eyes shut as her voice called to him from beyond the black void of his mind. Another time, another place she had danced around him and he'd pinned her.

"Please, Jack. Mercy."

This voice was not sorrowful or pleading. It was filled with light. The darkness recoiled at the brightness, not enough for him to see by, but enough for him to glimpse that a possibility existed beyond.

Jack. His name was Jack.

SEVEN

"SURELY YOU REMEMBER THIS ONE. WE FOX-TROTTED TO IT IN THE BALL-room. You with your bare feet and me in my stockings so we wouldn't scuff the polished floor and earn Dolly's wrath. She's always so particular about that floor."

The woman—Ivy, she called herself—stood across from Jack in the cell. She always kept distance between them. Music played from a machine she'd wheeled in on a trolley the past three mornings. Record after record of songs she knew every word to, but all he heard was noise.

She watched him, waiting. She was always watching, those keen eyes alert to every tic he made. Not that he made many. Movement and resistance had been cut from him. He moved only when ordered.

"Not ringing any bells? Or maybe you're not in a foxtrot mood. Let's try something slower." She replaced the record with a new one. The noise was slower in tempo. She stared again as if rooting in his mind for recognition.

"Please, Jack. Give me something. Anything to let me know you at least hear me."

He heard her. Heard the brightness in her voice greeting him each time she walked into the cell. Heard the brightness fading with each passing minute he didn't respond. Heard the brightness drop into a dejected sigh as she left. Could nearly hear the quick, shallow breaths, the thrumming of her heartbeat like that of a hare crouching in the brush as a wolf waited nearby.

Her worry was pointless. Unless attacked, he wouldn't move. The order to move came from authority, and that she did not have. So he waited. Anything else meant punishment. Pain that he could not escape.

"We listened to this on the rooftop once. I'd had a rather terrible day of Jefferson's constant ripostes to my every parry during a fencing lesson—you were the only one who could ever match him—and you hauled the gramophone all the way to the roof with Tchaikovsky, King Oliver, and Irving Berlin tucked under your arm. We sat and listened all night as the stars danced over our heads." Her hand, small but deadly, rested atop the metal horn from which the music came.

"I still go up there. The city sleeps at my feet and the heavens shimmer above me. Sometimes I feel those stars have been my only constant, calling to me with understanding while steadying me in place. Do you remember the stars?"

He heard her as he did before, but now something stirred within him to answer. He could not. He could only answer the order giver.

A blackened edge of his mind curled back. He stood on a ledge of darkness. Bright lights pierced the nothingness above. He longed to reach for the brightness but feared tainting them with his touch. They had called to him as she claimed they called to her. He waited for her to continue with words that might further peel away the blackness.

"I would stare at them for hours." Her voice moved over the music, edging apart the notes until he heard only her. "It was the only way I felt close to you, the only time I allowed the loneliness to steal over me. I have taken mission after mission to temper my pain and keep my thoughts from turning to destruction, but under the stars my pain and loneliness flow free like blood from a cut, pricked unmercifully by Orion, Perseus, and Polaris."

The stars had names? And she knew them. Something flared inside him. He didn't understand the feeling, only that it wasn't pain.

Bracing her back against the far wall, she slid to the floor. She wore green. As she had the past three days.

"You died shouting, yet the specter who took your place is silent. You sit before me, flesh and blood, yet it is not you. I am here with your ghost." She lifted her hand, fingers curling in the air as if reaching across the space between them, then slowly withdrew. "What must I do to bring you back?"

Nothing. He had tried to set free the screaming voice inside his head, the gaze that drifted to the night sky of bright lights, the fingers that clawed for release, but Dust beat them back, drowned them out, reduced them to no more than a stain seeping across his brain. She could not understand the blackness consuming him any more than he could recall the names of those stars.

"Have those monsters taken so much from you that a single word is too much? Perhaps you have forgotten words." She stood and placed another record on the machine. "Will this remind you?"

The needle scratched. Music filled the cell. Music he recognized. Not from the scorched blotches in his memory but because she played it each day. Her green eyes ever watchful for his reaction.

"All that I ask of you is love."

She waited until the last note faded before turning her eyes from him. He wished for one more note if only to keep her gaze on him, even in sorrow.

Each time the key turned in the lock, he would look up and wait for her to enter. Sometimes it was her and he would wait for her voice to fill the nothingness within him. Other times it was a bald man with questions, trays of food, and a change of clothes. The food he ate for necessity, but the clothes were untouched. Cleanliness had never been ordered or considered a necessity. Once a round man entered to draw blood with a needle while a tall red-headed man stood in the doorway, a gun on his belt. Jack sat unmoving and unspeaking through it all, as he was trained to do. Only when the woman, Ivy, came did he feel the pull to respond. If only he could.

After placing the record in its protective sleeve, she stacked it with the others at the bottom of the trolley. "I'll go and see about a tea tray. Perhaps that'll perk you up. Without the tea, of course, since you never could abide it. Flavored water you called it, but Cook will have a batch of lemonade ready, and I believe I smelled cookies baking."

The food trays taunted his nose with smells that made his mouth water for a single taste, but he touched only the glass of water, vegetable broth, and slice of bread. All of which he let sit for hours to turn cold and stale. Orders did not allow for warmth or freshness.

As she pushed the music machine out of the cell on its trolley, she cast him one last look. She sighed, a sound void of brightness, then locked the door behind her. The muscles in his mouth moved as if to call out, but no sound came. Not without orders.

Her footsteps faded away, each one tightening the walls around him. He shifted his gaze to where she had stood as the words from the song rang in his ears. He grasped for the notes and stabbed at the darkness in his mind, chipping away at the edges desperate to keep him out. The song held meaning to her. To Ivy. And to him, as she insisted. If only he could carve away enough of the blackness, he might understand.

He had worked his way through the chorus with little progress against the impregnable nothingness when the key turned in the lock. His attention snapped to the door. That strange eagerness to see her again battled against his instinctive alertness.

It wasn't her, but the man she called Philip. He had never entered the cell before, only looked through the door's cutout often enough.

At first he had said nothing, merely stared, but then the muttering had come. Baikal. Balaur Tsar. Torture. Betrayed. Abandoned.

The man—Philip—stepped inside and shut the door behind him. They never shut the door.

"Hello, Jack."

Each interaction was the same. The person would step in and greet him, then wait as if he could respond. When no reply came, they would carry on as if one had, asking their questions and presenting him with whatever temptation they brought—food, clothes, bedding—all the while remaining acutely sentient.

Philip moved with the agitated awareness of a wounded creature, slinking low to conserve its strength all the while setting its teeth for attack.

Resting his arms on his knees, Jack kept his attention on the far wall while calculating Philip's every breath, limb movement, eye shift, and nuanced tense of muscle. It was an assassin's instinct that told him a target's intention to bolt a split second before it happened. He tired of the predator and prey circle.

"Remember me? Your old pal Philip." A sad laugh escaped him. "Of course you don't. I didn't remember much either when I first came off the Dust. It has a way of eating away your mind bit by bit. It took months before my memories returned. Some in pieces and some not at all, not even after ten years. I'd be surprised if any of yours came back with the amount of Dust you've taken over the years.

"I see you're sleeping on the floor." Philip nodded to the thin blanket Jack had draped on the floor next to the bed. "A Riser still can't bring himself to sleep on a proper bed. Not allowed. At least you've a blanket. I had moldy wood shavings where they kept me at Poenari Castle."

Poenari Castle? No, there was no castle. Merely caves and tunnels dug deep into a mountain. An ancient underground stronghold built as a refuge against Ottoman attacks. A river and waterfall flowed above it. The rush of water loud enough to drown out the tortured screams buried in the earth.

The edges of Jack's blackened memory crackled. He clutched at the pieces falling like ash. Stone floors so cold that the moldy rivulets of water seeping from the ceiling would freeze in the floor cracks and frost his cheek as he curled atop a scrap of burlap in search of sleep. The stench of unwashed bodies. Gnawing hunger. Desperate cries for Dust to stop the pain burning in their veins. Jack had been one of many, but time passed and only he remained. By then his voice no longer cried for relief and silent obedience ruled.

Philip's attention moved to the pile of clothes folded neatly by the door. "Disregarding clean clothes as well. Cleanliness isn't a require-ment for assassinations, is it? Nothing matters but the mission. Not warmth, or comfort, or satisfying food. Humanity is a weakness to the Order, and Risers are anything but weak. Little by little they strip it from you. Your thoughts, your morals, the very fiber of your char-acter until there's nothing but what they've created." He kept close to the wall, well away from the predator, crossing his arms over his thin chest.

"I remember hunkering in that festering cell and whispering my name over and over so I wouldn't lose it. I knew if I did, I would be lost forever."

Jack had lost his name. Only just had it returned to him. He held fast to its possession like a man to his raft on a sea determined to drown him. Jack. His name was Jack Vale.

"When Ivy said it was you in London, I didn't believe her. I couldn't. Not after all these years. We watched you go over the cliff. No one could have survived that fall." Philip's words turned hard. "How are you alive, Jack?"

The sound of his name spoken aloud ground into Jack's ears. The muscles in his throat strained, desperate to reclaim the power of answering as himself. His tongue lifted, sluggish from disuse.

"I-I don't . . . know." The rusted words moved with uncertainty over his lips, the English foreign to his ears. Romanian had been the language of the Order, but now his born tongue clawed up the back of his throat, clamoring from the abyss to which it had been cut off.

"You speak." Philip seemed surprised, though not entirely caught off guard. "Parts of you remain."

"My mind." Jack tapped the side of his head where the blotches still held fast to his memories—all but the outer rims that slowly disintegrated like gunpowder spilled from a cracked cartridge. His fingers caught in snarls of hair coated thick with dirt and grease.

An odd sensation simmered under his skin. It prickled the hairs on his arms and scalp until he could no longer stand the filth beneath his fingertips. This wasn't an odd sensation, but a very old one long held captive. One his senses had been hardened against under the layers of weapons and blood and death.

Disgust.

"My mind. It traps me. You know. You understand."

"Yes, I understand."

"The woman, does she understand?"

"The woman—you mean Ivy? Has she not told you who she is?" He sounded genuinely surprised this time.

A yes grappled up Jack's throat, but it stuck behind his teeth. Had she told him who she was? He gripped his head in his hands, squeezing as if the pressure might loosen the black shrouds. She talked a great deal of the past. They had spent much time together. Music. Dancing. Stars. Why was the only freed memory one of those green eyes staring at him in horror on the edge of a cliff?

"She watched me die."

"Yes, she did. Nearly died herself." A long sigh. "It hasn't been easy on Ivy. She went through some dark days, and there were times I didn't think she'd make it back. Especially those first few months . . . She didn't want to go on, but I managed to pull her back from the edge. That's what brothers do." Hardness chipped Philip's voice. The muscles in his body tensed.

"Why did it take you so long to show yourself? Why did you not break free?"

"I could not."

"You couldn't. Is that what you said after Baikal? When Miles was flung into that freezing water, his last gasps pleas for his life? When Balaur dragged me away as I screamed for you to save me? Was that what you said when you didn't save us? You just couldn't?"

Jack pressed his head harder. Baikal. A lake of frozen water and a Snow Queen. Men all in black, but one man more terrible than the rest with colorless eyes. There was gunfire and screaming. Ice cracking. An explosion.

Pain throbbed behind his eyes as the unrelenting pressure of his hands bored through his skull, but not deep enough to hammer out the most blackened memories.

Philip took a jerky step. The air shuddered with agitation. A sky ominous before the thunder.

"You claimed we were brothers. Together to the end. Only you weren't there when I needed you most. I know now all your words were lies. You used me to get closer to Ivy. Then you abandoned me. You betrayed our so-called bond.

"I needed you and you left me in the hands of Balaur Tsar to be tortured night and day, to have his filthy claws reaching into my brain and scrambling all the goodness until I heard only his voice. And my *brother* wasn't there to stop him because he'd abandoned me on the ice of Baikal." His teeth scraped together. "I wasn't good enough to be one of Balaur's precious Risers. He wanted true soldiers that would fulfill the Order's objective to purge the world of the unworthy and raise themselves up. You were what he was looking for. The shadow of Jack Vale is long and all-encompassing. No one can hope to step out of it."

The blackness hissed as Philip's words scorched the edges of Jack's memory. They uncovered a rusted chair with straps. Straps that cut his skin when cinched tight against his struggle. A leather muzzle with metal slats for breathing would come around his mouth, so fierce it drew blood from his teeth pressed against his lips to cut off his screams.

Protests, screams, cursing, restraints. He *did* try to fight back. He *did* resist.

Jack scoured his fingers through his hair, dragging welts of pain across his scalp. What had happened? Why had he not escaped?

"Dust." He looked up. "They pumped us full of Dust until our veins demanded more. Risers could not do without it."

Philip's eyes were wild. Like those of prey when it thinks of besting the predator.

"That's right. They got you addicted so you would be completely dependent on them for the next dose. A successful mission meant the next hit. Fail and they'd let you lapse into a withdrawal so bad you'd want to claw the blood from your body. Each injection wiped away who you were until only the mindless compliance of a Riser remained. A weapon of death. Isn't that what you are, Jack? Death."

My name is Death. Jack Vale had been stamped out. Namelessness was what they gave him.

My weapon is Death. He was sharpened into a knife's blade until it was welded to his bones.

My purpose is Death. He existed for no other reason than to kill.

The blackness in his mind stretched out flat and frozen. Ice cracked beneath his feet and wind whipped against his chapped cheeks. Men in black with red crowns and dragons dripping like blood on their chests. A man on his knees in the center of the ice. Women screaming. The man being dragged away. An explosion.

Jack's head snapped up. He caught and held Philip's gaze.

"I remember you."

Philip crossed the chamber and dropped to a crouch in front of Jack. Close, intimate, and dangerous.

"Do you? What is it you remember? Promising to have my back no matter what or watching me being dragged away? Which of those do you remember? Because I remember nothing good of you."

"There was ice and an explosion."

"Yes, right where you abandoned me. Then I was tortured, beaten, brainwashed, and forced to kill innocent people with no ability to refuse. I waited for you to come rescue me. Day after day, but you never came. You left me there. Jack Vale, everyone's hero, was no hero to me." Philip's jaw worked back and forth, his expression hardening.

"I wanted you to feel the hopelessness I felt. I wanted you to know what it was like to be without friends or rescue. I wanted you to know the anguish of having the person you trust most betray you. Do you remember what happened on that mountainside after we left Poenari Castle?"

"The woman—Ivy—told me we were attacked. There was a gunshot. I fell off the cliff."

"There were *two* gunshots. One for the attacker. One for *you*."

Jack touched the spot near his collarbone where a bullet wound had scarred over. "You shot me."

"That's right. I had no choice. Not after seeing you for the enemy you are. Mine and Ivy's lives would have been better off without you showing up to pull us apart and then break her heart. It became obvious that you needed to be removed from our lives. So I did what I did. I didn't know if you'd survive the fall or if the Silver One would fish you from the river. Either way, I didn't care. You were gone, and Ivy and I could get back to the way things used to be."

The man—Philip—rocked back and forth on his heels. "Imagine my surprise when you turned up alive and well in London. Should've known the mighty Jack Vale would defeat the odds and survive. Go on to become the Order's top assassin." His nostrils flared. "You should have stayed dead. For Ivy's sake. Now I'll have to watch her suffer all over again."

"She doesn't know you shot me off the cliff."

"No, and she's never going to. It was a convenient shot that made the attacker look like he took you over with him. I had to protect her from you. It was for her own good, because she could never see you for what you are. You coerced us into a lifestyle where people want to kill us, and then we got in too deep to escape Talon. Not to mention you wanting me out of the way so you could gain all the glory. And Ivy."

"You claim you were my brother."

"Once. But I'm her brother first, and I choose her." Philip's face inched closer, his breath hissing through clenched teeth. Wetness sheened his eyes.

"The Order found me again after we captured you. They gave me a choice. Either I hand over Ivy for punishment for all the Order members she's killed, or I return you, their Riser. I won't allow them to hurt her because of you. I know your orders were to destroy Talon headquarters, but we caught you at the juice joint. It's time to complete your mission."

A flash of metal, then a needle pierced Jack's neck before he could react.

"Goodbye, Jack."

Jack sprang off the bed, clawing at his stinging skin.

"No! I will not go back to that."

He swung wildly at Philip, but already the white thickness swelled in his veins like a bullet shooting through a muzzle. Hot lead devoured his blood. It fired into his brain, blacking out the ice and the cold.

It blacked out the memory of Philip being dragged away by Balaur Tsar before choking around the last holdout: the woman, Ivy.

Jack reached for the memory of her, holding her gaze through the inferno of pain until the Dust burned him out and swallowed her whole.

He stared at the wall of nothingness before him. And waited.

"Riser." A man spoke from the corner of the chamber.

"*Da.*"

The man placed the empty syringe in his pocket as he came forward. He stopped inches away.

"Who are you?"

"*Eu sunt moartea.*"

"Well, then. I have your next mission, Death."

EIGHT

"You haven't told him you're his wife?" Dolly whirled from the oven with the baking sheet precariously tipping the hot cookies to the edge.

"It's not exactly something you spring on a man who's been brainwashed for the evil side for the past ten years. 'Oh, hello. Remember me? Ivy Vale, your wife and the woman you promised to love and honor all the days of your life before sealing it with a wedding band?'"

Ivy glanced over the latest report of possible Order activity as she rolled a piece of freshly washed hair and pinned it in place. Forty-four precise pin curls so far. Three more to go.

"I'm afraid the vow 'until death do us part' may have a different meaning to history's deadliest assassin."

After giving Cook the afternoon off, Dolly had taken over the kitchen. She always baked when stressed, and ever since the new occupant in the holding cell arrived, everyone at Talon headquarters had been balancing on knife tips. At least Dolly's outlet was delicious, even if she was heavy-handed with the despicable vanilla extract.

Washington had decided to rearrange the books in the library by publishing date according to the Julian calendar, while Jefferson prowled the garden whacking at weeds with his fencing rapier.

"Then what have you been telling him?" Dolly dropped the

baking sheet on the kitchen's worn worktable. A cookie bounced off toward where Ivy sat on the opposite side.

Ivy picked up the cookie and tossed it back on the sheet. Drops of melted chocolate burned her fingertips, and she licked off the sweetness before reaching for another hairpin.

"Little things in hopes of jogging his memory. Hamilton says the best thing to do for a person with psychological issues is allow them to come to conclusions on their own. Our duty is only to lay the path because forcing the issue may cause more of a setback or irreparable damage."

Dolly closed the oven door. "Far be it from me to argue with Talon's resident psychologist. You've the patience of a saint and the perseverance of an army general. Our Jack will come round in no time."

Frowning, she gazed over Ivy's hair. "How you accomplish that without a mirror amazes me."

"Multitasking is the mistress of necessity. A mirror only slows me down." Ivy pinned the last curl in place, then tied a silk scarf around her head. She closed the report file and shuffled it in with the others stacked beneath her gun, which had tiny flecks of red rubbed into the metal. A testament to her early days of checking her weapon after painting her nails. Sighing over her novice mistake, she dragged the bottle of red nail polish closer.

More than anything, she wanted her Jack back. The Jack who lit up when she entered the room. The Jack who could recall every star in the sky and quote lyrics to her favorite songs. The best friend who teased her and the lover who held her. Yet day after day she could not find him in that stranger's cold stare.

Her heart broke each minute she spent in that dreary cell with him until she was certain there were no pieces left to break. Yet each time the fragments would fasten themselves back together, only to crumble all over again. Her biggest fear was not that he would remain a Riser, for at least then she might cling to hope of breaking the fortress of his mind. The terror gripping her in its unrelenting claws was that Jack would come back, but not as the man she'd known. Instead, he'd be a man who no longer had a place for her in his memory or his heart.

"What if he doesn't love me anymore?" The fear escaped in a whisper, but it might as well have deafened the room with the force of a howitzer, blasting out before Ivy had a chance to stop it. Horrid emotion stung her eyes with the impact of hearing the words aloud.

Dolly leveled her no-nonsense gaze at Ivy. "Never have I seen two people more of the same soul. The road isn't paved for smoothness, but you'll find your way back to each other." She turned and rescued the spatula from the back of a drawer. "Jack loved you. *Loves* you. It may be buried under ten years of hardship, but truth like that doesn't die. Just give it time to find its roots again."

"What if the roots have been severed? What if he never returns?"

"Then we'll manage that day when it comes."

Ivy blinked away the tears and swiped the red paint over her final nail. She'd not allowed herself the vulnerability of breaking down in a long time, and she wasn't about to encourage the habit. If that floodgate opened, she might not be able to close it again, and her marbles would be declared lost for good.

Capping the polish, she blew on her wet nails. "Has anyone told you you're quite the romantic?"

"Poppycock. As if I'd allow such a ridiculous notion to cross anyone's mind."

"Is that why you've never been married? Too ridiculous?"

Dolly scooped a cookie off the pan and shook the spatula at Ivy's nose. "I'll tell you what's ridiculous. Keeping after that Washington. Proximity to that man for thirty years is enough to put any woman off husband hunting."

"Then my plan has been successful in saving the men of the free world from matrimony with your sharp tongue. Not a one would last a month, so I took the burden upon myself to dissuade you of this husband hunting." Washington's words of retaliation strode into the kitchen two seconds before the rest of him did.

"How grateful we are for your contribution." Dolly glared at him as she wielded her weapon of choice, which dripped with melted chocolate.

"You're quite welcome, but I've found another who might give you a run for your money." He circled the table and dropped a green folder in front of Ivy, eyeing her pinned and wrapped hair but wisely saying nothing. It wasn't the first time the kitchen had doubled as a beauty salon.

Careful of her not-quite-dry nails, Ivy opened the folder and gasped at the photograph clipped to the front of dozens of papers and reports. Long face, flat lips, flat nose, hair frizzing out from beneath a head shawl. The sepia tones only added to the earthiness of her skin and the hypnotic focus of her eyes.

"I know this woman, though that noun is a bit indulgent. More of a creature. I saw her at Dobryzov Castle in 1917." The day they thought Jack had killed Balaur Tsar only for him to return from the dead weeks later. The day so many things went terribly wrong.

"Helena Dragavei. Also known as the Silver One." Washington flipped through the pages and pulled out a single sheet with a drawing of a black flag sporting a silver moon, a gold star, and words written in a language that should have died long ago.

Translation: *The Next Step Is Not Enough.*

"Order of the Rising Moon's top banana."

A million questions raced through Ivy's head as she stared at the photograph. The woman had been within their grasp all along.

"How long has she been head of the Order?"

"Since 1890 when she resurrected it from the shadows. The Order was dormant for nearly two hundred years after moving underground in the eighteenth century, and it wasn't until right before the war that they started to stretch their legs again. If you recall, that was when we had our first run-in with Balaur Tsar, who went by the name Yuri at the time. He held no power then, but it didn't take long for him to climb through the ranks."

Ivy remembered all right. She and Philip—still living on the streets at the time—had sought refuge from the rain in a tunnel and found themselves smack dab in the middle of a sting operation that ended with her choking Jack and then being offered a job at Talon. She had not a single regret, but this woman—Ivy tapped a finger on the creature's slab of a forehead—had thrown her life to hell. That forehead was the perfect target for a bullet. Then two more, one through each of those hypnotic devil eyes.

"How have we not known about her until now?"

"Vlad III established the Order on a hierarchy where Dragavei now perches at the top. It seems her method is to put others out front while she remains hidden behind the curtain pulling the strings. But the war made her restless, and in her eagerness for the Order to reign supreme, she's shown her hand."

He reached for a warm cookie and earned a smack on his hand with the spatula, which earned Dolly a glare. She ignored it and continued plating the cookies.

"With Balaur dead we assumed the Order was dead as well. Our fault entirely for dropping the ball on that one. It wasn't until the recent string of political assassinations that we began to theorize their return from the dead. Again. Jack's reappearance solidified it."

Dolly placed a small plate with two gooey cookies in front of Ivy, but food was the last thing her roiling stomach could handle. Jack. The initiator, the prolonger, and the key forged to unlock this creature's Pandora's box.

Washington swiped one of the cookies and shoveled it into his mouth as Dolly moved to the sink for washing up. He chewed and swallowed quickly before she could catch him.

"Dragavei is the last of the line of original leaders put in charge by Vlad," he said. "The role of the Silver One has always been passed through blood succession. Rumor has it she poisoned her father so she wouldn't have to wait for the mantle."

"Charming."

"This photograph was taken last month in Budapest by one of our Hungarian agents." Washington shuffled out another photograph. Dragavei and a man standing in a park, deep in conversation, unaware they were being watched.

"The man is Balaur's replacement and the Order's weapons procurer. He was taken out shortly after this meeting, and our agent found a list of cities in his pocket. Cities where presidents, mobsters, and powerful businessmen have been assassinated over the past few months. London was next on the list, so I sent Philip to confer with Britannia."

"Three decades she's pulled the strings and allowed others to do the dirty work. Why show herself now?"

Washington braced his hands on the table, cookies within reach, but he made no move for them, his razor-sharp focus seeming trained on the discussion at hand.

"As I said, she's grown restless, and restlessness provokes recklessness. The Order of the Rising Moon is life and death to this woman. She cares for nothing but to see her legacy fulfilled. She has ordered the genocide of entire villages, the theft of weapons materials, the detonation of railways, the slaying of armies, and the assassinations of high-ranking political figures. She is wiping the slate of humanity clean for the Order to take its place in world government."

"And she's used Jack to do it."

Washington spared her an agreeing nod and packed the papers back into the folder. "I've already begun a list of preparations to be distributed to our international headquarters so they can aid us in tracking down this abominable harpy—"

"Keep your lists. I'm going after her now." Ivy grabbed her gun and slid off the chair, resolve slicing through the knots in her stomach.

"We don't know where she is."

"Everything we need to know is trapped in Jack's head. I'm going to get it out. After I do, I'm hunting down that piece of filth and putting a bullet in her for every second of torment she's caused him."

Washington's eyebrows slanted as he very precisely closed the folder.

"You have not been given those orders." Each clipped word echoed in the silence now pervading the kitchen. Even the clock on the wall seemed to hesitate in its ticking.

Ivy wasn't hesitating. Not anymore. "I am beyond orders at this point. I want my husband back and I want Dragavei dead."

"You cannot storm out of here with guns blazing. It's reckless, and such rashness will get you killed. Or another agent. You pull another stunt and disobey orders like you did in London, and so help me I'll lock you in a cell buried so far beneath this floor that worms dare not crawl so low. Put aside the Maiden. She'll be the death of you."

"I'm too angry to be killed."

His eyes, always on the precipice of cutting, sharpened to the point of a knife tip. One prick and he could slice her in two. "And now you're irrational. I taught you to think better than that."

"I'm tired of thinking. I want to *do*." She slammed her fist on the table, clattering the plate of cookies.

"You want revenge."

"Yes!"

"As do I for every life her evilness has snuffed out and for every bit of darkness she has cast across our lands, but I will *not* lose another agent in this pursuit of destruction."

Ting! Ting! Ting! The fire alarm sounded.

The blade in Washington's eyes sheathed. He jerked a finger to

Dolly. "Woman, have you tripped the alarm with your infernal cooking? I told you not to give Cook the afternoon off."

"This is none of my doing." Dolly plunked soapy hands on her hips and scowled. "Do you see smoke pouring from this room? No. Most likely it's Franklin in his lab."

Ivy stepped out into the hall. The air smelled of ash and smoke.

"I don't think it's Franklin."

"Fire!" Panicked voices crashed all around.

Ivy sprinted down the corridor toward the shout with Washington fast on her heels and found Hamilton banging on doors.

"Fire!"

Washington dodged as an agent bolted from one of the doors. "What's happened?"

Hamilton kept banging as he went down the hall. "Fire started. Smoke pouring up from the basement."

Jack. Ivy turned for the stairs that would take her belowground.

Washington caught her elbow. "Get outside. Now. I'll get him."

"I haven't cleared the top floors yet," Hamilton said.

Ivy pulled from Washington's grasp. "You get the top floors. I'm going below."

He shouted after her, but she was already running around the corner and disappearing through the concealed portal to the stairs before he could stop her.

Smoke stung her eyes as it drifted up the tight passageway. She ripped the scarf from her head and held it over her mouth. She had to pass through the underground training area before another set of stairs led down to the interrogation cells. Nothing would stop her from getting there.

"Ivy!" Philip barreled from the smoke and grabbed her shoulders. Ash smeared his face. "Get out of here!"

"Jack's down there." She wrestled out of his grip.

"It's too late! The fire is too much." He reached for her again and tugged her back toward the stairs from whence she'd come. "We have to get out of here!"

"Not without Jack!"

"It's too dangerous!"

"Then get yourself out." She wrenched herself from his hold and sprinted for the next set of stairs.

Philip's shouts echoed after her. "Ivy! Ivy, wait!"

She wasn't waiting for anything. *Hold on, Jack. I'm coming.*

Talon's training space was carved from the brick and dirt of the city's underbelly with chambers cordoned off for archery, fencing, explosives, and all other manner of deadly arts. On a typical day the walls rang with steel, dynamite, and grunts of exertion, but all of that was scorched in tongues of flame as the fire spewed up from the interrogation level and crackled across weapon racks and maps tacked to the walls. Ivy coughed and ducked below the swell of smoke.

A pole spewing flames flew at her head. She hit the ground flat and rolled, her scarf fluttering free from her hand. Fire singed the tip of a flyaway curl.

The flamethrower, taken from the battlefield of Verdun during the Great War, blasted orange and red fire. She rolled sideways, sprang to her feet, and kicked the deadly contraption from its bearer's hands. Before the device had time to clatter against the wall, a fist struck at her from the smoke. She dodged and danced sideways.

Please, please don't let it be who I think it is.

Another fist came at her and without hesitation she moved to counter it. As she'd done in the familiar dance a thousand times before.

"Stop trying to kill me every time we're together!"

The man who emerged from the flames and smoke wasn't Jack.

It was the cold-eyed Riser with nothing short of murder on his brainwashed mind. But how? The Dust was gone from his system. And how had he gotten out of his cell?

Their sparring shadows tangled along the walls and ceiling wreathed in fire. Maps and files curled and charred black. Rifle barrels melted, their wooden stocks bursting like tinder.

This was madness. Tears streamed from Ivy's eyes as smoke blurred her vision. If—no, not if—*when* the fire reached the gunpowder storage . . .

"Come on! You want to kill me? You'll have to catch me first." She sprinted for the stairs. They had mere minutes to outrun the coming explosion.

She raced up the steps, pushed through the portrait entrance, and burst into the grand hall—and straight into another blaze.

Fire dripped from the great banners, licking red tongues over mahogany-paneled walls and marble columns as it climbed to rake over the chandeliers, flames reflecting on each crystal facet. Over it all watched Talon's golden eagle from its perch high on the wall, its sharp eyes keen and glowing against the backdrop of its flag, its wings spread wide to the pyre below. Centuries of history. Gone with the flick of a match. But how? The fire from downstairs had yet to blaze this far aboveground, though it wouldn't be long as smoke poured out from the open portal.

Jack emerged from the stairs and stalked toward her. Not a smoke-weighted tear from his eye or a singed hair on his head. Weakness was stamped out with cold ruthlessness. A hunter oblivious to all but the prey in his sights. For all the twistedness of the situation, this prey thought only to save the hunter.

"That's right. Just come this way." She backed toward the front door as heat blazed against her face. "Let's take this round outside, shall we?"

Without breaking stride, he grabbed a flagpole and hurled it at her. It struck her legs and she stumbled, sprawling across the ash-coated floor.

He jumped at her. She met him with a knee to the chest.

He answered with a smack across the face that ripped her head sideways. The taste of blood trickled over her lip. She spat it out, grabbed his arm, and twisted it back. The force was enough to yank the arm from the socket and a howl of pain from any man. Jack merely grunted and shoved it back in place before slamming her down. She hooked her legs around his and wrenched his feet out from under him.

"Stop fighting me! I'm your wife. Do you hear? I am your wife, Ivy!" She slapped him hard across the face. Blood puckered through a slit on his lip. "Your name is Jack Lawrence Vale. You are my husband, and I will have you back."

Reddish-brown eyebrows, so straight and cutting, slanted down over cold eyes. A flicker, but enough to break his murderous concentration.

"I didn't spend the last decade believing you dead only to find you now and die in a fire, but if you're going to be the death of me, I'll have you know me first."

Fire gobbled up the walls with a heat that nearly burned her skin, but she didn't dare lose her grip on him. She might never come this close again.

The icy stare cracked. Orange light spilled across the deep blue like kerosene on the ocean's surface, rippling through the blackness crushed in the depths below. A memory? A recognition?

The crack turned jagged, brittle as a blade's edge. His teeth flashed in a snarl.

"I don't know you." He swung wildly, his voice harsh as nails scraping over the strung-out wires of her heart. "I don't know you."

Ivy leaped back out of his reach. Her feet caught on the discarded flagpole and she fell. She scrambled backward as Jack came toward her, fist raised for a final deliverance. Her back rammed into a pillar, blocking escape.

She stared up at her husband, the man she'd vowed to love until her dying breath. It hurt to watch him. He shone brighter than anything she'd ever witnessed. It was difficult to look at him and even more difficult to look away, for though death was in his eyes, they were still the only pair she longed to gaze into.

"Mercy, Jack."

His arm swung through the air and stopped inches from her. The coldness crackled into a confusion of blue as he stared at her.

Slowly, his hand began to lower.

An arm snaked around Jack's chest and yanked him back. Jefferson.

Jack twisted like a snake and struck his former mentor with a punch that should've sent Jefferson's detached head spinning across the room, but the man was tougher than old boot leather and returned each volley.

Fists, kicks, elbows, punches, flips, every move to tear a man apart, yet they grappled on like vicious titans of indestructible agreement, each refusing to fall until the other did.

The Talon flag peeled away from the wall and took flight. The eagle's golden wings sparked bright with embers that gobbled through the feathers and mighty claws until the bird collapsed on the grand hall's floor in charred bits of ash. Unlike the phoenix, life would not spring forth. All that awaited was death.

Ivy scrambled to her feet. "Jefferson! We have to leave before the gunpowder goes off!"

Jefferson nimbly missed a kick to the gut. "Get yourself out! I'll be right behind with Jack."

"I'm not leav—" The ceiling splintered. Wood and plaster crashed down in a shower of fire, cutting her off from the two men.

Jefferson's ash-coated face lurched over the blaze, eyes as intense as the inferno. "Get out!"

Appearing behind him, streaked in gray and black with blood trickling from his mouth, Jack grabbed his mentor by the forehead and jaw and twisted. Jefferson's neck snapped. He slumped to the floor, dead.

A scream ripped from Ivy's throat, but it was lost in the explosion of gunpowder erupting beneath their feet. The floor ripped open and ceiling beams caved.

And then blackness.

★★★

He stepped over the body at his feet and shielded his eyes against the fire ringing around him as the woman's scream echoed through the explosion. The entire building would collapse soon. He needed to get out.

The woman had backed toward a door, but it was blocked now with rubble. He looked around, calculating routes. There. A corridor barely intact, but not entirely consumed in fire. He moved toward it, then stopped and looked back.

The woman lay on the other side of the blaze, unconscious and trapped under debris.

"I'll have you know me first."

Her words coiled through him, reaching for a hold amid the nothingness. He curled his fists against it.

"You know me."

Her words cleaved into the dark cavern, gutting him with her assurance.

He leaped through the blaze and pulled the debris off her. Two interlocking rings on a chain spilled from the top of her blouse and lay on her chest. Each shallow breath showed a wink of orange fire on the silver. His hand reached for his own chest and pressed against the space over his heart, where two matching rings were inked into the skin.

"Mercy, Jack."

Jack. Jack Lawrence Vale. That was his name, and she knew it. The woman, Ivy, knew him, and here was proof he knew her too. Whatever this was, he could not allow it to end here.

He hoisted her into his arms, then ducked around the flames and raced down the corridor, bolting through a door that opened to a wide garden smoking with ash. He pushed through a gate into an alley.

Night tumbled between the buildings on each side, throwing shadows at odd angles. The alarm would be raised by now and they would come looking for him. He lowered her to the ground and watched for a moment as her breaths came short and shallow. The necklace hung limp around her neck, but it called to him through the nothingness.

He reached to touch it. Shouts sounded through the garden as the burning walls caved.

Straightening, he gave her one last glance, then disappeared into the night.

NINE

AGAINST TIME THAT WOULD CHISEL HER AWAY, SHE WITHSTANDS. AGAINST the forces that would cut her down, she survives. The Silver One is patient above all else. Like Death, she has bided the hours, waiting to strike at the precise moment.

Standing atop the battlement, she gazes upon the ancient stone gathered by her ancestors into this protective structure. It sits in a deep bowl surrounded by the foreboding mountains that have protected her people for centuries. It is a sacred place, a stronghold of ideals with a foundation of deep earth and a backbone carved from the granite slopes. It is here where her final plans are being set into motion.

"Tell me again," she commands the boy huddling behind her. A boy he is not, but neither is he a man with his blatant weakness leeching what purpose he can.

"Talon has burned. Your Riser has risen." His voice is little more than a dull razor pathetically sharpened. Still, he has proven his usefulness.

"My Riser has risen." She closes her eyes, savoring the tingle of saliva that rushes to her mouth in anticipation. Soon she will lead him home.

Her Riser has done great things for her. He is destined to do more. He is her symbol of true power, one she will use to show the world her strength on the appointed day not far off. Leaders of the world will be dragged before her, and she will hear not their pleas for mercy. At her command, her Riser will cut them down, and the world will know there is nothing but the Order.

Opening her eyes, she draws her shawl close and turns to face the weakling. A woman stands serenely next to him. Small of stature with reddish-gold hair and even green eyes if the moon were inclined to reveal the shade. She is a member of their holy Order and was selected with great care to stand here. Faithful, she should be called, for the Silver One does not recall her true name. Nor the boy's. He must possess one, but she does not stop to ponder it.

Her mouth turns down. "My Riser has risen, and you have returned without him."

His eyes slant away as if he cannot abide gazing upon her.

"You were commanded to set that Talon rats' nest ablaze and return with my Riser. Yet he slipped from your grasp and disappeared into the night—and with but a taste of Dust burning in his veins. You were not given enough for a complete dose, and now the effects will wear off and allow his mind to right itself, you spineless worm!"

Her fingers curl against her skirts. "His mind does not belong to him. It belongs to me, and I have taken great care in blighting out everything familiar he might cling to, leaving only the Order to fill the gaps. How am I to fill gaps when you did not bring him to me?"

"There was too much smoke. Once the fire caught, the whole building became a crumbling inferno. He got away from me."

She sees through his lies. He left her Riser to perish so he would not be forced to face the truth of what he has done to his friend. "You should have followed him."

"Followed him? Talon needs to think I died in that fire! If they ever find out I'm the one who poured the gasoline and struck the match, I'll be hanged without a second thought. I couldn't stick around, and now I can never go back there." He twists his hands. "I had nowhere else to turn, so I came here."

Guilt, too, has driven him here to beg at her feet. Fear rolls off him in rotting waves with a tang of hate putrefying in the deeper depths. It made his mind easy to twist into believing his supposed best friend is the enemy. This boy was a failure for Dust experiments at Poenari Castle, but he proved perfect in mental manipulations when her Yuri managed to recast his fears and insecurities, warping them into hatred of the one he calls Jack. She cares not for his hate. It is a means to her end that she will use to her advantage. The Order will succeed in exchange for his pettiness.

His gaze flickers to her, then quickly away. "Ivy—you'll leave her alone, won't you? I did as you commanded so she'll be safe now."

As if she has any intention of holding true to that arrangement. It is why she did not tell him her Riser was ordered to burn Talon *and* kill the girl. When it comes to her, the boy is pathetic, and the Order may yet need his obedience. He was not difficult for her followers to blackmail, the syringe of Dust too easily placed in his hand. *"Deliver the Maiden or the Riser."* She knew all along what his choice would be. The girl will be caught in time and punished for her crimes.

"All that matters is my Riser." *For now.*

"Come. Both of you." Hands spread wide on each side, she turns and stares out at the deepening shadows, coaxed out of hiding by the cloud-swept night. Her Riser has risen. Now he, too, must be coaxed from hiding and brought back to where he belongs. At her side.

"Tell me what you see."

"It's night and the moon's hiding. There is nothing to see," the weakling says as he stands to her right.

The woman joins her on the left. Her voice is soft on the air.

"I see a land cleansed of evil. I see a true leader stepping forth. I see the vision of our Order."

"Da, my child. There is much to see." The Silver One places a

hand between the woman's shoulder blades and shoves. The woman topples over the short wall and plunges to the earth below. Her body breaks in angles upon the rocks. The Silver One does not spare her a second glance before speaking to the boy.

"Now you, too, see what is at stake."

He gasps in horror and shrinks away from the wall. "H-how could you?"

"You dare ask me that when you have so easily done the same? Lives are mine to command. When you accept this, you will know peace and do what is necessary."

He clutches at his chest as if the skin strangles him. His eyes dart from the wall to her, and slowly he nods.

She smiles. The time has come to find her Riser and prepare him for the next step.

PART 2

Watch me.
I will go to my own Sun.
And if I am burned by its fire,
I will fly on scorched wings.

—SEGOVIA AMIL

TEN

THREE WEEKS LATER

OLD TOWN ALEXANDRIA WAS A REAL DARB OF A PLACE CONJURED straight out of colonial America with its cobblestone streets and rows of clapboard houses. Gas lamps flickered invitingly in the early evening light, while dogs barked from behind their wrought iron gates as the briny scent of the Potomac River drifted up the street from several blocks away.

Sunset over the river was a magical time when the sun cast shades of orange and pink against DC to the north and rippled over the river's water flowing south to eventually collide into Chesapeake Bay.

On that particular evening, Ivy didn't give two figs about the historical piles of bricks or the sun except to say good riddance to its oppressive heat for the day. The Virginia summer could be a sweltering beast when it wished, and apparently the beast wished it.

Turning off King Street onto Royal, Ivy peeled the collar of her cotton dress from her damp neck and flapped her rattan handbag to generate a breeze, but all she managed was to further irritate the mugginess. She paused at the corner of Cameron and Royal in front of a three-story redbrick building with three dormer windows perched on the roof like lookouts. A white front door with a gable roof and a short set of worn-smooth stone steps greeted guests to the otherwise plain edifice. Gadsby's Tavern. Serving ale and fare since the founding fathers sat at the square tables clinking tankards to the demise of King George.

A man and woman passed her and started up the stairs, he in a smart suit and she with a feather boa wrapped around her silk dress. He paused at the door with his hand on the knob and smiled back at the woman. She reached up and straightened his tie, then tickled his cheek with her feathers. Laughing, they headed inside, and Ivy did her best to act like it had no effect on her to watch a young couple crazy about each other enjoying a night on the town. She lasted all of three seconds before the lack of effect welled in her throat and threatened to undo her mascara.

Swallowing her misery and loneliness, she rounded the corner of the main entrance and took the stairs leading down to the delivery entrance below street level.

"Good evening, Mike," she called as she dodged stacked crates of potatoes and carrots waiting to be diced up for the evening meals and served in the dining room above.

"Evening, Ivy." Mike saluted with his meat cleaver before turning back to hack at the bloody steaks on his chopping board. "Nice night for a stroll?"

"It's a real dripper out there. Best to stay in the cave where it's cooler." She gestured to the cooking chamber, affectionately called the cave for obvious reasons.

"With all the other trolls just like me, eh?" He laughed along with the other kitchen workers peeling vegetables and mixing sauces. A motley band of army brothers from the Great War, their disfigured faces and missing appendages made them undesirable workers to most of the world, but the tavern owner respected their need for work after having served their country and hired them when too many other business owners turned them away.

Skirting around to the far corner, she ducked into an unused hearth and pressed the hidden lever. The fireplace's back wall slid open and Ivy ducked through. The door closed behind her with a grating of bricks. She blinked to adjust her eyes to the darkness.

"Maybe one day we'll meet where the sun actually shines."

Pricks of light guided her down a stone corridor, which opened into a large chamber that served as a hub with several spokes branching off into smaller chambers. Talon's newest headquarters. Well, new in that it was the first time they'd met in this location in the twentieth century.

Gadsby's Tavern was where George Washington first met with his spymaster, Benjamin Tallmadge, to establish Talon, and the dining room's alcoves were where they chose their first agents. These belowground chambers were where agents received their missions and where they limped back to after said missions were complete before the new headquarters was moved to Leesburg and finally settled into the building on Massachusetts Avenue. A building now burned to ash with naught but a few corners of brick left like skeletons in a ghoulish reminder of what once was.

So many things lost that night. So many things and all that was ever important to Ivy. Once more she was without, and the sorrow was breaking her in half.

She walked into the central chamber full of agents sitting atop crates and leaning against the brick walls with matching expressions of anticipation. Washington strode in from one of the smaller antechambers and paused to scan the room. Spotting Ivy, he made his way to her.

"Ah, good. You've returned. We can begin."

Ivy's heart lurched. "I thought you read it earlier."

"Nonsense. All agents must be present for the reading of the will so that it may be read only once before its secrets are given to the flame." He placed the scrolled parchment under his arm, then strode to the center of the chamber and called for attention.

Finding a seat on one of the empty dynamite crates that had yet to be cleared out as the underground chambers had served as a storage area for nearly two centuries, Ivy scanned the faces around her. Franklin, Hamilton, Dolly, and Millie, their latest recruit who'd proved a whiz at document resourcing, and half a dozen other somber faces filled the chamber, but not the ones she most longed to see.

Washington cleared his throat and unrolled the parchment. "The last will and testament of Horatio Sullivan Braumhauser, hereto known as Agent Jefferson . . ."

Washington's voice faded to a drone as Ivy's gaze drifted to the portrait on the wall behind him. It was of a man captured in a formal sitting with the Talon and American flags draped like bunting behind him. The colors were somber with a touch of the Romantic masters in all the portrait's fine detail save for the face, which had been scrubbed out with turpentine. Obscurity even in death. The bronze nameplate nailed to the bottom of the portrait simply said Jefferson. A sheen of tears covered her eyes. Had his name truly been Horatio Braumhauser? Such a superfluous moniker for such a serious man.

Heat branding her cheeks, Ivy dropped her attention to her lap and peeled the wet netted gloves from her sweating fingers before anyone noticed or blamed the guilty party for daring to grieve. After all, it was her fault their grand instructor and colleague was dead. Perhaps not by her own hand, but certainly by her doing. If she hadn't brought a Rising Moon assassin into their midst . . .

She quickly looked to another wall, but not before her eyes snagged on the other portrait. The same formal pose of a gentleman, bunting, and washed-out face; however, this nameplate read Philip.

The body of her best friend had not been recovered from the burned-out wreckage. She had waited day after day for him to come strolling down Massachusetts Avenue and complain that she'd worried too much like her typical cluck-cluck self. As the days dragged into weeks, her hope of ever seeing her friend again faded to ash. His bones were buried beneath the ruined memories of the only true home they'd ever shared. She had possibly been the last one to see him alive, and what had she done? She'd rushed by him, her thoughts desperate for Jack.

Hot tears stung her eyes. Had Philip been scared and alone when the flames closed in around him? Had he felt his greatest fear of abandonment? A fear she had promised him would never be realized.

Washington droned on. ". . . bequeathed to one Hamilton all fencing swords and boxing gloves, while textbooks of warfare nature shall be donated to Washington's library of choosing. Concerning a singular account at National Bank box 2284 containing my earthly value in a tidy sum, bequeathed to one Jack Vale."

A collective gasp ricocheted around the chamber. Ivy stared at Washington, too shocked to look away. He stared back, clearly surprised at the revelation. She felt all eyes on her and the unspoken accusations hurtling through everyone's mind.

Rewarding his own killer.

So much for Jack being his blue-eyed boy.

A disgrace to Jefferson's legacy.

Murderer!

Bodies shifted. Crates creaked. Any second now the derision would boil over into outright protest at the mockery of their slain comrade's memory being trounced by an agent of the enemy. An enemy she had waltzed into their sacred halls in hopes of reforming. Her fingers bunched into the thin material of her skirt. She wanted to scream that it wasn't his fault. It wasn't Jack who killed Jefferson but a horrible monster created by the Order. People in times of anguish were less likely to look upon circumstances with logical calm and too often gave in to the emotional need for a scapegoat, a target for their fury. A name, a face, was all the proof their emotions required, never considering the damaged mind beneath it.

Washington must have sensed the discord shattering the true

intention of their gathering and quickly read off the parting words of the will.

"This is my true and final statement given this day the twenty-fifth of July nineteen hundred and fifteen. Signed Horatio Sullivan Braumhauser."

Washington rolled up the parchment and tossed it into the fireplace, which was little more than a hole in the stone wall.

"Seek and ye shall find. Find and ye shall protect."

Ivy repeated Talon's motto through numb lips along with the other agents. Noble words, but when the time came to prove them, she had failed. She had not been able to protect, and the guilt would haunt her for the rest of her days. She stood rooted in place as the parchment caught fire and crackled to black and the rigid black words that personified Jefferson the man sizzled to a pile of ash. Would there ever be anything in this world but ash?

Washington spoke for a few minutes with Hamilton and Dolly, then came to stand next to Ivy as everyone else gave her a wide berth and side-eyed glares. Clasping his hands behind his back, he stood silent for a moment before finally speaking.

"It's good you returned."

It was the closest he would come to concern, and for that she was grateful. Dolly had fussed over her for a full hour with comments on how pale and skinny she was and how much good a long nap would do her, and while three months ago Ivy might have given in to the mothering, such comforts were beyond her now.

"I thought there might be something near Norfolk." The beach. Warm and sunny, the kind of place she and Jack once dreamed of going after so many frozen months in Russia. The kind of place they never had a chance to visit. "It was a dead end." Like all the other places she had searched since that horrible night when everything went up in flames. Jack was nowhere to be found.

"Where are you heading next?"

"Farther south." More beaches, warmer weather. "Unless you've heard from Europe."

Washington shook his head, dousing any spark of hope. "I'm pushing all the resources I can, but our overseas offices are caught up in a Red scare thanks to the Bolsheviks rumbling around. Jack is a master of slipping around unseen. He won't take any unnecessary steps that would get him caught or lead a trail back to the Order's headquarters." He glanced sideways at her and rushed on as her mouth sank down. "Worry not. Talon is proficient at finding the proverbial needle in the haystack."

Ivy tamped down her frustration and stuffed her gloves into her handbag. She'd have to remember to take them out for drying later or the smell would never come out of the bag's satin lining.

"I fear this needle has no intention of being found."

"It hasn't stopped you before."

"Nor will it now. I will find Jack and then I will find Dragavei and put her head on a pike. A fitting end to her cursed bloodline." Ivy snapped her bag closed, imagining that evil woman's head crushed between the metal clasps.

"Rather imaginative. And rash."

"Rash? Her demise was sealed ten years ago. I assure you there is nothing rash in my carrying it out."

Washington's already wafer-thin lips flattened further. A sure sign of oncoming disapproval.

"If we go after her with pitchforks quivering with revenge, we are blinding ourselves with bloodthirst and calling it justice. The Order of the Rising Moon is a global organization with roots digging deep. When we strike, it must be a coordinated attack to destroy them all at once so there is no chance of even an inch of root remaining to spread ever again."

He talked of pruning as if the Order were naught more than a weed growing in a walled garden. Where was the cry for slash and burn? The acrid lust for scorched earth? Why did she stand as the only one with a scythe in hand while the others had yet to take up so much as a trowel?

"We've had ten years to root them out. Ten years! I've had enough of waiting around."

Heads turned their way and all side conversations halted as attention locked onto the gathering thundercloud in the center of the room. No doubt hoping for a well-aimed lightning bolt to strike her down.

"Keep your voice down." Washington's admonition rumbled like low thunder.

"Why? Because my voice is too irrational for you?"

Taking her arm, Washington propelled her down a corridor and into a small chamber that he had commandeered for his office. Somehow he'd managed to wedge an eighteenth-century desk and two Queen Anne chairs into the space. Most likely leftovers from the first days of Talon. A stack of sideways crates served as a crude bookcase with a paltry collection of titles to choose from.

He closed the door and released her arm to walk behind his desk. A better position from which to glare at her.

"No. Because you're drawing unwanted attention to yourself. You're on thin enough ice as it is."

Ivy matched him glare for glare, uncaring about adding one more crack to the so-called ice. It wasn't as if she could sink any further than she had over the past ten years.

"You think I don't know everyone here hates me? That they all blame me for Jefferson and Philip?"

"What happened was a terrible tragedy, but every Talon agent understands the risks when they sign the contract. Our duty now is to prevent it from happening again."

"By serving justice and putting Dragavei's head on a pike."

"Dragavei could never bleed enough to fulfill the vision of justice you seek." Placing his fists on the desk, Washington leaned forward. The single lamp hanging above bounced light off his smooth head. "I will not allow a personal vendetta to jeopardize the overall mission of bringing down the entire Order."

Ivy scoffed. If the ice was determined to crack beneath her feet, she might as well go down with the ship full sail and colors flying.

"So now I'm a liability? You didn't seem to think so when you sent me to Argentina when the guerrilla wars began. Or when the Blackshirts marched on Rome. Or when I went to Sudan to confiscate weapons from the warlords terrorizing the local tribes."

"I realize now what a mistake it was. At the time I thought I was doing you a favor by permitting you to go on assignments because if I hadn't, you would have just gone anyway. You needed occupation, and I thought it would help assuage your grief, but instead it made you harder, closed off. At times reckless, like that stunt you pulled in London when you had express orders to return stateside after Spain. Talon is not reckless, and you have pushed the boundaries one too many times. Need I remind you of the bounty on your head as the Maiden?"

"They haven't caught me yet."

He shook his head. "I am sorry, Ivy, but when the time comes you will not go near Dragavei."

The situation was slipping from her grasp. She scrabbled for the rope that tethered her to all she'd known since that fateful day at Poenari Castle. The rope she had twisted together into a noose destined to slip over Dragavei's neck and string her up.

"Sir, I have the right, more than anyone here, to take down that woman."

"Talon does not operate on who has what right or personal acts of revenge. If allowed individual hit lists, we would lower ourselves to the dregs of mobs and dictators we have sworn to fight against. Chaos would ensue and set the entire world to suffering."

"You have no idea what I have suffered and lost."

Warning flashed in his eyes. Low and dark, it held more threat than a pistol pressed to her skull.

"Do not think for one instant that you alone have been dealt a blow in service to Talon. Dragavei and the Order will be dealt with, but not by you."

The ice cracked to a fissure beneath her feet, cold air rushing up to freeze her blood.

"Are you putting me on probation?"

"Think of it more as a time to reflect."

Her anger boiled through the freeze, hissing and spitting in a red mist. She slammed her fist on the desk.

"I've had a decade of reflecting and you even longer! You sat within your four walls surrounded by your books and papers, never stepping foot outside to understand the so-called recklessness required to see a mission complete. You think me crippled with emotion, but you, sir, are fettered by an unwillingness to take action until all the pieces fall into your order of logic. I for one refuse to hide from what needs to be done."

Eyes narrowing to slits, Washington slowly pulled his fists from the desktop and straightened to his full height. He stared at her a long minute, pressing her with the weight of his silence. At last the pale line of his mouth fractured to clip out his command.

"Dismissed, Vale."

Ivy slammed the door behind her. Infuriating, obstinate, unrelenting old boot heel. Her footsteps thumped off the stone walls, solid thunks to each of Washington's insufferable traits. After all these years of proving herself and completing mission after mission, he chose now to accuse her of operating on emotions and marginalize her for supposed vigilante intentions.

Well, not entirely supposed if her escapade in London held any weight, which apparently it did, but when had emotions been deemed a detriment to character? Oh yes, since the powers that be used emotion as a trump card to suppress anything they disapproved of. As if her objectives in South America or the Balkans had anything to do with emotions. Those objectives had been carried out with cool professionalism.

Unlike her actions moments ago.

A drop of water plopped on her head. "Ugh." A leaky pipe from the kitchens overhead.

She swiped the wetness rolling down her hair. Selfish, stubborn, insubordinate—the entire conversation with Washington had lasted less than five minutes and yet she'd managed to unleash every despicable attribute that clawed to the top. She'd done what she never wanted to do, and that was to behave childishly. Hardly a way to prove herself able to carry out orders.

She turned back toward Washington's office, stopped, and turned around.

Splendid, Ives. Destroy what relationships you do have left while making certain you're chained to a desk for the foreseeable future. Absolutely swell move.

She slumped against the wall, the stone offering a refreshing coolness through the thin cotton of her dress. Washington would most likely spit her over open coals if she returned now, even with an apology. If she was entirely honest with herself, she was only partially apologetic for what she'd said. Not that he needed to know that.

Pushing off the wall, she smacked into someone carrying a stack of papers. The thin white sheets fluttered about like feathers from a shot goose, cartwheeling and looping in the air until finally floating to the floor in a jumble of typed words.

Once the papers settled, all that remained was a beet-faced Millie, the document whiz.

"Oh, Agent Vale! I'm so sorry. How clumsy of me." She dropped to her knees and began scooping up the papers.

"No, the apologies are mine. I wasn't paying attention." Ivy knelt beside her. "Let me help you."

In a matter of minutes, they had corralled the wayward documents back into Millie's arms. The bright red had dimmed to pink on her round young face offset by a frizzy black bob.

"Gee, Agent Vale, I can't thank you enough for helping me."

"It was entirely my fault to begin with, and please call me Ivy."

The pink glowed back to red. "Gee, ever since I first came to Talon I've heard stories about you. How you took down Balaur Tsar, all the languages you speak, how you pretended to be a Turkish princess to infiltrate the Sultan's palace. You've completed more successful missions than any other woman in Talon history. You are the absolute bee's knees!"

Ivy summoned a smile she didn't feel. It was never easy receiving praise, especially considering her little scene moments ago in Washington's office.

"Thank you, Millie. I'm proud to serve in a long line of talented agents."

"I was sorry to hear about your husband. Then delighted to hear he was alive, but then sad again because of . . . well, you know."

Not knowing how to respond to that nor wishing to dwell on the painful truth, Ivy moved to go around her.

"If you'll excuse me, I have a few files to go over."

Short as the girl was, Millie swerved to block her path. "Before you go, I thought you should know that I took it upon myself after the fire to start sorting through worldwide newspapers, tax files, property disputes, business licenses, and any other clues that might lead us to the Order. So far I've found nothing on that account, but yesterday I came across a playbill advertising for a 1905 vaudeville show in Chicago starring the Valiant Vales, Agatha and Frank Vale."

If Ivy's day hadn't already slipped past the point of no return, those names gave it the final shove into irrevocably damaged.

"Jack's parents," Ivy said woodenly, her mouth too dry to rage.

Deciding three was a crowd for the limelight, they had abandoned their six-year-old son into the hands of a crabby aunt and made their way up the Eastern Seaboard working any stage that would open its curtains to them. A few years ago Ivy had followed their stale trail on a whim to a seedy joint in Queens where vaudeville had taken its last gasping breaths. As had the Valiant Vales thanks to boozed livers and tuberculosis.

"It looks like they died in 1921." Millie paused for a sympathetic moment, but when Ivy didn't react to the news of those lowlives, she pressed on. "I scoured around a bit and found property still listed under a Ms. Ethel Vale, aunt of Frank Vale, near Charlottesville, Virginia."

"Did the county not appropriate the land after her death? It's been nearly twenty years."

"It's in the sticks of Virginia. Who knows what goes on out there?" Millie shrugged as if the lack of civilization explained everything. But not—

A match struck and Ivy's dying insides sparked to life. It was a long shot to be sure, but so far the Eastern Seaboard had proven fruitless. Perhaps it was time for a change of scenery.

"Millie, you're brilliant! Finding a rabbit hole I didn't even think of searching for." She squeezed Millie's shoulders. "Thank you!"

"Wait! Where are you going?" Millie called after her as she hurried down the passage.

Ivy waved over her shoulder. "The sticks!"

ELEVEN

Ivy stepped off the dirt road and dropped her suitcase in the grass, then sank onto a fallen log. She unbuckled her heeled oxfords and let her stockinged feet slide into the cool green blades. Bliss.

The Virginia summer air hung hot and heavy, stifled below the canopy of the surrounding woods. She unpinned her straw hat, lifted it from her head, and flapped it in front of her face, if for no other reason than to cool the drips of sweat on her neck. DC summers could be boiling with all the brick, stone, and concrete reflecting like the sun and the air choked by the exhaust from hundreds of automobiles puffing up and down the avenues. Here it was downright muggy. She closed her eyes and filled her ears with the silence broken only by birds chirping and squirrels rustling in the branches. A smile curled her lips. She would take this over honking horns and hustling pedestrians any day of the week and twice on Sunday.

Peeling her eyes open, she glanced at her wristwatch. Nearly two hours had passed since the bus dropped her off in Charlottesville after six sweltering hours of riding from Alexandria, and one hour had passed since she last saw a motorcar. Good. Where she was going she didn't need neighbors nosing around. She slid her shoes back on and rebuckled them, then carried on down the road.

Another half hour went by and the sun passed its zenith, tilting shadows to her right without the decency to shave off a few degrees of heat. No matter. She would arrive shortly and the temperature would become the least of her concerns.

A narrow swath of trees had been shaved down through the woods to her left. At one time it must have served as a private drive, but twenty years of neglect had urged vines and bushes to branch over the intrusion. Ivy's heart hammered loud enough to be mistaken for one of the woodpeckers banging on nearby tree trunks.

She'd searched hundreds of places over the years, anticipation building with each step into a new foray. *This* would be the one. *This* would be where she found him. But like a trapdoor swung wide, the anticipation always gave way to plummeting disappointment. Like all the times before, her anticipation mounted with each step down the overgrown path, but *this* time it was different. The very air pulsed against her skin, raking her hairs to stand on end, and whispered to her senses that more awaited just beyond these woods.

The trees thinned to reveal a large clearing set against a backdrop of rolling hills. An old farmhouse with chipped white paint stood nestled among the uncut blades of grass. A barn leaned farther behind near a stream that rolled along the back edge of the property and disappeared into the trees like a ribbon threading back to its spool.

Ivy approached the house and climbed the front steps, careful of the missing top plank. Heart in her throat, she knocked on the front door.

Nothing. She knocked again. Seconds ticked by without so much as a squeaky floorboard sounding inside. She left the porch and rounded the house to survey the yard. A blanket and two shirts fluttered from a rope strung between a pole and what looked like a pitchfork wedged into the ground, while a fishing pole and rusted tackle box leaned against the barn.

She ascended the steps to the back porch and noted a pile of empty corn husks next to a rocking chair missing one of its rockers. A few of the husks were green enough to have been shucked that day. She waited for the trapdoor to shift beneath her feet, readying for the plunge to defeat her once again, but her footing remained sure.

"Hello?" She rapped her knuckles on the screened back door. "Anyone home?"

No answer. She pushed open the door, its groaning hinges signaling her trespassing to anyone within a mile radius, and stepped into the kitchen. Cupboards sagged with weariness toward a chipped countertop while a round table, propped up on two sides with bricks, sat like an island in the center of the room, a lone chair its only companion. A plate, two bowls, and a cracked cup were stacked neatly next to a deep farmhouse sink along with a bowl of sand, a top-drawer substitute for scrubbing.

Ivy lowered her suitcase to the peeling linoleum floor, then walked through a short hallway riddled with termite damage and emerged into the front sitting room. Victorian-era drapes drooped over the windows like grande dames long past their prime. The air was musty. The floor had been swept clean and the chintz-and-damask-printed furniture pushed against the front wall, blocking the front door in a defensive position. In the far corner tucked up next to a brick fireplace were two folded quilts and a flat pillow that appeared to be leftovers from the Civil War. A single candle and a book—its title too faded to discern—rested next to the bedding.

The trapdoor remained firmly shut, and she *knew*. Her search had ended. The clean dishes stacked next to the sink, the husks of corn, the folded blankets, the book. All scraped together from films of dust and misuse to create a semblance of normality. Pieces collected to form a life.

Stooping, she brushed her fingers over the pillow. Unnamed longings for all that had been lost shook within the closed boundaries of her heart, demanding their existence be acknowledged at long last.

"Oh, Jack."

Then the air changed. It zinged along her skin like a brush of lightning. Her muscles tensed, bracing for the threat as her fingers twitched on impulse for her Beretta.

She stood and took a deep breath.

"Hello, Jack." She slowly turned to face her husband standing mere feet behind her.

Dressed in faded tan trousers, dusty boots, and a thin cotton button-down, he fit the part of the country he had settled into. His dark brown hair was still unkept and reached past the open collar of his shirt where a patch of tan skin matched the golden glow of his forearms, exposed by his rolled-up sleeves. Gone was the sickly pallor from his face, which now radiated a diet of fresh air and summer sun, despite still being lined with wariness.

All of this was enough to make her weep with joy, but his eyes bolstered her enough to stand. Clear, blue, and watchful.

No threat. Her muscles, taut and ready for impact, relaxed a fraction, though she kept her distance.

"Do you know who I am?" Her breath was pinned in her lungs as she waited for the coldness to freeze over him.

A second ticked by. Then another as all possibilities of hope and despair tumbled together. Another second passed.

The blue of his eyes remained clear as he stepped into the room.

"You're my wife."

★★★

He'd become aware of her while he was in the woods checking rabbit snares. He'd felt something on the breeze, an unfamiliar presence drifting through the trees like that of a deer wandering far from its marked territory. She was as cautious as one, too, as she approached the house with the straight line of her shoulders doing little to betray the quickening of her pulse. Even from his distance hidden among the trees he could count the erratic beat. His own pulse hastened in response, and he tugged at his collar as it stuck uncomfortably against his neck. It felt too much like a muzzle controlling him.

His eyes followed her, seeking out the features he'd once known as well as his own. The way she smoothed a strawberry-blonde lock away from her cheek before knocking on his door. Her short stride as she moved around to the back of the house, different from his longer stride as he crept close and entered the back door silently behind her. The green eyes that took in his sparse kitchen in a single sweep.

"I—" His voice caught on her name. A name he had not spoken in such a long time but that came rushing over him in a mighty surge of remembrance. "You're my wife."

A gasp slipped from her lips. Surprise, delight, and disbelief wavered across her face, but she quickly reinstated a guarded expression. "Am I?"

The years had chiseled a confidence into her bearing, an assurance of control over all situations—except for that tiny tic at the corner of her mouth that gave her away. Her twisted nerves rivaled his own at their reunion.

"You wear a necklace with two interlocking grenade pins that we exchanged as wedding bands. I wanted to give you a proper ring, but you said you wouldn't trade it for all the diamonds in the world." He tapped a finger to the space over his heart. "I had them tattooed on my chest. By a one-eyed Greek sailor sporting a rather voluptuous mermaid on his thigh, if memory serves me. Though I can't say it's been the most reliable of late."

With a half-strangled laugh, she moved toward him. "Jack."

He stepped back, hand raised.

She stopped and the laugh slid behind that guard of restraint. "I'm sorry."

He lowered his hand to his side and forced the tension to drain from his bunched muscles. Bracing for attack had become his state of existence, but the Riser was no more. That belonged to the past, yet he was not prepared to move forward and take up the mantle of old expectations. He was caught somewhere in between on unsure footing.

"No, I'm sorry. I can't simply be the man you knew before."

"You don't need to explain or do anything you're not comfortable with. In your own time." She clasped her hands together in a show of calm acceptance, but the truth was branded on her white knuckles. "I'm content to stand in the same room without you trying to kill me."

The truth was worse than taking a hail of bullets. It pierced him straight through, shattering him with holes through which memories began to leak. A scattering of good from his past that tried to rise to the top but was sunk by the voracious evil. So many deaths he was responsible for—his hands were crusted black by blood.

"I didn't mean to upset you." Those green eyes saw every festering inch of him despite his efforts to hide. Why did she not turn away in disgust? "Heaven knows I've tried to kill you on several occasions. I'd say we're even."

"On the scales of judgment my sins far outweigh those of Judas." Sins he did not want to share with her. Deeds so dark no light of redemption could penetrate as they devoured all that dared come near. "Are you not afraid of me?"

"Dust in your veins was the only thing keeping you a Riser. I should hope any homicidal tendencies evaporated along with it."

"You would be foolish to put your trust in the good graces you once thought I possessed."

"I'll take my chances." She pulled a knife from her dress pocket before quickly slipping it away. "Just in case."

"You shouldn't be here."

"But I am here." The nervous tic at the corner of her mouth

curled up into a hint of a smile. She was foolish not to be afraid. "Are you hungry?"

Without waiting for an answer, she circled past him and headed to the kitchen. She looked out of place with her styled hair and pretty dress among the paltry attempts he'd made to repair the room with its wobbly table and broken crockery and piles of dust. Worn and cracked like him.

She withdrew a paper bag from her suitcase and placed its meager offerings on the table—a sandwich with the crusts torn off and an apple that had gone brown around a bite mark. A feast compared to the pathetic diet of corn and fish he'd consumed of late. His stomach rumbled in appreciation.

Should he offer her a glass of water? No, he'd forgotten to refill the bucket from the river that morning. Find a crate to sit on? No, that would require joining her at the table, and the nearness would prove too much. So he simply stood awkwardly and waited. Surely she had a plan because she'd left him at a loss.

"Go on then. Can't let it go to waste." After sitting in the only chair—with one leg shorter than the rest—she pushed the sandwich toward him and took the apple for herself.

Permission granted, Jack picked up the sandwich and forced himself to take a reserved bite. He chewed thoroughly and then swallowed. It was an unfamiliar sensation, this savoring of food bite by bite with no one threatening to snatch it from him at any second. His tongue was relearning the difference between salty and bitter now that he didn't have to swallow the food whole to get past the disgust of cold mush riddled with weevils.

"Smoked cheddar is your favorite."

It had been so long since he was permitted to have favorites. To have sole ownership of his mind, the freedom to choose one option over another.

"Is it?"

She nodded, turning the apple slowly in her hand. "You liked it best on a cracker."

"I don't recall the taste of crackers." He swallowed the last bite of the sandwich and refrained from licking the crumbs from his fingers like an animal, instead brushing them off over the sink. "The Dust no longer burns through my veins, but its effects on my memory linger. Little by little the memories crawl back to me, and I do the best I can to piece them together, but it's as if they belong to another man. A stranger I no longer know. The life he claimed cannot be reconciled with—" He gestured sharply to himself.

"Do you remember me at all? Us?"

His hands curled over the sink's lip, the cracked porcelain cool against his palms as her soft words soaked into him and spread the first warmth he'd felt in a long time.

He remembered them first meeting in the rain. He remembered the stories they read together about kelpies and winter witches. He remembered how she always smelled of roses, and even now the same delicate scent curled about the room with an enticement of longing. He remembered she wore green on their wedding day. She wore it now in a shade that perfectly matched her eyes—eyes that calculated his every twitch and intake of breath from behind a protective veil of lashes.

His fingers curled into fists. The short nails bit into his skin. "I remember that you were beautiful and everything good, which is why you're going to leave now and forget this place. Forget you ever knew me."

Her sigh stretched wearily between them. "Six hours on a cramped bus is a long time to occupy my imagination. In that time I settled on three different versions of how this reintroduction would go. The first one was my favorite, though I knew it to be the least likely. We would rush across an open field into each other's arms and drown the hours in kisses. Obviously that didn't happen. My second scenario involved you trying to break my neck. Again. However, it was the third option, the one I dreaded most, that has, in fact, come to call. Martyrdom."

Martyrdom. If that was what she wished to call it. He knew the blood-soaked truth of who he was. He turned to face her with his grip still anchoring him to the sink. A touchstone to keep him balanced since a gun no longer weighted his hand.

"You charge me with noble intentions, but the things I've done would make the devil weep."

Ivy stood. "It's taken me ten years to find you, Jack Vale. I won't allow you to fall on your sword now."

"You haven't enough sense to understand the danger you've put yourself in by attempting to save this lost cause. Take your bleeding heart elsewhere and let me be."

Reaching into the top of her dress, she pulled out the necklace with their wedding bands. "Well, that's the thing. I took a vow 'for better or for worse.' We've certainly seen better, and I doubt worse has any comparison to the hell of the past decade, so you see, I cannot go and let you be." She slid the chain between her fingers, the circles gently swinging back and forth, then coming to rest above the soft swell of her bosom. The rings winked at him in memories of silver. "I'll go find myself a room upstairs."

She picked up her suitcase and made her way up the stairs to the second floor. Boards creaked with each step she took. Did he not have enough torments without her here reminding him of what was before humanity had been stripped from him? Her presence would force him to confront truths he was unprepared to dig up. He was nothing more than a shadow of the monsters buried there, lost in the years and days when there was no escape from the darkness. He *was* the darkness.

He strode outside, the kitchen door slamming behind him, and fled to the woods. Away from her presence, away from the sun and its probing light, and into the cooling dimness that asked no questions and expected no reply.

★★★

Cool blackness drifted down from the hills as nighttime burrowed through the woods. Cricket songs hushed to a chirp as Jack stepped from the trees with a brace of rabbits in his hands. Stars pierced the inked sky like blazing candles where Hercules and Draco stretched their heroics to dominate the celestial view.

His gaze drifted across the quiet yard, the wild grass in need of a trim, to the house whose faded boards and broken windows blurred in the moonlight. He'd despised this place in his youth with its tedium and less than hospitable great-aunt chasing him around with a broom because he'd tracked mud across her carpets. It had merely been a place to rest his head until the day he packed his bag and headed to DC without a backward glance. He'd returned because he could think of no place else to go, and the dreariness that once crippled his spirit now wrapped his tattered edges like a balm. With a bit of care and patience, this place could be a home. If such a thing could ever exist for him.

A figure moved on the second-floor balcony. Caught in the shadow of the roof, Ivy stood silhouetted against the sky with moon slivers lighting on her pale hair, her face lifted to the stars. All those times he had stood on a mountain's ledge and watched the pinpricks of light shining over the nothingness, he'd wondered why he was drawn to them. Now he knew. It was her. Even lost in his own mind, deep down a part of him had known it was Ivy all along.

Perhaps in time they might reclaim—No, he wouldn't allow himself to think on it. She was here. They shared the night, and for now it was enough.

TWELVE

IVY DUMPED THE SCRUB BRUSH IN THE BUCKET, THEN BLEW A LOOSE HAIR out of her face and took a step back to admire her work. Three hours since the sun cracked over the horizon, and she'd worn the brush down to three bristles cleaning twenty years of grime off the kitchen floor and windows. They were now clean enough to eat off. Not that she would attempt it.

She'd had a restless night. Possibly due to the springs poking through the lumpy mattress or the rat-eaten sheets or the sinister spider crouched in its web above the door watching her with its eight beady eyes. The physical discomforts proved pitiful compared to the occupants of her mind. She'd spent the dark hours counting the stars and listening for any movement downstairs to indicate her husband had returned. He never had.

Through the window over the sink, she saw a figure step from the trees and stride across the yard. Her hands fluttered to the hairs escaping the kerchief she'd tied around her head.

Be calm. Jumping on your husband will only scare him off. Even in the name of affection.

He walked differently. As if his steps slowed him from his purpose. There was a time when he strolled with carefree abandon.

Now he seemed like the soldiers who came back from war. Some outwardly scarred and some not, but a sudden loud noise, an auto backfiring or a crowd roaring during a sports game, could knock them back into the trench of nightmares.

Worst of all were the ones spiraled back into battle. To kill or be killed. She'd read in a newspaper article years before about a man choking his uncle to death because he'd thought him a Hun. Would she wake up one morning with Jack choking the life from her with that cold, blank stare in his eyes? Not seeing her, not knowing her but as the enemy. Would she be forced to walk on eggshells in constant fear of setting him off?

Jack thudded up the back porch steps and opened the screen door.

"Good morning," she said. A little too brightly.

Any surprise he might have had at her greeting was smothered beneath the neutral acknowledgment of a curt nod.

"Breakfast." He held up two stripped and cleaned rabbits.

She offered a smile to cover her racing heart. "Shall we dine alfresco? I've spent too long in this kitchen and need some fresh air."

He turned on his heel and strode back out to the yard. Ivy whipped the kerchief from her head, attempted to fluff the flattened hairs with her fingers, and untied the apron she'd found stuffed in a musty cupboard before following him outside.

A much-used cooking pit was dug in a sunny spot next to the river where Jack knelt with flint in hand. When he struck the two rocks together, a spark leaped between his fingers. He touched it to the kindling in the center of the pit, and the fire caught and spread to the waiting sticks of wood. With deft skill, he spit the two rabbits and placed them over the fire.

Ivy sat on the opposite side of the pit and spread her skirt modestly over her knees. Dirty water stains splotched the hem.

"I see you dine out here quite often. It's a magnificent spot, green and cool with the soothing sound of the water."

He adjusted the spit, his long, untrimmed hair falling to curtain each side of his face. "Inside is too . . . confining."

Ivy clamped down the murmurs of pity gurgling up her throat. Pity was for the weak, and her husband was anything but weak. He had survived ten years of torment at the hands of pure evil. He'd been caged and beaten. It was no wonder he held a distrust of walls blocking him from freedom.

She plucked a blade of grass and rolled it between her fingers. "Not to mention crawling with unwelcome guests. I had more than one spider land in my hair this morning, and I'm fairly certain there are at least four generations of mice residing in the linen closet. I'll need to work up my bravado before tackling them."

All her life she'd imagined a home to care for, adding touches of herself to each corner and shingle. How lovely the house would be, painted a bright white with cheery green shutters and pink geraniums on the windowsills. For the first time in her life, she had a place she could nearly call home. Yet the heart within it did not beat because its two occupants acted like strangers.

On and on she rambled about the house and cleaning as she fought to control the jitters bubbling to the surface while Jack silently turned the browning rabbits. ". . . needs a fresh coat of paint. Later I'll check in the barn to see if any cans are left, but no, they would be at least twenty years old and dried up. No matter, the window shutters will need to be repaired first. Do you have any thoughts on the color? A white farmhouse would be wonderful with a bright green front door. I've always wanted my own front door to paint."

Her steady stream of nerves continued as Jack pulled the meat off the spits and placed it on large, flat river rocks that served well as plates. She babbled around bits of juicy meat until the bones were picked clean, eating mostly to keep herself occupied rather than from hunger. Jack barely touched his.

"Come spring, a new flower bed around the front porch—"

Jack dropped his rock. It hit the grass with a thud, rolling his breakfast right off. "How long are you staying?"

Placing her rock on the ground, Ivy straightened and quietly met his eyes. "I am never leaving you again, Jack."

His mouth pressed into a bloodless line. He surged to his feet and moved to the river's edge with his back to her. Once upon a time she had been able to read his every movement, every twitch, even the way his shirt crinkled between his shoulder blades. His shape was the same, a bit thickened by muscle perhaps, but now traces of a foreign presence banded through the familiar form. Where strength had been balanced by humor, he was now wary. Where his keen sniper's eyes had been softened with a wink, his stare was now haunted. The Riser might be gone, but the killer had not left without a fight, shredding Jack's insides and leaving behind permanent scars.

After several excruciating minutes of silence, broken only by the sound of water splashing over rocks, he spoke.

"What happened to Talon headquarters?"

He might as well have pressed one of those rocks straight into her chest. Its weight settled deep. Philip had told her that Dust fragmented memories or wiped them away completely. She had feared this moment when she would be asked to fill in the gaps, and she knew she could not avoid what was to come.

"It burned to the ground. We've since moved to another location in Alexandria."

"Gadsby's Tavern."

"Yes."

"I barely remember what happened. I was sitting in the cell waiting for you to return. Next thing, my mind was nothing—the cold nothingness that comes with Dust. There was fire everywhere and then a woman. The heat burned my skin and the ash choked my lungs, but I didn't stop. I never stop in the nothingness.

"Then the roof collapsed and the woman screamed. I knew I

should leave her, but I couldn't. I carried her from the fire to a back alley. Two rings dangled on a necklace hanging from her neck. Two interlocking rings that matched the tattoo on my chest. I didn't understand, didn't know what it meant, only that she needed to be saved. *You* needed to be saved."

The phantom rock eased off Ivy's chest. The Riser had not been in complete control. The Riser would have left her for dead, but a sliver of humanity had battled for survival. Jack fought back even though he was not himself, and he had fought for her. Never again would she allow those monsters to touch him and twist him to darkness. She would hunt down every last one of his nightmares until he knew peace again.

"Do you remember being injected or how the fire started?"

"There was a man. He talked to me. He knew my name."

"Do you know who the man was?"

"He was—" His expression contorted as if he were in pain before his head dropped on an exhausted sigh. "His face blends into the smoke. Each time I wrestle it to the forefront of my mind, it slithers away."

"Would you recognize him if you saw him again? Or heard his voice?"

"I was lucky to remember my own name after that last dose. It felt double the strength after not having an injection in nearly a week. Double the destruction I caused."

"What happened wasn't your fault. It wasn't you."

"All of it has been my fault. That night especially." His hands curled into fists, knuckle bones straining against the skin. "Jefferson . . ."

Ivy stood but didn't dare approach him. "Don't, Jack. Don't do that to yourself."

"His death is no one's fault but mine. Along with every single one of my other victims. My ears rattle with their dying screams; my hands are stained with their blood. No amount of penance will cleanse my sins." He turned to face her. Anguish twisted beneath the harshness scraping his voice. "Is that the kind of man you wish never to leave again?"

Fear nipped at her, its harsh teeth needling that she was a fool to believe this person could truly be her Jack again. She refused to cower under the first threat of opposition. "You are the man I love."

"To love me will be your ruin."

She saw it there as he stared at her, the blue sharpening to a cool distance and the bloodless line of defense setting his mouth. He would push her away as the guilt hollowed him until nothing was left but a shell. Unless she fought for him.

"Your love might be my damnation, but I will go to my grave with no regrets."

The blue eyes regarded her, no longer with distance yet not with welcome either. With a shake of his head, he disappeared into the woods.

Ivy's legs wobbled with the blow of rejection, but she stood her ground. Stood ready to fight.

★★★

The fishing lure bobbed peacefully on the river's surface as the afternoon current flowed past gently before turning around the bend and tumbling over rocks at a quicker speed. This had always been Jack's favorite part of the river growing up. Quiet, steady, and far enough from the house that he couldn't hear his aunt shrieking at him for whatever grievance she'd assigned him that day. It was a wonder he'd returned to this place, but then, he'd had nowhere else to go. Here he hoped to gather his memories amid the rotted floorboards and cobwebs with no one chasing him. Knowing the terrain as he did, there was no possibility of the Order discovering his whereabouts and taking him unawares.

"Hungry?"

Jack whipped back the fishing pole. The line sliced through the air, the lure glinting with deadly intent, then went limp.

Ivy stood behind him with a knife raised and the cut bit of line at her feet, her eyebrows slanted at him.

"Always looking for new ways to kill me. I'm glad you're trying to keep the spark alive in our marriage. Thankfully, I came prepared." She clipped the knife onto her belt and held out a picnic basket. "I brought lunch."

After laying out a freshly cleaned blanket, she sat and pulled two covered plates and a jug of water from the basket. Jack tossed his fishing pole next to the old tackle box, then sat beside her—not too close—and accepted his plate of hard-boiled quail eggs and freshly picked blackberries. From the purple stains on Ivy's fingers, she must have picked them and found the eggs that morning.

Ivy smoothed her light blue skirt over her knees. Her movements were always graceful; the delicacy of her slim fingers topped by finely shaped nails deceptively concealed her strength, whether she was putting on lipstick or sliding bullets into a chamber. He had yet to witness either since she'd arrived, but the juxtaposed memories flashed firmly in his mind, taking root in the thin cache he painstakingly raked through each day.

Ivy bit into her hard-boiled egg. "I've started a list of items to pick up at the store. We need more to eat than berries and fish. I'm no gourmet chef, but if there's anything you'd like me to make—"

"No."

"No, you don't fancy a roast or a pie? Or no, you're well enough existing on stolen corn from the farm two miles down the road?"

He'd wondered how long it would take her to mention that. "I left him rabbit furs in exchange."

"This is not the wild frontier where we trade in furs. I brought plenty of money to buy us proper groceries."

He popped a handful of berries into his mouth, his throat already working to swallow the juiciness whole, but he forced himself to stop and chew slowly. No one was coming to snatch the food from him.

He pushed aside his empty plate and hooked his arms around his bent knees. "I don't want to go to town. Interacting with people . . . I'm not ready for that." The last time he'd gone into a rural community had been in China—he couldn't remember when—but a group of humanitarians refused to surrender their land to the Order. No one was spared.

"It's no trouble for me to go alone," she said as she put away her empty plate. "I survived being stranded in Morocco for over a month with nothing more than a penknife. Charlottesville will be quite tame in comparison. You can go when you're up for it." She kept her tone light, gentle. Polite. As if she might scare him with anything less.

Wasn't that what they had been doing? Avoiding direct conversation by dancing around in well-mannered awkwardness? She was allowing him to take the lead, move forward at his own tempo, but what if he'd forgotten the steps? What if he could never find the confidence to dance again? What if the ability was beyond his reach?

"I don't know if I'll ever be ready."

She took his plate and placed it back in the basket with hers. Busy. She was always busy working, keeping her hands moving. Once upon a time they savored each other's presence without the nervousness.

"Time is a great healer." She closed the basket lid.

"Is it? Because so far I feel as raw as pure alcohol poured over an open wound again and again. My soul is weary from the weight of guilt, yet sleep is the last thing I want because the nightmares are there waiting."

She stilled. "Do you want to tell me about them?"

He was more aware of her in the calm than during any of her movements. Each breath, each heartbeat, each lingering second caught in her gaze. In their line of work, stillness was a cover for bottled-up tension when the trigger beneath their finger screamed to be squeezed. The killer was at his deadliest in that moment, deciding whether or not to fire. The more unmoving, the more lethal the assassin, and Jack was unprepared.

He matched her stillness. "That is not a horror I would pass on to anyone."

She inhaled a steadying breath, the kind the executioner did before taking the shot.

"We have both survived horrors over these past years, many of which will never leave us. We've been given a gift, Jack. A second chance to find peace and happiness."

Her hope shot him clean through.

"The man I was before might have known those things, but he no longer exists."

"I know you believe that right now." She didn't miss a beat. "We're no longer the same people we were before. Parts of me died ten years ago, but there are still old parts that remain. I see them in you too. If they hadn't survived, we wouldn't be sitting here now."

He eyed the knife on her belt. Brave words, but she remained armed around him. A telling truth if ever there was one. "You mean I would have killed you by now."

Her full lips twitched. "You might have tried. As you've seen, I'm more than capable as a match for you." She slid her legs beneath her, shifting into a kneeling position, then reached across the distance and touched his arm. "I grow lonely with my own pain. I only wish to share yours so we will no longer be alone."

Alone. Once the word had meant control. With no one to summon his emotions or sway his conscience, he was more easily dragged into the nothingness to become the Riser. Then he was left to stand among the piles of bodies, with empty bullet casings the only things to call his own as the Dust left his veins and pain struck hot and furious, its vicious teeth soothed only by more Dust.

In the moments between the nothingness and the pain, his memories prickled. Vague sounds and hazy images he could never quite grasp, yet he would lie in his cell waiting for a soft voice to tell him it was all over or for the blurry outline of a woman's mouth to smile at him. A thousand times he had wondered which was more painful, the nothingness or knowing the horror would never be over.

He glanced down at Ivy's hand on his arm, her touch so light it was barely there, yet he felt it in every nerve of his body, like parched ground absorbing the first drop of rain. His gaze moved up her arm to the rapid rise and fall of her chest, her heart matching the furious beat of his own as the mask of stillness dropped.

Two hearts reunited but offbeat. They needed to find their rhythm again despite its broken notes if they were to stand a chance of moving forward together. His gaze traveled over the necklace holding their rings, then up her neck until it found her eyes. Green with touches of gray, they reflected everything trembling within his own soul. Trepidation, hurt, sadness—and a longing for hope.

Lowering his eyes, he eased away from her touch lest the fresh rain flood his parched soul and wash away the tender roots seeking purchase.

"Remind me if I ever taught you to fish."

She blinked, the tenderness having turned to confusion before settling into acceptance at the sudden turn of the conversation.

"No, you never did. That was something you and Phil—" The name caught in her throat. She swallowed it with the merest tremor of her lip before curving it into a smile. "I'd love to learn."

He stood and offered her his hand. She hesitated, then slipped her fingers over his. His muscles strained to keep from shaking as he pulled her to her feet. She immediately let go and stepped back with a shy smile. How long would this dance go on with neither quite knowing how to act, how to balance all that was new with what had once been so familiar?

Jack grabbed his fishing pole and attached a new lure to the line she had severed, then moved to the edge of the river and handed her the fishing pole.

"Flick it over your shoulder three times, then release."

Ivy held the pole horizontally and briefly sighted down it like she would a rifle before setting it right again. "Why three times?"

"Once to aim, twice to clear the mind, and three times for luck."

"That's a bit superstitious."

An image of her standing in a doorway cut through his mind. The memory was as sharp and as real as if he were there now, smelling the sweetness dusting the air. "No more so than you tossing a pinch of face powder over your shoulder for luck. It's more pleasant smelling than salt, you said."

"I still do that." She smiled.

They stood close enough for the hem of her dress to brush against his trouser leg as the scent of rose soap lingering on her skin brushed under his nose, reminding him of the nights they'd lain together. He would kiss the back of her neck where the aroma had curled into the hollows behind her ears and the dips of her shoulders.

A long-dormant feeling shuddered, and air rushed into the corroded place inside him that he'd thought crumbled long ago. The desire to brush aside the shortened locks of strawberry-blonde hair and touch his lips to those secret places quickened through him. He only needed to lean a bit to the right and— He stopped short and stepped away. The disappointment flickering in her eyes knifed him, but not enough to overcome his fear of getting too close and hurting her.

Quiet minutes passed with nothing more than the rippling water to fill the silence as Ivy fished and Jack shredded a blade of grass between his fingers.

At last Ivy blew out a heavy sigh. "Either the fish are napping or I'm a very poor pupil."

"Philip didn't know a lure from a reel when I first taught him. He hooked more sunken tin cans and boots than fish, but after he got the hang of it, the fish would practically leap into his bucket." Where had that recollection come from? So many memories had been blotted out; a new one resurfacing was a welcome surprise. A rusty noise rumbled in Jack's throat. Had a laugh also managed to break free from the rubble of his mind?

"I remember one time he tried to set off detonators in the Potomac to see how high the water would blast, but they never went off."

Ivy's laughter tumbled free. "It amazes me still that you both survived those days with no missing fingers or noses."

"He always took the most chances. Like at Lake Baikal when he strapped on that bomb vest and threatened to blow us all to kingdom come." And just like that the rubble closed in on him once more. "I dreamed of him the other night. Snow and ice were everywhere. It was so cold we could barely move our limbs. Then everything was on fire. I felt nothing. Not the heat scorching my skin or the smoke choking my lungs. Philip was with me, trapped in the flames, and then like that"—he snapped his fingers—"he was gone."

"Oh, Jack. Philip died in the Talon fire. He loved you dearly. He was never the same after you fell from that cliff. Neither of us were." She was quiet a moment before speaking again. "In your dream you saw him in a fire. Do you think you saw him that night? Do you remember at all how the fire may have started?"

"Only snatches. I remember the gramophone playing and then a needle pierced my neck. The heat of the fire burned up the stairs behind me. A woman. No faces." Jack flicked the shredded grass from his palm. "Reclaiming my memories is like tracking a fox; every time I get close enough to capture one, it seems to vanish. It's maddening."

"You'll get there. One day at a time. Even if the memories don't fully return, we'll make new ones."

Jack shook his head in disbelief. "You make it sound so simple."

She gave a small tug on the fishing line and the lure bobbed closer. "I realize it's not simple. Nothing about any of this is, but I refuse to give up without a fight. I choose to fight for us."

"I don't know if I'm worth fighting for. They made me a monster. I ask myself again and again, if the monster always dies at the end of the story, why am I still alive?"

Casting off all pretense of fishing, Ivy dangled the pole from one hand as she spun to pin him with a direct stare. Horrible, uncompromising determination that he wished only to recoil from.

"Because the story isn't over, and you are *not* the monster. The monster is gone. It's still you in there. Changed, but still you, and if you can't see that man, I'll help you uncover him. When you hurt, I'll be here. Whatever you need, I will find it."

He met her sincerity without flinching. The cost of such vulnerability slit a hole straight through his gut.

"That's just it, though. I don't know what I need."

THIRTEEN

IN THE DAYS THAT FOLLOWED, THEY EXISTED IN A SERIES OF VIGNETTES OF feigned domesticity. A "Pass the butter and rolls, please," scene at breakfast; checking the trout line before lunch; and midafternoon he would help carry a bundle of freshly scrubbed towels to the clothes-line. The after-dinner performance was always a surprise.

Ivy would take needle and thread to a pair of trousers in need of patching or seek out an upstairs closet to scrub clean. He would go to the old barn to repair a chair or rummage through ancient junk for something useful or disappear into the woods to set overnight traps. For a dash of extra excitement, they would stand on the back porch staring up at the sky with snippets of polite chatter tripping between them, as if words found the whole situation too awkward to form themselves into meaningful conversation.

Until one night Jack dreamed of fire and pain and awoke screaming.

He jerked upright, sweat slicking his skin as he gasped for air. Blankets lay tangled around him on the floor like defeated foes after battle. Moonlight leaked through the cracked window of his upstairs bedchamber and crept across the bare floor, climbing up his legs, undershorts, and chest. The scars covering his skin shone silver in the pale light. Many of them he knew—a blade fight in Madrid with a Mark I trench knife, a lead pipe outside Singapore, a Mannlicher M1895 crossing into Bulgaria. Many more tallied fights he could not remember.

Feet ran down the hallway. He tensed at the swift knock on the door, but there was no need to reach for the blade beneath his pillow. The door clicked open.

"Jack?" Ivy moved in without waiting for a response, eager and light but not rushing. She knew better than to rush at him. Her white silk nightdress puffed around her as she knelt near him. The glint of a blade flashed in her hand before she covered it in the folds of her nightdress. Still fearful he would turn on her. The fresh scent of roses clashed with the staleness of his sweat permeating the room. She glanced at the clean bed she'd made for him days ago then down to the floor at the pallet of rumpled, worn blankets he preferred.

"Another nightmare?" She was washed in shades of silver and cool blue with shadows burrowing deep into the dips and hollows of her curves. Delicate and shifting; he could never hope to grasp her all at once.

Jack shoved a hand through his drenched hair and dragged away the long, wet ends clinging to his forehead and neck, then quickly dropped his hand to a fist against his thigh before she noticed the tremor. Who was he fooling? She noticed everything.

"Was it the fire? Or Dragavei?"

A bead of sweat rolled down his forehead and dripped off his nose. He turned his face away to the dark wall where the moonlight could not reach. Where he could not be exposed.

"I hope it wasn't the dinner I cooked." Her voice carried a teasing note. It curled around him, attempting to pluck out the darkness so heavy inside him. He craved her soft words while simultaneously wishing for an impenetrable wall to separate them. To protect her from him.

He swatted the sweat from his nose. He sensed her probing lightness sputter and fall away.

She shifted closer and the edge of her nightdress brushed against his knee.

"Will you tell me about it?"

Jack squeezed his eyes shut. The faces of his victims had been wreathed in fire. Their mouths gaped open, but the screams could not be heard above the sound of his firing bullets. He could feel the fire burning the leather mask on his face and melting the rifle barrel in his hands. Another drop of sweat trickled between his eyelashes. He swiped it away and opened his eyes.

"What is there to tell? I have bad dreams. So does everyone else."

"Not everyone wakes up screaming night after night. My own deeds have left me crying out in the middle of the night, but I know they must pale against what you've been through."

"I'm sorry for waking you from one of your rare nights of peaceful sleep." Brushing past her, he stood and walked to the window, careful to keep his reflection unexposed in the cracked glass. The night was pitch black save for the moon behind a smear of clouds. It was the perfect position and lighting for a hunt. Too many times he'd stood at a window like this, rifle in hand, waiting for hours without moving for his target to come into view. He curled his fingers tight against the ghost sensation of a ready trigger.

"Go back to bed."

The floorboards creaked as she rose and crossed the room toward him. She stood before the window, exposed for all to see in the pale light, her sorrowful face lifted to him. She'd left the knife next to the bed.

"Won't you tell me?"

Tell her? Tell her of the nightmares where he was the monster? Tell her of the blood so thick on his hands they were forever stained black? She would face him with more than sorrow after that. No, the devastation he'd wrought belonged to him alone, his torment to carry as punishment like Prometheus with his rock and liver-devouring eagle.

"If you're worried about frightening me, don't be. We're both killers who have destroyed parts of ourselves to survive."

"You are naive to think Talon deaths are in any way measurable against those of the Order."

"Death is death, and my conscience bleeds with my guilt. The memories scar over each day until my dreams rip them open again." Grasping the collar of her nightdress, she slowly pulled it off her shoulder to reveal skin so pale it was nearly translucent but also marred by pink welts. Her necklace with their wedding rings slipped out and dangled for a moment before resting against the pink satin ribbon barely holding the edges of her neckline together.

"So many seen and unseen, ripped open over and over. The scars thicken, but the pain of remembrance is always present." As she slid her nightdress back into place, her gaze fell from his face to the bare skin of his chest. She leaned forward and brushed her lips over the knot of scars on his shoulder. "I'll kiss every scar on your body and make you remember their beauty."

Her warm breath caressed his skin, rooting him to the spot despite the frantic pace of his heart. "There's nothing beautiful about what I did to get them."

"They're beautiful because you survived them."

The summer heat pressed heavily between them, hot and still to highlight each rasped intake of breath, each lash brushing against her cheek, the inches closing off individual space. He wanted her as she wanted him. He wanted her words, her voice, her smiles, her touch, her love. She was everything good and bright, and she loved him. At least, she loved the old Jack. The one who had been able to return her love with abandon. All he could offer her now was brokenness and darkness. He could never forgive himself if he were to tarnish her with his failures.

He stepped farther back into the shadows, mere inches, but they might as well have been miles. "Go back to your bed."

Hurt flashed in her eyes. Good. If she was hurt, she wouldn't reach for him again. His resistance might crumble if she did. He wrapped his blackening pain tighter, its burden a mocking comfort, but at least he knew its torments and could keep it from touching her. Opening himself to Ivy would be like standing with his arms spread wide to fend off a serrated knife attack. And her aim was deadly.

Her mouth opened on the tiniest quiver and attempted to form words. Jack held his breath, almost hoping she would protest or plead to stay.

Stay with me.

She pressed her lips into a firm line, turned to gather her blade, and left, quietly closing the door behind her. Her footsteps padded away from him, each step a beat of relief quickly followed by regret.

Come back.

The faint sound of her door clicking shut at the end of the hall thudded in his ears, leaving him alone with thoughts of what might have been and the approaching loneliness to swallow them whole.

★★★

Ivy pulled back the string on her bow and let the arrow fly. It zipped over the parched grass and slammed into the bottom of the target she'd constructed out of a deflated tractor tire and tarp. In the time she'd been out here, only three of the ten arrows reached the bull's-eye. The others lay scattered about in shameful disarray.

She never missed, yet her dead-on accuracy couldn't hit the wide side of a barn today. Or yesterday. Or the day before that, if she was counting. Which she was not. They all blurred together, nothing changing.

She and Jack existed, stuck in a limbo of polite torment. He was calm, indifferent, almost like an old acquaintance now forced to exist under the same roof. The roots that had woven them together seemed to have withered, and the brittleness left behind scratched away her faith in their bond ever regrowing.

What if Jack never fully recovered? What if the psychological damage was too severe and no amount of love or patience could alleviate it? Fear mocked her promises of eternal devotion. What if this was who they were now?

She nocked another arrow, drew back, and released. This one hit the tire's outer rim. She eyed the bow with malice.

"Maybe if you weren't a relic from the War between the States you'd actually shoot straight." Carved of solid yet aged hickory, the old bow had been rotting in the barn when she found it. She'd restrung it in hopes of channeling her frustration through the age-old art of shooting something, but the ancient piece only proved to exacerbate the tension she felt.

She dropped the weapon and crossed the yard to retrieve her wayward arrows. The dying grass crunched beneath her bare feet as thin gray clouds drifted across the sky. The slight breeze was a welcome relief from the August heat that sought to drown her in humidity.

A week had passed since Jack's scream awakened her in the middle of the night. She'd gone to comfort him. To let him know that no matter what, she was here. And he'd pushed her away. In the beginning her patience and understanding had been like thread from an endless spool, its length immeasurable and its strength capable of binding the greatest tears, but each day the thread was pulled farther and grew thinner until only a few wraps remained. The day was coming when the last bit would slip free, leaving only a hollow tube where there had once been abundance.

Doubt had begun tying her hope into knots. Might he be lost

forever? Another knot. What was the point of staying where she was not wanted? Another knot. Were they truly broken beyond repair? She hated the thoughts as they knotted in her heart and mind, but they were inescapable. Fear was as much a part of the human condition as love, but how long until one broke the other? How long before they both broke her?

She and Jack passed each other in the hall, careful not to touch, tight smiles on their weary faces. She heard him pacing the floor in his room at night where he still refused to sleep on the bed. Her heart broke to see that threadbare pallet on the floor when the space in her bed had been empty and cold for so long. Sometimes she would hear the kitchen door swing open and he would disappear into the night, not returning until the sun cracked over the horizon. She knew because she would lie awake listening for him, wondering if this was the time he wouldn't come back.

Arrows in hand, she marched back to her bow. She nocked an arrow and shot. Missed. How many times was she expected to reach out to him when he locked himself further away? She tried again. Missed. How many more cracks could her heart suffer before it crumbled beyond repair? Another arrow. Did he not feel the pain throbbing between them? The arrow stuck in a tree to the right. Did he think they could continue to exist like this? Another arrow. It jammed into the ground before the target. Another.

"You're not drawing back far enough."

Ivy jumped. The arrow sailed far left.

Jack stood just behind her. The silent stalker of her sanity. "Sorry. I didn't mean to make you lose your concentration."

"A bit late for that." The knots inside her tightened.

"You forgot to anchor at the corner of your mouth. I remember teaching you that. The string whacked the side of your nose. You still have the scar." His hand reached out as if to touch the tiny sliver of white on the side of her nose where the string had left its mark, but his fingers curled away, and he dropped his hand to his side. "If you don't anchor, there's no constant to judge the next shot."

It was as if time had wound backward and they were in Talon's training room again. Jack patient and efficient in his instruction; her the novice assassin missing the target on purpose so he would step closer and adjust her stance. How easily he slipped back into that role while the one of friend, confidant, lover, and husband eluded him. As did the ability to reciprocate making an effort, but who needed effort in a marriage? By all means, let them discuss target tactics instead.

"Yes. I know." Her words were sharp as she raised the armed bow.

"Keep your wrist straight." His finger gently tapped her wrist. The soft touch pierced her skin and filled her bones like floodwaters bulging against a dam. Another touch, another word, and all hell would break loose.

She yanked back the string, not bothering to anchor. The arrow shot far over the target and thunked into a tree. "Time to make supper."

Jack blinked at the sky as if he could read the sun behind the gathering clouds. "It's only four o'clock."

Blood thrumming in her ears, Ivy marched across the yard and up the back steps and stomped into the kitchen. The screen door slammed behind her with satisfying punctuation to her mood. Realizing she still gripped her weapon, she tossed the bow onto the kitchen table that no longer wobbled. Jack had carved a new leg, and the table now stood straight as a ruler. One she felt like kicking.

Slamming pots and pans, smacking dough with a roller, and chopping through a cabbage with a single whack should have quelled the heat roaring through her blood, but she only wanted to hit something harder. Like her husband's thick head. She dropped the pan of biscuits on the table, hoping the sound was loud enough for him to hear out in the yard. She plopped onto a chair and scraped butter over the burned corn cobs while the peas boiled on the stove.

An hour later her blood had managed to simmer down along with the gravy, and she called Jack in to the table. The sun had been obliterated by the gathering rain clouds, and she'd forgotten to light a candle to combat the darkened kitchen. Apparently barely suffused anger made one oblivious to such needs as light.

Jack lit a few stubby candles and the kerosene lamp, then sat across from her at the table, eyeing the shriveled peas, the corn that had gone cold, the burned biscuits, and the fried chicken that still had blood leaking through the crispy skin. Wisely, he said nothing and loaded his plate. Silence filled the room, punctuated by the oven's metal ticking as it cooled and the scraping of forks and knives across the china.

The food rolled tastelessly around Ivy's mouth as she swallowed automatically, the bites hitting her stomach with an ungratifying thud. *Say something. Anything.* The silence stretched on. *Ten years of loneliness and we have nothing to say.* Words and thoughts and feelings bubbled inside her from dawn to dusk until she thought she'd explode from the pressure of keeping them under lock and key.

Jack would talk when he was ready, and in the meantime, she would support him through patience and love. He would bid her good morning, and she would bite her tongue to keep from asking if he'd had any nightmares. They would discuss catching fish when she wanted to know if he'd ever tried to escape from the Order. He would ask her to hand him the hammer as he nailed the porch steps down while she burned to ask if he still loved her. Ten years of caged demons and heartache, and they hid it all behind a scattering of eggshells, never touching, never reaching for each other.

Feet shuffled under the table. Forks scratched across plates. Their shadows wavered against the four-walled box of a room as rain splattered against the windows. Eggshells crackled.

Ivy wanted to scream.

"Can you pass the peas, please?" Jack asked.

She stared at the bowl filled with the green blobs. It was by far the most offensive item on the table, its contents shriveled and discolored, and it was the one he'd asked for. The absurdness of it made her snap.

"That's it? That's all you have to say to me after ten years? Pass the peas?!" She jumped to her feet with enough force to send her chair flying backward as she glared at him across the table.

Vegetables, that was what he wanted. Not to know how she'd coped living as a widow. Not to ask if she'd looked for his body in the Argeș River until her fingers and toes were numb from the frigid water. Not to ask how she felt about him shutting her out of his pain day after day.

Coherent thought crashed into irrational emotion, and she seized the first thing that popped into her mind. "You haven't even mentioned my hair!"

He sat staring at her, slack-jawed, a forkful of pink chicken halfway to his mouth. "Um, you cut it."

"Yes, I cut it!" she hissed. "I've done a great many things in ten years, but you wouldn't know, would you, because you won't talk to me. You're fine to sit here in silence, only breaking it to ask for the damn peas!" She snatched the bowl and hurled it toward him.

He ducked just in time and it smashed against the wall behind him. Glass shattered and the globs dripped down the peeling wallpaper, leaving streaks of green smeared into the faded daffodil print.

He stared at her in disbelief. "Have you lost your senses? Or are you trying to kill me?"

"Wouldn't be the first time, nor am I likely the only one. I assume people have been trying to kill you for years, but I wouldn't know about any of that, would I?"

"Any of what?"

"What you've been doing or where you've been for the past ten years."

His shock disappeared and hardness dropped over his face. "You know exactly what I've been doing."

"How can I when you won't talk to me? Oh, I know about the Dust, and the Riser, and even Dragavei, but I don't know anything about *you* because you've closed yourself off from me."

"For good reason."

"You think I'm afraid of you? Of what you've done? What about the terrible things *I've* done? The blood I've spilled and the morals I've cast aside in the pursuit of trying to kill the person I was before. I very nearly succeeded too. Each life I ended scraped another sliver of humanity from me, and I was grateful. Because without my humanity I couldn't feel, I couldn't summon the burden to care. Then, when I'd nearly achieved complete numbness, you showed up like a hot wire, sparking me back to life. Except I'm not living. Neither of us is. We're caught in a hell of silent surrender to the worst parts of ourselves."

He knocked his chair sideways. The legs splintered off.

"What do you want from me? To fall to my knees and weep? To curse the sky I was born under? To tell you every single evil I've committed in a purging of my soul? So we might, what? Cry and hold each other in mutual understanding? Talk about the old days when I used to sit next to you under the stars, or attempt to resurrect the dreams we once had for our life together?" His voice crackled with ice as his eyes steeled with resolve. A Riser on the brink of unleashing.

"I am not that man. He was murdered and dumped into a pit too deep to climb out of. The Order saw to that. So tell me precisely what it is you want from me."

"I want you to fight! Fight to climb out of that pit. Fight to reclaim the pieces of yourself that I know are still in there. Fight for *us*! Just fight, damn you!" She grabbed the knife from her plate and speared it at him.

He whipped sideways and grabbed the handle. As smoothly and

as quickly as always. "The only way I know to fight leads to death and destruction. I refuse to let you be a part of that."

"Don't you understand? I would destroy myself to save you from fighting that way ever again."

"And what if I can't be saved? What if this is all I am now? A shell. And not even the shell of a man whose heart once beat, but a used-up bullet casing, an echo of all the horror I've inflicted. All I hear is the echo. The villain doesn't die. He doesn't remember how to die, so he doesn't. He doesn't remember how to live. So he doesn't. He's just a shell called Death." He flipped the knife to hold the blade, then flung it.

It struck the floor inches from her toes, the blade lodged deep in the wood plank, its handle quivering.

She should have been afraid. On his best days Jack was dangerous. On his worst he was absolutely ruthless. Perhaps she was braver than common sense dictated or perhaps just foolish enough to believe she stood a chance should he snap, but either way she refused to give ground.

"So that's it? You're content to remain in these echoes, pulling me along with you until we wither away from our pain? Side by side, but no closer than if you'd remained a memory beyond the grave."

"No one is forcing you to stay. In fact, no one asked you to come."

Rain crashed against the glass panes as thunder rumbled in warning.

"Well, I did come, and I am not leaving. I'm here because ten years ago I watched my husband slip over the side of a cliff and plunge to his death in a frozen river. You were gone and I screamed. I cried and wailed. I shouted so you would hear me on your way down and force yourself to come back to me.

"I'm here because time and time again I found myself on that cliff wanting to join you. The thought of finding you in this life or the next kept me going back, placing my bare toes on that ledge and staring down into that rushing river, but death refused to claim me. It led me here, to you. And now that I'm standing in front of you, I feel as if I'm back on that cliff with nothing but the frozen air around me, waiting for you to come back to me."

"Is this what you wanted to come back to you? This killer who didn't have control over his own mind to know who he was killing or why, only that he'd been ordered to? A monster kept on a leash and caged, made to lie in his own filth and clean the stains of blood from under his nails with rocks chipped from his cell wall?"

The shadowed hollows of his eyes, cheeks, and neck devoured the candlelight, carving his face with darkness as long hairs slashed over his eyes like knives. "My life was forfeited to a group of psychotic occultists whose founding patron used to set his subjects' heads on pikes for amusement. Don't think you were the only one waiting on a ledge wanting it all to end."

"Then why are we still standing there? Why are we standing *here*?" She gestured to the space between them. "There is so much breathing room between us, yet I can barely move. Why are we not moving, Jack?"

"I don't know how anymore." The muscles in his throat constricted as if the words had to force their way up. "If I take one step closer to you, I don't know if I can resist the ache to touch you—"

"Then touch me!"

"My touch brings death."

"Living without your touch kills me."

"And what happens if one day I snap and break your neck? Have you thought of that at all? Because I have."

"It's a risk I'm willing to take." She stepped toward him, but he moved back. Defensive. She grabbed her plate and smashed it on the floor in an explosion of anger that cracked her wide open.

"Stop breaking things!"

"I hate this china! I hate painted fruit."

"My aunt brought it all the way from New York."

"You hated your aunt!"

"I did—she was a terrible woman—but now we won't have anything to eat off of."

Their shouting drowned out the rainstorm.

Ivy kicked at the broken shards. "You muster more outrage for this repulsive antique disk than you do for our shattered relationship."

The steel blazed to fire in his eyes. Hot and devouring as if to scorch everything in its path. Including her. "You want to talk about love and finding happiness together, but they took it from me. Hope was a weakness to them, and I was remade with gunmetal in my bones and wolf's fangs. Everything good was burned out in their forge until only pieces of anger, hatred, and revenge remained. A hell with no escape."

"Then I'll drag you out with my teeth if I have to. I lost you once. I won't let it happen again."

"And I won't allow you to sacrifice yourself for me. There is every chance the Order will come for me. Those devils will shoot straight through you to get to me, and having your blood on my hands is not a guilt I can survive."

"You think to threaten me with the devil? What can the devil do to me that hasn't already been done?" Ivy held his fiery gaze. "No, Jack. The only hell worse than what you've been put through is this right here. This insistence that you deserve nothing else. Not happiness, not peace, and not love."

"I could not live with myself knowing you loved me more than anyone else in the entire world and I destroyed you."

They stood staring at each other, a thousand hurts and undeclared words between them with no bridge long enough to cross the vast distance. It was terrifying to ache alone, untouched and unspoken to. In her life she had been many people and worn many titles. Daughter, orphan, friend, agent, wife, widow. In that moment the pain stripped her of each and laid her to bare bones, nameless.

"Not once have you said my name." Her whispered words cracked at the end.

The fire in his eyes guttered. His shoulders sagged as if all that was lost between them had collapsed on him.

She turned on her heel, wrenched open the screen door, and shot across the yard. Raindrops continued streaming from the pent-up gray clouds, patting coolly against her heated face.

"Ivy, wait!"

She rushed on, ignoring his calls for her. Her name from his lips should have been a balm to her soul. How many nights had she lain in an empty bed longing to hear him call for her in the darkness? Praying to hear him say it once more. Now she couldn't make her feet turn back. She needed to be away from the pain.

Through the woods she ran until the river lay dark and flowing before her. An offering of peace.

She kicked off her shoes and rolled down her stockings with a feverishness that tore a hole straight through the silk. She shucked off her dress and waded into the water. It rushed up her calves, thighs, stomach, and finally lapped over her shoulders. The rain fell harder and pinged against the surface of the river, spitting drops into her eyes.

She sank, letting the water close over her head. Then she opened her mouth and screamed.

FOURTEEN

QUIET DARKNESS ENVELOPED THE HOUSE EXCEPT FOR A SINGLE CANDLE left burning on the kitchen table. In a kitchen that had been thoroughly cleaned. No shattered china on the floor, no dried streaks of peas on the wall, no black biscuit bits littering the counter. No evidence of what had erupted here hours before, save for a lingering stench of smoke.

Ivy shut the door behind her and tossed her sodden dress and ripped stockings over the back of a chair. Water slid down the material and splattered onto the floor in wet rings. She would tend to the mess tomorrow. Or perhaps not. So many things had been ruined— what was the point in caring about more? Goose bumps ravished her skin as rainwater rolled from her hair and slithered down her body, covered in nothing more than a thoroughly soaked chemise and step-in drawers.

After padding across the hall into the front room, her gaze slid to the corner. The pathetic pile of blankets had long since been laundered, folded, and put away, but the memory of seeing it when she'd first entered this house knifed white hot through her. To come so far without having moved forward. She turned away and started up the stairs, her bare feet leaving wet prints as each step groaned and creaked.

At the top of the stairs, she paused and glanced down the hallway to the door her traitorous eyes couldn't be stopped from staring at. Dark, cold, and closed. As always. Ignoring the fist of emotion squeezing her chest, she turned away toward her own room. The door was ajar with warm light spilling out. She took a deep breath to still the fist as it clenched tighter, tilted her chin to a couldn't-care-less angle, and walked in.

Jack stood at the window with his back to her. A candle burned on the nightstand, its glow fracturing off the raindrops pinging the glass pane.

"If you've come for another round, I'm all out of crockery and drenched to the bone. Come back tomorrow."

His breath fogged the window in slow, deep exhales. Feet braced apart and hands clasped behind his back, he stood ready for battle.

"The Silver One found me on the bank of the river half dead. I was frozen with water in my lungs and several broken bones and cuts from bashing against the rocks while I floated downstream. I remember the pain and a cold so deep I thought my bones had turned to ice. The attempts to reset my broken limbs were crude, and afterward I was tossed into a festering cell. Rats gnawed on me day and night because I was too weak to move. And then the fever came." His low voice rolled around the room in hypnotic waves. She couldn't have broken away from its tragic lull even if she'd wanted to.

"Time passed, though how much I couldn't guess because the hours and days were void from that level of hell. I was dragged from the cell into a cave-like chamber with hard earthen fragments hanging from the ceiling like spears. Water trickled down the walls into muddy pools, and the Silver One's hole-ridden robes dragged through the sludge, leaving streaks and the stench of decay in her wake. The last solid memory I have is of a needle pricking my arm and Dust flooding my veins. Then the nothingness."

His voice released its grievous hold on her, but its quiet surety left her shaking. He spoke of the horrors as if they were mere facts he had long since battled and failed to defeat.

He turned, shadows dipping across his face. "You're shivering. And, uh . . . your clothes."

Having forgotten her own state of affairs, Ivy glanced down at what was on obvious display thanks to her now-translucent under-pinnings. Grabbing the hem of her chemise, she wiggled to begin the tug of war to slip it over her head. Jack's face flamed and he spun around to face the window again.

A greedy mixture of sadness and disappointment spilled through her at his lack of . . . what? Appreciation? Desire? It had been too long since his eyes were on her, since the flame of longing burned bright in his blue eyes—a flame she'd ravenously returned. As quickly as the greed came, it vanished into shades of shame. She wanted his heart again above all else. The rest might come again in time.

She stepped behind the privacy screen made of cheap muslin fab-ric and reached for a towel from the basin stand but missed. She tried again with shaking fingers and clutched the towel to her chest, fight-ing for mastery over her teetering emotions. She inhaled a trembling breath, careful not to allow Jack to hear the nerves coursing through her. He'd summoned a great deal of bravery to bleed himself open like this, and the last thing he needed was her falling to pieces.

Ivy's fingernails clawed into the towel as she brisked it over her skin hard enough to leave red marks. "Helena Dragavei, this 'Silver One,' she controlled you."

"She controls all."

Shivering enough to make her teeth rattle, Ivy grabbed the extra quilt she'd washed and placed on top of the bureau, wrapped it around herself, and stepped out from behind the privacy screen. "Not all anymore."

Jack took a deep breath. "No, not anymore." He turned and leaned on the windowsill, his fists clenching and unclenching at his sides until he finally tucked them away by crossing his arms over his chest. Keeping his gaze fixed on the floor, he continued his story.

"For the next few years, Risers like me were created. We trained by fighting one another. Those whose bodies couldn't handle the Dust were easily killed—like splitting wilted cabbages with an axe. Over and over again we fought until I was the only Riser left standing. The Order's supreme creation. It didn't happen overnight. The monsters are created slowly like pottery, but instead of clay there is twisted gunmetal and cruel claws, painted with the blood of victims and hardened by death.

"The Silver One sharpened each claw and twisted each fiber of metal until her will was all that existed. A Riser has no thoughts and no voice beyond the one she commands. I would go for days on end with no water to quench my thirst, and she would stand outside my cage with a filled cup asking if I'd like a sip. I couldn't answer because she hadn't given me permission. Even if permission was given, I wouldn't answer because a Riser has no opinion, no will to agree or refuse, no needs, no wants. She would drain the cup to the last two drops then fling them at me. I lapped at those drops between the moldy floor cracks like a dog."

The strength left her legs and Ivy sagged onto the bed. She wanted to weep and wail for the cruelty of it all, but more than anything she wanted Helena Dragavei's head skewered and dropped into the deepest ravine they could find.

"She may have treated you like a beast, but that does not make you one."

"There are times when I still feel that leather mask on my face, suffocating me. I have to remind myself to chew my food because no one is coming to snatch it from my hands. I have to pick out a clean shirt each morning because now not only do I have clean clothes, but several pieces to choose from. *Choose*, when I thought the very word had been stricken from my existence. The only new wearable items the Order gave me were gun holsters or knife sheaths when the old ones broke or were lost in a fight. The clothes on my back were stiff with years' worth of grime, sweat, blood, and other disgusting filth. I was a weapon, and weapons don't require clean clothing."

Strike that. Not just skewered but impaled on a dull, splintered piece of wood crowded with thorns and lit on fire.

"If you were her prized pet, how could she keep you in such horrible conditions? Valuable weapons must be cleaned and oiled; otherwise they're useless in a fight. It's one of the first things we learned as assassins."

A wry smile twisted his mouth. "The Silver One isn't concerned about the art of proper arms handling and care. In fact, she has no concern for any person, not even herself. All that matters is the Order and bringing them to power, and to do that she needed a Riser to clear the path. Besides, the filth, the starvation, the lack of control meant nothing to me. Not with Dust flooding my veins, drowning out my own mind and everything else except the need to complete the next mission so I could get my next hit."

"An addiction."

"One you would do anything for if only to fight off the pain of not having it." He dropped his hands to his lap, twisting his fingers until the skin stretched white between his knuckles. "I fought as hard as I could, but in the end I couldn't overcome it, and for that I will always be ashamed."

The struggle to hold back her emotions knotted in Ivy's throat. "You fought back, and that's what matters. You cannot be ashamed for what was beyond your control. You are the bravest man I know."

"I'm not brave anymore, Ivy. I'm all broken. They changed me into a monster I never wanted to be." He ducked his head. The long curtain of hair shielded his face. "I still see the faces of all my victims. At night the dreams come, folding in on each other and forcing out things that were buried in the nothingness. Like a door unlocks in my mind and all the hellish things trapped within break free. I've tortured thousands. Razed entire villages to the ground. Slaughtered innocents and guilty alike. I wake up to their screaming."

She could fight it no longer as the need to touch him overwhelmed her. She pushed off the bed and went to kneel before him. "Unclench your fists, my darling. Your war is over."

She took his hands and kissed the scarred fingers, then turned them over and pressed more kisses into his palms. Palms so deeply ingrained with dirt and calluses from gun handles that smoothing them out would take a hundred lifetimes.

He stared down at their joined hands. "I've forgotten how to uncurl my fingers from the trigger. Fingers that drip red. I'm terrified of staining you with them."

"You keep saying that as if mine are pristine. As if I don't have horrors that will haunt me to the grave and sins to carry beyond." She squeezed his hands. "Do you know what scared me the most when I was out there on my own? It wasn't dying. It was knowing that the pistol once so heavy with justice in my hand had grown lighter and lighter until I no longer felt the weight. I felt nothing, Jack."

He pulled his hands free, still not meeting her eyes. "Every time a gun barrel pointed at me, do you know the only sliver of emotion that was able to break free amid all the chaos? Relief. One bullet to end it all, and I could be free. The Riser wasn't allowed defeat; I had to put a bullet in my opponent before he could put one in me. As I tried to put one in you." He stood and paced away.

Ivy rose, clutching the blanket tightly around her, and stepped toward him. There was no place to escape to. The demons had been loosed, and here she and Jack would face them. "You did, yet here I am. Here I will always be for you to tell me every terrible thing you have ever done and to let me love you anyway and anywhere."

He squeezed his eyes shut in a look of near despair. "Anywhere? What of my darkest places?"

"Especially there."

He drew a shaky breath and his eyes flashed open, at last finding hers. Brilliant and blue and tormented. "Pretty sentiments, but what do you expect will happen? That you pick up all my broken pieces and mold them back into the man you knew? Do you think any of those pieces are worthy of being your husband? Can any of them be fashioned into the life you deserve or the family you want?"

With a trembling hand, she brushed back the hair scraping his cheek. "*You* are the family I want."

"I know in your heart of hearts you want a child. We dreamed of that once."

The memory of all their hopes and dreams from so long ago lanced across her heart, slicing through tender wounds like a knife through a hard-boiled egg. The pain spilled over, raw and deep and consuming.

Tears streaming down her face, Ivy spoke slowly, her voice cracking. "You did give me a child. Once."

FIFTEEN

AGONY LIKE A BULLET RIPPING THROUGH HIS FLESH HIT JACK QUICK AND hard. He dropped to the bed.

She swiped at the tears on her cheeks. "I didn't know I carried our child when we tracked Balaur to Poenari Castle. After you went over the cliff . . . Well, I was rather banged up and Philip took me to the hospital in Braşov. I lost the baby two days later. Before I knew. Before I could love it."

"Ivy . . . I am so very sorry."

She went on as if she hadn't heard him, as if lost in her own dark world of remembrance. "There was no more baby. No more you. I had nothing to live for. Nothing I wanted to live for. The doctors kept me under watch for a time, and Philip never left my side. He's the only person who knows." Her mouth twisted.

"I returned to that cliff not long afterward. It was still covered in ice and snow. I took off my socks and shoes and stood there on the ledge, staring down into that icy river, imagining you waiting for me on the other side. I didn't feel the cold. I only saw you. Then Philip was there, urging me back. He asked me why I was so eager to die, and I told him it was the only way I could get to you."

Jack slid to the floor and lowered his head in his hands, fingers digging hard into his temples, but the anguish was relentless. "Please stop. You're breaking my heart," he whispered.

But she could no more stop the torment than he could fend it off. The open wound gaped between them, split raw and demanding attention.

"A few years ago I was injured. A takedown gone wrong in Serbia. A group of Rising Moon members had planned to assassinate a government official and put one of their own in his place. I got to him first, but they shot him straight through me." She sat on the edge of the bed, then pulled back part of the blanket wrapped around her to reveal a puckered white scar inches from her navel.

"The doctors did the best they could, but I can never have children. In a way I was glad it happened. I didn't want to have a family without you. *You* were my family."

Whatever remained unbroken in his soul now cleaved in two. Down and down the pieces fell. All they had lost. All that would never be restored. All they had sacrificed, struck down with nothing left to cling to but grief. A grief that could so easily be scrubbed away into nothingness if he let the darkness overtake him. How simple it would be to give in. No more pain, no howls of anguish scratching at his soul, no sorrow bleeding him dry.

He looked at Ivy. By candlelight her skin was cast like wax, a pale surface for the flame's reflection to flicker on. Her lips were pressed tightly together over a clenched jaw as she stared straight ahead through glassy eyes. The restraint was killing her. As it was him.

He let the tide of sorrow come, and a great rush drove the nothingness far below the crashing waves of agony. No matter the pain, it was worth it. To once again feel like a human being was worth it. *She* was worth it.

He started to reach for her, hesitated, and pulled back. His fingers cried out, needing to feel the peace of her touch. He reached again, this time placing his hands in her lap while touching his forehead to her knees. A reverent supplicant in need of grace.

"Oh, my own love," she whispered, then softly touched the top of his head. Before he could press a kiss to the blanket, her fingers kneaded through his hair until her nails scored his scalp and a sob escaped her throat. His arms wrapped around her and roughly pulled her onto his lap, and together they dissolved into tears for all that was lost between them. No words were necessary as the dam broke and their grief crashed together. They clung to each other as the only source of survival in the surge. Two broken hearts desperate to find a way to fit back together again.

As the racks of her body began to ease against his own, he held her quietly to him, filling his deprived senses with her scent and her softness.

"You're the only real thing I've ever touched." He dropped his head to the crook of her neck where the smells of river water and rain mixed with that of roses. He used to kiss her there. "How can you still want me? After what I've been. All I've done."

Her tear slid down the side of his neck as she took a shaky breath. "I know you, Jack. Through a thousand lifetimes and across millions of stars, I'd find you, never to leave you. Until death do us part."

"My warrior champion to the end." Lifting his head, he took her face in his hands and gently brushed away the tears with his thumbs. She was still his Ivy. Soft velvet draped over courageous steel. "You will never fight another battle alone. I swear it."

She gave him a watery smile. "How I've longed for you."

The smile welled into a fresh batch of tears, and she wrapped her arms around his neck. Jack held her close as she wept. No amount of tears or number of words could fill the cracks of heartache. Not for the child they never met, their withered intimacy, their youth and innocence, nor the half shells they were forced to become. Time relinquished its grip as they sat there suspended for a beating moment of restoration.

Minutes or hours passed before Jack found himself gazing out the window from his seat on the floor as midnight slowly rescinded her throne to the purple dawn. The rain had ceased, and a pinprick of stars blinked their last against the rising sun.

"When I was the Riser, I used to stare at the stars and wonder what their pull on me meant. Andromeda, Pegasus, Corona Borealis. I didn't understand their significance, but I was drawn to them."

"Deep down a part of you knew where you belonged." Having changed into a satin nightgown and matching robe, Ivy drew the shared blanket over their legs and cuddled into his side. Natural, effortless, as if she'd never left. In a way, she hadn't.

He leaned his head back against the bed, contentment rising like an intoxication, mellowing his bones and calming the blood that typically hissed in his veins. "It seems no matter how hard the Order tried to scrub my mind, some memories refused to die. They could never truly take you from me."

"I'm stubborn like that." She grinned up at him.

It was one of the traits he adored most about her. Without it they never would have met, she never would have survived as a Talon agent, nor would she have taken him down in a DC speakeasy. It was her tenacity that brought her down to his cell day after day as he writhed in withdrawal from Dust. Then she'd followed him here and pried open the cage trapping his pain and set it free. Now here he sat, drawing full, deep breaths again.

She began humming a sweet tune that rumbled in his ears and conjured many a night of holding her close and swaying under the midnight moon. "I know that song."

"As you should." She continued humming.

"To greatest heights or lowest depths, I'd go to be with you."

"How many hours did we spend dancing to this before each mission?"

"Hours in heaven can't be counted."

"A perfect response."

He brushed stray hairs from her temple where they had dried in frizzy waves. "A true response."

She was quiet for a moment, her fingers busy tapping the rhythm on the blanket across his knee and causing his gut to twist. Ten years she had lived as a widow. Ten years of loneliness when she should have had a man to hold her in her youth. He should be grateful that she might have found comfort. After all, her happiness was all he had hoped for since the moment they met. But the thought of her in another man's arms was enough to make him wish for oblivion.

When at last she spoke, her voice was low and threaded with memories. "I haven't danced in a very long time. A few of us agents would cut a rug at one of the dance halls from time to time—when we weren't tracking down crime lords or preventing a coup d'état—but I'd always sit out for the slow tunes. Couldn't abide them. And this song, well, I've tried not to think about it in ten years, but it would always find me. Usually in the quiet of night when shadows come out to haunt."

A better man might have responded with greater compassion, but he'd never claimed to be a better man when it came to wanting his wife only for himself, though he had the tact to keep his relief quiet.

"I don't know if I even remember how to dance." Dancing. Laughter. Music. Concepts suspended in memories from a lifetime ago.

"Then we'll take it slow and give our forgetful left feet a chance to catch up." He couldn't see her face, but he could hear the smile in her voice. A smile that clung to hope.

How he wanted to hold tight to that hope and make it his own, but it was infinitely fragile, and the weight of his monstrous claws still hung heavy.

"Will they catch up?"

"I have every faith that they will."

"Even if we're dancing in the dark of night?"

She ran her hands over him, lingering on the scars and torn edges of his heart, and touched her forehead to his. Her green eyes were the color of new birth in the breaking light.

"When have we ever been afraid of stepping into the night? That is where we have always found our stars."

SIXTEEN

AUGUST ROLLED INTO SEPTEMBER, SCORCHING THE LAND AND BLEACHING the sky to a dry blue. Birds chirped in the early morning hours and crickets sang at night, but midday was left to the heated stillness, and nothing was so oppressive as working indoors.

Jack gave the nail one final smack with the hammer and stood to examine his work on the wall. Termites had enjoyed free rein of the house for years, eating through floorboards and ceilings, but their biggest feast was in the wall in the central hallway that also served as a load-bearing wall. A little more snacking and the whole house was likely to crash down on them.

He'd done the best he could using a few planks he'd scrounged from the barn to shore up the wall. This was the one repair he and Ivy agreed on. The others were a matter of opinion. He didn't think the front porch steps needed fixing, nor the front door; sprucing up that area might appear to be an open invitation for visitors, which he vehemently opposed, but Ivy had insisted.

He had to admit the house had taken on a shine since her ministrations. Doors had been screwed onto their hinges, windows polished, shutters retacked, and furniture moved into nondefensive positions. His hands had finally found an occupation of restoration rather than destruction.

Smiling at that amiable thought, he packed up his ancient toolbox and walked through the kitchen to the back porch.

"You look like you could use a glass of lemonade." Ivy sat on the swing with one of the back support slats missing. She had an opened letter next to her. Two glasses of lemonade sat at her feet.

His heart stopped a little each time he saw her, especially when she smiled at him like that, as if she held a secret for him alone. He set down the toolbox and took one of the offered glasses of lemonade.

"I put the pitcher in the river to keep it cool, but by the time I carried it back to the house it was hot again." She laughed, setting the swing into a gentle sway.

His heart thumped at the delightful sound, soft yet vibrant like a ray of morning sunlight streaking into his soul. A week had passed since their night of confessions, and with it the shroud of heaviness engulfing them peeled away. Rawness still layered their exposure, but as with any wound, time would knit together the serrated edges. Only a scar would remain, knotted and silvery with remembrance but making the surface tougher than it had been before.

"Does the wall still stand?" Ivy asked.

He sipped his lemonade. "Barely. Tomorrow I'll start chopping trees to cut into new planks. The entire wall needs to be torn down and rebuilt."

"I'll help. Two of us will make the work go faster."

They spoke as any husband and wife would, discussing repairs to the house. *Their* house that was slowly becoming a home. This place that had once been a prison to him, trapping him with failures and loathing, had begun to fill in the holes with the sounds of Ivy's humming and the scent of fresh wildflowers from the field. They could start over here. Belong.

From the contented way she gazed at him, he knew the possibility dwelled in her mind too.

Before he jumped the gun on laying down permanent roots, he

sipped more lemonade, then nodded at her letter. "First time mail has been delivered here."

"A letter from a friend keeping me informed of the world at large while I do my best to disappear from it. Millie is her name; she's a new Talon recruit. She helped me locate this address."

"And what does the world at large have to say?"

"Oh, nothing out of the ordinary." She tucked the letter back into the torn envelope.

Her voice was unusually bright, which meant the news had nothing to do with anything ordinary.

"Let me guess. Operations are falling apart without you, and your skills are required to hunt down the latest terror threatening the free world."

"Not exactly."

"Whatever it is can't be that terrible. Not after everything we've confessed to each other. No more holding back, remember?"

Her forced brightness dimmed as she settled into resignation. "Do you remember when I told you I've been hunting Order members for the past ten years? Well, I didn't simply hunt them. I eviscerated them from existence and managed to earn a reputation among bounty hunters. It seems Talon captured two last week who were looking for me."

"What's the price up to?" Jack grinned then raised the glass to his mouth for another drink.

"Around four thousand dollars."

Jack spit out the lemonade. He quickly wiped the drops from his chin with the hem of his shirt. Four thousand dollars was enough to set up two lifetimes of comfort.

"Impressive."

"Thank you." She picked at the edge of envelope as the corners of her mouth turned down.

"There's more."

She tore the envelope's corner. "I'm worried they'll find us. That I'm bringing the nightmares to our door."

"Then they'll be forced to leave. I'm the only nightmare allowed to live here."

One corner of her mouth tipped up. "You've only ever been a dream to me."

"You have rather poor dreams then."

"They're mine and I plan to keep them, along with making new ones for the both of us. We owe it to ourselves."

He wanted to agree, to go along with whatever dream she spun for them, but he didn't trust himself not to ruin it. In time, she'd said. Would it ever be enough? Rather than disappoint her with his doubt while their rebuilding remained so fragile, he gave a noncommittal noise and set down his empty glass on the railing.

"I need to sharpen the axe before supper if I'm going to start cutting planks in the morning." He picked up the toolbox and started off the porch toward the barn.

She said nothing as he walked away, but he felt her eyes on him the entire way.

Later, after a light supper of creamed corn, late summer peaches, and grilled trout, Jack settled on the back porch with a lantern and his ancestor's flintlock pistol. With a soft cloth he began the soothing motions of cleaning the weapon, each swipe easing the day's tension from his muscles and calming the distractions rattling around in his mind.

"Whew! Is it hot in there." The screen door swung open and Ivy stepped out onto the porch. The soft sounds of a record playing followed her out. "Might have to sleep in the river simply to stay cool tonight."

"The roof isn't bad as long as it doesn't rain—and you stay away from the chimney where it's pitched steep. You're liable to wake up sliding straight off."

"You slept on the roof? I can't imagine it was very comfortable."

"No, but it was more enticing than listening to another of my aunt's lectures about how the saints were going to crown her in heaven for taking on the likes of me. Woke up a few times with the shingles sliding right out beneath me. If I hadn't grabbed the gutter I would have gone over."

"Always one for adventure, even as a little boy." Ivy laughed and sat next to him on the step. Close enough to touch. If they wanted to. "I haven't seen that piece before."

She leaned closer, brushing her arm against his. He inhaled her sweet rosy scent. If he turned his head an inch or so, he could press his lips to the skin just behind her ear. A thousand times he had kissed her there, but it had been so long. Too long. He needed to woo her as he had once before, not sling her over his shoulder and carry her off upstairs. She deserved romance.

"Does it still fire?"

He snapped out of his reverie. "Yes." Clearing the telling huskiness from his voice, he tried again. "It's a 1750 flintlock pistol made by Thomas Cadell of Doune, who built some of the best iron pistols to be found. Nine-inch barrel with a .57 caliber. My great-great-great-grandfather's. He was said to have brought it over from Scotland and used it to fight the redcoats during the Revolution. See this nick here?" He turned it over in the lantern light and pointed at a thin slash on the barrel. "Caught the cutting edge of a saber." He held it out to her.

Holding it, she tested the weight, sighted down the barrel, and brushed her finger over the hammer where a sharp piece of flint would be clamped in tight if the pistol were in use. She traced along the intricate engravings curling the entire body length.

"It's beautiful. And heavy."

"Seventeenth-century Scotland preferred to make their dags—pistols, that is—from pure brass or iron."

Her eyebrow hiked with condescension. "I'm aware of Scots weapon etymology. How is it you can recite the lineage of any weapon placed in your hand yet never once mentioned that your people hail from Alba?"

"It was so long ago it seemed of little importance. Unlike this gun, which is still with us." Tangible and relevant. A man needed nothing more.

She snorted with historical outrage. "*Vale* is from fourteenth-century Middle English and borrowed from the Anglo-French *val*, meaning dale or valley. All this time I thought you were French." She frowned and handed back the pistol. "Though the French and Scottish did share an alliance against the English during the Jacobean rebellions. Perhaps that's where your ancestry crossed the Channel."

"I'll leave that mystery for you to unravel."

"I'll unravel it as soon as we return to Alexandria. The Library of Congress is bound to have ship passenger lists and enlistment records." She tugged at the collar of her blouse. A trumpet solo crooned on the record, momentarily quieting the serenade of crickets.

"I'm in no rush to return, though. Summer in the city is miserable. Perhaps we should come here for the summer like all the rich swells do when the heat becomes unbearable. Swimming in the river, no shoes to stifle our feet, blackberry picking, and fresh fish for supper. Doesn't that sound heavenly?"

Dread filled Jack's belly, dark and heavy and threatening to pull him back into the Dust-created nothingness. The bubble of contentment finally popped.

"I can't return with you," he whispered. "It's madness to turn me loose again, an assassin in the midst of thousands of people."

She leaned her shoulder into his and dropped her voice to a conspiratorial whisper. "In case you forgot, there are many of us assassins on the loose."

"Your kind are the sort that kills my kind."

The teasing light faded from her eyes. She took the gun from his hand and placed it behind them. "You're still part of Talon.

Washington, Hamilton, and all of the instructors want to see you return. It's our home."

The omission of Jefferson cut him quick as a knife. "Talon is no longer my home. Not after what I've done, and I certainly don't expect anyone to welcome me back with open arms. I have nowhere to belong."

"You belong with me—"

"Do you honestly believe things could ever be the same at Talon? That I could stroll into those training rooms under the Alexandria streets where they were forced to relocate because *I* burned the old ones to the ground? Do you think no one would stare at me in contempt? Living day after day surrounded by the shame of murdering those I was once closest to." He shoved a length of hair behind his ear. "I thought out here we could start over. You and me and only the memories we allow. We can be happy with no need to ever return."

"If you would have allowed me to finish, I was going to say that you belong with me, and I belong with you. Wherever *we* decide that may be."

She made it sound as simple as making a wish and having it all come true. As if they wouldn't have to fight for every single moment of peace every single day. He was so tired of fighting.

"I can't go back, Ivy. I can't go back to that life where I'm only one kill shot away from turning into the Riser. What if I lost control?" He raked his hand through his hair and squeezed the back of his neck as tension strained through the muscles.

"Dust is what controlled you," she said. "Without it you simply cannot snap back into the Riser."

"Are you so sure? All those years under control, I wouldn't be surprised if the instincts still lurked inside me." He dropped his hand. "Some days I feel as if the devil's very tattoo is drumming inside my head, and it's going to break me again, a thousand times over."

"I won't allow you to break. If any give must be had, we shall bend together."

The chaos in his mind calmed. How she affected him, stilling the torment of thoughts come to steal his sanity.

"Why do you see the good in me?"

"Sweet, sweet love of mine. I see the good and the bad. I see the wars within you, the cuts and the bruises, and I love you all the more for them. Because you're mine."

Drawing a deep breath, he touched his forehead to hers with a desperate need to shut out the interfering distance between them. "So you'll stay?"

With a soft smile, she pulled the chain from around her neck. Their rings dangled from the end. "Always."

Jack touched the inked circles over his heart. Perfect matches. Ivy reached out and curled her fingers lightly over his.

"After ten years apart, you must be crackers to think I would ever leave you. Are you crackers, Jack?"

"Somehow I think it wouldn't matter to you if I was."

"Not one bit. It would keep the adventure in our relationship, and you know how I adore adventure."

Jack dipped his head and brushed a kiss on her fingers resting over his heart.

"That I do."

★★★

Ivy forced her pen to the paper.

Dear Washington,

I'm writing to you from our countryside retreat where we've found a semblance of peace and contentment—

She threw the pen on the makeshift desk, then wadded up the paper and tossed it to the floor to join the half dozen other crumpled attempts. No matter which words she tried, none managed to arrange themselves into what she needed to say. To her utter dread, written words were failing her.

Write! her head screamed, yet in her heart of hearts lurked a more primal need. Her gaze strayed to her Beretta on the nightstand. *Vengeance*, it seemed to whisper. Vengeance for anyone who ever hurt him, for everything that kept them apart, for the horrors that preyed on him still.

She cocked her ear to the door, listening for any sound of disturbed sleep down the hall, but Jack slept quietly. The peace of it settled deep within her as a promise. A new life. A new chance at happiness and growing old together far away from the violence that had ripped them apart.

She pulled out a fresh sheet of paper and smoothed it flat, then balanced the pen between her fingers.

Tonight was a night of battle; her mind was at war with her heart. A fight between what she knew to be true, what she felt could be, and what she knew she had to do. She glanced up through the window, grateful for the moon's luminescence shining on what was important, as well as its concealment, hiding what she did not wish to dwell on. At times, the hardest decisions were best made under the light of the moon.

Dear Washington,

This has not been an easy journey, but at last I have found what I sought for so long. The future now beckons us to a new path, a path of peace and contentment that could not be taken if we were to remain where we once stood.

With deep sorrow I must bid you adieu, yet I beg you to hold fast to the knowledge that I carry with me the fondest memories and deepest gratitude for your guidance and the home you welcomed me into. I found myself, and now I have found one who needs me more.

Gratefully,

Mrs. Jack Vale

SEVENTEEN

JACK WIPED HIS SWEATING PALMS AGAINST THE KNEES OF HIS PRESSED trousers and dragged in a fortifying breath to steel his nerves. If only he had a gun or a blade. There was nothing like the solid weight of a rifle stock to steady the buffs, but there would be no weapon carrying on this occasion. Tonight he was armed only with a skill likely to prove rusted beyond repair.

He checked his setup, ensuring each detail was secure in its place. Success would live or die by it.

Setting sun.

Check.

Gramophone.

Check.

Record.

Che—he pulled the black disc from its paper sleeve and set it on the turntable.

Check.

Good. All he needed now was the girl.

He cranked the gramophone handle until music sputtered through the horn, then he crossed the backyard and knocked on the kitchen door. A few seconds later feet sounded across the floor inside right before the door swung open.

Ivy hit him with a full-force smile. "I always appreciate a gentleman who comes to call right on time." Dressed in peach and satin, she glowed with the hazy incandescence of a Southern summer night.

"And I appreciate a lady who has her eyes closed as she was instructed to do before opening the door."

"Oops." She giggled and closed her eyes. "Promise, I didn't see a thing."

Taking her hand, he looped it into the crook of his elbow. Her fingers settled into the crease with delicate assurance. He waited for her tremble of unease, the flash of her eyes snapping open in panic, the bunching of muscles as she prepared to flee, but none came. His presence no longer elicited the fear of immediate death. Here she stood with her eyes shut—a tip-off if ever there was one. No self-respecting assassin released their target from sight. It was enough to make a man feel himself again.

"Is the surprise to see how long we can stand on the porch?" she teased.

"I've sat buried in a mound of snow waiting for a kill shot for thirteen hours before. Standing on a porch should prove no difficulty, but it would be less entertaining." He led her onto the grass toward the strains of the record humming over the cricket orchestra as the fading rays of daylight shifted through the trees. His nerves jangled and he forced himself to take a slow, deep breath. The kind that had kept him alive while buried under that mound of snow.

"I know this tune," she said. "It's from one of the new records I picked up in town the other day along with the groceries. Well, I say *new*, but that's a relative term to a country-shop owner. The Song and Supper Club hasn't been a popular band in nearly a decade."

He clasped her hand while sliding his other arm around her waist. Dancing position. "Keep your eyes closed."

He waited for the right beat, then stepped out. It would have been all too easy to imagine the first reunion of Ivy swaying in his arms with matching steps and sliding rhythms, but the truth proved a stumbling of feet and rushing the beat. On his part at least. Ivy matched him step for step, right or wrong, like a ripple following the plunk of a stone in water. He had thought, had hoped, muscle memory would guide him and they could rekindle the ease they once shared. It had been the most natural thing in the world when they danced as time loosened its grip and their cares drifted away. The only thing falling away now was his hope of salvaging this attempt to woo his wife.

A memory wavered to the surface. They were becoming more frequent as Ivy helped patch in the holes. Some were good and some bad—he didn't want her to leave out anything for the sake of his peace of mind. Everything fit together to create a whole picture of who he was.

"I remember enjoying this band. They sang one about a boat ride through Central Park."

"'By the Banks.'"

"'By the Banks,' yes. There was a trombone solo that sounded like a duck." The song was all the rage in 1914. Thirteen years had passed, and the world kept spinning, yet he felt as unmoved as a relic buried in time. "I'm sure you think all that too old-fashioned by now. Perhaps my tastes aren't suited for these snappier times, as you call them."

"I like old-fashioned." Her eyes cracked open to reveal a glimmer of cool gray-green.

"No, keep them closed. I want you to remember the good days. When we danced on the rooftops with the city at our feet."

"Jack." She opened her eyes fully. "The memories of those times are wonderful, but I want to see what's before me right now. So dance with me and let's watch the world fall away."

He was caught between a dueling past of happiness and pain and a future cautious of confidence, but this was a moment he could plant his feet on, certain of what he wanted. She moved lightly in his arms, her footsteps an extension of his own as he guided her over the grass. Ever so slowly the anxious beat pounding in his head eased. There was no battle to figure out, no right or wrong. This moment was as it should be. A man finding his way, guided by the woman in his arms. A woman who gazed at him with love, content to follow his lead.

The sun had sunk behind the trees by the time the record scratched to an end. Reluctantly, Jack released Ivy and went about lighting the lanterns to combat the growing darkness while she selected new music.

"Let's try this one: "Tiger Rag" by the New Orleans Rhythm Kings. It's the smartest one the shop had. Owner said he'd ordered a crate of gospel records and this showed up instead. None of his customers would touch it, so he sold it to me for half price. That old man wouldn't recognize good music if it bit him on the ear." She placed the shiny black disc on the turntable with glee. "We can fox-trot to it."

Jack blew out the match after lighting the last lantern. "Fox-trot? Is that similar to the Grizzly Bear or the Turkey Trot or any of those other animal-named dances?"

"The Grizzly and Turkey are for those stuffy prewar dances. The Foxtrot is simply the One-Step but jazzier." At his look of confusion, she snapped her fingers and bounced on her feet. "Hotter, livelier. Jazz, baby."

Before the anxiety of modern invention could send him ducking for cover, he tossed the spent matchstick aside and held out his hand to her. "Would you honor me with an instructional dance"—he paused and let the next words pull themselves from the past and into the present—"Mrs. Vale?"

Ivy's eyes widened in delight. "My pleasure, *Mr.* Vale."

They started off well enough, though anything would go well when she stood pressed up against him. But as the beat bounced on, so did Ivy. She moved faster and faster until he thought her likely to launch out of his hold.

"You said this was supposed to be the One-Step. Shouldn't that mean going round and round with one simple step?"

"I also said it was jazz. You're doing swell. Here, try this." She stepped forward then back, brushed her hands over her knees, then stepped forward and back again. "The Charleston. It's the cat's pajamas!"

He attempted to mimic her movements, which resulted in nothing short of him looking ridiculous, but the more it made her smile, the harder he tried until his feet were swinging and kicking right along with hers. At least until the tempo changed and his foot kicked instead of swung and tangled right into Ivy's. Their arms flailed out for balance, lost the fight, and together they toppled over.

She landed on top of him, and his entrenched fight instinct kicked in. Without thinking he flipped her onto her back, pinning her hands down.

She blew a curl from her eyes. "Don't you dare try to kill me, Jack Vale."

Guilt flooded him. He immediately released her and shifted his hands to the grass on each side of her shoulders. "Sorry. Habit."

"Bad dancing was never your habit, so I'm left to assume you mean the grappling move."

"Are you saying my dancing was bad?"

"Let's just say we weren't Vernon and Irene Castle there at the end with their deft footwork." She tweaked his cheek. "Though I doubt very much they could match your professional assassin skills. To each their own talents."

"Were you not bragging minutes ago about these fancy steps you'd learned since the last time we stepped out?"

"True, but I've also picked up a few moves you haven't seen yet." Hooking her arm under his, she twisted and slid her body out from under him, then threw her freed legs around his back.

Before he knew what was happening, Jack found himself again on his back. Ivy grinned down from her seat on top of him.

"Like the art of jiujitsu."

He fought the urge to retaliate—the Riser's need to control and dominate its target. One by one he forced the muscles in his body to relax. The only target in his sights tonight was pursuing his wife. Not choking off her air supply.

"Pray tell, what is this jiujitsu art? Besides you taking me by complete surprise and knocking the wind out of me. A task not easily done, mind you."

"Its origins are actually Japanese. One uses levers, torsions, and pressure to take their opponent to the ground. It translates to 'gentle art.' Washington taught the skill to his old Rough Rider friend Theodore Roosevelt, who was enthralled by it. After Roosevelt became president, he liked to practice on robust visitors to the White House."

"Bully for Teddy, but I doubt he was so gentle about his takedowns. Some things are better left to a woman's touch."

The humor in her eyes swept away like a tide, exposing the rawness between them. The green depths of her gaze rippled with a new current brimming with longing.

Leaning down, she brushed her lips over his. The briefest touch, yet it set his skin afire and he was helpless to control the burn as he lay there branded in place. Mere inches separated them, and he couldn't tear his gaze from hers. This moment, this locking of eyes—not hands clasped or lips touching or bodies united—proved the most intimate connection in his mind. To reach out and touch another's soul. No hiding, no escaping, no cowering. He saw her, and she saw him.

Her fingers trailed up his check. He flinched, unaccustomed to a touch on his face that did not inflict pain. Quickly he pressed her hand back to his cheek before she could pull away. With his other hand, he reached around her neck and slipped his fingers into the soft hair curling damply against her skin. The silky red-and-gold strands had fallen wild and loose from their combs thanks to the dancing exertions. He preferred it this way, preferred *her* this way. Spontaneous and untamed.

She leaned forward again, hovering over his mouth.

"Do you want me to stop?" The pulse in the side of her neck beat furiously—a beat that echoed the anticipation in his own thrumming blood.

"No. I don't want you to stop," he said, his voice husky.

For all he might have anticipated after so many years of deprivation, the reality of her kiss pierced him into pieces. Her hand on his cheek. Her body sighing against his. Her scent mingling with his own.

Broken moments slowly stitched themselves back together, and when the picture was completed, he realized it was not of what was but merely the beginning of what could be. She was fire in his bones. Water to his parched soul. Every part of him that came from the grave was alive again.

"How many times have you kissed me?" he asked when her lips parted from his.

"Thousands."

"How many times have I kissed you?"

"Thousands."

"When was the first time I kissed you?"

"Nineteen sixteen." Her shaky breath caressed his lips, still warm from hers. "In the woods just outside Petrograd. I was worth the wait, you said."

Yes. It had been snowing and twilight had turned the world blue.

With trembling fingers, he brushed a loose hair from her cheek just as he had done then. "And you were."

"Then you kissed me again. Afterward you told me you loved me."

His fingers faltered. There it was. Suspended between them, hovering in the inches from her lips to his. A word powerful enough to bind hearts, launch wars, shatter pride, and bring the world to its knees. He had been brought to his knees, but by a force so ugly, so shameful, that rising to his feet again and reclaiming that word was a privilege he felt unworthy of.

"Unclench your hands, my love. Your war is over."

He sat up, easing Ivy off his lap. "My war will never truly be over. The fragments of gunmetal are buried too deep. They've torn holes through the one word I long to speak to you, just as I did in the woods all those years ago. But now it can't . . . I can't . . ." The word strangled in his throat. Desperate to break free, yet the dregs within him sucked it back into the deplorable pit he struggled to escape. How would he ever find the worthiness to speak it to her again?

"Shh." Her warm fingertips touched his lips. "I know what's in your heart, Jack, and you know what's in mine. For now, it's enough."

His hair had fallen across his eyes, and she reached out to tuck it behind his ear, then trailed her fingers along the back of his neck. Sparks shot across his skin.

"Sometimes we should take advantage of moments that don't require words."

His body tensed, but not in the way he expected. He needed to touch her, to feel her pulse quickening with his, to retrace the fullness of her mouth, to rediscover the sensitive spot behind her ear that always smelled of roses. He needed her in his arms, and not only to hold her close while dancing.

Cradling her lovely face between his hands, he brought her mouth to his with the tentative fear that he might have lost what talent he once possessed when it came to kissing. Then her lips parted against his and instinctual desire took over. She belonged to him and he to her, and he accepted her offering as if he were a starving man at a banquet.

"Ahem." A man cleared his throat. "My deepest apologies for the interruption."

Jack and Ivy sprang to their feet, blades from hidden places magically appearing in their hands.

Every sense on alert, Jack moved in front of his wife. If the Order had finally caught up with him, he'd meet the devils first.

"You're trespassing."

"Again, my apologies, but I assure you it is with good reason."

Ivy lowered Jack's knife hand. "Washington?" Disbelief rang in her voice.

The man stepped into the ring of lantern light. He was dressed in a suit and tie better attuned to city life than the backcountry, but then, the master of Talon had always preferred attiring himself for a lecture hall no matter the circumstance.

Jack relaxed his stance but didn't follow Ivy's lead in putting away his knife. His old headmaster Washington may have been, as well as the man who took him in off the streets and gave him a home and a future, but Jack had burned that home to the ground. He'd also murdered the man's best friend. Those kinds of actions tended to burn hatred into a man's heart hot enough to seek justice. Jack deserved whatever punishment the man sought to dole out, but he wasn't going down without a fight. If nothing else, he would take the brunt should Washington attempt to punish Ivy for siding with him.

"How did you find us?" Ivy asked.

"My dear, I have been in charge of the world's foremost secret agency of spies and assassins for twenty-five years. Finding two rogue agents is a mere afternoon puzzle. That, and Millie, the new research girl, showed me the deed to the property." Washington flicked a glance at the house. "I failed to realize how far from town it was. Hence the late hour of my calling."

"Did you walk all this way from the bus stop?" Ivy asked.

"The kind lady at the diner offered me her son's bicycle, for which I gladly offered her five dollars in payment." The faint silver rims of a bicycle reflected in the lantern light behind Washington. Bending over, he unrolled his pant legs.

When he straightened, his eyes landed on Jack. Keen and sharp as a sword point. "Hello, Jack."

Jack inclined his head but said nothing as he stood watching, waiting.

Ever the one to seek peace amid tension, Ivy put on her best hostess face. "Shall we go into the house? I made a pie earlier, and you're surely hungry after that ride from town."

"Once again, I must apologize. This is not a social call. I'm here to inform you that the Order of the Rising Moon is on the hunt and killing everyone in their path until what was lost is found again."

Ivy gripped Jack's hand. "What was lost?"

Washington's stare bored into Jack. "Him."

EIGHTEEN

Ivy SET A SECOND GLASS OF MILK ON THE KITCHEN TABLE IN FRONT OF Washington, then sat in the chair opposite him. "Why are they hunting Jack?"

"He is their Riser. They want him returned."

"Well, they can't have him."

Washington sipped his milk and politely made no comment when she couldn't offer him the perfunctory tea or coffee since she kept neither in the house.

"Three weeks ago a village near the Romanian and Hungarian border was burned to the ground. The elders were found impaled with notes pinned to their chests. Each was written in a different language, but all contained the same message: Bring us our Riser. A few days later a peace envoy in France was attacked. There were no survivors. The next targets were a British diplomat, some Canadian Red Cross workers, a Japanese party leader, and a congressman from New York. Hits all over the world and the same message left with each: Bring us our Riser."

"And how is the world responding?" Ivy asked.

"With confusion mostly. Many believe it to be the Fascists, who have been gaining popularity since the war. Others believe the acts are a retaliation against the Allies from rather sore losers of the war.

A few conspiracy theories are floating around too, of course, and believe it or not, those are closest to the truth."

Ivy curled her hands to fists in her lap. "What is Talon doing to stop the murders?"

"Sitting on our laurels, twiddling our thumbs, and hoping the Order of the Rising Moon will politely come knock on our door one sunny morning." Washington gulped the last of his milk and set down the empty glass with a thud.

"Honestly, Mrs. Vale. You have been gone a mere two months and have already forgotten our procedures. Our agents have not stopped looking for Dragavei or her minions. There is a great deal of finger pointing in the political rings right now, and that is where Talon wants it contained. While the leaders are distracted slinging mud at one another, we have the opportunity to eliminate the true threat before another world war breaks out, but we must act quickly."

Forcing her fingers to uncurl and remove her nails from biting into her palms, Ivy clamped down the rage threatening to spin out of control.

"The Order was silent for centuries until rearing its ugly head during the Great War. They are masters at entrenching underground to bide their time. What makes you think they'll be caught now?"

"They cannot hide forever. Not from Talon. Not from you."

For ten years she hunted the Order to the darkest corners of the map. One by one in Jack's name. Ivy had been Talon's greatest assassin, yet no matter how much blood she spilled, it was never enough. There was always more.

As long as Dragavei lived, Ivy could never rest.

Washington pushed aside his glass and leaned forward, linking his hands. "Three days ago we intercepted an Order member in Hollywood. He'd been sent to kill Mary Pickford and Douglas Fairbanks."

Ivy gasped. "Actors carry unprecedented power these days. Their deaths would make a larger splash in the news rags than the deaths of heads of state."

"Indeed. Such a hit would draw the outrage of the entire world. A boon for the Order to attract attention to their search for Jack— the outraged public would call for his blood if only to keep their beloved starlets safe. As you can imagine, such attention would be detrimental to Talon. We caught their failed assassin and are currently holding him at our Alexandria headquarters. So far he remains uncooperative."

"Then make him cooperate. Force him to tell us where Dragavei hides." Ivy's rage bubbled up again. The news was like hovering her finger over the trigger while her target sidled just out of range.

"Yes, well, that has been rather difficult since his tongue was cut out sometime long ago. The only lead we've ascertained is from parchment and ink tucked into his jacket. Matching writing utensils were found on the deceased. Franklin has traced the ink to a small factory on the outskirts of Constanta, Romania. Talon agents are en route now."

"Do you think the Order's stronghold is there?"

"We'll know soon enough, but perhaps if we had more information—any clue that could lead us to the correct location . . ." Washington's gaze drifted to where Jack stood braced against the sink with his head tilted slightly forward. His carefully combed hair from earlier in the evening now hung in spiked strands around his face like a mask.

Silence crackled the air.

Then she saw it—saw what Jack had been trained to do as a Riser. He was waiting. Waiting for his prey to reveal its move before he shot it down. Or rather, his hunters this time.

There had been enough battles in this kitchen. Ivy wasn't about to allow a shoot-out. "The Order did its best to sever Jack from all of his memories. A few are returning, but his recollection is slow and not always clear. Including the exact whereabouts of the Order's stronghold."

One of Washington's long fingers, the same fingers that could flip through the pages of a book faster than a blink, calmly tapped the back of his other hand. A tell for his forthcoming superior analysis.

"Having holes in one's memory is a common psychological result from trauma. It is the brain's way of protecting itself from further damage and harm. Time is a great healer, but I fear in the case of the Order, time is not on our side. The killings will continue. However, I think there is a better way to flush them out of hiding." His finger tapped once as he shifted his pointed stare to Jack.

"We offer them what they seek."

"You want to give them Jack? Are you out of your mind? Absolutely not!"

"Agent Vale, if you recall our semantics lessons, you will remember there is a difference between offering and giving. We dangle the carrot before their nose, and Dragavei will stop at nothing to obtain it. To reclaim her Riser."

Ivy gritted her teeth to hold back the anger ready to explode.

"Jack. Is. *Not*. A Riser. Not anymore."

The candlelight reflecting off the kitchen window caught in Washington's dark eyes. It blazed like fire battling a storm.

"You have spent the last ten years hunting down every lead and link to this organization with substantial results. Yet they persist like spores of mold hiding throughout the cracks of society at home and abroad. What if I could guarantee once and for all a cleansing that will smite the Order of the Rising Moon to nothing more than a smudge of blackened ash buried in some obscure book of history? What if we finally catch the head of the dragon? You can have Dragavei's head on a silver platter, Agent Vale."

The storm charged between them and swept over her, wrenching her this way and that. Tantalizing currents beat against drowning waves. Her foes—*their* foes—vanquished at long last! Yet a hollow-ness pitted her stomach. Upstairs, fifteen shiny bullets were lined up on top of her dresser like soldiers patiently awaiting orders to be loaded into her Beretta and fired into Helena Dragavei's skull.

Ivy had wanted the thrill of the hunt, of closing in on her prey and seeing the fear claw into the woman's—the *creature's*—hateful eyes. With each bullet Ivy intended to remind her prey of the pain and torment she had caused Jack. Then, only when the vile creature's screams of agony turned to pathetic whimpering, would Ivy press the cold metal between those horrid eyes and discharge the final round.

But at what cost to her husband's tormented soul? If he stepped back on the playing field, he may not survive it.

She turned in her chair. The choice was his alone. "Jack?"

Silence. Seconds ticked by. Dimness beyond the single lamp shot through the strands of hair barricading his face. Light and dark at war. She saw no relief, nor disgust, nor even anger. He was unmoved. Cold.

"Jack?" She whispered this time.

The intensity of his gaze landed on her for a long moment. What passed through his mind she could not read before he looked to Washington, his expression harsh and deadly as jagged glass.

"No."

He walked out the back door.

Ivy was on his heels in seconds. "Jack, wait! Talk to me."

"I will not go back out there. Talon can do its job without leading me like a pig to slaughter." He stalked across the grass. The shadows of night settled into deep recesses of blue and inky black. Somewhere among the trees crickets scratched their lonesome melodies.

Her heeled T-straps sank into the grass as she hurried after him. "They won't lead you to slaughter. Washington thinks—"

"I heard well enough what Washington thinks. He would have me trot out before those dogs to make them salivate, and then, just when their vicious teeth clamped around my throat, Talon would spring into action, defeat the evil dragon, and save the day. Who can bother with the carnage when the mission is successful in the end?" He began collecting the lanterns from their impromptu dance floor, blowing out the flames. The lights extinguished one by one and with them the last warmth of the summer night.

"You will not be carnage. I will not allow it."

"Allow?" Disbelief choked the word as he reached for the last lantern. "You stand here after seeing what the Order did to me, knowing the things *I* did as a drug-addicted, brainwashed Riser, and you expect me to go running straight back into it."

"Of course I don't."

"There are things carved so deep into my soul no light can ever penetrate them, nor do I want it to for the shame they've branded on me. I thought here—" He spread his arms wide to the cool night air and tilted his head back. The hair fell away from his face, freeing his pained expression from its mask. "I thought I could learn to breathe again without the weight pressing down on me every second of every day. Why can't we forget everything else and be happy here? I don't want to resurrect demons; there are plenty still scratching inside me. Talon can do what it's supposed to do—what we failed to do at Lake Baikal and Poenari Castle. They can end it, because I'm tired of fighting." Cradling the last lantern, he stepped closer to her. The shifting shades of anger, disbelief, and coldness had fallen into the wearied creases of his face. "I'm so tired, Ivy. Aren't you tired?"

She took the lantern from his hands, her fingers brushing his. An hour before, that lantern had filled the evening with a glow of happiness, shone on dancing feet, and witnessed kisses full of promise. She blew out the flame and held the lantern in her arms where the heated glass prickled her chilled skin. Now it was nothing more than a snuffed-out reminder of what could have been had the outside world not intruded on their forged Eden.

"In truth, I don't know how I feel. I've longed for and been reluctant to see this day come. Tracking down the Order was my sole purpose for the past ten years, and now to play no hand in their final destruction . . ." She slowly shook her head as opposing desires battled for control. "I want to wrap you in a bulletproof blanket and keep you safe. Always. I want to hide here and never let the outside world find us. I'm tired of always having one more kill, one more kill, yet I could fight through eternity if it would stop the Order. I want to personally end Dragavei. For you, for us. I know you must want the same revenge, that final act of justice."

"I don't do that anymore. I made a vow never to become that killer again."

"Then let me do it for you."

Sadness outlined his smile. So different from the one he had looked at her with when she'd been in his arms earlier.

"I've never been the man to stop you, and I won't now. Go if you need to. I'll be here waiting for you when you're ready to come home." He pressed a soft kiss to her cheek, then trudged back to the house where Washington stood silently on the porch. She watched as Jack brushed past him before glancing back over his shoulder.

"You can stay the night, but the discussion is over."

Ivy retraced her steps across the grass and climbed the porch steps. Every bone in her body stretched restlessly against her too-tight skin. If only she could tear free of its mortal restraints and scatter herself across the paths of revenge and peace, never forced to give herself wholly to one or the other.

Standing straight and tall in his fine city suit, Washington looked as out of place on her country porch as the letter *J* in the Greek alphabet, yet he was never a man who allowed his surroundings to dictate his comportment.

"My intention in coming here was not to cause an upset."

Not to mention her ruined romance. "Rather pointless considering there was no other possible outcome." So much for breaking down the final proverbial wall in her marriage that night. That hope was now firmly ground into the dust.

"I suppose so, but my intentions were—*are*—honorable. As they always have been for Talon and every agent under my leadership."

Ivy peered at him under the dark eaves. Here was the man she had looked up to for half of her life. The man who taught her the bravery of words and language, who gave her a home and offered her purpose when her life had stretched bleak and pointless before her. He had been the paragon of intelligence and honor, a man who could never crumble, but when she looked at him now, truly and without awe-tinted glasses, the facade was stripped away. Doubt and uncertainty clouded his eyes while fear crooked the spine that never wavered.

"You're a good leader, sir, despite what I said to you that day in your office."

"Ah, the day when last we parted. I haven't had such a dressing down since 1907 when Dolly accused me of using all the coffee to finish a late-night reading of *The Education of Henry Adams*. Which I did, mind you, but will never admit to her. How she expected me to read such a dense tome without a strong brew is beyond my comprehension, but there you have it."

Ivy smiled. She'd witnessed many a scolding between the two and had been on the receiving end of her fair share. How she missed those voices ringing through Talon's corridors, the smell of gunpowder clinging to the drapes, Philip's laughter as he chased her across the roof during those early days. Talon was home and everything that was good in her life.

Her smile faded. So many things had changed. *She* had changed. "Still, I owe you an apology, sir. I was angry and spoke out of turn."

"You spoke your heart, Agent Vale, and for that I will accept no apology." Half turning, he looked toward the house behind him. To where Jack had disappeared. "We are all entitled to follow our own conscience . . ."

Ivy stepped around him, blocking his view. "You can't have Jack."

"Perhaps if you spoke to him. Tried to explain that we are running out of options. Surely he sees the efficiency, the immediacy with which this plan must be executed." Desperation cracked his armor. "The Order has been killing innocent people for centuries, all so they may topple the world power and place themselves in charge. They have murdered and tortured Talon agents and burned us out of our home, and by God I will have justice for it. I will not stand by and watch until there is no goodness left in the world to fight back against the evil. What they did to Jack is unforgivable, and I will use every means at my disposal to ensure it never happens again. Not to anyone."

Ivy squared her shoulders and stepped closer. Close enough to see the pinpricks of revenge burning in his eyes.

"You cannot have Jack. But you can have me."

NINETEEN

THE PREDAWN HOUR APPROACHED AS THE WORLD SLUMBERED AND THE first smear of gray blotted away the night's darkness. Dew covered the grass in slick wet droplets while birds rustled in the treetops, eager to spread their wings and greet the new day.

New day be damned. Jack was still living a nightmare.

He shoved off the barn door, turning away from the sleeping house, and moved to his workbench. He picked up the worn hand plane and slid it over a long plank of walnut. Back and forth. Muscles straining. Chunky slices of wood fell at his feet, not the delicate shavings meant to come from the plane's blade. He had no use for delicacy today. Back and forth. Another chunk hit the floor, jagged as the hell Washington had ushered into his precariously balanced world mere hours ago.

Ivy was leaving. She had yet to say the words, but Jack knew. He saw it in the tight smile she gave him when she came inside last night. Saw it in the clothes stacked on her bureau. In the bullets that lined her windowsill. She was leaving and might never return to him. Not because she didn't want to, but because one of those bullets might very well have her name on it. She would take that bullet and die believing it was for him.

He glanced over his shoulder where long coils of rope hung on the wall. He could tie her down and force her to stay, but they both knew he wasn't the kind of man to stop her from doing what she believed best. Besides, she knew how to untie herself from every knot imaginable, so rope proved useless in thwarting her. He could kidnap her and run, but then, she'd been trained to escape hostage situations. He could kiss her until her lips bruised while drowning her in words of love. It would buy him time, time they so desperately needed together to recount all the ways they loved each other. Ways he longed to express. Yet instead of knocking down her door last night and ending their separation, he had holed up alone in his room like a coward. Paralyzed by his own fear, by the cold, dank smell of his old cell creeping up his nostrils. By the feel of dried blood caked under his nails. By the echoes of his screams filling his ears. He'd lain on the bare floor like a wounded dog, too afraid to rise lest the nightmares return to beat him.

Back and forth he shoved the plane. Chunk after chunk of wood. The comforting scent of woodsy musk and sweat filled the barn. It churned his gut. He needed the taste of bitter metallic and the raging force of Dust to shudder through his body and jar the chaos loose from his mind as it forced him into the nothingness.

He tossed aside the plane and reached for the sledgehammer.

Over and over he slammed the metal head against the plank. Wood splintered and cracked, and the demons within howled at the exertion.

A woman's scream cut through the noise. Ivy.

He dropped the sledgehammer and raced out of the barn toward the house. He tore the screen door off its hinges and threw himself inside.

"Ivy!"

Bam!

A gunshot from the second floor.

"Ivy!" Jack flew to the stairs.

On the upstairs landing clad in her silky nightdress with pin curls in her hair, his wife was pinned to the floor by an enormous hulk of a man. His hands were around her throat.

She wrapped her legs around the man, hooked an arm under his thigh, and flipped him onto his back. Grasping at her nightdress, she yanked the eighteenth-century pistol out from beneath the silk and bashed it against the side of his head. He howled in pain, his hands breaking free from her neck. She surged to her feet, grabbed his legs, and tipped him backward down the stairs. He landed with a moaning thud at Jack's feet.

"Take care of that, will you, darling? He shot Washington, who is bleeding all over the guest room." She blew Jack a kiss and disappeared down the hall.

Jack stared at the man trying to crawl past him. The intruder who had violated his house. Who had attacked his wife. Who had brought violence to their threshold. All rationale switched off. Like the swift chop of a white-hot ax, gone was Jack's conscience and in its place was cold deadness.

He grabbed the man by the scruff of his neck, then slammed him against the hallway wall. The man's bulk smashed out bits of plaster to reveal crawling termites and chewed wood. Jack slammed him again. Part of the wall crumbled, and the man fell backward into the kitchen.

Jack stepped through the hole as the man scrambled to his feet and swung wildly with his fist. Jack dodged, lifted a chair, and hurled it at him. The man shook off the blow like a dazed bull, then charged straight into Jack. They crashed onto the table. It collapsed in a great cracking of wood, and they hit the floor.

Jack grabbed a piece of the splintered table and rolled to his feet, swinging it at the man's head. The intruder shot his leg out and kicked Jack in the knee. Pain shot up Jack's leg as he stumbled backward and buckled.

"The great Riser, *da*." The man laughed, a sound like gravel scraped over rusted metal. Blood leaked from his nose. "The once unstoppable dog of destruction. Look at you. *Slab. Jalnic*. You make me sick."

Weak. Pathetic. Spoken in a language that unleashed Jack's nightmares. Dark and cruel, it swarmed around him, suffocating the good he had tried to become. It taunted him with nothingness.

"How did you find me?" Jack matched the spoken tongue. A rumble came from the hall that trembled through the house's frame. Ivy thumped down the stairs hauling what sounded like Washington's heavy body.

"She wants you back, Riser."

"How did you find me?"

The man laughed. Spittle and blood flew from his dry lips, mixing with the rusted gravel of his laughter into a wet slopping noise.

"*Slab. Jalnic*. Come. Come, Riser. Give in to who you truly are. You cannot fight it. You will not win. I will take your resistance from you."

The darkness pitched around Jack. He breathed it in and let it fuel his rage. Launching himself forward, he locked his arms around the man's meaty waist and knocked them through the back door and into the yard. Nothing existed beyond the flesh beneath his pounding fist, the blood flying from busted cheeks and broken teeth, the numbing sense of death prowling as life leaked from his prey's eyes.

In the distance he heard a woman's voice. A voice he'd heard a long time ago from a cliff high above him. "Jack!"

The darkness cut it off, releasing him to the black deeds of his ferocity. He'd fought against it, yet it found him, and he would stop at nothing to keep the nothingness from taking him fully. Bones crunched beneath his fists. He would not go back to it. Blood splattered his face. He would not be that again.

"Enough." A large hand clamped onto his arm midswing.

Jack blinked. The darkness swelling within him snarled and retreated like an animal kept from the victory of its kill.

Around him, the smoky dawn came into focus. Wet grass seeped through the fabric over his knees, chilling his skin. His raised fist glowed like a red hammer.

Strong fingers tightened like a vise around his arm. "Enough now, son." Washington lay sprawled on the grass next to him. His face was pale in the weak morning light, but his eyes glittered like daggers ready to strike.

Jack stared at the motionless man beneath him. His face was a raw pulp. Warm blood trickled between Jack's clenched fingers. He'd done this. In his desperation to fight against being dragged back into the nothingness, he'd called upon the very darkness that fed it.

Slumping onto the grass, Jack wiped his hand over the wet blades, staining the green with red. "I swore I'd never kill again."

Washington tapped a finger to the man's fleshy neck. "Despite all appearances, you have not broken your vow. The miscreant lives."

Ivy knelt beside Washington. "How did that ugly bull get in our house? He tried to shoot me while I was unpinning my hair. Does he have any idea—"

Heavy wood cracked and splintered, followed by a deafening rumble that shook the house. The entire frame quivered as if struck by an earthquake. The roof collapsed, smashing the walls in a filthy spew of splinters and dust and crumbling mortar.

Jack stared in silence until only the back porch steps remained intact. "I knew we should have repaired that load-bearing wall first." Or maybe he should have chosen a different wall to smash a man through.

"So not only did this rat disrupt my hair routine"—Ivy's eyes narrowed to slits—"but now he's destroyed my house. Who is he exactly?"

"He's from the Order," Jack said.

The V on her forehead creased to a sharp point. "How did he find us?"

"I don't know."

"His timing leaves a lot to be desired, but I am in need of target practice, so I won't quibble on appropriate calling hours." She pulled her pistol from her satin nightdress and flipped off the safety before fitting the sight on her target.

"We can't shoot him."

"Whyever not?"

"We need answers. Such as how he tracked us and if more are coming."

Rising from her kneeling position, she studied Jack for a long moment. Her desire to maim seemed to battle good sense in her expression until finally a weary victor emerged. Arching an eyebrow in disagreement, she clicked on the gun's safety.

"Have it your way." She knelt once more between the unconscious intruder and Washington, careful to place the gun well out of the enemy's reach. "Are you certain he's alive?"

Jack stared down at the battered face. He felt nothing for the man. Not rage, not anger, and certainly not guilt. Only regret for the humanity he had shed in those red-stained minutes. "He is. Barely."

Ivy glanced at him, a barrage of questions deftly hidden behind a mask, then she turned to Washington. "And you. Getting shot like that. A man your age should not be jumping in front of bullets."

Washington levered himself up on his elbow. "You were lucky to miss his first one, but he would have had you with the second if my geriatric form hadn't caught his attention." His gaze skittered over Ivy's barely there attire before flitting to the sky. Red splotched his pale cheeks. "Transpiring events have diverted proprieties, but as we are no longer in mortal danger, you may wish to cover yourself, Agent Vale."

"Applesauce and crackers. Pull yourself together. You can dress a knife wound without batting an eye, so don't turn blushing virgin on me at the sight of a woman in her nightie. Let me see where he shot you." She carefully pried at the hole in Washington's trousers. "A clean shot through the hip. More show of blood than anything to truly worry about. A few inches to the left and he would have hit the intestines or bone."

"I've had worse."

"Not in a long time. You haven't been in the field in many years."

Washington gritted his teeth as Ivy continued to prod the area. "Yes, and look what happens. First time out and I get shot. Not even a worthy hit, merely a padding of skin and fat."

"The next time a man comes to shoot us in our pajamas, I'll be sure to put you right in front of the bullet. Which internal organ is admirable enough for you?" She arched an eyebrow with enough condescension to make Washington's mouth close with an audible snap. "Jack, hand me your shirt. I need to make a bandage."

Absently, Jack shrugged out of his shirt and put it in his wife's hand, and she set about bandaging Washington.

Their banter carried on while Jack stared at the collapsed rubble of the house that carried too many memories. Bad ones with his hateful aunt. Bittersweet ones as he'd crawled here to leave his Riser past behind and lick his wounds. Fragile good ones he'd been building with Ivy. Gone.

"How did he attack you?" he asked.

"I was in the washroom doing my hair." Ivy kept her eyes on the task at hand as she wrapped strips of Jack's shirt around Washington's hips. "I heard the floorboards creak, then saw a pistol pointing at me from the mirror. It all happened quickly after that. Washington threw himself at the intruder. Took the second shot. He aimed at me again, but I ducked and a tussle ensued, which concluded with him destroying our home." She stood and touched his arm. "We can rebuild."

A dry, bitter noise scratched from his throat. "How can we

rebuild knowing any minute the foundation could be wiped out from beneath us? This was supposed to be a safe place, yet he found us."

"Then we stop hiding and go find them."

Crouching, Jack grabbed the unconscious man's shirtfront and yanked him into a sitting position.

"Wake up." He smacked him across the face. "I said, wake up." He backhanded him. The man's lip split. Blood dribbled out.

Wheezing, he cracked open an eye.

"Good. I have your attention." Jack slapped him again. "You're going to answer a few questions for me."

The man spat out a tooth. *"Nu."*

Jack settled closer, pulling the man until he was inches from his face. "You know I can extract the information I want. And you know how." He waited as the terrible knowledge skittered across the man's defiance like poisonous spiders.

"How did you know where I was?" The man's gaze flitted to Washington. Jack twisted his shirt, tightening the grimy collar around the man's thick neck. "Don't look at him. Look at me and answer. *Acum!"*

The voice, strong as metal and cold as a blade, came from deep within Jack. From someplace dark but not forgotten. Where death dwelled. *I am Death.*

The man's eyes widened with fear. "I-I was in California for a mission. My partner was intercepted by his people"—he jerked his head to Washington—"before we pulled off the hit. I waited outside, watching. A few hours later this man came out, and I followed him here."

"Who else is with you?"

"No one. My partner is probably dead by now, which means I get all the reward money when I take you back to the Silver One. She has placed a bounty on your head. Five hundred thousand lei to anyone who brings you to her alive."

That name coiled like a venomous snake in Jack's belly, twisting its scales and latching its fangs into his tender parts. "Helena Dragavei. The devil herself in skirts."

The fear cowering in the man's eyes ignited to fury. His hands clawed into the dirt. "You dare speak her name? You, dog, are unworthy to meet her eye, much less lick her boots. You are her beast of war, her weapon to wield for our great Order. Nothing more."

"For being nothing she certainly seems to need me a great deal. Can she not achieve significance without her weapon? Will the Order never take its place at the world's helm without me to slick the prow red with the blood of the innocent?"

"You are her symbol. You will take the heads of the powerful and serve them at her feet."

"She's the one who's lost her head if she thinks I'll do anything of the sort."

The man seethed. "Insolent! The noble Order of the Rising Moon has destiny—"

Another slap. More blood. "Where is Dragavei?"

The man coughed, then began to laugh. Blood drained from his nose into his mouth, streaking his teeth. "You do not remember how to find her. She took your memories. She took *her*." He jerked his chin at Ivy, then flicked a wild glance to where the house once stood. "She took this place. She took everything you had, and you belong to her. You have tried to start again, but she will take that from you too. She will come, and there will be no escape, Riser. You belong to her. You *will* bend to the Order."

A gun clicked over Jack's shoulder.

"Move aside, darling." Ivy pointed her pistol between the man's eyes. "Jack Vale belongs to me alone. You tell that devil I said so when I send her to join you in hell."

Jack didn't move. "First he's going to tell me where to find Dragavei."

The man stared back at Jack, locking them into a chamber of wills with no escape, only mirrors to reflect the hackles of their inner demons. "I tell you and the fun will be taken from this game. Find the Silver One yourself before she finds you. Because she will. Turn to the blackness, Riser. Let it consume you. Only then will you truly know where you belong."

"I will never go back to that darkness."

The man smiled. Red dribbled between his teeth. "But you have already started."

"Doesn't mean I'm going to finish it." Jack stepped away and took a deep breath. Air filled his lungs. It crowded out the black tar threatening to suffocate him. Closing his eyes against the images of blood all around him, he inhaled again, driving the frenzy from his blood.

A soft hand touched his arm. Ivy. "Are you all right?"

He cracked open his eyes. "I will be."

"If we need to—"

Bam!

They spun around to find the man dead on the grass with a hole on each side of his head.

Washington lowered his gun. "I protect my agents. I failed you both before, and I led him here. He was my hit to take." Grunting, he stood and pressed a hand to his side swathed in makeshift bandages. "There's no need for you to ever step into that darkness again, Vale. We'll find another way. This I vow to you."

★★★

Ivy tossed another log onto the fire and scooted closer to the warmth. "Whatever happened to your declaration of Talon not operating on personal acts of revenge or individual hit lists?"

"A good leader will stand by his rules to keep the boat steady, but he also knows it is time to break such rules when a wave crashes over the stern. Talon has not survived this long without learning to bend a bit. A lesson I have taken rather too long a time to digest." Washington leaned back against the log he sat by and crossed his feet at the ankle. "Besides, that bastard had it coming."

"When was the last time you were in the field?" Ivy asked.

"McKinley was in office. I had an assignment in Cuba."

Night had fallen and with it the temperature dipped into September coolness. They had salvaged what they could from the rubble of the house, but beyond a few items of clothing, nothing was worth scrounging for. Whether through foresight or simply the exceptional ability to always be immaculately dressed in a crisis, Washington had been fully and properly attired when he was shot that morning.

Curling into a towel that had been drying on the line, Ivy poked the log in the center. "Do you miss it? Being in the field?"

"After today, no." Washington grimaced and set a hand on his bandaged side. The wound wasn't deep, but the bleeding had taken some time to stop. "My deepest and sincerest apologies for leading that man here and shattering your peace. I should have been more careful. I should have noticed a tail. I should have"—his mouth twisted with anger—"I should have done better by you and Jack."

"Don't do that to yourself. We knew what this life would be when we pledged ourselves to Talon. Every one of us has regrets in one shape or another, but we do the best we can and carry on."

"Words of wisdom. Keep talking like that and you'll be a Talon professor before long."

"That's not for me. I prefer the doing, not the teaching." She poked at an ashy log. It crumbled to gray powder. "If I'm being honest, though, the doing has lost a bit of its luster. It's become more of a nickel I keep in my pocket, worrying between my fingers until the grooves are worn down."

"Are you saying you want to toss the nickel into the proverbial fountain and make a wish?"

Ivy glanced at her Beretta lying peacefully next to her on the grass. Red firelight danced across its glossy black surface. Inside slumbered fifteen bullets, ready for their last mission against the Order of the Rising Moon.

"I want revenge. I want justice. But more than anything, I want Jack. Whatever it takes or costs, I want him."

"Do not lose yourself to vengeance. It drove Hamlet mad."

"With all due respect to Shakespeare, he never had a husband brainwashed. 'This is the very ecstasy of love. Whose violent property fordoes itself. And leads the will to desperate undertakings.'"

"You dare to quote Shakespeare to me?"

"You've done it often enough to me, *Macbeth* being a particular favorite."

"Nothing else will suffice when one dwells in a world of assassins."

A figure emerged from the darkness. Jack walked toward them holding what appeared to be sheep shears. He sat on the opposite side of the fire and began to run the rusty blades over a whetstone in methodic *shush-shush* sweeps.

"It's been a rather long day." Washington stood, lightly touching his bandaged hip. "I shall bid you good evening." He headed into the barn where they had wrangled a few musty horse blankets for pallets to sleep on.

Ivy waited until the barn door creaked closed and the crickets resumed their serenade. "I've been thinking about what our next step—"

"We leave in the morning."

"*We?*"

"The world has many demons in it. I am one of them. I have tried to fool myself into believing I could live in peace, but hiding is all I've been doing while the demons out there continued their slaying. Their destruction ends now." *Shush-shush* went the blade. Rust scraped off, catching fire shadows on its red flecks as it floated to the ground, scattering across the grass.

"The Order turned me into a beast of nightmares. That's precisely what I plan to give them." He held up the shears to his eyes. Some rust still clung to parts of the blades, but the edges shone sharp. Jack grabbed a handful of his hair and moved it between the blades. *Snip.*

The chunk of long brown hair seemed to defy gravity for a moment, as if shocked it had been cut away from its source. It caught the light in a blaze of red, then faded to umber and at last dull brown as it dropped to the ground and curled like a brittle leaf.

Jack's gaze caught hers across the fire. Hard and determined, it seized her heart. Without a word, she rose and took the shears from his hand. They were heavy and cold, an unfamiliar weapon, but one she could wield with more violent intent than any weapon before.

Snip.

Long hairs fell between her fingers.

Snip.

Long hairs grown from captivity. Strands harboring blood and pain and guilt.

Snip.

The hairs caught at her skin like hooks, desperate in clinging to one last fraction of domination from their years of barbaric rule. She shook them off. Down, down they fell, deadweights no more. She moved quicker. Shearing off chunks. The newly exposed skin on the back of his neck shone pale in the moonlight, revealing new patterns of scars. So much of him was familiar beneath her fingers, yet so much obscurity had marked him during their years of separation. Parts of him she would have to learn anew.

At last she stepped back to examine her work. It was like the hands of a clock rotating back in time. His cheeks were no longer hidden behind the lank curtain. His eyes were wider and his jaw more angled.

She brushed a piece of cut hair from his left ear, allowing her fingertips to linger over the slight crimp at the top that he'd earned in a boxing match long before they met.

"It's a bit choppy, but I think you'll do."

Reaching a hand up, he ran it over his short locks, slowly, as if not quite believing the change. Inch by inch his shoulders straightened without the added weight pressing them down. Ivy's heart swelled at the transformation, but she reined in the threat of tears by using the shears' handle to dig a small hole. Gathering the hair, she shoved it into the hole.

Jack knelt beside her and scraped dirt over the top of it. Buried and forgotten.

"The beast nearly took me today. Its foul breath stung my neck, its scales drawing the darkness around me. I felt its fangs sink into my skin like needles filled with Dust." His fingers dug into the dirt, strangling it between his knuckles. "I wanted that man's blood on my hands before he could drag me back. I became what I hated to prevent it from happening."

"The Order will never stop hunting for you."

"Which is why I will hunt them. Until they are destroyed."

Ivy had been in the game long enough to know the rules. To succeed was to outmaneuver an opponent and take the kill shot before they placed a bead on you. Peace was short-lived while the enemy still prowled.

She was chomping at the bit to have Dragavei's head on a spike, but every bone in her body balked at allowing Jack anywhere near that evil creature's claws.

Yet Jack was their best bet at tracking down and putting an end to the Order of the Rising Moon once and for all. Without him, Ivy and Talon would continue their wild-goose chase until they were picked off one by one.

She placed her hand over his dirty one. Grit rubbed between their palms. "Are you certain you want to do this?"

He linked his fingers through hers. "Yes."

Her husband's face told her how much he needed this. Needed to look his fear in the eye and put a bullet in it. The Order had controlled him for so long, but bit by bit he'd reclaimed himself. He decided his actions. He chose what he ate. He cut his hair. Ending the Order was the last piece in making himself whole again.

Ivy took a deep breath, then pulled the worn note from the pocket she'd sewn into her chemise. Carefully, she unfolded the yellowed paper that was nearly translucent in places from her holding it. The penned words were scratched forever into her mind.

You must go on, love. For me. For us.

"There's something we need to do first." She handed him the letter.

His brow furrowed then smoothed as he read the faded ink. "I hoped you would never have to read this. So many times I broke the pen in my hands as I struggled to put down each sentence. There I was penning a goodbye letter on our honeymoon. What man should be forced to do that?"

"I hated it at first. I hated you for writing it and for telling me I could only read it should the worst come. I wanted to give up, but this"—she touched the corner—"kept me alive. Now you're here with me, and I no longer need ink stains to force me to go on."

Cupping her hand under his, she guided him over to the flames. The paper glowed orange as it wavered over the heat. Jack's fingers spread wide and the paper tipped into the fire. It blazed bright for an instant, then curled black at the edges. Ten years of sadness, longing, anger, and desperation crumbled to ash.

Jack's arms circled her and pulled her close to face him. His forehead leaned against hers, and she watched as the firelight turned to blue flames in his eyes. Heated and alive, it burned through her like a living flame. She could burn alive from his touch and never heed the consummation.

His hand moved up her back, over her shoulder, and trailed up her neck. Cradling her face, he touched his lips to hers. Gentle at first and then as if a great urgency broke free of its restraints. His mouth was her sanctuary, and she gave in instinctually, offering as much as was demanded. If they'd possessed the capability to look down from above, they might have noticed their melded shadow on the ground, its edges brightly lit and shimmering.

As it was, they were too engaged to notice.

PART 3

I have weighed love in the balance and found it
maddening.
But for all of this, I would die again for love.

—J. C.

TWENTY

IF IVY THOUGHT RETURNING JACK TO THE FOLD OF TALON WAS GOING TO be a snap, she was sadly mistaken. At best the other agents ignored him or treated him with wary caution. At worst they held their guns and knives within a finger's reach and eyed him with homicidal intent.

Raising her Beretta in a fluid motion, she aimed at the paper target downrange and fired. Bull's-eye.

No, that wasn't the worst. She'd heard taunts as he walked the underground tunnels of Talon headquarters. *Murderer. Monster. Jefferson's killer. Order spy.* It had taken every ounce of self-control not to put their necks under her boot. That and Washington's restraining hand.

Finished with practice for the day, she swept up her spent casings and dumped them in the trash bin along with the obliterated target sheet. Now all she had to do was spend the rest of the evening cleaning her gun. As she did every night since returning to HQ nearly a week before. Wowzers, being a secret assassin was nonstop excitement. Maybe tonight she'd clean the gun blindfolded if only to shake up the routine.

"Heading out so soon, Agent Vale?" Beatrix sauntered into the brick chamber and placed her pistol and magazines on the stand, nudging Ivy's to the edge. Dressed in a purple number with a drop waist and white sash, her lips stained a deep vamp that was all the rage, she looked like she'd come straight off the streets of New York City, not drab, communist Leningrad. She also looked wildly inappropriate for a firearms exercise.

"Here I was hoping we could have a friendly little competition. You must be in need of practice after all those lazy summer days in the country. Where was it you disappeared to? A retreat? Spa? Sanitorium?"

Ignoring the jab, Ivy glided a hand over her marcel waves. They had taken hours to perfect, and she was already missing the softer bob she'd sported in the country.

"I gladly leave the firing range to you. All these years in Russia must have turned your bullets to icicles. I wouldn't want to take advantage since you've never had to fire your weapon before. Why *are* you here?"

"Washington's orders. Seems he requires more trusted help in going after the Order than he could scrounge together here."

"I notice he didn't order your fiancé back. Too drunk to get his feet beneath him?"

Beatrix's dark lips flattened. "Victor has his own assignments in Russia to complete. Stalin isn't exactly the easiest man to kill, what with his paranoia and all." Pushing her mouth into a less severe shape, she feigned great interest in lining up her magazines on the stand. "Tell me, is Jack still the best sniper, or does he prefer killing with his bare hands these days?"

"Jack uses his skills only when necessary. As do we all."

"Against the enemy. Not our own." Beatrix knocked one of her magazines down with a tap of her nail.

Ivy swiped her belongings from the stand before Beatrix could send them clattering off and placed them in her bag.

"What he did all those years wasn't him. The Order poisoned him to be their weapon."

"A convenient excuse, don't you think? Kill hundreds of innocent people, murder your own mentor, burn down Talon, and then blame a decade of slaughter on your brain for incorrect functioning. And here you are defending him. Did you think Talon would welcome back either of you with open arms, all wrongs forgiven?"

Ivy dropped her bag to the floor. It hit with a thud. "Shut. Up."

"Or what? You'll break my neck the same way your *Riser* broke Jefferson's? Or maybe burn me out like he did his supposed best friend. Have you so quickly forgotten Phil—"

In the blink of an eye, Ivy had yanked out her hairpin and slid it under Beatrix's chin, tipping her snooty little pointed nose to the ceiling. The pearl-and-diamond tip glimmered as brightly as it had the day Dolly gifted it to her. A treasured tradition for Talon ladies.

"We've skated along well enough so far, but one day you and I will have a go."

Slow as a cat stretching, Beatrix reached back and pulled the hairpin from her own red locks. Hers was tipped with a ruby. "Why wait?"

"Because you need to practice first." Ivy pierced the delicate skin the tiniest bit, drawing a small bead of blood on the end of her hairpin. "I want it to be a fair fight." After wiping the drop on Beatrix's mauve lace sleeve, Ivy returned her hairpin to its hidden pocket in her blouse—the pin was completely useless for her fashionable hairstyle—and picked up her weapons bag.

"You're a fool, Ivy. Trusting in the heart as if it doesn't lie. Jack is a monster. Nothing can change that no matter how desperately you believe otherwise."

Ivy kept her chin up and shoulders back as she left the chamber at a dignified pace. Once in the corridor and out of sight, she sagged against the musty brick wall. *Monster. Murderer.* The taunts exploded in her head. She pressed her forehead to the cool bricks to drive out the horrible accusations.

Only they weren't merely accusations. They were the truth. Jack as the Riser had been something else entirely. A man not himself. Why could the others not accept that? Where was their compassion for his suffering? Where was Philip to stand with her against the hate? She could fend them off with Philip at her side, but alone . . . she felt her strength wavering.

"A-Agent Vale? Are you all right?"

Ivy jerked away from the wall. "Oh, hello, Millie. Just a bit of a headache. All that shooting, you know."

Millie shook her head, her frizzy black hair swinging against her round cheeks. "I don't, actually. Hamilton won't allow me near the broad side of a barn with a weapon, so I remain Talon's filing clerk and operations assistant. The most action I see is a paper cut."

"Do you want to go out in the field?"

"More than anything! I'm no good at maps, and my decoding is atrocious, but I do a bang-up job of blending in, and that has to be part of an agent's skill at some point."

The girl was intelligent, efficient, and eager. Talon agents had been recruited on less. Ivy herself had little more than a primary education and scrapper instincts from living on the streets before she joined. It was heart that mattered. Everything else could be taught.

And right then Ivy desperately needed a project to keep her from going crazy while Washington assembled details for their mission.

"How about I give you a few pointers in fighting and weapons handling? Tomorrow maybe?"

Millie's smile erupted like a firework. "Gee, thanks, Agent Vale! That'd be swell."

"I'll get you within spitting distance of that barn, and then Hamilton will have to change his tune about training you." Ivy patted the girl on the shoulder and moved to continue down the corridor before stopping. "By the way, thank you for finding that place in the country for me. I never would have known on my own."

Millie bobbed her head in acknowledgment, then her eyes sobered. "I'm sorry about what happened to your husband. From all the reports I read, he seemed to be a good man. No one should have gone through what he did, but it's a true test of his character that he survived. I hope you two will be all right."

Emotion flooded Ivy's throat. She swallowed it. "Thank you, Millie. As do I."

A noise, mellow yet commanding, echoed down the corridor.

Ivy looked around. The sound seemed to shimmer from the very walls. "What is that?"

"A Cambodian gong. Franklin picked it up in Chinatown not long after you left. It announces the all-hands meetings."

"Why a gong?"

Millie shrugged. "He said a siren was too loud and flashing lights too confusing since they sometimes flicker in and out depending on the weather."

Agents were gathering into the central hub of their underground headquarters, and Ivy sidled along the back wall as the other agents took seats on the mismatched chairs. During her absence, the place had been scrubbed clean of mold and centuries-old rubbish and dynamite crates. Maps were tacked to the brick walls and strings of humming lights hung from the nails. The cool scent of underground stone and gunpowder tainted the air.

"Quiet down." Washington strode into the chamber with a folder stuffed under his arm. "I'll keep this brief. In ten days on October the second, the Treaty of Nations will be meeting in Paris to discuss a global limitation of armaments now that a new threat has come to their attention. The Order of the Rising Moon."

"How comforting that they only notice murder once Tinseltown is targeted," someone muttered.

"Their ignorance is notable, but that's government for you. Hiding what the left hand is doing from the right hand, all the while never bothering to glance behind them for the creeping threat." Washington opened the folder and pulled out a green leaf the size of his hand with gold printing on it. "An invitation found at Mary Pickford's house after we intercepted the assassin sent to kill her and Douglas Fairbent."

"Fairbanks," Millie offered cheerfully from her perch next to Ivy. "Their house is called Pickfair, and it sits like a castle atop a hill where the Hollywood glamour set go to pay homage—"

"Splendid." Washington's unblinking stare did little to diminish Millie's excitement at providing pertinent facts about the situation. He continued, "The invitation is for a party being held the night before the armament conference at a private residence a half hour outside of Paris. Members of the Treaty of Nations along with a few from the, ahem, glamour set"—his dark eyes cut to Millie—"will be in attendance."

"Who's hosting?" Beatrix asked. She leaned against the opposite wall, as far from Ivy as she could get.

Washington scanned the leaf. "A Miss J. Baker."

Beatrix's mouth flopped open. *"Josephine* Baker?"

"The Christian name is not printed." Frowning, Washington flipped the leaf over and back as if the mystery might be solved on a waxy vein. "At a gathering such as this—"

"Is she an Order member?"

Cries of dismay echoed around the chamber. Causing scandals with suggestive dance moves and banana costumes on the stage was one thing, but being a cult member was quite another.

"At this time there is no J. Baker on our list of suspects. She is simply the soiree hostess. That being said, we have every reason to believe Order members will be among the guests. They've hidden in plain sight and risen through the ranks of power in all industries.

Our mission is to find out from them where the Silver One keeps her secret base. All of you know that for years we have tried in vain to determine the location of the Order's headquarters. This will be our biggest lead so far." His gaze flickered to the back wall.

Ivy's gaze followed and landed on Jack. He stood in shadow with his back pressed tightly against the brick as if wishing to blend into it. She wanted to go to him but held her place, her heart aching. Joining him would only draw attention when he clearly wished to go unnoticed.

"Franklin has expertly removed the names from the invitation and scripted it for a Hollywood agent and two aspiring actresses. Beatrix, Ivy, and Jack. This is your mission. The rest of you are dismissed."

A deafening silence followed.

Stares as sharp as daggers zeroed in on Jack. His shoulders tensed, his head tipped down not submissively but ready for attack. Then the murmurs of dissent started to ripple.

"That's enough of that." Hamilton cut off all attempts to rally to disagreement and spite. "You are dismissed."

Agents filed out one by one with Hamilton picking up the rear. Before passing Jack, he offered a curt nod, but the coolness in his eyes didn't thaw. He, Franklin, and Dolly had welcomed the prodigal back with more congeniality than the rest of the group. Franklin with a cheeriness he reserved for all and Dolly with a great deal of weeping and motherly hugs. Hamilton had offered slight resistance but bowed to Washington's decision. That was something at least.

"Are you out of your mind?" Beatrix practically spat the instant the chamber cleared and only she, Ivy, Jack, and Washington remained.

Washington spiked a dark eyebrow. It was like a spear under-cutting the bare skin of his head. "Mind your tone."

Beatrix's dark red lips twisted as if attempting to summon

contriteness. "Sir, I must protest the judgment of allowing *him*"—she flung a pointed finger at Jack—"on any assignment, least of all this one."

Blood boiling, Ivy took up defense. "How dare you? If anyone has the right to go after the Order, it's Jack."

Washington held up a silencing hand. "Are you questioning my judgment, Agent Dew?"

The freckles covering Beatrix's skin melted into her bright flush of red. "No, sir. Merely *his*." She might as well have said *this monster's*. "The Order brainwashed him for a decade, and now we're sending him straight back to their waiting clutches. What kind of killing spree can he accomplish if he falls to them again? How do we know he won't snap into Riser mode under stress? I cannot go on a mission if I cannot trust my teammates."

"Then you must trust me and my judgment. The three of you have the most knowledge of the Order, minus Fielding who is on assignment in Argentina and Victor who is supposed to be on Stalin's coattails. You've seen the Order in action and know what they are capable of. You are the best I have to send up against them."

"Easy to say when you'll be sitting safely on the other side of an ocean." Scowling, Beatrix crossed her arms. How she had managed to charm a man into an engagement was beyond comprehension.

"Not this time. I'm going with you." Washington smoothed down the buttons on his vest, looking much more the bookish master than an assassin. "I've been complacent in my library for far too long, and the Order is a thorn that must be plucked from civilization once and for all. They have festered long enough."

Ivy was first to recover from the shocked silence. "When do we leave?"

"Tomorrow morning. We have passage booked on the USS *Leviathan*, which incidentally belonged to the Huns until we captured it during the war. I'm curious to see if they left any hidden transmitters or the like before they all jumped ship before seizure." The Talon leader looked giddy at the prospect.

"A shame we can't take one of those flying machines like Charles Lindbergh took a few months ago. I read it only took him thirty-three hours to make it from New York City to Paris. Can you imagine being able to travel so fast from one place to the next?"

At this, Washington's giddiness bottomed out. "If the Almighty had intended us to fly, He would have provided us with wings. Mark my words, this air contraption will never take off."

"That's what they said about the horseless carriage."

With no fight left to pick, Beatrix offered Ivy and Washington a tight smile and turned to leave. "Well, I'm off to pack. Can't arrive in Paris with nothing to wear." She took the chamber exit farthest from where Jack stood motionless against the wall, not sparing him a glance.

Ivy didn't waste another thought on her. There would be plenty of time cramped together on the boat to shoot eye daggers at each other. "It's a surprising honor that you'll be joining us on assignment, sir. Considering your recent brush with death." She nodded pointedly at his hip.

A sly smile slipped across Washington's face. "Not so long ago a rather insightful if not obstinate agent referred to me as 'fettered by an unwillingness to take action until all the pieces fall into my order of logic.'" He sobered. "As a result, I failed more than one of my agents. It will not happen again. I will see this through. And as far as my flesh wound, it is healing quite nicely. Excuse me, please. Jack, I have a few items to speak with you about if you might spare me a moment." With a slight nod of his shiny head to Ivy, Washington crossed the chamber toward Jack and indicated the exit leading off the main space to the chamber where he kept his office.

Jack paused and looked to Ivy.

With an encouraging smile, she nodded. The corners of his mouth lifted in return, but the wariness of a cornered animal guarded him. He followed Washington and disappeared down the dim corridor.

Ivy's smile dropped. She looked around the empty chamber, breathing in the damp stone and mustiness of sealed air. Centuries' worth of secrets were chipped into these bricks, the cause of good over evil its mortar. She ran a hand over the wall, the rough blocks scratching her palm in silent recognition. Soon she would add her own brick of revenge and seal it with justice.

I am coming for you, Dragavei. For all the demons who haunt him. For all the ones who mangled his stars into darkness. You forced him to become a nightmare. Now I will become yours. And I am coming.

TWENTY-ONE

Le Vesinet, France
October 1, 1927

Lights blazed from every window of the French villa, and music belted from the open front door like a dance hall jazzing up the autumn night. Ivy fizzed with excitement.

"Stop fiddling." Beatrix smiled through her dark-stained lips as they followed the crush of party guests up the stone steps and under the glass-and-metal-framed awning.

Less concerned with appealing to the vanity of the rich swells surrounding them, Washington continued tugging at his neckwear. "It has been some time since I've worn a starched bib and dress shirt. Allow me a moment as I resign myself to the fashion once more."

Ivy hooked her arm tightly in his elbow while playing up her act as a wide-eyed ingenue starlet. "The party begs your forgiveness in not allowing sweater vests, Professor Higgins, but as a Hollywood agent scouting his next big talent, you should be accustomed to wearing such things and not pulling at it like a top on a string."

"I'll have you know I cut a fine figure in black-tie dress before the war. I do say, though, these new tuxedo jackets are quite the thing. The old tailcoats made me look like a penguin from behind."

"Well, you're simply the bee's knees tonight, sir."

Lifting an eyebrow, he glanced down at his smart black jacket and trousers. "Do you think so?"

"*Le plus beau.*"

Squaring back his shoulders with feigned arrogance, their fearless leader escorted them through a foyer with colorful tile floors, whitewashed walls, eye-catching plaster molding, and a dripping chandelier. The details were rather fuzzy, covered in a thick veil of cigarette smoke with a throng of jostling bodies eager to see and be seen.

"Invitations over there, s'il vous plaît," a stoic man, looking official in tie and tails, intoned near the door.

He indicated a large tree positioned in front of the intricately carved staircase. The tree was made of wire with brown plaster wrapped around it to simulate a trunk and limbs.

"Take one of these and clip your invitation anywhere along the limbs." A smiling servant girl in a lacy cap and apron handed Ivy a yellow clip shaped like a banana.

Washington attached their leaf invitation to a branch next to dozens of others. The tree was practically full, and the party had only just started. By the end of the evening, the tree stood a good chance of tipping right over.

Invitation secured, Washington led them dead center of the large parlor, then took a step away while raising his hands like a conductor readying to display his showmanship. For that was precisely what followed.

Beatrix shimmied until her mink coat slipped off her white shoulders and puddled at her feet to reveal a black-and-silver gown that sparkled with sequins and tassels. The chandelier light sparked red flames in her hair, styled in a faux bob and slicked into finger waves. Propping one black-gloved hand on her hip, she cocked an eyebrow at Ivy as if to say, *Beat that, Vale.*

Ivy pushed her crimson lips into a full smirk, perfected by

watching Clara Bow at the pictures, then dropped one shoulder. Her golden fox-fur stole slid down the length of her body and curled around her emerald satin shoes. Her emerald gown dotted with gold sequins twinkled like a crown jewel. She tilted her head just so, as she'd seen Miss Bow do a hundred times, ensuring the pearl-and-diamond bandeau wrapped around her head reflected the light. Not to mention both of her eyes.

She felt the crowd breathe in. Rounding out the curve of her lips, she settled into the weighted awe as if it were nothing less than expected.

Washington snapped his fingers in the air, and a serving boy appeared at his elbow. "Take these away." He waved with feigned annoyance at the sloughed-off furs as if they were mere rags.

"Yes, sir." The boy clicked his heels smartly and gathered up the pieces into a mountain of fur.

Ivy forced her expression not to reveal her sorrow as the beautiful stole bobbed through the crowd and disappeared into a back room. Miss Clara Bow never pouted over a departed wrap and neither would she. If all went according to plan, she would retrieve it again by night's end. But this was a Talon mission. In all likelihood the plan would get chucked out the window in favor of shooting from the hip.

"Come, girls," Washington drawled. "We're here to mingle." He offered Beatrix and Ivy each of his elbows, then paraded them from room to room. The front sitting room held marvelous antique furniture, the salon boasted scrolled chaises and velvet drapes, the library walls were stacked high with books, and the conservatory showcased a gurgling fountain—already a prime spot for the more amorous couples.

Slinking from room to room as she smiled and cooed, Ivy remembered the first time she'd begged to play the honey at Dobryzov Castle ten years ago when they hunted Balaur Tsar. Jack had given her more than one piece of his high-handed opinion on the matter while threatening to tie her to a tree if she ever suggested such a ludicrous part again. She'd gone on to play the seductress with great success over the years, yet each time his voice rang in her ears.

On this night, their first foray back into the field together, he hadn't so much as offered a raised eyebrow of protest. To her surprise, he'd whispered that he regretted not being able to witness her performance as he was tasked to patrol the perimeter. Then he'd kissed her cheek and told her to knock 'em dead. She'd fought hard to keep her eyes from welling up and ruining her mascara at the glimmer of flirtation, the old Jack peeking through.

After the trio's second pass through the foyer, Washington positioned them in the library doorway for the best vantage point.

"There are two Order members now." He kept his voice low as he raised his eyebrows over a glass of champagne. "Along with Pierre LeBlanc, chairman of the Treaty of Nations."

Talon kept a long list of the world's who's who in politics, power, and threats. Nothing was more thrilling than striking off a threat with a fresh red pen.

Turning to catch a waiter before he moved on with the tray of pastries, Ivy wiggled her fingers over the selections.

"Canelés with vanilla crème," the waiter said.

Ivy pulled her fingers back. Vanilla. The bane of all dessert selections. "*Non, merci.*" She waved him away and snagged a glass of champagne from another passing tray, then noted the men slinking past the invitation tree and up the stairs.

"I'll follow the gentlemen." She sipped the golden bubbles. The liquid fizzed on her tongue and glided down the back of her throat. "You two keep scouting down here."

"Mind your head," Washington warned. For bullets and blows, not short doorways.

Grinning, Ivy tossed back the rest of her champagne and plonked the empty glass on a nearby fern. "Oh, drat! That glass took the last of my lipstick, and I can't meet the next sip with bare lips. I'll need to reapply. Excuse me for a bit, darlings."

Tiny beaded bag in hand, she ducked under the tree and swayed her way up the stairs. At the top of the landing, she looked over the railing and wiggled her fingers in parting salute, then turned right down a corridor. And straight into a man stubbing out a cigarette on a miniature Venus statue.

"Clumsy little—well, hello there, beautiful." He spoke French. The man's immediate frown righted itself in his full beard as he looked her over with interest.

Ivy started to reply in his native tongue before immediately correcting with English and a smattering of bad French. What Hollywood starlet just so happened to speak impeccable French? She opened her eyes wide and batted her mascara-caked lashes.

"Parley-voo, excuse me! These heels are new and rather tricky to navigate up all those steps." She flashed him a peek of her satin heels. "I was just looking for the *la toilette*. Do you happen to know where I might find it? I'm a bit shiny." She touched the tip of her nose and added a giggle for good measure.

The man's smile oozed under his thick mustache. "*Oui*. I take you. You come with me." His broken English was heavily accented and might have been charming if he hadn't been trying to seduce her into a dark room.

Giggling again, she slipped easily from his grasp. "I don't think the powder room usually has a bed in it."

"This one does." He reached for her, whisky and smoke heavy on his breath. "What a beautiful inspiration you make for my canvas."

"You want to paint little old *moi*? That's an offer I simply can't refuse, but only after I powder my nose."

"I wait here."

Irksome as a flea. If she had any hope of trailing those Order members, she needed to get rid of him. Fast. "No, no. Wait for *moi* in the garden. My agent is downstairs, and he'll be suspicious if I don't come down right away. He's such a bore. Even at parties he doesn't want me to have fun." She pushed her lower lip into a pout. "Meet *moi* outside in *dix* minutes and I'll give him the slip."

"What is this slip?"

"I'll sneak past him. I hear there's a lot of woodlands to get lost in on this estate. He'll never find *moi* out there with all the trees and bushes."

The man's roving eyes lit up. Drawing a fresh cigarette from a gold case marked with the initials H. M., he sucked in a lungful of smoke and exhaled in what he likely considered a seductive puff. "Ten minutes. No second more."

She grinned and tweaked his cheek. "No second more. Aw revoir." Wiggling her fingers in goodbye, she sashayed down the corridor while keeping her ears alert should he change his mind and make the bad decision of following her.

"Men," she muttered, straightening her walk when she was certain she was alone. "Thinking we all want to be pawed at in dark hallways."

"It's because they're animals," came a silky voice from the stairs above her. "Think they can hunt and kill as they please. It's why we should keep them outside or on a leash where they belong. Including the very talented Matisse."

Ivy craned her neck to locate the owner of the voice. The woman came down the stairs in sections. Long legs, curves, elegant neck, and lush eyes heavily rimmed in kohl.

"Josephine Baker." This time Ivy didn't have to act. She was genuinely starstruck. "I mean, Miss Baker. I can't believe I'm in your home."

"Josephine, please. Or Jo." The woman didn't walk; she rolled on air. A gown of cheetah print trimmed in deep green poured over her body like molten silk. "And you're welcome here anytime, honey. American, yes?"

"Yes. DC originally." *Keep up the act, you blathering idiot.* Ivy propped a hand on her hip. "Now I'm trying my hand in Hollywood. My agent says my big break is coming soon."

Sympathy flickered in Josephine's eyes. "Honey, I learned something a long time ago, and I'm going to pass on this piece of advice to you. All those bigwigs will tell you everything you want to hear and never mean a word of it. You gotta go where the people love you and want you."

Ivy dropped her hand, and with it a bit of her act. "Is that why you moved to France?"

Josephine smiled brilliantly. A million-watt smile that would reach all the way to the guests in the dance hall. "That, and the wine." A shadow passed over her lovely face, dimming the light in her eyes. She reached up to touch her short black hair, the tiny curls forming a kind of fringe across her forehead. "Seems my skin was too dark for America's taste, but the people of France have opened their arms to me, and I adore them for it, so here is where I'll stay as the queen of Paris."

Ivy's heart ached. Loneliness, no matter the source, was possibly the cruelest burden. Ivy had found her acceptance at Talon, and it seemed the famous Miss Baker, performer extraordinaire, had found hers in Paris.

"I hope to be as brave and wonderful as you one day. See my name in lights."

"Tell you what, I've got a picture coming out in December. *Siren of the Tropics.* I'll get you tickets for it. In the meantime, you come by the Folies Bergère in Paris and see my show *Un Vent de Folie.* Leave your modesty at the door." Josephine winked and raised a wicked eyebrow. "Most of the people here tonight expected me to turn up in my banana skirt because of that show. I got the last laugh though. Did you see the invitation tree?"

Ivy peeked over the railing at the wire tree covered in fat green leaf invitations and yellow clips. A banana tree. She laughed. "Very clever."

"That's all the bananas they're getting from me tonight. They can buy a ticket for everything else." Josephine grinned. "Gotta be one step ahead if you want to stay on top. That's my second piece of advice for you—I don't even know your name. Where have my manners gone?"

"Clara." Ivy held out her hand.

Josephine shook it. "Well, Miss Clara. It was a pleasure meeting you, but I'd better be a good hostess and go see to my other guests. I'll be sure to send that animal who tried to paw you to the far end of the woods. Maybe we'll get lucky and he'll fall into the stream." She started down the steps, then turned back. "Use my private bathroom for powdering your nose. Fourth door on the left."

"Thank you, Josephine."

Suppressing her giddiness at having met a real-life star, Ivy turned her mind back to the mission and the Order members she was supposed to be tracking. She checked the first room, then moved down the corridor. All empty. When she entered the last room, a faint light glowed beneath a connecting door.

Based on the elegant bed and personal items scattered about, it could only be Josephine's bedroom, and the light was most likely coming from the bathroom. In her line of work "most likely" wasn't a sure bet. She reached into her handbag and wrapped her fingers around her chirper gun. Better safe than sorry.

She slipped across the dark room, then rapped on the partially open door. "*Excusez-moi!* Is this room in use?"

No answer.

She pushed open the door and breezed in, heels clicking on the tile. "It's been difficult to find a quiet place to—"

A noise rustled from the enormous marble and silver bathtub.

Sharpness on metal. Then the sound of deep, heavy breathing. The kind of breathing made by someone twice her size. A head poked out of the bathtub. Sleek and golden with black spots, it rested on top of the marble edge.

Golden eyes rimmed in black stared at Ivy. A massive yawn revealed rows of white pointed teeth. Perfect for ripping apart meat.

Ivy froze. "N-nice k-kitty."

The cat—cheetah? leopard? man-eater?—leaped from the tub and blocked her escape. Its long body flexed with muscle as it stalked toward her, its golden eyes unblinking.

She pulled the gun from her bag and took a step back. Her foot caught on a pile of discarded towels. She tumbled backward and landed hard on her bottom. Her gun skittered across the tile and under the sink, far out of reach.

The cat didn't stop.

Ivy tried to scramble away, but her feet tangled in her gown's hem. "Nice k-kitty. G-good kitty c-cat."

The cat's heavy paw stepped on her dress. The spots danced on its shiny coat as the killer muscles tensed for striking. Ivy would have a second, if not less, to latch onto its neck and attempt a choke.

If she got past the teeth and claws. Of all the ways to die—a bullet, beat, hanged, dropped off a cliff—being eaten by an exotic cat had never made the list.

The animal's hot breath clawed up her bare arms, chest, neck, and face. Wet drops clung to its razor-sharp teeth. Salivating for its anticipated meal. The golden eyes were inches away, unwavering and deadly as they locked onto their target.

The cat lowered its head and headbutted her.

The scream strangling up Ivy's throat collapsed into a muffled sob. The animal headbutted her again. First her cheek, then chin, and finally it rubbed against her neck. A deep purr rumbled up its throat.

"You w-want to be p-petted?" In answer it rubbed its cheek against her shoulder. Lest she offend the wild creature, Ivy raised a shaking hand and scratched between its velvety ears. "You'd better not be m-marking me as a late-night snack."

The cat dipped its head, sending Ivy's fingers to its neck. And a collar made of diamonds that spelled Chiquita. Ivy's mouth flapped open. Some folks kept canaries. Josephine kept a jungle cat.

"As lovely as this introduction has been, Chiquita"—the purring intensified—"I really must be going. I have evil men to interrogate and a husband sneaking around the garden who has yet to compliment my gown."

Extricating herself from the affectionate feline proved useless as Chiquita took it upon herself to remain glued to Ivy's side as she retrieved her gun and walked out of the bathroom. The cat continued following her beyond the bedroom door and up to the next floor. The noise of the party dimmed, punctuated only by shrill laughter or a blaring trumpet note. At the end of the hallway, yellow light spilled out from under the last door. Ivy crept closer, Chiquita serenely at her side, and pressed her ear to the closed door. The distinct sound of a needle scratched over a record.

Readying her gun, she turned the doorknob. It opened without resistance. She stepped quickly inside to what was a private study dressed in rich woods, creams, and greens. An antique scrolled desk perched in front of large double windows while bookshelves lined two of the walls. The marble-topped fireplace was ablaze, and facing the hearth sat two gold wingback chairs with a low table between them. Three glasses, two full of amber liquid, sat on the table.

Taking matters into her own paws, Chiquita prowled straight to the chairs and sat in front of the one closest to the empty glass. Her tail flicked with impatience. Ivy joined her in front of the chair where a man was slumped on the cushions. His eyes were glassy, skin a sickly gray, and foam flecked his lips.

She knew before she even checked his absent pulse. She picked up the empty glass and sniffed. Brandy with the faint scent of almond.

Pierre LeBlanc, chairman of the Treaty of Nations, had been poisoned.

★★★

Jack pushed a branch from in front of his face and scanned the lawn. Black ties, fancy dresses, laughter, and booze. A typical evening for the rich and powerful in their element of excess.

He'd been tasked with circling the perimeter to locate Order members from the list. How he was supposed to identify them while crouching in the bushes he hadn't figured out yet, but he kept his ears tuned and eyes peeled. Eyes that kept flicking back to the house. Ivy was in there somewhere, among the pulsing jazz notes and cigarette smoke. He wanted to be with her.

Not here though. It was bad enough for his body to be tense at all times, bracing for what might be coming. Staying alert for so many years had taken its toll, and the armor was not so easily discarded. Bringing him along was questionable to begin with, but waltzing straight into a crowd of people with members of the Order likely to recognize him was a disaster waiting to happen. The last thing this night needed was a triggered Riser on the loose.

The acrid stench of cigar smoke curled under his nose and rooted into his brain, digging out a corroded memory. It had been dark and chilly, much like this night, when he'd stood on a roof-top. Below him stretched a city. Which one? A body lay at his feet. A match struck behind him, and cigar smoke crawled over his shoulder.

"Well done, Katona." The cigar man spoke Czech. No. Hungarian. *"With the ambassador dead, I will take his place. Long live the Order. The next step is not enough."*

Jack pulled back from the memory only to see the past before him. Six feet away stood the cigar man. Order member and Hungarian ambassador to France for the past seven years. Since Jack had killed his innocent predecessor.

Crouching through the bushes in his own evening wear, Jack lined himself up within striking distance. One quick snatch and he'd have the man by the throat with no drunken revelers around to notice.

One. Two—

"Good evening, gentlemen." Cigar man raised a hand in greeting to two approaching figures. His French was horrendously threaded with a Hungarian accent. "Splendid party, is it not?"

"*Oui.* Josephine knows how to throw a *magnifique fête,*" one of the men said. He was tall and slender with silver hair. "I told her to try a more refined guest list next time, but what can one do? She prefers an eclectic gathering of power and art."

"Ever the snob, Alphonse."

Alphonse, the silver-haired man, sniffed with disdain. "One must have standards, and when those standards are not met, matters must be taken in hand."

"So it is done then?"

Alphonse glanced back to the house and nodded. "As of tonight, I have taken position as the new chairman of the Treaty of Nations. It will be announced tomorrow that Pierre LeBlanc died unexpectedly—I am certain those newspapers we bankroll will have some clever title ready—and that I, as assistant chairman, will come forward to take his seat."

"And not a day too soon," the other man said, wiping a pudgy hand across his sweating brow. "With the Treaty convening tomorrow and LeBlanc still in charge, they would have voted for a global limitation on armaments. Now Alphonse can ensure the Order will obtain what weapons we need."

Cigar man puffed on his cigar, huffing rings of smoke into the air above their heads. "The Silver One will be pleased."

Fury ignited in Jack's veins. *The Silver One.* His finger coiled around an imaginary trigger.

Alphonse preened. "Indeed. She will be when I inform her this evening."

Cigar man choked, sputtering out gasps of smoke. "You speak with her? Directly?"

"As incumbent chairman of the Treaty of Nations, how can I not? You will see for yourself later tonight at the gathering." Alphonse smirked. "The Silver One personally charged me with this duty, and after years of patiently waiting for the opportune moment, tonight I succeeded. With this organization now under full command of the Order, we are but a hairsbreadth away from ushering in a new era where we are master of all."

"May we save your adulating speeches until the gathering, Alphonse? There has been enough seriousness for one hour." The pudgy man made a drinking motion and nodded toward the house. "This is a party. We are meant to be seen enjoying ourselves."

Jack's muscles tensed, ready to spring, but three against one was bound to call attention. He'd need to take the smoother route of cornering them without witnesses. Rising from a crouch, he pressed a hand to the front of his white buttoned shirt, the restraining top button unfashionably undone, and shook the leaves from his sleeves as he tried to recall what it was like to step into a crowd as if he belonged there. As if he were part of the set. His head buzzed with anticipation. His heart hammered with trepidation.

You are not the Riser. You will not hurt anyone.

He stepped from the bushes and moved after the group, dodging between dancers, ducking around drink-laden trays, stepping over toes, and twisting away from flailing hands tipped with red-hot cigarettes. A veritable minefield.

The evil trio bobbed ahead in a lazy zigzag with the bar as their destination, while Jack kept as close to the crowd's edge as possible. The drinks setup was difficult to miss. A stone fountain bubbled with champagne where guests were encouraged to dip their glasses for a refill. Tables on either side glittered like gemstones with bottles of amber whisky, crystal vodka, burgundy wine, and tawny brandy, while ice could be chipped from two glacial Eiffel Towers with diamonds frozen inside them.

Jack had always wanted to present Ivy with a diamond ring—no. Interrogation first. Romance later.

A figure low to the ground slinked in front of him. He glanced down, expecting to find a woman crawling on the ground in search of a lost glove or some such thing. Nothing. He stepped closer to the bar. The figure moved before him again. And again he could see nothing.

Then a rope coiled around his leg. The fight armor that never left him clicked into position. Touching the handle of the knife concealed on his belt, he yanked his foot free of the trap.

A low growl rumbled behind him.

Turning, he came face-to-face with unblinking yellow eyes, spots, a whipping tail, and sharp white teeth. Jack curled his fingers around the knife and slowly pulled it from his belt. A drunken guest searching for a glove most definitely would have been preferable.

The enormous cat stalked toward him. A hiss escaped between its teeth.

"There you are! I've been looking all over." Like a glittering candle, his wife materialized from the crowd. Of all the catastrophic timing, she had to come looking for him now.

"Ivy, stay back."

"Whatever for—Oh! You're out here too." At the sound of her voice, the predator sat on its haunches and purred. Ivy glided by, scratched the animal on its head, and stopped in front of Jack.

"Pierre LeBlanc is dead," she whispered. "Poisoned by two Order members who must have slipped out here because I can't find them anywhere in the house. Jack? What's the matter?"

He seized her by the shoulders and shoved her behind him. "That's a wild animal! Perhaps you thought it an oversize house cat or mistook it for a dog, but I can assure you this creature is aiming for a jugular."

"Chiquita?" His wife had the nerve to sound flabbergasted. "She's an absolute sweetie. Listen to her purr." Ivy skirted around him and started scratching the cat's chin. The animal closed its eyes in bliss and lifted its head to provide better access.

"You've met this killer before?"

"She gave me quite the fright in the bathroom earlier, but we're *bonne amie* now. Right, Chiquita? Now you must be friends with *mon amour*. Go on, tell him bonjour."

Chiquita walked around Jack, rubbing her cheek against his legs and trailing her tail around his ankles.

"Uh, it's a pleasure to meet you, Chiquita." He turned his attention back to the matter at hand. "Pierre LeBlanc is dead, you say?"

"Yes. Arsenic-laced brandy. I followed two Order members upstairs. They escaped before I could corner them." She threw a mock glare at the cat. "I found LeBlanc in a study on the top floor where they poisoned him before ducking out."

"They're here." Jack leaned his head toward the bar where the men were taking their time sampling each of the libations on offer.

"Good. Let's get them."

As she started to move toward them, Jack grabbed her arm. "Wait. There's something you should know first." The words stuck in his throat like grappling hooks, their ropes knotted tight around the black deeds buried deep within him. Deeds he never wanted to come to light but that were uprooting themselves nonetheless. His fingers dug into her arm. "That man over there with the cigar, I know him. Or rather, he knows me."

Ivy twisted her head to look at the bar then back at him. Understanding filled her expression. "As the Riser."

"What if he . . ." Jack swallowed to dislodge the hooks in his throat. "There's a bounty on my head. If he or any of these other Order members catches me, you know what will happen. This party will turn into a bloodbath."

"We can't allow that to happen, now, can we? A bloodbath will ruin all this wonderful champagne and most likely my magnificent gown, which you have yet to comment on." Her teasing smile faded as she reached up to cup his cheek. "No one will touch you. No one."

"What would I do without you?"

"Turn into a reckless blight of a man. Oh wait. You've already done that, so there's no use in repeating the ruse." With a wicked wink, she pressed a full kiss to his mouth. This time his blood pounded far more pleasantly than with trepidation. "Wait here, and I'll get our man. You can have the job of knocking him around."

"Which one?"

She called over her shoulder, "Doesn't matter. One is all we need for threatening." Putting her hips into a luxurious swing that set her gown of sequins to dancing, she swayed across the lawn and tapped Alphonse on the shoulder. He looked down, whisky glass halfway to his lips. Surprised at first, then delighted, and finally leering like a wolf at a lamb who had wandered into his den.

Ivy said something and laughed. Alphonse leaned closer and trailed a finger along the exposed skin of her arm. She smiled like a proper coquette and playfully swatted his hand away, which he took as an invitation to snake his arm around her waist.

Jack would kill him outright. No drawn-out interrogation required. Beside him, Chiquita growled her agreement.

Leaning up on tiptoe, Ivy whispered into Alphonse's ear. He eagerly nodded. With a polite bow and a bit of nudging his compatriots, Alphonse guided her through the crowd, grabbing a bottle of champagne from a waiter as they went.

Jack trailed along the throng's edge, Ivy ever in his sights. Skipping over the cool grass, she pulled Alphonse into the glass aviary framed in white wood. Jack quietly slipped in behind them a moment later with Chiquita on his heels. Bright moonlight shone through the glass panes that drew to a point overhead, drifting down to brush silver across pots of planted trees. The soft rustling of feathers and curious chirps sounded between leaves as the colorful winged inhabitants hopped from one branch to another.

"Do not play the shy maiden with me, *ma lapine*," Alphonse cooed as he leaned around one of the trees. "Not after your whisperings."

Ivy giggled as her green and gold sequins flashed from behind the tree. "A gentleman would not repeat such things."

"Perhaps I am no gentleman, but then, that may be why you sought me out, *oui*?" He ducked around another tree, but the sequins shimmied out of his reach. "Come now. Let us not waste this seclusion or bottle of fine champagne. I should like to watch it froth between your ample—"

"Mind if I take a sip?" Jack closed the door behind him and leaned back against it. "I promise not to be nearly so reticent as the lady here."

Swerving around a branch and startling its feathery occupants into a squawk, Alphonse scowled.

"This is a closed party, monsieur. You are not welcome." It might have been a regal rebuke with his white bow tie and cold disdain if not for the canary feather clinging to his pomaded hair.

Ivy strode out from her hiding place and plunked her hands on her hips, squaring off to Jack. "Who are you calling reticent? I'll have you know that was one of the most forward proposals I've been forced to lower myself into suggesting."

"One of?" Jack's eyebrows spiked to his hairline. "How many others should I know about?"

She waved a hand dismissively. "Doesn't matter. I had to break all of their necks."

"You trollop." Alphonse growled at Ivy. "Thinking to lure me out here only to pit me against an inferior man. Dueling was outlawed centuries ago, and even if it hadn't been, you are hardly the sort of *salope* worth scrapping over. You are nothing more than a *femme sans cervelle*."

Smiling sweetly, Ivy approached and brushed the feather from Alphonse's hair. Then she grasped his shoulders and jerked her knee straight up into his groin.

He keeled over with a shuddering groan.

"Yet you are the one storing your brains in an, ah . . . most fragile appendage. Tsk-tsk."

"I thought I would be the one knocking him around." Jack shoved off the door. "Are you quite done defending your honor?"

"Yes, dear. I leave the rest to you."

Jack dug his foot under Alphonse's belly and nudged him onto his back. His knees seized up in a puny effort to ward off further injury to his throbbing bits.

"Where is the Silver One?"

"Wh-what?" Alphonse wheezed. Pain twisted his face red.

"Helena Dragavei. Leader of the Order of the Rising Moon. Where is she?"

"I-I don't know what y-you speak of."

Jack groaned. "Why do they always take the route of feigned ignorance?" He snatched the champagne bottle that Alphonse had the presence of mind to hold on to despite his indecorous fall. Cristal. Perfectly aged from 1919.

"Because their ilk are not intelligent enough to realize they do not have the upper hand." Ivy's skirts rustled over the mulch covering the aviary floor as she went to sit on a stone bench nestled under a bushy palm. Chiquita settled at her feet. The tip of her tail flicked with annoyance.

Squatting near Alphonse's head, Jack pulled out his knife and ran it around the gold foil enclosing the bottle's spout and neck. It fluttered to the ground with a shiny crackle.

"Allow me to explain how this is going to go. We can have a back-and-forth with me accusing and you denying until at last you break and confess everything I need to know." He slid the blade against the side of the cork. A sliver curled off and landed on Alphonse's chest.

"I'm a patient man with limitless options for how to break you, but to be perfectly honest, Alphonse, I don't want to be at this party. The sooner I can take off this monkey suit the better because what I really want to be doing is hunting." Another cork sliver fell.

"I intend to mount that hag's head on a wall, so the sooner you tell me where she's hiding, the sooner this will all be over with."

Recognition flashed through the pain in the prostrate man's eyes. His knees lowered from their defensive position. "You are him. Her Riser."

Her Riser. Always belonging to someone like a dog on a leash. Never a man but a thing, a weapon to be used at another's will. Jack slid his knife through the cork, smooth as butter under the sharp blade.

"Good. Then you know what I'm capable of." A sliver fell onto Alphonse's pale neck.

"There is a bounty on your head. Enough to set up a man for ten lifetimes. That is how precious you are to her. To our cause."

"I was but one in a hundred killers for her."

"There are none like you. She has tried dozens of times to create more Risers, but they were utter failures. Their bodies were too weak for the serum and their instincts not honed to those of a true killer. Not like yours." A dark, devilish gleam flickered in Alphonse's eye, brushing his face with hellfire.

A hellfire blazing to consume Jack. "Where. Is. Dragavei."

"I heard you have over five hundred kills to your name. Single-handed. *Impressionnant*. Even more impressive is that more than half were at close range. Tell me, Riser, what is it like to plunge a knife into a man's heart knowing his only crime was to stand against the Order?"

With a flick of his blade, Jack stabbed out the remaining cork. Golden foam exploded from the bottle. He wrenched Alphonse's jaw down and poured the streaming brew into his mouth.

Alphonse gagged and choked against the onslaught of liquid. He thrashed and beat his arms against Jack. Ivy whistled low and Chiquita moved to stretch languidly across Alphonse's legs, pinning them in place.

"I don't take pleasure in ending a life," Jack said, wiping champagne droplets from his hand onto Alphonse's expensive jacket. "But there are times when it is quite satisfying to grind my heel over a loathsome insect such as yourself. Now, are you still thirsty, or do you wish to answer my question?"

Alphonse twisted his head to the side and spewed out the contents swimming in his lungs. *"B-blaireau! Tête de noeud!"*

Jack dumped the rest of the bottle's contents into the man's mouth. "The lady already warned you about keeping your manners." He smashed the end of the empty bottle against the ground, then ran the jagged circle down Alphonse's shirt. The silk tore like tissue paper.

"Last chance. Where. Is. The Silver One."

"T-tonight!" Alphonse coughed. Spit and champagne erupted from his gasping mouth as his purple face faded to red. Chiquita hissed at the disturbance. *"Aux tr-travailleurs munici-cipaux."*

"Municipal workers." Jack held up the bottle. Moonlight twisted through the sharp green glass. "Don't offer me half facts, Alphonse."

A half gurgle, half sob escaped from the drenched man's throat as the cat began to lick his hand. "Père La-Lachaise."

Jack glanced at Ivy.

"It's a necropolis in Paris," she said.

"In the twentieth arrondissement, to be precise." Beatrix sailed into the aviary with Washington on her heels.

"Ah, you found one of them. Excellent." Washington shut the door behind them before startling with a cry. "What is that?"

"Chiquita," Ivy said. "Josephine's pet. She likes to be scratched under the chin."

"I'll take your word for it." He looked unconvinced.

"Where have you two been?"

Swatting away a dove that flew too close to her head, Beatrix circled around Alphonse and stopped next to where Ivy sat on the bench. "Our stubborn leader was tempted into a game of wit and quip with some bombastic fellow who proclaimed a temperament of sobriety no matter how much scotch he consumed. And consume he did, downing a shot per quip. When we left the house, he was zozzled under a piano upon which a flapper named Zelda was pirouetting."

"Hemingway is a showman." Washington made a disgruntled noise. "He'll do anything for attention, as his last novel proves."

Ivy grinned. "As I see you are on your feet, I take it you were last man standing."

"A well-read man will always stand victorious. Now, who do we have here?" With Chiquita's unblinking gaze rooting him to the spot, Washington peered from his position by the door. "Alphonse Monte. Assistant chairman to Pierre LeBlanc."

"Chairman now. LeBlanc is dead," Ivy said.

"As we heard no gunshot or scream, I assume strangulation or poison."

"Arsenic."

"Always a popular choice. I store a pinch here should the occasion of need arise." Washington touched one of his golden cuff links. "As we cannot allow Monsieur Monte to roam free and stir up trouble for the Order, we'll hand him over to the Talon French agents while we seek to fry our larger fish. I shall go telephone them now."

As Washington slipped off to call in reinforcements and Beatrix knelt to scratch Chiquita, who still lay contentedly across Alphonse's legs, Jack tossed the spent bottle aside and stood to unkink his muscles. He hadn't interrogated, let alone tortured, anyone for many months, and maintaining his crouch had caused his muscles to cramp. A tremor started in his hand. *I don't do that anymore.* But apparently he did.

Ivy rose from her bench and skirted around Alphonse to stand next to Jack. She spoke in a low voice. "Are you all right?"

Pushing his shaking hand into his pocket, he nodded. "Ready to get on with this witch hunt."

She glanced to where his hand had disappeared. Concern creased between her eyebrows. "If it's too much . . . If you think you can't—"

"That woman has killed hundreds of innocents and ruined our lives. I intend to ruin her. It ends tonight." His mouth twisted with a wry smile. "How appropriate the setting is a cemetery."

The creases on her forehead smoothed to dramatic reluctance. "Here we are on our first night back on the town, and you want to take me to a cemetery. How romantic." Sighing, she ran a hand over her gown. "I suppose I'll have to change."

Jack trailed a finger over the emerald sequins scattered down one of the gown's straps. "A shame. You look pretty tonight."

"Only tonight?"

Smiling, he bent close to her ear. Roses scented her hair. "The prettiest assassin-slash-seductress on any night."

"I'm sure that's what Monsieur Matisse thought when he suggested I pose for his painting."

His smile evaporated. "Who is this?"

Ivy ran a hand up his shirt and patted his chest. "No one you need to beat up, darling. Just a simple artist. Besides, I already sent him on a wild-goose chase into the trees. With any luck he's been caught in the brambles by now."

Grasping her fingers, he pressed them against his chest over the interlocking rings tattoo and forced his lips to curve up good-naturedly. This Matisse josser was one lucky man—only because Jack didn't have another champagne bottle within reach.

TWENTY-TWO

PÈRE LACHAISE CEMETERY

DEAD LEAVES SCURRIED ACROSS THE WINDING BRICK PATHS BETWEEN ornate tombs that crowded together like uneven rows of decaying teeth. Blackened with age, the tombs sank crookedly into the earth as if the weight of the dead below dragged them down. Stone crosses and carved busts atop the pointed roofs seemed to cry out to the heavens for saving.

Some thought cemeteries peaceful. Jack found them creepy.

After local Talon agents discreetly carted away Alphonse, the American agents quickly changed into clothing more appropriate for slipping around unnoticed before gathering a few supplies from a Talon warehouse on the outskirts of Paris. The benefits of a worldwide agency meant an expansion of stock far beyond money and weapons shoved into a bank box.

"It's down this way." Beatrix led them past dozens more artfully chiseled monuments while Washington and Ivy paused every few feet to ooh and aah over some famous buried person they'd read about. Sarah Bernhardt. Isadora Duncan. Oscar Wilde. Rossini. Chopin.

"Pipe down with your tourist fascination," Beatrix hissed. "We're nearly there."

Walking in front of Jack, Washington and Ivy exchanged irritated glances but continued in silence. Jack made a mental note to bring Ivy back one day so she might browse the dead at her leisure no matter how many shivers it gave him. Anyplace she wished to go, he would take her. After he killed Dragavei. He brushed his fingers against the knife on his belt. After he buried the blade in her twisted heart and could finally rest.

Stopping in the shadows before a roundabout, Beatrix pointed ahead to a monument in the center. *"Le Monument aux travailleurs municipaux."*

An obelisk amid a ring of bushes protected by a low stone wall. A female figure sitting on a seal was carved into the front side of the monument. Words were inscribed over her head, but the midnight hour made it impossible to read them. At the base of the tall, pointed structure was a cement block with double gray doors.

"It's underground," Jack said.

Washington peered at the doors then at the brick walk circling the monument. "Are you certain?"

"Dragavei prefers to do her dirty work belowground." The muscles in Jack's arms tensed as if preparing for the sting of a needle. A memory of dirt and wet stone drifted under his nose. The scents were carved into his nightmares from being locked in a cage underground, only released to be strapped into a chair for the injection of Dust that would leash his mind to her bidding.

A hand on his arm drew him from the depths of memory. Ivy. "Steady now."

His arms relaxed, earning a brief smile from her. She was worried about him. Again. He needed to pull himself together, otherwise neither of them would be able to focus on the mission. Any lack of concentration going into this would spell catastrophe.

"Looks like we're not the only latecomers," Washington whispered as he pointed to a man and some women crossing the roundabout and slipping beyond the gray doors.

"Would have been easier to arrive with the crowd." Ivy tugged at the scarf wrapped around her hair. Not the best disguise, but combined with the darkness, it would do. Walking into such a chamber as the Maiden was bound to gain the notice of a bounty hunter or two. "We could have gone unnoticed."

"Too late for could-haves now." Washington adjusted his belt, which was weighed down with small flasks of gasoline. "Ready?"

They all nodded as one. Dressed in plain street clothes of black and gray, they at least had the comfort of blending in with the shadows. Washington walked across the cobblestones with purpose, as if they belonged there, and stepped firmly through the doors. Beatrix and Ivy followed with Jack at the rear.

Torches built into the stone walls illuminated a steep path of steps leading down. The air chilled with every inch of their descent. Dead vines twisted between the crumbling bricks, and spiderwebs filled the nooks and crannies. A cold hand clutched at Jack's lungs, squeezing until his breaths were quick and shaky.

What he wouldn't give to have his old rifle, Reaper, heavy and solid in his hands. He hadn't held that beauty in ten years, and he missed the reassuring bulk of it, the way it molded to his arm and shoulder. The crack shot it gave him. But Reaper wasn't easy to disguise, so he'd packed his second favorite weapon, his pistol, Undertaker, for this trip into the city of the dead. Miraculously, Ivy had saved it all this time. Small and lethal, Undertaker clung to his hip, waiting for its moment. The thought of putting a bullet into Dragavei's skull eased the choking hand from his lungs.

At the bottom of the stairs was a small chamber with a single sarcophagus in the center, behind which stood two men with machine guns strapped to their chests.

"Password!" one of them barked in French.

Ivy stepped forward. "'The next step is not enough.'" That terrible Dacian language rolled smoothly from her tongue.

The guard pressed the foot of the body engraved on the sarcophagus, and a door concealed in the wall behind him swung open. After they walked through, the door closed with a grating sound behind them. They stood in a rectangular corridor with an arched ceiling and blazing torches hanging from chains nailed into the stone walls. Squares were cut along both walls with names chiseled onto each one.

"It's a crypt," Beatrix said.

Ivy walked slowly, reading the names out loud. "Visegrád. Braşov. Constantinople. Snagov. Milvian. Grunwald. Fontenoy. Austerlitz." She paused at a name in the center. A crescent was carved into the stone above the name. "Târgovişte."

"These aren't names." Washington ran his fingers over one of the squares. "They're battles throughout history."

"They're Order of the Rising Moon," Jack said. "Uprisings for their takeover under the guise of battle. A favorite ploy and one Dragavei likes to torment her captives with by reciting each fight and the number of people killed or fallen in the name of her glorious cause."

"So they've been in the history pages all along," Washington mused as he stopped at each title, his expression painted with keen interest. "Behind emperors, kings, redrawn borders . . . each step bringing them closer to their goal."

Beatrix scoffed as she toed a fallen torch ember. "Obviously they're not a force to be reckoned with if it's taken them thousands of years to gain power and they still haven't taken it."

"It's like a long game of chess played out over the centuries. They've been waiting for the right moment to call checkmate."

Jack followed behind Ivy, reading the inscriptions. Mărăşeşti. Istanbul. London. Washington, DC. Dread filled his belly. He knew these places. The dread roiled to dismay. These had been his missions as a Riser. He raised his shaking hand and traced the letters of London as a memory stole over him. A memory of these letters being chiseled into this stone.

"I've been here before," he whispered.

Ivy turned to him. "When?"

"After I assassinated the secretary of state for war in London." He dropped his hand and met her steady gaze. "After I saw you." Moving around her, he walked to the end of the corridor and pulled down the last torch holder. A block of crypts grated open like a door.

Entering first, Jack stepped into a subterranean amphitheater that he now remembered had served as a gathering place for Order members for hundreds of years. The space was roughly the size of Ford's Theater with four tiers leading down to a floor serving as central stage that was surrounded by enormous flaming braziers. Hunks of granite had been carved and hauled in from the countryside to build this den of evil while uniquely placed tombs on the ground above had been fitted with skylights to allow the moonlight to stream in and flood the space with gray and silver coolness.

They stood at the back of the top tier where a walking path circled the perimeter. Hundreds of people stood shoulder to shoulder on the varying stone levels. Their voices filled the air like droning, bouncing off the stone walls and ceiling and echoing back at twice the volume. The noise drilled into Jack's bones.

He tugged up the collar of his jacket to hide his lower face. The last time he entered this place his hair was long, and he wore leather confines and buckles as Dragavei's Riser. Though he'd managed a shave and clean clothes since then, he wasn't taking any chances of being recognized.

He scanned the chamber. "Dragavei isn't here. Yet. She prefers to build anticipation before appearing." He wanted her to see him first. It would be the last thing she ever saw.

Washington quickly took in the scene, his mind no doubt processing and calculating. "Ivy. Beatrix. Wait until I start a controlled fire, then fan out and drop the smoke bombs once Dragavei addresses her followers. The crowd will panic and stampede for the exit." He turned to Jack. "You get to the monster for the kill."

The team waited for Jack's response. All eyes on him, judging, wondering if he was truly ready. Waiting for him to snap, or worse, trigger back into the Riser. He would rather die than allow that to happen.

Jack nodded.

Relief flickered in Washington's eyes. "Wait for my signal."

Ivy squeezed Jack's hand before slipping off into the crowd opposite Beatrix. Washington started to turn away, but Jack grabbed his arm.

"If this goes bad, swear to me you'll put me down." Washington started to protest, but Jack's fingers dug into the man's arm. "I will *not* be a Riser again, and I can't ask Ivy to do it. It has to be you. Swear to me."

The horror on Washington's face hardened to understanding. "I swear."

Jack released him and walked along the back wall as his teammates moved into position. A few people from the crowd turned to look at him, but he hunkered into the upturned collar of his jacket and shifted his gaze downward. Anything resembling a stare, a trait of hunters and perfected by a Riser, would draw suspicion.

Soon a hush fell over the crowd and a cloaked figure with a hood drawn low to obscure his features stepped onto the circular ground floor. The flaming braziers threw orange and red light on him, but the colors were absorbed into the blackness of his robes. He raised his arms and the heavy sleeves fell back to reveal skinny arms.

"*Madames et monsieurs. Damen und herren.* Ladies and gentlemen. We gather tonight as members of our righteous Order. Our calling to rid the world of its chaff and start again with those who are worthy. Those who are we."

The crowd breathed in as if his very words gave them life. Their mouths panted for the next gulp of poison.

"We have never been so close to achieving our true purpose and destiny as when our Order was founded four hundred and sixty-five years ago by our Prince Dracul. He alone had the wisdom and foresight to purge the earth of wastrels, the weak, the corrupt, and the useless. Once they have been toppled from power, we of the Order will rise up and rule these lands as they were meant to be ruled." He stretched his arms wide as if to encompass the entire chamber. "The next step is not enough."

"The next step is not enough!" the crowd cried out.

The words crawled over Jack's skin, but he tuned out their chant and their eyes hungry for destruction. He'd seen and heard enough of it to last a lifetime twice over.

As dirt shook loose from overhead from the rising cries, the robed man waved his exposed arms for silence. The crowd stilled and leaned forward in anticipation.

"We are blessed to have our leader among us this night," the robed man droned. "The one who will lead us from the darkness into the light of a new day for our Order. For that is her calling, our Silver One."

Torches were doused all along the tiers, drowning the amphitheater in darkness save for the braziers surrounding the central stage. One by one, the roaring flames turned blue. A memory pounded at the back of Jack's skull. He had seen that trick before in a chemical lab at Talon, then again at a different lab. Next to where Dust was created.

The flames jumped and hissed, burning white at their greedy hearts. The entire chamber glowed with their brilliance. Then another figure stepped to the very center of the room. Surrounded by fire on all sides with dragging skirts and shawl covered in the rollicking shadows. Frazzled gray hair stuck out around a fleshy face that sagged onto her neck.

The creature of his nightmares. The Silver One.

Dragavei.

The air shaved across Jack's skin like razor blades, passing through his lips to drop into his lungs like lead. He felt bruises welting on his back as if the strap had lashed its memories across him. He felt the sting of the needle pierce his skin and the straining of muscles against the scorching in his veins. He felt the blackness crowding the edges of his fractured mind.

He pressed his hand to the cool handle of his pistol.

I *control this now. Not the Riser. I control my mind. Not her.*

Lungs easing, he moved away from the wall and slipped into the crowd. Row by row he gradually inched toward his target.

She was stout and hunched, her shadow wide and swallowing all the light around it. On the street she might be mistaken for something that had rolled from the gutter, but here she was viewed as a paragon with followers eager to throw themselves at her feet. Or into a world war. Whichever she desired.

"The time is upon us, dear ones." Her voice was like peeling paint, rasping against the ears. "The time for us to bring the world to its knees just as we did at our origins. When we lit the fires in Rome, when we set the plagued rats upon the ships to infest the world with the Black Death, when we accused the witches, and when an Order-bound member shot a bullet into an archduke, setting off a war such as the world had never seen.

"Even now we have members in Germany working to establish a political party based on our most treasured beliefs. A purge is coming. One that will winnow away the undesirables and leave only the favored to rule under our Order." She drifted around the stage like a dried leaf, brittle from the passage of time.

"I come to you now not as your leader, but as the last living drop of blood spared by Drăculea. My ancestor was commissioned by the Dragon himself to begin this Order as a catalyst to the reformation of decadent civilizations. Civilizations that have reached their pinnacle of profligacy. It is our duty to carry out his mission and restore the balance until there is nothing but the Order."

Pausing on the third tier, Jack scanned the crowd. Ivy stood among the crowd across from him. Beatrix was to his left. He dared not look behind him to where Washington waited to mark the signal, lest he draw undesired attention. How long would Washington allow the creature to rattle on? Were his ears not bleeding enough?

Dragavei lifted her hands to the streams of moonlight. Her baggy black sleeves drooped like the wings of an old bat. "The stars are nearly aligned as the Fates decreed. Once they are in configuration, we must rise up and seize power. I command each of you now, on the appointed day a single month hence, to assail the leaders of your countries. Arise and overtake them. Bring them to me for execution. The world will watch and know that the Order is truly the only one with power."

Execution. That was why she wanted him—wanted the Riser so desperately. Not only because she believed he belonged to her, but because she needed him as the blade at her side. A blade no man or woman would ever dare cross once slick with the blood of governments. He was to be her executioner.

Jack pressed the heel of his hand to his forehead to stop the splinters of horror from shredding apart his attention on the target. Sliding between two people entranced by the monster's speech, he moved down to the second tier. Dragavei was no more than twenty feet away. Perfect range for a bullet. He could even shoot from this distance and hit the connecting point between both ventricles of her heart and split the withered thing in two, but that would be a waste of a good bullet. Only an empty cavity could exist within a monster such as her.

Dragavei lowered her arms, her sleeves falling limp at her sides. She began to circle the stage once more, her moth-eaten skirts dragging behind her like a dead animal. "Do you believe, my children of the moon?"

"Yes!" echoed around the chamber in a multitude of languages.

"Do you believe?"

"Yes!" they cried.

She continued circling. Shadows of the silver-and-blue flames flashed across her like fangs. "I see some here tonight who do not allow our cries of jubilation to cross their lips. Some who do not believe in the purpose our great leader, Vlad Dracul, ordained us for."

The crowd began shifting with unease, murmurs of surprise rippling from one tier to the next. Pulse spiking, Jack now stood behind the final row of people blocking him from Dragavei.

She stopped in the center of the floor. Cold, round eyes stared out from the fringed shawl covering her head.

"There are impostors here tonight." Her right arm raised, her stubby forefinger unfurling from her fist to point directly where Jack stood. "Led by one of our own. Did you think you could slip by me? Did you think I would not feel you near, my Riser?"

A gasp exploded around the chamber. The people standing in front of Jack clambered away to reveal him. He sprang to the floor and stared back at her. Separated by no more than ten paces of open air. Air seeping with poison and hatred.

He wanted her dead. Wanted her body riddled with bullets. Wanted to drive a stake through her heartless chest and mount her head on a pike for all the world to spit on. He wanted to stab her for every second of pain she had ever inflicted on him and watch her crawl around a festering cell like a beast as her mind shredded to madness.

He brushed aside the edge of his jacket to reveal his gun. "Hello, you monstrous hag." In an instantaneous move he drew his pistol and took aim.

Her cracked lips formed a misshapen O of pure delight. She took a trembling step toward him.

"Fire!" Washington's shout carried down the tiers like a swift storm, followed by thick clouds of acrid smoke billowing from the second and third tiers. Ivy and Beatrix.

Orange flames licked their way across the stone floor and caught on the gasoline Washington had trickled down the amphitheater steps while the crowd was riveted to the stage drama.

Women screamed and men pushed bodies aside as they rushed toward the exit.

Jack didn't move. Neither did Dragavei.

Her lips stretched up to form a sinister smile. "I've missed you, my Riser."

He curled his finger around the trigger. "I've come to send you to hell."

She flung a handful of powder into the braziers separating them. A wall of blue fire blazed up between them.

Jack fired into it.

No heavy thud followed to announce her fallen body. He'd have to jump through the fire.

He cursed as the heat burned across his face. He might not walk away from such an idiotic move, but he would ensure she didn't either.

One. Two. Thr—

The blaze died. In the snap of a finger, its searing flames dropped to ashes. Standing before him was a man. Dark blond curls skimmed eyes that burned into Jack. Jack's memory worked in a frenzy to stitch the holes together. He knew this man.

"I know you," he said.

The man stared at him without blinking.

The forgotten pieces clicked together.

Snow had covered the mountainside as he trudged away from a castle . . . Which one? Dobryzov? Bran? Poenari! Ivy was with him. And this man.

This man, who had shot him. This man, who spoke to him in a cell. Who injected him with Dust.

"You turned me into the Riser again."

The man's eyes narrowed. "I did."

Ivy's scream echoed across the chamber. "Philip!"

TWENTY-THREE

PHILIP WAS DEAD, TAKEN IN THE FLAMES THAT CONSUMED TALON HEAD-quarters. Or so Ivy had thought. Yet he stood before her now very much alive and wreathed by dying blue flames.

At her shout his head snapped to where she stood on the second tier. His stare was cold and hard, that of a stranger. It felt like a sharp icicle spearing into her heart.

He turned on his heel and fled through a small door. Jack took off after him. Ivy raced down the stone steps and bolted across the floor and through the door that led into a dim corridor with brick walls that shrank in around her.

Sputtering torches were nailed into the brick every few yards and crowded the narrow space with smoke. Skulls were slotted into gaps between the bricks, and bones crunched beneath her feet as she ran. A catacomb of sorts.

Footsteps echoed ahead, urging her onward. Without warning the ground sloped up. Her toe caught on an uneven brick and she pitched forward. She flung out her hand to the wall to steady herself and brushed against a jawbone missing half its teeth. Swallowing her cry of disgust, she ran on.

Far ahead a cool draft spiraled toward her and set the torches to sparking. Embers flicked her arms as she raced by. Wind whistled through an open door. Lungs burning, she flew along the final yards and burst into the crisp night air where a set of wide steps led up to ground level.

Across the one-lane street ahead were rows of tombs hidden beneath the boughs of towering trees. There was no sound, no movement, save the wind rustling the leaves.

Ivy spun to find a Byzantine Revival columbarium flanked by four wings housing funerary urns. Near the columbarium stood a gray-stoned courtyard upon which Jack and Philip squared off.

Ivy ran toward her friend. "Philip!"

Philip took a step back, keeping several yards of distance between them. He was pale and much too thin with dark smudges under his eyes—so similar to the way he looked when they were children starving on the streets.

"H-how are you alive? You died in the Talon fire," she said.

"Did you bother looking for my body?"

"Yes. Washington and I scoured the ashes for any trace of you but found nothing. I was devastated." Tears gathered in her eyes. "We assumed you were caught in the flames and buried underground. How— Why—"

"I should have let myself burn that night. It would have been better. Talon would have flayed me alive if they discovered I was the one who started the fire and set loose the Riser. I couldn't stay. So I ran. The Order was the only place that could protect me from Talon's wrath."

"Y-you started the fire?" Ivy's voice cracked. "Oh, Philip. No. Please, no."

"I'm sorry I hurt you, Ives. You were never supposed to be caught up in this." The hardness of his expression faltered with sadness.

Here was her friend who once helped her carry soggy newspapers from one block to another. Here was the brother who always insisted they were their own family.

"The Order didn't give me a choice after we caught Jack in DC. Not really. They wanted you or him. I gave them the Riser."

Ivy stared, unwilling to accept his words. "No. The Philip I know would never do something so despicable. Especially not to the people he loves."

"I was trying to protect you, Ives. Like I've always done." His stare frosted over. "Until *he* came along."

Stealthy as a shadow, Jack moved to stand next to Ivy. One shoulder and one foot angled forward, he stood in a defensive position.

"You call it protection when you shot me over the side of a cliff?" Jack's voice was low and dark. "You told me in that holding cell that I was nothing more than your enemy, that you had no choice but to take me down."

Ivy gasped. "No! That can't be true. We were attacked and you fell." She looked from one to the other. "Philip, tell him what you told me. That you shot Balaur Tsar's man who ambushed us. He grabbed onto Jack as he fell. Tell him there was nothing you could have done to save your best friend." A sob wrung from her throat. "Tell him!"

"Tell him what, hmm? That he was who the Silver One wanted all along?" Bitterness crackled in Philip's eyes as he pinned them on Jack. "*You* were always the chosen one. At Talon, with the Order, as the Riser."

"I wasn't *chosen* as the Riser." Jack's voice growled with barely controlled fury. "I was beaten, tortured, and drugged into a murdering monster. Do you think that was something I wanted? Betrayed by my best friend and turned into a beast. If you were any kind of friend, you would have shot me dead before giving me over to such a fate."

"Fate. Ah, yes. Tell me, was it fate or simply bad leadership when you abandoned me on the ice of Lake Baikal?"

Jack flinched as if the accusation were a physical blow. "That day will haunt me until I die."

After Baikal all those years ago, Jack had beaten himself up with guilt. The words *failure* and *betrayal* acting as lashes against any hope he had of redemption. He'd chosen to save *her* from plunging into the freezing water instead of chasing after Balaur Tsar, which likely would have resulted in the entire team being blown to kingdom come.

"That night when we rescued you from Balaur, I told you of my deepest agony in being unable to save you from the ice. 'There's nothing more to be said,' you claimed." Jack's voice shook. "Was it all a lie so you could slip closer and stab a knife into my back?"

Philip pressed the heel of his hand to his forehead, as if fighting a pain inside. "You are not the tortured hero you presume to be."

"It was not abandonment, Philip," Ivy said. "It was a situation with no winning choice. Can you not see how Dragavei and the Order have twisted this misunderstood tragedy to their advantage? They have used you."

"The only thing the Silver One has done is open my eyes to the enemy he truly is. Everything bad that has happened is because of him. Everything he touches is destroyed. It's why I had to shoot him before he could destroy us. I had to protect you, Ivy."

"Protect me by shooting my *husband*?" Ivy's insides went cold. "Ten years you lied to me. You saw my grief and pretended to be my friend. How could you lie to my face all this time?"

"It was for your own good! He would have hurt you. That's what he does, but he knew he would have to get me out of the way first. I had no choice but to remove him from you forever." Each word was like brick after brick of reinforcement until all rationality was walled off and paranoia slithered about, whispering fear into his ear. Fear that seethed with anger that he unleashed on Jack with a feral growl. "But you hurt her anyway. Even after you were gone. She got sick—nearly died trying to find your body in the river. Then grief drove her to almost jump from the edge of that same cliff. *I* was the one who was there for her, pulling her back from the pain *you* caused! That's the only reason I remained at Talon, to make certain she was always safe. That the pain didn't take her."

The gun shook in Jack's hand. "There would have been no pain if you hadn't shot me off a cliff."

"I thought the pain you caused would disappear after you were gone, but no. You still managed to cause destruction by turning her into a vicious, vengeful executioner hunting down Order members. With the bounty on her head now, she's worth more dead than alive."

"I turned myself into a huntress. No one else," Ivy said.

"Because of *him!*" Wildness flared in Philip's eyes. "Don't you see how much danger he puts you in? *He* is the enemy. He always has been, but I was too blind to see it at first. My eyes have been opened to the truth. You must see it too. You have to get away from him, Ivy. Now!" He held out his hand, beckoning her to him.

She ignored his plea. "The truth? What are you talking about? Jack would never hurt me—or you."

Jack moved slightly in front of her. "The Dust could have affected him differently somehow than it did me. They must have used it to brainwash him. Balaur Tsar manipulated and twisted his fears until I became the enemy. Until he was driven to hate me. Is that not what they did to you, old friend?" His voice was empty of emotion as he aimed his pistol at Philip.

"I might forgive you if I knew he scrambled your brains, but you were lucid enough to stick me with Dust in that holding cell and set fire to Talon headquarters. And you seem coherent now."

"That's right. I had no qualms giving the Order exactly what they wanted—you. Their precious Riser. They would have killed Ivy otherwise."

"Just as I plan to kill you after you tell me where Dragavei has fled."

"See, Ives? Nothing more than a cold-blooded murderer." Venom hissed in Philip's taunt, as if a mad animal had overtaken him. "The

Silver One will see you again soon. One month, Riser. You have one month."

Ivy grasped her husband's arm. "If he's been brainwashed, he's not in his right mind. Please, Jack. He needs help."

But Jack was past the point of listening. "Why not bring me in yourself and gather the reward? I'll tell you why not. Because you're a coward. A jealous, petty coward still trembling for a scrap of acceptance. Talon won't give it to you, not now, but the Order might. At least until you're no longer of use to them." He tipped the pistol's muzzle down a fraction. "I'm warning you. *Where* is her hideout?"

Philip stood silent.

Jack fired. The bullet hit an inch from Philip's toe, spraying shards of brick onto his shoes.

Ivy dug her fingers into Jack's arm. "Please! He needs help!"

Philip jerked his hand at her, begging her to cross to him. "Come with me, Ives! We can hide, start over. Just you and me. Forget about him."

"You're insane to think I'm letting you anywhere near her." Moving to fully block Ivy, Jack aimed once more for Philip's heart. "Tell me where to find Dragavei."

Philip flicked panicked eyes between her and Jack like a trapped animal. He started to back away, digging in his pocket. "You've been exposed. All the Order members gathered here tonight saw your face, and now they will hunt you, *Riser*. The Silver One will have you one way or another."

Ivy looked at him in horror as air hissed between Jack's teeth. "Son of a—"

Philip threw a grenade at them, spun on his heel, and ran.

Jack whirled and pushed her. They hit the ground, Jack's body pinning her down.

Bam!

In the split second the grenade went off, Ivy held her breath as she waited for the explosion to rip through her body, for metal to slice her skin or fire to consume them. Instead, smoke choked the air and seeped into her lungs, causing a coughing fit.

Jack peeled himself off her and helped her up.

"Are you all right?" He batted the fumes away from their faces.

Unable to speak through the coughing, she nodded.

"Philip!" Roaring with curse after curse, Jack scanned what he could see of the area. "I'll find you! I swear it."

Silence was the only answer.

Ivy staggered away from the courtyard to a small patch of grass across the cobbled lane and slumped against a tree as fresh air eased into her lungs. Anger crackled around her heart like a live wire, hissing and spitting.

Philip had sent Jack to his doom. For ten years he stood beside her as she grieved the loss of her husband and child. He was the one who pulled her back from the brink of eternal destruction. He had helped her smile again, encouraged her to piece back together a semblance of life for herself.

For ten years he had lied to her. Claiming it was for her own good. The anger ignited and exploded through her bones, rending her heart in two. Broken. Shattered.

Jack bent over and riffled through the debris on the ground. His fingers hovered and then picked something up. He stared at it a moment before pocketing it and crossing the street to her. Mouth grim, he squatted and said nothing. No emotion of any kind reflected in his eyes beyond a cool acceptance of the situation.

If only it were that easy for her.

"He was our friend." Her eyes burned with lingering smoke and tears. "He was my family."

"And now he's given himself to the enemy."

"They took his mind from him. That was not the Philip we knew."

Jack grunted. "The Order has a way of wringing out the good in a person so all that's left is blind obedience and hate."

She brushed away a trickling tear, refusing to allow it to drown out the single flicker of hope that remained.

"He was brainwashed. Like you were. Surely he can come back like you did. With time."

Sorrow gleamed in Jack's eyes. Whether it was sorrow at the way she clung to a thread of hope or sorrow at the terrible truth, she could not decipher.

"He might have been brainwashed when he shot me off that cliff, but he was in his right mind when he covered up what he did and let you believe it was an accident. He also knew what he was doing when he injected me with Dust and ordered me to attack Talon agents while he lit the match to cover his tracks. There's no coming back from that. No forgiveness."

Could *she* forgive him?

When she'd had nothing, she still had Philip. Her brother in all the ways that mattered. When they joined Talon, their tiny family had expanded. They'd found a home, people who cared about them, and at long last a place that offered them safety. It was all she had ever wanted. How many times must she endure the utter heartache of losing it all? First her parents, then Jack, and now Philip. Stripped away from her one by one.

"I knew he was still distressed from his imprisonment at Poenari Castle. Franklin calls it a mental struggle similar to soldiers' shell shock." She picked a dried blade of grass from her trouser leg. "Philip had trouble sleeping. Sometimes he would stare off into the distance for long periods of time. His moods could be unpredictable, and I often caught him looking over his shoulder as if he expected a threat to jump out at any second. Even within the safety of headquarters. But I thought he was getting better the last few years—at least, outwardly he seemed to be more in control of himself. After the London mission, the paranoia returned. I saw it and I didn't do anything to help him."

Jack shifted his weight. "He was angry with me that night we freed him from Balaur's dungeon. I told him how sorry I was for leaving him on the ice, begged for forgiveness. I thought he had forgiven me that night. Or at least that we could find a way past it. But looking back, he wasn't acting like himself that night. He was unnaturally still, except for his twitching eyelids and indifference to the cold. Then his abrupt departure to look for firewood . . . At the time I took it as signs of trauma, but now I believe it was more than that. Dragavei and Balaur took his hurt, his feelings about me abandoning him at Lake Baikal, and twisted the pain to hatred. Poisoned words are her specialty. I witnessed it many times."

Ivy placed her hand on his knee. Solid and warm, it was a reassurance that he had been returned to her. All those years she sought it at the breakfast table, where he should have been sitting across from her. At night she would press her body to the blanket and find only coldness. In the silence she would wait to hear his voice.

He had returned to her a hollow thing, carved out and echoing within. She'd poured her memories into him, filling him with their shared pain, sorrow, joy, and love until at last no echo remained.

Did she owe the same allegiance to Philip? After the betrayals and lies, could she find enough goodness to pour back into him? "If he has been warped, perhaps we can undo the damage. It took time, but your mind returned from the darkness. And your captivity was so much longer than the months he suffered."

"No. Philip has chosen the other side. This is not a case where we can simply hang him out to dry as you did me." His words were tight and clipped, the projection of a mind already decided. "He is beyond our reach."

Voices called from the darkness. Ivy and Jack sprang to their feet with pistols in hand. If Order members were already hunting them, they would be sorely mistaken in thinking to capture willing prisoners.

Two shadows rounded a nearby tomb. "Ivy? Jack?"

Jack lowered his pistol at the familiar voice. "We're here."

"There you are." Relief lit Washington's face in the moonlight as he and Beatrix hurried toward them. "We've been searching all over for you."

Ivy cast her gaze east to where the Order's secret door stood hidden behind rows of tombs and trees. They must have chased Philip at least six hundred feet through the tunnels.

"The fire?"

Washington whipped a silk handkerchief from his breast pocket and patted at the sweat slicking his bald head. All he managed to do was smear around the flakes of ash that had landed there. "Contained within the tomb. We managed to slip out with the others. I daresay they've scattered all about without taking any notice of us, but we shouldn't take advantage of their panic and linger. No doubt they will regroup and begin their search for us in earnest."

They moved west along the lane, keeping to the shadows of the towering trees lest any Order members had fled that direction.

Beatrix stared at Jack's back as he walked ahead of her. "Was that Philip I saw before you two disappeared? And why didn't you shoot that old hag? You had the shot."

"The hag will die soon enough. I've a bullet with her name engraved on it." Jack glanced this way and that, alert to nearby danger. "Philip is no longer on our side."

If looks were knives, Beatrix would have sliced him to bloody ribbons. "Then what was the point of this whole night? We had a target and you lost it." She turned on Washington next to her. "Did I not tell you he would be a liability? Part of him is still the loyal monster. That's why he couldn't shoot Dragavei. What makes you think she won't trigger him again into slicing our throats while we sleep?"

Yanking the hairpin from her scarf, Ivy grabbed Beatrix's arm and yanked her around so they were face to face. "I told you what would happen if you didn't keep your trap shut." The tip of the pin glittered with threatening intent.

"If I may." Washington stepped smoothly between them and unlatched Ivy's grip on Beatrix's arm. "Walloping one another in a graveyard—"

"A graveyard is attached to a church," Ivy corrected on impulse. "A cemetery is not."

"Yes, well, fighting among ourselves does us no good wherever we may be. Save the sparring for after the mission." With an intimidating schoolmaster glare at each of them, Washington continued toward the exit.

Beatrix rubbed her arm in silence while managing to write every spiteful thought across her face before she trudged after Washington.

Jack watched Ivy, his expression balanced on a razor's edge between thrill and danger. "You don't always have to defend me, you know. I am who I am, and I've done what I've done. There is no way to change that, just as there is no reason for you to pull out that hairpin every time someone starts whispering. We already have one killer in this marriage. We don't need another."

"As an assassin myself, and a rather good one at that, I take offense at your presumption of what constitutes our marriage." Ivy stuck her pin back into the scarf and retied the ends that had loosened during the chase. The stench of smoke clung to the thin material.

A half smile tilted Jack's lips. He brushed the scarf's ends over her shoulder, grazing her neck with his fingertips. "Fair enough, but maybe we should refrain from punching or stabbing those who are trying to help us."

Helping was a complicated word when it came to Beatrix, just like everything else about her. Even so, Jack had a point. Him and his logic.

"Tonight was nothing more than a ploy to lure me out of hiding," Jack said as they caught up to Washington and Beatrix at a T-shaped intersection. On the other side stood tall black gates that led out of the cemetery. "Dragavei executed her plan well from the moment Josephine Baker sent out those party invitations. In the end she got what she wanted. She got me here to show my face."

Washington dabbed at his forehead before tucking the dirty hankie into his pocket. "There's been a reward on your head for some time."

"Few knew my face before. I always wore a mask of some kind. Now everyone who was here tonight will be able to recognize me. She wants them to hunt me for sport, knowing all the while that I'll be coming for her."

"While you were a large draw, do not forget one vital detail," Washington said. "We now have a one-month deadline until she starts a mass execution."

"And we all know who the executioner is set to be," Beatrix muttered.

Ivy thought back to all the places she'd tracked Order members, wiping out their existence one by one from the ledger of humanity. Too many cities, woods, and underground hideouts to count.

"I've spent the past decade combing the ends of the earth to root out the Order's leader with no luck. How are we supposed to find her again in one month when we haven't a clue where she's holed up?"

"You didn't have this." Jack reached into his pocket and held up a small stick. "Celestine. A mineral found all over the world, but there's only one place where it's carved into a grenade pin."

Ivy took the slim stick that was nearly the size of her little finger and held it in her palm. She rolled it back and forth, catching the moonlight on its delicate blue surface.

"Is this from Philip's smoke bomb? He always had a knack for creative explosions."

Washington leaned close to exam the piece. "Explosions are one thing. This skill is something else entirely. I've never seen the like."

"I would be surprised if you had." Jack stared wearily at the pin as if looking at an opponent he was reluctant to meet again. "It's a skill mastered by one man alone."

Beatrix started toward the gates. "Let's go pay him a call, shall we?"

"It's not that simple. He's deep in the Tatra Mountains of Czechoslovakia, his place nearly inaccessible, and he's not exactly friendly toward strangers. Or acquaintances. Me in particular."

"You tried to kill him, didn't you?" Ivy wrapped her fingers around the pin and safely tucked it in her pocket.

Jack nodded. "On several occasions."

TWENTY-FOUR

HE IS PANTING, PACING LIKE A CAGED ANIMAL. THE SILVER ONE WATCHES from beneath hooded eyes as he kicks over a rack of weapons. She is dispassionate to his rants, for he is little more than a child having caught sight of his favorite toy only for it to be snatched away before his fist could close around it.

"He was there! Right there!" The weakling hurls a box of bullets across the room. Bright gold casings clatter across the floor and roll over the chalked outline of the Square. "I could have ended it all right there!"

Her guards move to collect the scattered bullets, but none dare step across the chalk. The Square is entered only to fight, leaving one victorious and one dead. Only then may the victor leave the Square.

Here in the ancient castle's bailey beats the heart of her arsenal. The metal arm of the Order readying to be called into service. Guns, knives, grenades, and chemical potions to outfit an entire army fill the shelves of the large stone chamber. It was grand once with fluttering flags and shields adorning the towering walls, but always purposed for what is required of its members. Much blood has been spilled here, and if the weakling does not cease his tantrum, his will be added to strengthen the stones.

"I did not order you to end it," she says at last. "My Riser must return here."

"And then my revenge will be had."

The boy does not know what he desires. His pain boils for revenge, but his fool heart cries for acceptance. The conflict that will not allow him to deal the death blow. It is his greatest weakness and one she will use to her advantage to draw her Riser back into the fold.

Without her ultimate weapon the arsenal is inconsequential. He must lead the army, for though she commands the Order, it is only her honed arm of destruction with his massive kill tally that they will follow into battle. And battle is needed for complete purification.

She moves around the Square, the ragged hem of her skirt stirring chalk dust into the air. "My Riser is no doubt tracking us. He will be here before long. Along with his companions."

"You promised you wouldn't hurt her." The boy thinks this concession will somehow absolve him of treachery.

She, however, never gave a promise not to hurt the green-eyed woman. She merely allowed him to believe that the woman was not needed for the Order's purpose. Let him continue twisting the meaning to his own desperate beliefs. She is not inclined to clear up his misunderstanding, for the woman is very much the linchpin to bring the Riser to heel. And heel he must.

She circles the chamber. Chemicals bubble in laboratory tubes, their toxic fumes controlled by cork stoppers and precise measurements. Scientists and guards sort through crates of explosives and guns, assigning them to shelves of like kind.

Purpose floods the room, floods her being as she runs a hand along the cold stone walls. Generations of her people's blood and beliefs are soaked into the very mortar, fortifying the sacred nest against all who would oppose the Order.

Mortar granulates beneath her fingers. The centuries are taking their toll.

Her Riser must be brought to heel. She rubs the decaying dregs of mortar on her skirt before her guards take notice.

The greater good of history and the future depend on him.

TWENTY-FIVE

Vel'ké Hincovo pleso, Czechoslovakia

THIS WAS NOT A PLACE JACK HAD EVER EXPECTED TO RETURN TO. WHAT assassin was foolish enough to return to the scene of his failed mission?

Apparently he was.

The team stood gazing down into the valley. They were hidden behind a rocky outcrop where they'd parked their motorized snow bikes—recently invented by a man named Carl Eliason, according to Ivy, who also made certain he knew Franklin's own prototype beat Eliason's by four years.

A ring of mountains towered all around them, their pointed peaks like sharpened teeth ready to devour the orange blaze of the setting sun. A crystal bowl of water lay before them, the deepest glacial mountain lake in the Tatra Mountains. Frozen most of the year and icy cold during the other days—cold enough to freeze the air in a man's lungs and burn straight into his bones. The loss of feeling in his pinkie toe was testament to that after a harrowing incident four—no, five—years ago when he'd been forced to plunge into the icy depths to avoid a spray of bullets aimed straight at his head.

Andìl Horváth had been a bastard back then, and Jack doubted time had mellowed the old con man.

Dressed in dark trousers tucked into tall leather boots and a black Sherpa-lined coat to keep out the biting temperature, Ivy looked ready for a clandestine trek across the Arctic itself. She stood next to him, the back of her gloved hand grazing his. He liked these small touches she gave him, a brush over the back of his hand, a finger trailed along his shoulders as she walked by, a smoothing of his hair. Simple questions passed between the two of them through touch. He had fumbled at first, ashamed that his touch for so long had meant only death. But as with most things, his wife was persistent, and it wasn't long before he could not resist returning her touch.

He answered her now by spreading his own gloved fingers and locking hers within them, earning a smile from her.

"Legend claims these *plesá*, or lakes," she said, "were created by a powerful being who wished to bring his happiness to the Fairy Queen of the High Tatras after she was captured and locked away by the cruel ruler of the North Sea who wanted her for his wife. Her friend formed these lakes so she might have a way to see her old home through their waters."

"Where did you read that? One of the books in Washington's library?" As soon as the words fell from his lips, they tasted of bitter ash. Ash from a fire he'd caused, leaving Washington's precious library a smoldering ruin.

As was her way, Ivy continued to smile through the pain of memory. "I picked up a book in Prague when we changed trains from Paris. A children's book—" Her smile wavered at the ashes now falling from her own lips. A book for the children they would never have together. With a shake of her head, she forced her brightness back into place. "I find those are the best places to discover a good story. Philip once told me—"

Her expression faltered again, but this time there was no swift recovery to perk her up. Over the past week since they had left Paris, neither of them had mentioned Philip's name, but he had been there, lurking in darkened corners and shifting through the recesses of their minds. It was an unspoken agreement to speak only of Dragavei, the Order, and how to stop them. Every topic seemed to circle around the traitor without ever acknowledging him aloud.

Philip's betrayal was a bullet straight through Jack's heart. A .45 caliber jacketed hollow point that burst open upon impact, its mushroomed lead ripping out his soft parts until there was nothing left but pulpy bits. The hole left nothing. Not forgiveness, not understanding, not even sadness or anger. Merely an emptiness.

Jack knew better than anyone what it was like to be held prisoner against the rationale of his own mind. Philip's rationale had been broken by Jack's abandonment on Lake Baikal, and then his mind was twisted by Dragavei into that of a hideous beast raging hatred. Even that might have been forgiven. It was Philip's knowing what Jack would become, knowing the torture and torment intended for him. The hundreds of cold-blooded murders he would commit. His identity blotted out. The loss of the woman he loved. The child they might have had. Those things he could not forgive.

Parts of him and Ivy had been stolen, never to be reclaimed, and for that Jack welcomed the emptiness; otherwise he would be forced to remember the friend he once had. The friend who stood at his side during the good times and defended his back during the worst.

He glanced down at his wife. Her lovely face was pale and wearied with lines as if she'd drawn into herself to seek solace from the pain.

Squeezing her hand, he turned his attention back to the lake and the timbered building perched onshore.

"Ready for this?"

The troubled lines on her brow smoothed and she cocked her

head to an arrogant angle. "I'm always ready. In fact, I'm looking for a spot of trouble tonight."

"Good thing you've brought me along. I'm bound to stir up quite a bit of trouble."

Worry lines dug back into her brow, furrowing with such sorrow that he nearly called the mission off right then and there.

"You don't have to do this, Jack. We can find another way."

"There is no other way." His vow mocked him. *I will not be that again.* He smoothed his thumb over her brow, the caress pleading for her to trust him. As if her trust alone could hold him back from slipping completely over the edge to what he needed to become.

"He needs to be terrified, and we need answers. The Riser showing up on Andìl Horváth's doorstep is the way to do it."

Beatrix seized that moment to stroll in front of them in her tidy black jacket and boots. "The plan is foolproof. If I were one of Dragavei's goons, you'd better believe I'd jump at the chance to turn him in and claim the reward money."

Ivy summoned a smile that could cut glass. "How comforting your confidence is."

"Huzzah for team morale."

"She's right, you know," Jack said. "I'd fetch a handsome price. Set you up in comfort for the rest of your life."

"Darling husband of mine, don't you know by now that you're all the comfort I will ever need?"

He pulled up the fur-lined hood to cover her head, fitting it around her face until all that peeked out was a pair of green-gray eyes, a very red nose, and lips on the verge of turning blue.

"Some comfort I am. Can't even give you a proper roof without having to watch it collapse."

Her hand smoothed up the rough black material of his jacket—the closest thing they'd been able to find to what he'd worn as a Riser—and stopped over his heart.

"Perhaps we could think about starting a fire now. For comfort." Her fingers splayed over his hidden tattoo—a question—her shivering lips curved into an invitation.

"Ahem." Washington cleared his throat behind them. Bundled from head to toe in the most expensive fur coat they could find in Prague—one that declared him an important man of finance—he looked as out of place as a slingshot at the shooting range.

"If you would be so kind as to contain any infernos until a later time, it would be much appreciated so as not to distract from our true purpose of visiting this godforsaken mountaintop in less than welcoming temperatures."

"Missing your books in front of the hearth already?" Beatrix called as she checked the magazine in her gun. "Oh wait. Those were destroyed in a raging inferno caused by none other than these two."

"Beatrix, if you do not dull that pointed tongue of yours, I will personally hold you under that freezing lake water until you are too numb to speak again." Ignoring her slack-jawed surprise, Washington rubbed his gloved hands together as if to inspire warmth. "Now, are we all ready?"

Four against who knew how many of the roughest sort of criminals gathered west of the Carpathians. Jack had taken far worse odds.

"All set, sir."

The sun had receded behind the jagged mountains, casting a gray shroud by the time they traversed the steep path to the lake and the solitary building squatting on its edge. It was a two-story affair that had been cobbled together by drunkards with whatever materials they found lying about. Hulls of boats, boulders from the mountains, roughly cut wood from a nearby forest, all wattled together and held in place by questionable-looking mortar likely made of more spit and beer than actual cement. Somehow it had withstood the freezing water and bitter wind for more than a century to welcome all manner of miscreants seeking sour beer, loaded dice, marked cards, black-market deals, or a man to kill.

An outlaw's sanctuary. And Andìl Horváth ruled over this slipshod hovel like a king. Considering their last encounter, Jack didn't relish stepping foot inside again.

His team crept down the mountain, ducking behind rocks before they slipped around to the back of the building that protruded over the frozen lake.

"Andìl's office is there." Jack pointed to two large windows taking up the second-story left corner. Yellow light seeped between a gap in the drawn curtains. "It's at the end of a corridor lined with rooms hosting more private affairs. At the end of the hall are the stairs leading down to the main barroom."

"Which appears to be in full swing," Beatrix said as voices and clinking glasses carried through the chinks in the walls. "What happens if Andìl is in his office? He'll run out screaming for help."

"At eleven o'clock every night he makes his rounds in the barroom, collecting debts and rumors, telling lies, and ensuring the kegs are primed to get his customers drunk enough to spill their valuables," Jack said. "What time is it?"

Washington consulted his pocket watch. "Eleven fifty-one."

"We have nine minutes to get into his office and wait. He returns promptly at midnight to continue working on hatching his next evil plan."

"Rather thorough for a miscreant." Washington snapped his watch closed. "Right. You and Ivy climb up and have a little chat with this Angel. Beatrix and I will remain here on watch."

Beatrix brushed past them and peered around the corner of the building. "Don't forget to club him when you're done. Can't have him raising the alarm as you try to shimmy back out the window."

"Believe it or not, this is not my first attempt at breaking and entering." Ivy pulled out a length of rope that she'd secured around her waist. "Though it has been some time, and I'm rather excited about it."

Jack unfolded the prongs of a grappling hook and secured it to one end of the rope. "Stand back." After swinging the hooked end for momentum, he released his hold. It sailed through the air and caught the ledge of the window. A quick tug ensured it was secure.

He climbed up the rope and pressed his ear to the window. All quiet. No shadows moving in the light. The office was empty.

He pulled a slender file from his pocket and wedged it beneath the window, then pried it up until he was able to slip into the room. Ivy clambered in quickly after him, leaving the window slightly open but the curtains drawn should they need a quick escape.

The space was large and crowded with treasures procured from less than fair trading practices or outright theft. A writing desk that once belonged to the tsar of Russia commanded the center of the room, while thick Persian rugs—once used to smother chills creeping across Windsor Castle's floors—muffled their footsteps. Ivy settled herself behind the massive desk and propped her feet on top of it. Jack stood next to the door, out of eyesight for when Andil made his appearance.

Footsteps sounded beyond the closed door.

Wiping his face blank of all expression, Jack bunched his shoulders and dropped his arms straight down, hands curled into fists. The posture was stiff from disuse and as uncomfortable as ill-stretched skin, but one he knew how to mold his body to like a predator sinking its teeth into the hide of its prey. The restricted stance cut any excess from his movements, honing them only to what was needed like sanding grit from a blade. His lungs squeezed out air in shallow spurts. Not even breath was wasted. A Riser wasted nothing.

A key slid into the door's lock. It clicked and the door pushed open.

The thick scent of unwashed men barreled up from the barroom and into the office. Like a two-by-four straight to the face, rotted with pungent knots of sweat and skinned animal clothing. The under-currents of cheap whisky and vodka came after that, quickly followed by the dry ash of cigarettes. The bloated underbelly of it all reeked of desperation and danger.

In walked Andìl Horváth. The dark king lording over his dark kingdom with surprising flair that one might otherwise reserve for the circus. Swarthy as coal and rugged as the mountains, he had wrestled time and place for his own purposes and bore the savage marks across his face. The long, curling black hair of his Roma people was tied back with a purple ribbon that matched his purple waistcoat and trousers. A silver handkerchief was tied around his throat at a jaunty angle with tasseled ends brushing against the open collar of his black shirt.

He paused and stared at Ivy. His surprise was quickly replaced with darkly glittering fascination.

"If you seek a job, there's an empty chamber next door. The last girl died from the pox, but we changed out the mattress."

"Charming offer, but I'm here on another business matter." Ivy leaned back in the leather chair. "Andìl Horváth, I take it?"

"At your service, *zlatko*." Andìl placed one hand over his heart and dipped his head. Gold rings twinkled on his fingers. "May I have the pleasure of knowing who my most beautiful visitor is?"

"A lady is allowed her secrets, and that is one I wish to keep."

"A *lady* does not walk into a place such as this." Andìl's voice was silk cut with a blade.

"I'm a different kind of lady," Ivy said.

"So I observe." Andìl stroked the pointed tip of his mustache. "Business, you say. I only do business with those what can make it worth my while."

"Good thing I can, and much more." A bold smirk stole across Ivy's lips. She'd painted them dark crimson for the meeting, coloring herself with mystery and seduction. A deadly combination that Andìl predictably fell for.

"My attention you have." Reaching back to close the door, he spotted Jack. The man yelped and stumbled backward.

Jack slammed the door and stepped forward.

Andìl glanced at Ivy. "You dare to bring the Riser here?"

"Best not to worry about him," Ivy said from her lounging position. "He's quite harmless unless called upon to act." She paused for dramatic effect. "Is there need for him to act?"

Andìl stopped backing away as his black eyes swept Jack up and down. "He-he is under your command?" Ivy remained silent, allowing Andìl to draw his own conclusions.

Never a man given to emotions, Andìl moved only in currents conducive to his own gain. If he profited from you somehow, he was the most gracious of hosts for as long as it suited him. If there was nothing in it for him, he would offer just as wide a smile while slitting your throat. He'd tried it often enough on Jack and still seemed to harbor a grudge against his escaped opponent.

Andìl approached Jack, circling around his back and stopping at his side. He reached out a hand as if to touch Jack before abruptly pulling back.

"He's cut his hair and managed a shave. He looks almost civilized since the animal I last encountered."

"I prefer him tidy." Ivy crossed her ankles atop the desk. "Lice, you know."

"Ah, but this." Gaining confidence, Andìl gestured to the undone buttons on Jack's jacket. "This looks careless, and we cannot have that. One might think standards are slipping in our weapons handling." He jerked the buttons through the holes.

Distress slashed through Jack's body, cutting off his air supply as the last button was secured beneath his chin. Choking him into submission.

"Do you wish to sit, Riser?" Andil indicated an unoccupied chaise next to a gilded statue of Zeus.

Jack didn't move. Didn't so much as acknowledge the offer. A Riser was never asked. He was commanded. And he certainly did not wish for anything. Nor would he give in to the blood heating in his veins for a fight.

So he waited.

Knowing this full well, Andil smirked and lifted a glass decanter from a shelf lined with amber-filled bottles and glittering glasses. Removing the stopper, he passed the decanter under his nose and inhaled.

"Coconut arrack from Sri Lanka. It is distilled from the sap of unopened coconut palm flowers." He poured a finger's worth into a beveled glass and held it up to the light glowing from a candelabra. Lines of ruby and gold streaked through the liquid. "Some consider it an aphrodisiac when paired with ginger beer." He swallowed the contents in one loud gulp before offering a second glass to Ivy.

"I'm allergic to ginger," she said. "Now that we've gotten that unpleasantness out of the way, on to business."

"Forgive me, lady, but your charm only extends so far past the threshold of my office. In my country it is customary for guests to drink a toast while entertaining their host with stories from the travels that brought them to their host's door. You sweep in here and occupy my desk without honoring such hospitable customs and expect me to sign along whatever dotted line you present without so much as offering me your name."

"My name is of no import."

Andil flashed his full set of white teeth. "A nameless woman who travels into a wolf's den with a beast of her own. My, my. What secrets are you keeping?"

"None that require explanation." Ivy began plucking at the tips of her glove, sliding out each red-nailed finger one by one.

"You have never darkened my door, of that I am certain, but I cannot disguise a sense of familiarity. Has one of my men threatened you before? Perhaps we met in Budapest? I have much business there."

"I'm afraid you haven't had the pleasure of either." She dropped her freed glove in her lap and set to work on the other one.

"Traded your goods on the black market? Smeared your mother's reputation?"

"No."

"Have I shot at you in a dark alley?"

"I would have shot you long before you could have pulled your trigger." Her second hand now free, she smoothed both leather gloves across her lap.

Andil huffed with laughter. "It will come to me."

He poured himself another glass, then settled into a red silk chair in front of his desk and propped his own feet on top. Inches from Ivy's toes. His boots were made of the finest Italian leather with turned-down cuffs that would raise the jealousy of a flamboyant musketeer.

"Very well, my lovely. To business." Sipping his drink, he gestured for her to begin.

Ivy reached into her coat pocket and pulled out the celestine grenade pin and placed it on the desk.

Andil's feet dropped to the floor. He leaned forward, clasping his hands on the desktop. The tips of his mustache quivered. "Where did you get that?"

Ivy's eyebrow slid up sharply like a rapier parrying an uncouth attack.

"I did not hike to this treacherous wasteland to answer boring questions, so *I* will be doing the asking. Where is Helena Dragavei, otherwise known as the Silver One?"

A tremor raced down Jack's spine. That name had caused the most savage of men to tremble and shrink in fear, but not her. He knew the name had been carved into her so deep that the pain of it had deadened her nerves like a fire-hot knife on flesh. He still awoke in chills and sweats, that name twisting like a live wire against his insides. Even now it scraped across his skin, scratching its poison along his veins. He longed to inch closer to Ivy and have her marble coolness brace him against the venom, but he forced himself to remain motionless despite the warfare on his sanity.

"What do you want with her?" Andìl's voice was all silk. All the more dangerous.

"She's stepped in my way. I want her removed."

"What makes you think I know where she is?" His gaze slid to Jack. "More curiously, how is *her* Riser now under your control?"

"As I stated earlier, I do not offer explanations to my secrets."

"But that means you have Dust—"

"Again with the tedious questions. Come now. We're both much too clever to play at avoidance." She flicked the crystal pin across the desk as if it were an irksome fly. "Back to the business at hand."

Andìl caught the crystal and rolled it back and forth beneath his ring-bedecked fingers.

"Clever or not we may be, but the Silver One is much more so. She will not be found unless she wishes it."

"Ah. She hasn't deemed you important enough to know her location, despite your business transactions with her." At his scowl Ivy reached into her other pocket and pulled out a thick stack of bills. She dropped them on the desk. "I'll pay for your information."

"Tempting as it is, no amount of money would cover the cost of what the Silver One would do should she discover I tipped you off." He pocketed the crystal pin. "I need a greater payment. Something that ensures I come out on top."

Ivy stared at him for a moment before replying.

"Fine. Along with the money, I'll give you him." Swinging her legs off the desk, she flicked her gaze at Jack. "He works wonderfully well at ensuring his master remains on top."

"Surely after serving the Silver One for so many years, he could lead you to her."

Ivy sighed. "Alas, his mind has been scrambled and no longer holds memories, merely commands. Otherwise I would have knocked on Dragavei's door long before coming here." She wrinkled her nose as if the fumes from downstairs wafted up through the floorboards.

Wickedness gleamed in Andìl's eyes like oil on dark water. "What makes you think I won't slit your throat right here and now, then hand over the Riser for the reward? Dragavei would pay me thrice what you offer, along with the continued protection of her supporters. I make a move against her, and there won't be a corner of this earth where I can hide from her followers commanded to avenge her."

"We both know you wouldn't make it two steps toward me without a knife in your gut. Want to try? Be my guest." She raised a finger as if to signal her Riser. "As long as I control him, your threats are less than meaningless. They're childish and insipid." She slowly lowered her finger. "Lure Dragavei out from her hole. I kill her and you get the Riser. You could take your place as the new leader of the Order. All those followers belong to you."

Andìl made a dismissive gesture. "What do I want with that draconian regime? My allegiance is to myself alone and what profits me, no matter which side I need to play. Though I will say, the less honorable side pays better."

"Fine. Burn the lot of them. Keep to your own loyalties. Or continue to rake in your dishonorable funds. The choice is yours if only you give me Dragavei."

"And if I don't?"

"You know precisely what will happen. Only this time my Riser will finish the job and remove your head."

Rising, Andìl tugged the silver handkerchief away from his neck to reveal an angry pink scar wrapping all the way around. His dark eyes locked on Jack.

"Remember this, Riser? A chain garrote." He dangled the material over Jack's face. It brushed his eyes, his nose, his mouth, each touch a suffocating nightmare he could not rip away.

Andil chuckled from the other side of the cloth, a sinister recognition of the torment he wielded. Jack held his breath and waited. A Riser always endured.

At last the handkerchief dropped, and Andil, his fun not to be concluded, draped the material around Jack's neck. Jack clamped his back teeth together to maintain his composure, despite his throat spasming as if he were choking.

Andil's eyes shone. "Remember this?" He unbuttoned the top two buttons of his shirt to reveal a round scar above his heart.

"You knew right where to shoot for maximum pain without the kill. Surely you remember this bit of handiwork." He brushed aside a mass of black curls from where his left ear should have been. "Quite the history you've knifed across me, beast. Someday I should like to return the favor."

He let the hair fall back into place, patted it over his missing ear, and looked back to Ivy. "You are very brave to come here tonight and demand the Silver One's whereabouts. There are at least fifty sworn members of the Order downstairs as we speak. Every single one of them knows about the bounty placed on this Riser's head, and every single one of them would sell his departed mother's eyeteeth to collect that bounty. One word from me, and they would tear you limb from limb before allowing you near their precious leader."

"I've faced down enough Order members in my time. That drunken lot poses little threat." Ivy laughed from her seat behind the desk. A sound like brittle ice. "Call them if you like."

"Why spoil our little party by inviting in the boors just now? Let them wait." He strolled across the room to a cabinet filled with trinkets and lifted the lid of a gold box. Pulling out a thin rolled cigarette, he waved it back and forth beneath his nose.

"I knew it would come to me eventually. The reason you are so familiar, and how you knew where to find me. You are the one they call the Maiden."

Ivy's fingers twitched on top of her gloves on the desk. "So I am."

The Maiden? The name burned through Jack as hotly as the handkerchief still looped around his neck. Ivy had told him what she'd become and about the cold ruthlessness her mourning had stoked. Because of him. Never once had she whispered her murderess title. It seemed they were never to escape the monsters they had become.

"You have quite the bounty on your own head, my lady." Clamping the cigarette between his generous teeth, Andìl struck a match. Fire flared and he held it to catch the end of the cigarette. "You've hunted and killed hundreds of Order members—many of them my good customers—over the past decade because of a broken heart, they say. Your husband, was it? How cruelly your enemies taunt you by bestowing the alias Maiden. As if this man never existed. Must have been quite the love affair to tally such a kill list." Dragging in a deep lungful, he held it in for a long moment before puffing out the smoke in a lazy ring.

"True love never dies, but revenge is gratifying," she said.

"And your greatest revenge will be Dragavei."

"There you go proving you're not as dumb as you look."

"It is not wise for you to insult me."

Rising from her seat, Ivy walked around the desk and smiled at him. "Then don't make it so easy." She pulled the cigarette from his lips and dropped it on the Persian rug, then ground it to ash with the toe of her boot.

A knife unleashed itself from Andìl's sleeve. It slid into his hand and pressed against Ivy's throat.

"Do not force me to cut the smile from your pretty face, lady Maiden. It would be a shame for the world to lose such a beauty, but then, perhaps it might not be such a travesty to you if I were to cut deeper. Deep enough for a reunion with your dead husband perhaps?"

A thin sliver of red trickled down her neck.

It took every ounce of control for Jack to remain motionless and not snap the man's neck in a hundred different places.

"Crassness is a mark of the petty." Ivy pushed the tip of the knife away with her finger as her other hand brought her own knife's point to his belly. "Tell me where Dragavei is and I won't gut you like a sour fish."

"I have no intention of helping you, Maiden. The Silver One will pay a king's ransom to finally have the woman who has been hunting down her followers. Payment for you plus him will set me up for three lifetimes."

Andìl moved fast. He was at the window tossing down the grappling hook before Jack could take an uncommanded step forward.

Their way out was gone.

"Who needs a Riser when I will own the world?"

Ivy launched herself at him with the knife. He spun, whipping a silken rope from his jacket and lashing it around her throat.

He yanked the rope and dragged her across the floor. Ivy heaved and clawed at the cord as it cinched tighter, her face turning bright red.

"What will you do now, Riser, when she is incapable of commanding you?"

"Kill you most likely." Jack drew his pistol and shot Andìl's hand. Two fingers blew off. Andìl screamed and the rope fell from his bleeding stub of a hand.

Ivy dropped to all fours and jerked the binding from her neck as she wheezed for air.

Jack charged across the room and grabbed Andìl by the neck, then slammed him against the wall. It was all too easy to slip back into fight mode. His body moved with killing intent, yet his mind fought for compromise. His skin seemed to tighten as if sensing his hesitation to allow it full control. There was no negotiating with a Riser.

Slowly, he squeezed. Muscles strained and blood pounded beneath his fingers. Raw heat charged through Jack, scorching the hesitancy and self-loathing that had kept him in check, kept him from what he was truly capable of.

Ivy grasped his leg as she pulled herself to standing. Face still red and gulping for air, she placed a hand on his arm.

"Jack." So soft, his name was a plea. "We need him alive."

The heat eased back from his fingers, which loosened their grip around Andìl's throat. Jack felt air trickle into the man's lungs. The demons inside Jack hissed at being deprived of their cruelty.

Shouts ricocheted up the stairs, quickly followed by feet pounding closer. Jack cursed. With the clarity of hindsight, he knew the silence of a knife would have been the wiser choice for Andìl instead of alerting the entire bar with a gunshot.

A feral light gleamed in Andìl's bulging eyes.

"You," he rasped, pinning his dark stare on Jack. "*You* are . . . the husband . . . turned master . . . assassin. How perfect." Sick laughter gurgled from his mouth as he worked to draw in more air past the fingers crushing his throat. The sound rankled in Jack's ears like nails, puncturing his hopes of becoming a good man again.

"The Silver One will pay mightily for this turn of events. No doubt she will have a special torment in mind for your murderous wife. I know I would."

Jack's demons rejoiced as their talons tore deeper into his fleeting humanity.

He grabbed the handkerchief from his shoulder and twisted it around Andìl's neck.

"No one hurts my wife. Ever." He yanked the material's ends. Andìl's eyes bugged out farther as he clawed at his throat and gasped.

A ball of gray robes crashed through the door, hurtling into the room. The figure collided into Jack, knocking him off balance.

Two goons flew in on his heels with fists swinging.

The robed man blocked a punch before knocking the first goon out cold. "Just couldn't slip in and out quietly, could you?"

Jack slammed his fist into the second assailant's face. The man's head snapped back as teeth flew from his busted mouth. "Who the devil are you?"

Seizing the distraction, Andìl ripped the handkerchief from his neck and shot out the open door, shouting, "The Riser is here! He's brought the Maiden!"

Jack pointed his gun at the hooded figure. "You cost me my lead."

"Haven't changed much since our Russian days, have you, Jackie boy?" The man threw back his hood to reveal shaggy black hair and a wild beard covering a familiar face. "Always quick to the trigger."

"Victor?" Ivy gasped.

He slung off his robe and tugged his forelock. "The one and only. My *kotyonok* called for backup, and here I present myself in your hour of need. Only I went through the front door."

"I didn't realize Beatrix had contacted you."

"My darling soon-to-be wife and I cannot go more than a few days without speaking or writing. We are both sick with love." Victor hiked an eyebrow at Jack. "Mind lowering that, mate? You're making me nervous."

Jack started for the door as angry voices clamored up the stairs. "I'm going after Andìl."

Victor gripped his shoulder. "Every man down there is gunning for you both. I'll lead. You two follow me this time." Grinning, he slipped out the door.

Voices and gunshots echoed down the corridor. Jack's demons cackled in anticipation.

Do it! Become the Riser.

"Jack?" Ivy clicked off the safety on her pistol. "Ready?"

More scuffling. More gunshots. *Become the monster.*

"I hear the devil's tattoo. Beating over and over in my head."

"You know his drumming, and you have mastered it. It's time to let your demons run." She flashed him a brilliant grin, then tore out the door, calling over her shoulder, "Let's see if you can keep up with me!"

The demons hissed and clawed for release, digging their talons into his mind and begging for control. But their reign was over. It was time Jack took back what was his own. He was a fighter, not a Riser. The inner monsters were a part of him, but from that moment on they would submit to his command. Their hissing flared to a cracking whip. Jack latched on and twisted, leashing them to his will.

He stepped out the door and over fallen bodies as he approached the top of the stairs. On the barroom floor below, Washington and Victor were ringed in by fighters while Ivy slid across the floor on her knees between a charging brute's legs and kicked his feet out from beneath him.

Glancing up, she caught Jack's eye and grinned. "Going to stand there all night or join the fun?"

She was as good and as fast as he remembered. Of course she was. He'd trained her that way.

They'd both been punished long enough, and it was time to do what they did best. Gripping his demons' leash, he shut down the fury in his blood, the worry, and separated himself from the monster. This time he would beat his own tattoo.

He stalked down the steps, eager to join the fray.

TWENTY-SIX

JACK WAS EVEN BETTER THAN SHE REMEMBERED. FASTER. STRONGER. AS if his muscles had been shaved of excess movement and restricted to precise action. Ivy marveled at every single one of those actions.

The last time she bore witness to those stealthy punches and jaw-cracking kicks, her husband had been hell-bent on killing her, an objective now transferred to the forty-odd Order members attacking them with murderous glee.

An all-out battle consumed the barroom with fearsome opponents—pirates, thieves, murderers, black-market dealers, and all manner of lowlifes—all trying to outdo the others to claim the Riser and his Maiden. Chairs sailed like mortars across a battlefield. Tables shattered. Bodies broke.

Ivy ducked, punched, and kicked once her stock of bullets ran dry. The hooligans put up a good fight fueled by copious amounts of some foul-smelling liquor that had them grunting and charging like wild bulls.

She grinned, taunting them forward as life and excitement flooded through her veins, washing away the cobwebs of the past decade. Making his way toward her and tossing men aside left and right, Jack caught her attention. Gone were the drawn pale-ness and the cold stare. In their place burned a bright ferocity—a controlled approach—that pierced her soul. *They* were doing what they did best. Together again. At last.

He plowed over the last man standing between them. His eyes flamed brighter as he looked at her.

"How's that for keeping up with you?"

"Not bad. I've seen you do worse." She hurled a knife into a man choking Victor. "But I've also seen you do better. Not getting rusty, I hope."

"You tell me." Jack grabbed her around the waist and swung. On instinct she flung out her feet and whacked several heads together. She regained her footing, and he gave her cheek a quick kiss before releasing her.

They moved closer to where Victor punched and kicked bodies away from the door, and Washington, sporting a swollen eye, walloped every attacker who got close enough with his briefcase.

"We need to get out of here!" he shouted.

A man with only one arm came at Ivy swinging a black knife. She twisted sideways as he lurched by and slammed the butt of her pistol against his skull.

"I'm not leaving until every last one of these devils has been dispatched."

"I've got something to end them all in one fell swoop. Out the door *now!*"

Ivy whipped her pistol against another assailant in answer. She'd spent a decade hunting down these miscreants, and she wasn't about to let a single one of them escape.

"Not until—"

Jack hooked an arm around her waist and hefted her up. "Now's not the time to be stubborn, love. Out we go."

Carrying her, Jack darted through the hole Washington and Victor made, then through the door and outside. Thick white snowflakes splattered against her face as snow tumbled off the mountaintops.

Washington and Victor ran out after them. Washington heaved his briefcase back inside and slammed the door closed. Jack deposited Ivy unceremoniously on the ground, then grabbed an oar next to an abandoned boat and shoved the solid piece of wood through the handles as men inside threw themselves against the door.

"Run before it blows!" Washington threw out his arms, urging them forward.

Ivy scrambled to her feet and started running up the hill toward the snow bikes, but a faint voice caught her ear.

"Wait for me!"

Beatrix! She raced out from behind the building, her feet skidding across the icy lake.

Victor turned back, horror washing over his face. "*Kotyonok!* Move! Quickly!"

Boom!

A red ball of flame burst through the shack's frame, exploding it like matchsticks. The thunderous noise pelted against the surrounding mountains, causing rocks to shift from their precipices and hurtle into the valley.

Ice cracked, the sound like that of razored whips against glass.

"Victor!" Beatrix screamed.

Illuminated by the inferno, her figure tottered on the breaking ice. Fiery beams from the shack crashed all around her as she flung her arms out to keep her balance.

"Beatrix! Hold on, my darling!"

Victor sprinted toward her, but Jack flew faster. His stride seemed to extend twice the length of a normal man's as he raced across the ice. Ivy's breath froze in her lungs as his feet touched from earth to ice without slowing. How many times would an icy lake threaten to end them?

A mighty snap rang out and the ice split. Great frozen sheets shifted apart and smashed together. Burning timbers fell into the water beneath, hissing and spitting up steam.

Beatrix wobbled and fell, disappearing from view. Jack leaped over the remnants of a charred table and was swallowed into a haze of smoke.

A second later he emerged carrying Beatrix. Jumping the cracked ice and dodging blazing debris, he made his way to them on land. Finally he transferred her safely into Victor's waiting arms at the edge of the lake.

"What were you doing so far out there on the ice? You were supposed to watch the front door." Victor cradled her against his chest and kissed all over her face.

Beatrix managed to look pleased with his attentions while batting his lips away at the same time.

"I saw a man running from behind the building. I thought he was probably the one we were here to interrogate, so I went after him, but he escaped to the other side of the lake on something that looked like a small boat with a sail."

"Iceboating?" Ivy offered. "It's a popular way of transporting cargo, especially around the Baltic Sea area."

"Fascinating as always." Beatrix winced as Victor adjusted his hold on her. "My foot slipped into a crack. I think my ankle is broken."

"If that is your only injury, I shall gladly take it." He kissed her face again despite her protests, then looked to Jack.

"Thank you, mate. It seems your legs are faster than my own, though they flew with the speed of Cupid's wings."

"Yes. Thank you. Jack." Beatrix's jaw shifted as if the words passed like foreigners across her lips.

Orange flames reflected in her eyes as she met Ivy's gaze, and the accusations of betrayer, murderer, and traitor crackled silently between them. After a moment the words crumbled into the past, forgotten.

"Truly."

Jack gave a tight nod as if trying to brush away the gratitude.

Ivy resisted the urge to cup his chin and keep it raised. His goodness deserved to be recognized even if he refused to see it himself.

"Everyone sorted now?" Washington pulled leather gloves from his pocket and slid them onto his hands, wriggling his fingers into place. "We'll take the snow machines around to the other side of the lake where Andil—"

He pointed across the lake. Half a dozen headlights bounced across the ice headed straight for them.

"On second thought, perhaps we fashion a plan B, as I fear retribution fast approaches."

"It's the midnight crowd," Victor said. "They'll be none too happy to find their degenerate hole has been blown sky-high."

"Then we shall not allow them time for their anger to sour upon us. Let us away!"

They ran up the slope to where their snow motorbikes were stashed behind a boulder. Victor carefully balanced Beatrix on the back of his bike while Ivy jumped behind Jack on a second. Washington took the third. The machines roared to life, and they sped off, tires spitting snow and rocks behind them.

As they raced along the worn mountain path leading away from the lake, Ivy twisted her head to look back.

"They're not slowing down!" she shouted over the roaring wind.

"How many?" Jack shouted back, keeping his eyes on the path ahead.

"Four. Two stopped at the fire. Too dark to count riders."

Slowing to allow Washington and Victor the lead, Jack maneuvered their bike around a hairpin curve that was better suited for a goat's sure footing than two rubber tires covered in rusted metal chains.

Low clouds obliterated the moon and stars as specks of more snow swirled off the mountaintops.

Tightening one arm around Jack's waist, Ivy pulled out her pistol and turned her upper body for better aim.

"Keep it steady!"

Aiming at one of the tailing headlights, she fired. Missed. She took aim and fired again. Glass shattered and the light died. Cursing echoed from the dark shape as the bike's engine cut off. He couldn't follow without a light to guide him over the treacherous road.

One down. Three to go.

Shots rang out seconds before bullets showered the ground around their back tire.

"Fire at me? I don't think so." She aimed a few inches below the closest headlight and fired.

The bike's tire burst, and screams faded behind the roar of the remaining two bikes as they raced forward to regain the ground lost by their fallen comrades.

"Go faster!" she yelled.

Jack cocked his head. "What?"

"Faster!" she shouted in his ear.

They crested a ridge overlooking a shallow, flat valley with a dark ribbon twisting at the bottom. A river.

Lights glowed from a long steamboat docked at a single pier. Victor's and Washington's headlights grew smaller as they looped down the rocky road below into the valley, making straight for the river.

"Hold on!" Jack whirled the bike around, skidding to the side of the path and throwing Ivy sideways. Her legs tightened and she latched onto Jack's arm before she was flung off completely.

He tossed a grin over his shoulder. "Told you to hold on."

The first bike soared over the ridge. Ivy shot the front tire.

The bike cartwheeled and tumbled down the side of the mountain just as the second bike sped into view. Jack let them pass before throwing their bike in gear and tailing after them.

The rear rider took a second to realize that the fleeing prey had become the hunter and scrambled to aim his weapon behind him.

"You better get him with the first shot," Jack shouted over the rushing wind. "I don't fancy a bullet in the face."

"You worry about driving." Ivy batted snowflakes from her face before steadying her hand on his shoulder and firing.

The rider jerked and toppled off the bike. The driver swiveled toward the empty air behind him and lost his balance. The bike wobbled and tipped.

Jack zoomed past as the driver cursed, his legs pinned beneath the heavy machine.

Laughter bubbled up inside Ivy until it burst out. Tilting her face to the chill of night, she let the laughter ring out bright and clear with the thrill that only traipsing so close to death could bring. Adrenaline rushed through her veins, pounding in her blood and heating her entire body. Her soul felt untethered from its chains deep inside, finally flung free, bare and alive.

Jack's laughter joined hers. Hesitant and off pitch after being chained for so long to the Riser's inhumanity, it rolled out in great bursts. It was the sweetest sound she had ever heard.

Ivy stowed her pistol, then slipped her arms around her husband and rested her cheek against his back, savoring the rise and fall of each muscle in his back as he breathed. In and out. In and out. Alive. Ivy smiled and hugged him tighter. Alive and together.

At the bottom of the mountain, they followed the trail through the valley to where the steamboat was docked. The ship had three levels with an observation deck on top. Two tall smokestacks belched fumes into the air as the boiler chugged to burn enough coal to move the water beast through the freezing water. Most likely the boat served as a passenger vessel during the summer months when water was easier to travel by than the mountainous terrain. These flat-bottom boats were also ideal for navigating the sometimes-shallow water.

Jack shut off the bike and leaped off. He grabbed Ivy and swung her around.

"You were magnificent, my brilliant girl."

"You weren't so shabby yourself." He released her and she ruffled the snow from his hair, then locked her hands behind his head. "I'd forgotten how thrilling a getaway could be."

He pulled her close until her body brushed lightly against his. "I'd forgotten how thrilling *we* could be."

"Did you see Andil?" Washington's voice called as if through a tunnel. A very hazy tunnel Ivy had no desire to acknowledge. "Up on the mountain—was he one of the riders?" His voice pushed through the haze into her and Jack's moment.

Ivy tore her gaze away from Jack's deeply blue eyes to find Washington standing no more than a foot away from them. She unlocked her hands from around her husband's neck and tugged her jacket back into place.

"I couldn't make out their faces."

"Andil wasn't there," Jack said. "He never chases, only flees. He'll be in another country by now."

Washington's eyes cut to him. "Which country?"

"He mentioned having business in Budapest," Ivy offered. "Perhaps he has contacts there we can question."

Washington marched down the pier toward a rugged man in a long coat. "Captain, we desire transport to Budapest." His switch to Hungarian was as easy as a hot knife slicing a stick of butter.

"It'll cost you." The captain propped back the furry ushanka on his head and scratched his thatch of straw-colored hair. "More passengers I take, the less cargo I pick up on the route. Cargo is my only source of income during winter months."

Washington motioned to Victor, who pulled a leather purse from his jacket pocket and handed it to the captain.

"Fifty gold pieces now. Another fifty when we arrive in Budapest. No questions and no answers, *igen?*"

The captain took the purse and hefted it between his tar-stained hands. "*Igen.*" He nodded and shoved the money in his pocket, then motioned them to his ship. "This way."

Eager to leave their troubles behind should they come calling again, the team hurried aboard and followed the captain up a flight of stairs to the middle deck.

"She doesn't boast as many comforts as during the summer months when we ferry more passengers on holiday, but she's sturdy, and it looks like your lot is used to a bit of roughness." He led them down a long corridor lined with doors.

"Deck below is for chow. Serve yourself when you hear the bell." He pointed to a stairwell in passing. "Up is observation deck. Stay out of the crew areas and stay out of the way." He began pointing at doors. "These two quarters for the ladies. Next three for the gentlemen." He kept walking. "Need anything else, find it yourselves."

"Might you have a doctor onboard, Captain?" Victor asked as he opened Beatrix's door for her. She leaned heavily against him on her good foot. "The lady has a broken ankle."

The captain glanced back without a flicker of emotion. "I'll send ol' Sawbones to you after he finishes cleaning up the galley." With that threat he disappeared around a corner.

The thrill of adventure running through her, Ivy sailed past the door where Victor stood and stopped at the last door.

"This one will suit us fine." She twisted the knob and pushed the door open. Excitement pounded in her blood, making her dizzy as she looked over her shoulder at her husband.

"Coming?"

TWENTY-SEVEN

JACK STEPPED INTO THE ROOM AND CLOSED THE DOOR BEHIND HIM. AS HE leaned against the smooth wood frame, a tremor ran down his throat as he swallowed.

Ivy roamed about the chamber, trailing her small white hand over the thick fur blanket across the foot of the bed and the bureau with a pitcher and washbasin. Outside the round portal window, the clouds shifted and moonlight filtered in, casting the world in shades of silver.

It glowed across Ivy's skin as she crossed to a small table where an oil lamp sat. She struck a match and touched it to the wick. The light bloomed with warmth and melted into recesses the moonlight couldn't touch. Her eyes met his over the burning match as its flame flickered down the slender length of wood. Lazily, she blew it out before turning her back to him to drop it on the table.

The air quickened in his lungs as a new thrill intensified in his blood, heating and spiraling through his veins until standing still was no longer an option—standing apart was no longer an option. He couldn't bear a moment more of not touching her.

He closed the distance in a matter of strides, each step a banishment of the separation, death, loneliness, and loss that had lingered too long between them. He wrapped his arms around her, one around her middle and the other anchoring her shoulders, pulling her back against his chest.

He buried his face in her hair, inhaling the sweet scent of roses and icy cold that clung to the tips of her strawberry-blonde strands. She curved her hands over his, lacing her fingers between his own. His lips skimmed over her smooth cheek, working their way to her neck where the rose scent had settled into the indent of her collarbone. With a ragged sigh, she allowed her head to fall back against his chest, exposing the tender skin of her throat that flushed a satisfying red as her blood responded to his touch.

Turning her face up, she cupped the back of his neck and brought his lips down to meet hers. She felt like fire and ice, freezing and scorching him in equal measure, driving him to the edge of madness. If this was madness, he wished never to return from it.

He clawed at the buttons on her coat, tearing them off. They pinged across the floor, quickly joined by her coat, shed like an unwanted skin. She spun in his arms and offered him the same courtesy, ripping open his coat before flinging it to join hers someplace neither bothered to notice.

The darkened parts of his soul that had lain crippled and forgotten now blazed with life. Yet it wasn't enough. He needed more.

He twisted his hand in her hair with urgency, and she matched his kiss with a ferocity that would fell a weaker man, but Jack had never been that man. He claimed each kiss, each stroke of her hand as a brilliant flame shattered the last of his reserve.

Tearing her mouth from his, she pressed her lips in a fiery trail down his throat as her fingers made quick work of undoing the buttons on his shirt. Cold air rushed against his exposed skin but was instantly banished by her warm breath fanning across his chest, caressing the patchwork of scars and burns branded into his body. Scars that had known only pain and hatred. Beneath her hands they became like smoke, still visible but only as a reminder of what had once burned in agony.

He captured her mouth once more, desperate to sear her as she did him. He wanted to make the world stop spinning. To draw her into the moment where only they existed. To carve his name into her skin with the longing in his fingertips. He wanted to pull her over the edge and let their bodies fall into the inferno, fire springing into their bones.

He broke away for an agonizing moment to slip off her outer garments and underthings before pulling her tightly to him.

The necklace holding their wedding rings, warmed from her body, pressed between them. Their breaths shuddered into each other; their gazes locked as if to look away meant being lost forever. He wanted desperately to cast his starving gaze over her, to drink in the bounty that had so long been denied him, but he needed touch more. Her full body pressed against his cried out to him. *Mine. Yours.*

He hoisted her in his arms and carried her to the bed, then stretched them out over the fur throw. His heart pounded as the lamplight flickered across her bare shoulders, dipping into the hollows as if begging him to explore. And explore he had, hundreds of times, but it had been so long since they'd seized those timeless hours of mutual passion and possession.

Hesitation stole in as she stared up at him through long lashes. He feared they might move as strangers, but he knew her. Knew her as his own.

"Jack," she whispered. A single name spun in quivering threads of longing, questions, impatience, and surrender. She rose up and kissed him, molding her lips to his as her eyes fluttered closed.

"Don't close your eyes," he murmured, shaking off the constraints of shyness and giving himself over to the intimacy of their union. "I want you to watch me come undone. I want you to see what you do to me."

★★★

"You didn't tell me you had an alias. Maiden," Jack said as he lay on his back.

Ivy lay next to him, curled on her side, her head propped on her hand as contentment washed through her. "We've had much to relearn about each other over the past couple of months, and I didn't want to burden you with all the brash antics of my old assignments."

His brows rose. "'Brash antics'? Closer to 'nefariously thorough' from what you've told me, yet you've never mentioned the Maiden."

"My enemies chose to mock my heartache with that title. I would have preferred something more dashing like Lady Death or Queen of Revenge, but I was never consulted in the matter."

"Guess that's something we'll need to amend since you're no longer a widow and certainly no maiden. That and your appetite. You need to eat more." His hand skimmed over her side, lingering over her bare hip. "Fill out these curves."

"Trekking across the globe and scrounging for food while on assignment for years on end is not conducive to maintaining a womanly frame," she said, reaching for the last slice of stale bread. Jack had braved the cold air and left their room in search of food from the galley when they found themselves rather famished some time ago.

She smiled with fulfillment, their other ravenous appetites having been satiated. Momentarily.

"Besides, curves are out and straight flat lines are *haute de rigueur* according to *Harper's Bazaar*."

"I don't know who this Harper person is, but he's gone out of his right mind. No man wants to hold a toothpick." He winked and playfully pinched her where a good amount of roundness remained.

She stifled a squeal and pretended to scoot away, but he hooked a hand over her and drew her closer. The fur tickled her stomach as she glided back to the sanctuary of his warmth.

Relaxation flooded every part of her. Her skin hummed in tiny ripples like those of still water after a stone breaks its surface. Her muscles and bones stretched loose. Her blood glided smoothly, thick as honey through her veins, replete in her languorous state. She had thought—and had thought about it a great deal—that their first reunion of intimacy would be shy and awkward as they fumbled to relearn each other. Thinking always got in the way. Without the interference of an analyzing mind, her body knew him. Knew his touch, his breath, his wordless seeking, and answered in a language all their own.

The ship rocked gently to the rhythm of the river as the winter wind rolled down the surrounding mountains and blew across the water. Lamplight flickered and swayed with the motion, loosening shadows against the wall in dull golds and softened blacks.

Ivy furrowed her fingers through the bear's thick pelt beneath them until she brushed against Jack's chest. She traced the ring tattoo, one circle interlocking the other, earning a slight shiver from him. Pleased with the result of her touch, she trailed her fingers upward to tangle in the dark brown hair curling over his pale skin.

A memory curled her lips. Dark brown inside amid the quiet dimness, but a gleaming auburn in sunlight. Her hand curved left and glided over his shoulder and down the length of his arm. Hard muscles flexed beneath her palm.

He had always been fit, but before, his body had displayed the graceful muscularity of a stalking tiger. Heavy but fluid. The passing years had bunched those lean lines into hard-packed solidness, grinding softness between the bones until not an inch was given over to waste.

Her hand scooped around to his firm backside. Not an ounce of softness to pinch, much to her dismay.

"The same could be said of you. Nothing but skin and bones."

"Could a man of mere skin and bones do this to you?" In one swift movement he rolled on top of her, pinning her flat.

She tried to laugh, but it came out as a grunt. "Get off!"

"That's not what you were saying earlier." He settled more comfortably with his full weight sinking down on her. And it was a great deal of weight. Dense muscle. Long bones. Taut skin. And one thick cranium. "In fact, I distinctly remember you using all manner of limbs to hold me right as I am now."

"I was a drowning woman needing the whole of you as my soul's salvation. Right now you're more of a sinking stone."

He propped himself up on his elbows, elevating the brunt of his weight from her. A lock of reddish-brown hair fell rakishly across his forehead.

"Sinking to the depths of love."

"You are impossible." Laughing, she shoved him off and immediately regretted the rash act as cold air lashed against her exposed skin. "No, wait!" She scrambled to pull him close again. "Come back or I'll freeze to death."

"Drowning. Freezing. Sinking. Make up your mind, woman. Here, wait before you yank my arm out of its socket." Gently, he turned her away from him and curled his body around her before pulling the edge of the fur blanket over them. "Better?"

"Much." She wriggled into him as closely as she could and sank into the perfect fit of their nested bodies. His warmth unfurled along her skin and seeped into her core like a soothing current that drew her into its drowsy depths. Her eyelids grew heavy, the weight of her lashes seeming too much to bear. The light of the room grew dimmer, like a candle drawn behind a curtain.

Some moments later that seemed to have escaped the passing of time, Jack's arm tightened around her as his voice rumbled in her ear.

"It is love, isn't it. After all this time?"

She felt for his hand and brought it to rest over her heart. "It's that and more. It's freedom."

He softly kissed her neck, then his breathing grew lighter and then even with the surrender to sleep. Ivy smiled and gave herself over to the gentle pull of slumber, safe and content at last in her husband's arms.

★★★

At some point in the night Jack stirred. The lamp had burned out. Beyond their window the clouds had shifted, allowing moonlight to pour through the window, bathing the chamber in quiet blue.

Ivy must have felt him move. She turned to him and brushed her fingers over the pulse in his neck. A wordless question. In answer he pulled her to him and made love to her with an unspeaking tenderness that left them lying peacefully satisfied, again in possession of all they had lost. He was afraid to move, afraid to shatter the perfection between them as each twitch of her muscles and the in and out of her breaths registered in his awareness.

He hadn't lain this still in a long time. His body was rusty to the pleasure of deep sleep, his mind too accustomed to anticipating the next threat, his ear always cocked to the door. A gun lay beneath his pillow even now.

But she gave him rest.

A curled lock of hair rested on her smooth cheek. He picked it up and gently rubbed its silkiness between his fingers. He remembered when it fell nearly to her waist in long gold-and-strawberry waves that she would twist into intricate knots to keep out of her face during target practice. No thanks to this Harper Bazaar person, she had lopped it off to fall above her shoulders, meeting the newest fashion craze. He tucked the lock behind her ear and drifted his fingers into the finer hairs along the nape of her neck. Long hair or short, she would always be beautiful.

"What are you doing?" Her long black lashes fluttered open to reveal catlike eyes staring up at him. Customarily a greenish gray like winter settling over a field, now they were painted with smoke in the moonlight.

"Memorizing you." His fingers trailed along her jaw. "Filling in the blanks of my mind where you were stolen from me. Adding to what I thought I remembered but can now see so vividly."

"Have I changed that much?" she whispered.

"I can't name what I felt when I touched you." His eyes traveled over her, finding an echo of yearning. He had roamed freely over the planes and valleys and contours of her body in a rediscovery of terrain he had once navigated with ease. She still giggled at the ticklish spot on her rib cage, and three freckles formed a nearly perfect Orion's Belt on top of her thigh, but a strangeness now marked her in the shapes of furrowed scars and webbed-over indentations.

"It's like coming home again after an absence of far too long. The familiar is all around me, comforting and safe. But there are changes too. Small differences to mark the passing of time. The losses endured." His hand covered the jagged scar below her belly. The mark of their lost child.

Her fingers brushed over his, a brief touch as if she were afraid of lingering too long. She swung her legs off the bed and grabbed his discarded shirt, slipping it on before padding barefoot across the floor to stand at the porthole. Gilded in blue and silver, she seemed carved from marble.

"The day I didn't die with you was my biggest failure."

"If you'd died that day, you wouldn't be here to save me."

"We saved each other."

"No, not *saved*. That's too trite a word." He climbed out of bed and pulled on his trousers. Crossing the room, he stopped behind her and rested his hands on her shoulders. "What was it you said earlier? Freeing? We freed each other."

Turning, she wrapped her arms around his waist and rested her cheek against his chest.

"'To greatest heights or lowest depths, I'd go to be with you.'"

Jack held her close, savoring everything she was to him.

"'And I swear by all the stars I'll be forever true. All that I ask of you is love.'"

They hummed the melody of their song in the chilled air around them, swaying to a single heartbeat, the stars their only witnesses to freedom.

TWENTY-EIGHT

Ivy THREADED HER NEEDLE AND STARTED ON THE NEXT BUTTON. A GRAND total of ten buttons she had ripped from Jack's coat in her eagerness the previous evening. Not one did she regret.

After a tasteless but filling breakfast of porridge, she had borrowed a sewing kit from one of the ship's crew and begun the tedious yet fulfilling task of mending her husband's clothes. A secret smile crossed her lips as she ran a finger over the last hole. Perhaps she would leave one not mended as a reminder of their night together and the joy of more to come.

Assignments were often grueling and demanded absolute dedication if agents hoped to survive another day, but once in a while a moment came along when cares could be pocketed like pebbles to be tossed across the morrow's river of troubles. For today, she would enjoy the midmorning flush of the watery blue sunlight after the previous evening's snow clouds.

Braving the chill, she had opted for a chair and heavy wool blanket on the ship's observation deck rather than remain confined in the dim room below. Besides, without Jack's company it held little appeal for her. He and Victor had gathered in Washington's room to take inventory of what weapons they had left and what needed to be purchased once they reached Budapest. Beatrix remained resting in bed after the ship's cook and part-time doctor confirmed her broken ankle.

Looping the thread once more, Ivy tied it off and snipped the tails. If she could ignore the chill on her nose, toes, and fingers, and the rocking of the ship, she could almost pretend she was back in the Virginia countryside sitting on the porch swing, blissful in her domesticity. Perhaps someday soon, after she'd killed Dragavei, she and Jack could return there. Rebuild a home of their own with a red front door and lace curtains in the kitchen. Smiling over the patterns she imagined on her dishes, she threaded the needle and began on the next button.

"We have four guns between us and ten blades of varying sizes." Washington's voice was punctuated with each step up the metal stairs to the observation deck. "After we gather money and IDs from the deposit box at the Budapest bank, we'll need to find a weapons dealer."

"I know one near Kossuth Square," Jack said as he followed behind Washington. "He's discreet." Without his coat for an extra layer of warmth, he'd buttoned his shirt all the way to his chin and flipped up the collar to warm his neck. He cut quite the dashing, devil-may-care figure.

Spotting Ivy, he beelined toward her as a grin split his face. He stopped next to her and leaned down to kiss her with a claim of possessiveness.

"Hello, love," he whispered.

Heat stirred all the way to her toes. "Hello to you too," she whispered back.

"Ah, the art of discretion. Important, is it not, Jackie boy? Keeps people from knowing what you've been up to." Cigarette clamped between his teeth, Victor strolled past them and winked with about as much imprudence as a brass band.

"Discretion is key," Washington said as he settled atop a tarp-covered crate. Sunlight shone weakly off his bald head, like the luster worn off a brass doorknob that had been handled too much. His eyes pinned Jack. "How do you know this dealer?"

Jack straightened, keeping his hand on the back of Ivy's chair. "I threatened him once. Before . . ." No further explanation was needed.

Victor propped himself against the rail and puffed his cigarette. Smoke streamed away on the breeze. "While I appreciate your vast list of contacts, the last one you provided didn't end so well. He got away and my fiancée now has a broken ankle."

"This one has wooden legs," Jack said. "He won't get far, but don't insult his cat or his mother. He fit hidden rifles into his legs. I watched him shoot a man who pulled the cat's tail. That was after I burned down his first shop."

"So you'll have fond memories to rehash while we raid his cupboards. Splendid."

Ivy leaned back to see Jack's face. "Would it not be better to do business with a dealer who hasn't met you before? If he recognizes you and knows about the reward, we're asking for trouble."

"There are a few other dealers, but old Zimmerman has the best supplies coming straight in from Germany. You want it, he has it. You think you want it, he has it. You don't know you need it, he has it." As she opened her mouth to argue further, he lightly squeezed her shoulder. "I'll stay hidden while you go inside if that makes the transaction easier."

A relief, but not entirely safe. She turned to Washington. "Why not go to Talon's Hungarian headquarters? They'll no doubt have what we need, and we could certainly use backup. And if Andíl is hiding in town, they'll know where to find him."

Washington shifted atop his crate, pulling the edges of his coat closer as the wind picked up. "No. Talon they may be, but we can't run the risk of having them seize Jack. Like it or not, he's still wanted as a Riser, and Talon agents are obligated to take him into custody. I'd rather avoid all that red tape and paperwork and do this ourselves."

Victor puffed his cigarette. "What would be simpler is for *someone* to suddenly remember where he was held captive for the past decade, allowing us to cut out the middleman altogether."

All eyes drifted to Jack. He bore it all, not flinching from the expectation. "I told you all I remember, and it's not much. There were mountains covered in snow and a cave with water overhead."

"So we're looking for a cave in the mountains near a river or waterfall." Washington's thin lips twisted. "That narrows it down to nearly every eastern European country."

Once more, all eyes shifted to Jack. They hoped as she did to spark a memory or clue that could lead to a precise target. As it stood, they were aiming in the dark.

Crossing his arms, he shrugged. "Sorry. Take it up with the black holes she drilled in my memory."

Ivy extracted herself from the wool blanket and stood. She wriggled her fingers under his elbow where his hand was clamped tight. "It's more than we've had to go on all these years."

He looked at her as if silently arguing against her attempt to wash him free of guilt while simultaneously blaming himself for not being able to offer more. If they were going to stand around arguing about blame, none of them was getting off the hook. Years of working for Talon had left each of their hands grimed with dirt. The best thing to do was press on with what they had.

Washington cleared his throat. "In the meantime we shall continue planning for all eventualities and narrow our search for Andil and his contacts." Ever levelheaded, he was unfazed by the holes in their mission. His confidence had the habit of overriding any difficulty as soon as it presented itself. The man could catch on fire at the breakfast table and calmly request a glass of water with which to put out the flames without setting down the *Washington Post*. Unnerving was what it was.

"'Eventualities.' Such as Philip turning traitor?" Victor tossed his spent cigarette into the choppy water, turned, and leaned his elbows back on the rail. "What's going to happen to him?"

Ivy's hand slipped from Jack's elbow. "What do you mean what will happen to him?" Her voice came out louder and shriller than intended. She clasped her hands together to stem the rising alarm.

"He's one of us. We'll take him home and treat his mental instability. He needs people to care for him and remind him that true friends are not the enemy."

Victor snapped his fingers. "Just like that, eh? Bring him back and all is forgiven. Just like Jack." Victor shrugged apologetically at Jack. "No offense, friend. You know I think you're the bee's jazz, but you did burn down headquarters and bump off a few people."

"Because of Dust!" She was without a doubt loud and shrill. She took a step away from them.

"Philip wasn't on Dust when he betrayed us," Jack said quietly. "Or when he shot me, making me fall off the ledge."

After the shock of seeing Philip alive in Paris and learning of his treachery, Ivy had not dared to breathe his name, though her heart cried for him. For the friend and brother she knew. Not the man who had stared at her husband with a vehemence that struck like poison in her bones. No one in the group had mentioned him, but there he was, just below the surface in their collective mind like a ticking bomb. At some point she knew the bomb would explode, and she would be forced to acknowledge the magnitude of his actions and the destruction he'd wrought. But as long as it was pushed to the corner out of sight, she would ignore it. Ignore the irrevocable changes when all she longed for was a return to what was.

The bomb ticked louder in Ivy's head. "Not Dust, but neither was he in his right mind." *Tick. Tick.* She crossed her arms. A useless gesture to protect against what was coming.

Jack's gaze was cool and dispassionate. *Tick. Tick.* "I intend to see justice served for what he's done. To the fullest extent of Talon's consequences."

Boom!

Not a growled threat or a fervent cry. His words were a calm statement. A fact sharpened to a razor's cold edge that slashed straight across her heart. Talon consequences ran the gamut from reprimand to probation to hanging. A trial by one's fellow agents and then sentencing in accordance with the severity of the crime. Philip would never be released with a simple reprimand.

"Jack, you cannot mean that. Philip is our—"

"Our what? Friend? Comrade in arms? Best man at our wedding? Your generous heart is commendable, my love, but he deserves none of it. He is a traitor, a liar, and a murderer. All unforgivable offenses that I will not allow to be neglected."

"His mind has been warped. If we could only speak with him—"

"We did. At Pére Lachaise. You saw he could not be reasoned with. Do not offer excuses for a traitor simply because you refuse to face the truth." Not one muscle flinched in his face. Not one glint of mercy shone in his eye. It was as if a mask had dropped into place, hardening him from the inside out.

She rushed to reclaim the tender man before the rigidity walled him off. "How do we even know what the truth is when the Order and Dragavei have twisted it to their own benefit?"

"I know what they do. I have lived their hell and become their devil, and now I want nothing more than to end every last one of them. I thought you did too, but now as we stand on the cusp, you waver." The mask cracked. "Do you even know what you want? Last night I thought it was me."

"Of course it's you! It's always been you." From the corner of

311

her eye, she saw Washington motion to Victor. They crept silently away, leaving husband and wife to the privacy of their heartbreaking convictions.

"What do you think I've been doing all these years? Hunting and killing and numbing myself to the pain, all the while wishing I had perished with you over that cliff. But we've been given another chance." She gripped his arm, hard as wood beneath her cold fingers.

The mask fell back into place. "And now you want that second chance for the coward who lied to our faces with friendship only to stab me in the back. He lied to you for ten years, Ivy! He condemned me to torture for ten years. And he did it intentionally." He wrenched his arm from her and slammed his fist against the rail. The metal gave a dull twang.

"Then help me make this right. Please." That day months ago when she'd stood in Washington's Alexandria office and demanded justice played through her mind. He'd told her that people could never bleed enough to fulfill her vision of justice.

How self-righteous she had been then.

But Philip blurred the lines. And Jack knew it.

"My thirst for revenge is stronger than my need to make things right." His eyebrows caved together as if the entire world weighed between them. Their world. "You want so badly to forgive and forget and make everything return to how it used to be that you have deliberately blinded yourself to his guilt."

It was her turn to bang on the rail. "That is not true! I know what he's done, but I also know who he is in his heart of hearts, and that is something I cannot simply turn my back on. As I did not turn my back on you."

"*Trusting in the heart as if it doesn't lie.*" She pushed Beatrix's mocking words aside. They thought her mad, but Ivy couldn't give up on those she loved.

"Dragavei and every minion she commands in the Order deserve death for what they have done—to us and the world. But this is *Philip*. I have to believe that the Philip I've known since we were children must still be in there. And if he is, there is a chance to save him."

"Listen to yourself! 'His heart of hearts,' whatever it may have been, is now stained black. The bond we three shared is broken."

Broken. The word cut sharp and deep. First her family was broken, severed by disease. Then her shelter, taken away when she was expelled from the orphanage to the cold streets of DC. She had stitched herself back together with the threads she found in Philip, and then came Jack and Talon, only to be cut in two when Jack fell from the cliff. Shattered when she lost their child. Then Jack returned and healing began. But now the threads had completely unraveled to reveal her ragged, broken pieces once again. Her cobbled-together family broken again.

One by one she gathered the pieces of herself—pieces Talon had shaped, pieces Philip had protected, pieces Jack had inscribed his name on—her heart clenching tight around them.

"It may be broken, but that does not mean it is beyond saving."

Her heart bled out as sorrow at her disloyalty flickered in her husband's eyes.

"You may believe in his salvation, but I do not. When the time comes, I will do what is necessary."

The wind whipped down from the mountains, scuttling across the river and pelting icy water across Ivy's face. She barely felt it because of the pain splintering inside her, splitting her heart to expose her greatest fear: she couldn't have them both.

Jack had chosen her again and again. Above his own comfort, above the mission, above his own life. He chose to save her that day on Lake Baikal, resulting in Philip's kidnapping. She felt as if they were back there on that frozen surface. As if the ice were cracking beneath her feet all over again.

He stared at her for a long moment, his gaze singular with resolution until the hard blue wavered the tiniest bit. Sadness.

He took her face, one large hand pressed tightly to each of her cheeks, and lowered his forehead to hers until she was swallowed by the blue sadness.

"Do you know what went through my head as I fell?" His voice was rough with emotion as his fingertips dug into her cheekbones.

Words strangled in her throat. "Jack."

"Thank God it's me and not you." He pressed his lips to hers. Quick and hard, bruising her with heartache.

Then he released her, clenched his hands at his sides, and walked away.

TWENTY-NINE

BUDAPEST, HUNGARY

THE DANUBE RIVER CUT THROUGH THE HEART OF HUNGARY'S CAPITAL city, slicing it in two.

Ivy stood on the observation deck buttoned tightly into her wool-lined velvet coat to ward off the frigid morning breeze kicking up from the river and watched as history unfolded itself across the cityscape—the land initially settled by the Celts, the roads cut by the Romans, the baths carved from marble by the Ottomans, and the Renaissance and Baroque architecture topped with Eastern European flair.

There was Buda Castle, where she had taken out an Order member among the precious plants of the royal gardens. That had been not long after the Great War ended. To the left stood St. Stephen's Basilica, where she had taken refuge from a thunderstorm six years after her first visit and discovered the incorruptible right hand of Saint Stephen I of Hungary himself housed in the reliquary. She'd had three Order followers who moonlighted as Parliament members to eliminate on that trip. Perhaps one day she might visit as a tourist.

As the crew bustled around readying to make port, Washington joined her at the rail. "'Danube so blue, so bright and blue, through vale and field you flow so calm.'" He frowned at the muddy water chopping against the side of the ship. "Not quite truthful, those lyrics."

"'The Brown Danube' isn't quite as romantic as 'The Blue Danube,'" she said.

"Romance is nothing but cutting corners to spare someone's feelings."

"An adage that proves why you remain a bachelor."

"And happy to be so." He sighed. "Marie Therese saw to that."

Ivy's eyebrows shot up. Never had she heard him speak a woman's name with a sigh.

"Who is she?"

He didn't reply until she elbowed him twice.

"She was another life ago. Ah, Parliament." He pointed to the Gothic Revival style building with its symmetrical facade and central dome spread along the left bank. "Do you know there is a hidden labyrinth of vaults beneath it? Some scrolls date back to the Romans. One can access it only with one of three existing keys. A key I once held in my possession but which Dolly misplaced some time ago while dusting my office. Fool woman."

"Who has the other two?"

"The Hungarian president and the pope."

As the cool, crisp scent of the mountains faded, the facets of a bustling city took over in billows of industry smoke, automobile exhaust, animal carts driven by country farmers hauling their goods to market, and filthy water slapping against the concrete and brick funneling it into submission. Docks stuck out from the barrier walls with ships and boats of all sizes bobbing next to them. All around were the shouts of commerce, people loading and unloading its abundance in heavy crates and nets with wriggling fish.

Their ship angled toward an empty dock.

Movement scuffled below, and Ivy peered over the rail to see Victor and Beatrix shifting out of the crew's way as they prepared to lower the gangway. Victor fussed over her, trying to get her to sit while she demurred and leaned into him with a coy smile. He immediately stopped fussing.

Ivy's gaze slid farther down the rail and found two blue eyes staring up at her. Her heart clenched. Jack. She offered a small wave to which he politely responded with a tilt of his head.

For four days they'd gone on like that with polite words and movements that undercut the relationship they had worked so hard to reclaim. Philip was not mentioned again, but he was present like an eddy tugging at them from below the surface. Both seemed reluctant to toss the first pebble and break that surface to release the chaos beneath, so they merely circled around warily, waiting.

How could they be so close and stare so deeply into each other yet feel the distance of strangers? No, not strangers. That was too impersonal, and one had the option of walking away. This was very much personal with neither able to walk away. They were too stubborn for that, which turned out to be a rather annoying and fatal flaw in their line of work. Then again, could she love a man who did not stand for his convictions? Flawed and hardheaded certainly, but weak? Definitely not.

Next to her, Washington settled against the rail. "Since I met Jack, he has carried more pain than a thousand deaths could ever bear. Betrayed, tortured, beaten. He has surely trod hell. Yet where darkness once burned, I now see peace in his eyes. But only when he looks at you. *You* are the reason he's still alive."

"I've hurt him terribly."

"Yes, you have. You're also doing what you think is right."

Her heart sped up. "So you agree with me? About Philip?"

"Oh, I didn't say that."

"Then you agree with Jack?"

"I did not say that either." He turned his razor-sharp gaze to her. "My agreement is in the best interest of Talon."

"And what might that be?"

"What it needs to be when the time comes." He glanced away. "I have always tried to guide Talon based on its founding principles of helping those who cannot help themselves. Oftentimes my personal convictions have been at odds with Talon's, but I swore an oath that I do not take lightly. My yoke of leadership is both a privilege and a curse.

"I lead the finest, bravest hearts, yet hearts are not infallible. They crack. They lose courage. They grow weary. It is at these times when my burden is heaviest. Do I watch the heart crack further and break into irretrievable pieces because that is what my oath swore me to? Or do I examine the oath from a new angle? Especially if one of our own is in trouble." He straightened from the rail. "Ah, here we are at last."

With the ship securely docked and the gangway lowered, she, Washington, Jack, Beatrix, and Victor were quickly shuffled off after paying the remaining fee to the captain. They jostled through the teeming wharf lined with merchant stalls and warehouses all serving business from the river.

"I shall go hire a taxi to take us to the dealer's shop," Victor said after leading Beatrix to sit on a crate in the shade of a harbor building bordering the dock area. "I'll return momentarily."

As he walked toward the main street, the crowd thickened around them. Mules hee-hawed as they pulled heavy wagons. Sailors squatted around blazing braziers to keep warm against the chill while mending their nets, and fishmongers called out their day's catch.

Squealing metal sounded above all the noise.

"Watch out!" The warning came seconds before a net hoisting boxed cargo split and its contents plummeted to the ground. The boxes burst open, spewing out black granules.

"Gunpowder! Run!"

"Get those mules out of here!"

"Quick! Sweep away the powder before it reaches the braziers!"

"Douse those fires!"

Commands clashed with shouts as panic overtook the crowd. Mule wagons collided, the drivers whipping their animals to turn away. Dockworkers scrambled to sweep away the gunpowder while merchants knocked them over, fleeing in terror.

"Let's get out of here before we're trampled." Ivy ducked as a tray loaded with pickled herring swung toward her head.

Washington helped Beatrix to her unsteady feet. "Come along, ladies. This is no time to stand around gawking."

"Wait. Where's Jack?" Ivy jumped onto Beatrix's vacated crate and scanned the pandemonium. "Jack!"

Washington yanked on her arm. "Get down from there! We need to leave."

She pulled free of his grasp, searching the throng. "Where's Jack? Jack! I don't see him." A new sort of panic ricocheted through her body.

Victor hurtled around the side of the building and gathered Beatrix in his arms. "This way. Quickly." He frowned up at Ivy. "I thought you were with Jack."

Dread thumped in her heart. "What do you mean?"

"He raced by me a moment ago saying someone had claimed you were swept away by the crowd. He's looking for you in front of the warehouses."

Ivy jumped off the crate and knocked past people. Insults were flung at her back as she raced through the crowd, weaving her way down an alley. She burst into the open on the other side of the dock warehouses where those fleeing had begun to congest the street.

"Ivy!"

Across the street four men hauled Jack toward an idling open-top Sunbeam automobile. They carried him by his arms and legs.

He twisted and jerked against their hold to no avail. The driver ran around the auto and pulled a syringe from his pocket.

Jack's eyes bulged, the veins in his neck throbbing.

"No! No! Do not!"

The needle jabbed into his arm, ripping a cry of torment from him.

Pulling out her Beretta, Ivy fired at the man, clipping his arm as she sprinted toward the car.

The men threw him into the back seat and jumped in on either side to prevent his escape. The auto throttled into motion.

Ivy shot at their tires, the engine, anything to stop them, but her bullets merely pierced the side doors to little effect.

From nowhere, Washington appeared alongside her, firing his own gun. His bullets cracked the front windshield, but the auto sped on.

Jack twisted around in the back seat. Pain contorted his face as he locked eyes with Washington.

"Kill me! You swore!"

Washington stumbled to a halt and took aim. His finger shook over the trigger.

The auto swerved around a corner and disappeared.

Washington fired. The bullet struck the corner of the building where Jack's head had just been.

He grabbed Ivy's elbow as she attempted to race past him and yanked her to a stop. "This . . . is . . . ." He panted for air. "We'll . . . never . . . catch them on . . . foot."

She wrenched away. "Those are Order members! If you think I'm going to stand here while they kidnap my hus—"

He grabbed her by the shoulders. "There's another way. I wanted to avoid it, but we have no choice now."

THIRTY

TALON'S HUNGARIAN HEADQUARTERS WAS LITTLE MORE THAN A SQUAT two-story building painted a sad yellow with smudged windows that gave the appearance of a slumbering bum. The inside fared only slightly better with patched-over bullet holes from the Great War and mismatched furniture that appeared to have escaped eclectic estate sales.

Vajda, the office's head agent, had been surprised to say the least when their ragtag American counterparts knocked on the front door. Being an agent of Talon, he took it in stride and ushered them inside to his office.

"We are at your service, *úr*. I only wish I knew of your arrival sooner, and we might have made better arrangements to meet you." Vajda presented them with a tray of tea and *kakaós csiga*, rolled-up pastries spiraled with chocolate.

They crowded into the small space and squished together on a lumpy couch that appeared to double as Vajda's sleeping area. Beatrix toyed with her deadly hairpin, her broken ankle propped on a cushion on Victor's lap. Ivy sat flicking the safety of her pistol on and off. Washington took a wooden chair near the solitary desk.

He declined the so-called chocolate snails, accepting the offered teacup instead.

"Had I known of our predicament I certainly would have sent word, but you understand this business we're in. Hardly any missions are predictable."

Vajda squeezed his gangly frame behind the wobbly desk, piled high with folders and stacks of paper, and plopped into his chair. "May I ask the details of your mission?"

"No, you may not."

Vajda blinked behind his spectacles. "I see." He pushed aside a stack of folders and rested his elbows on the scarred desktop. "As you are now in Hungary, perhaps it is best if my office takes over. This being our jurisdiction."

"I understand this is your territory, but our mission is of a personal nature." Washington sipped his tea.

Ivy continued flicking the safety. On. Off. On. Off. The man was maddeningly calm, and they needed to get to the point.

"You see, one of our agents has been abducted, and we seek to find and rescue him."

"Abducted by whom?"

"The Order of the Rising Moon."

Vajda's sparse eyebrows shot up into his greasy hairline. "They have been rumbling a great deal of late. Last month two Hungarian Parliament members were assassinated outside their offices. I hear reports every week of government officials killed around the world. The Order is taking them down and quietly refilling the seats with their own members."

"Yes. Their attempts have become desperate, which means they are in a hurry to see the completion of Dragavei's plan. I believe she's been waiting on one vital asset before playing her final move for control." Washington sipped the last of his tea and placed it aside.

"Final piece?"

"My agent."

"What is so important about this agent that makes him the

linchpin of the Order's plan to take over each country worldwide?" Vajda reached for a *kakaós csiga*.

Ivy snapped the safety on. "He's my husband. Is that important enough for you?"

Vajda's fingers slowly retracted, sans pastry. He stared at Ivy for a long minute, processing what this meant for his agency, before turning back to Washington. "What precisely do you need from me?"

"I need to know where Dragavei's secret lair is," Washington said.

Vajda barked with laughter. "Forgive me, but do you not think that if I knew where the Order hides, I would have smoked them out long ago? They are like an army of shadows. Slipping and slithering here and there, nearly impossible to catch. We have tried in vain over the years, but always the Order eludes us."

"Only because we didn't have certain clues before. Now we do. We are looking for a cave high in the mountains near a waterfall or body of water."

Vajda chuckled again before quickly smothering it. "*Úr*, that describes half of Europe."

Washington rumbled under his breath, something about having his own words fed back to him.

"Be that as it may, you know this terrain. Together we might finally pinpoint the location."

"My agents have pored over maps to no avail—"

"They didn't have me." Beatrix fluffed the cushion under her foot.

Vajda tugged at his lopsided tie, clearly unaccustomed to having things demanded of him in his own office.

"Very well. I'll see what we have on hand." He shimmied out from behind his desk and left, softly closing the door behind him.

Washington rounded on his less than impressed crew. "What happened to letting me do the talking?"

Ivy matched his wilting stare. It had intimidated her once. But not today. Today the devil himself wouldn't dare cross her.

"The longer we sit here sipping tea over pleasantries, the less chance we have of rescuing Jack in time."

"The best chance we have of that is through pleasant diplomacy. Insults do not earn cooperation. We cannot fight the Order and Talon foreign offices at the same time."

They waited in charged silence until Vajda returned with an armload of rolled maps. He looked at his desk, then turned to Washington. "Would you mind holding these. *Kérek*." Without waiting for a response, he dumped the maps into Washington's lap then hastily unloaded the folders and stacks of paper onto the floor. He regathered the maps and laid them on the desk with a sweep of his arm.

"All the maps we have, though I do not know what use they will be when my agents have combed everything you see before you."

"That's where my specialty comes in." Beatrix swung her foot down and hopped toward the desk. Washington quickly offered her his chair. After settling herself, she unrolled the first map. "Let's see what we have here. Mountains. Waterfalls." She glided her finger all over eastern Europe. "So many to choose from."

Ivy rose and looked over Beatrix's shoulder. "Yes, but Dragavei doesn't choose at random. She's methodical. Strength, control, legacy. These are important to her. No doubt she will have chosen her prime location to serve the purpose of each. Much as Balaur Tsar chose Poenari Castle for its link to Vlad Dracul."

Victor lit a cigarette from where he continued to lounge on the couch. Smoke purled through his nose. "Then all we have to do is figure out what translates to Dragavei's Dragon Lair."

Beatrix tossed aside the first map and unrolled a second. "Where is your big red X marking the spot, you old hag?" she muttered to herself, lost in her own world of longitude and terrain.

Ivy snagged a *kakaós csiga* and bit into it for clarity. Food was a tremendous help in times of trouble. Fact-bloated lists and pages of history flashed through her mind, pertinent points leaping out and categorizing themselves into a new configuration of possibilities. She turned over each bit of information, examining each of her nails as was her habit when recalling facts. One painted nail equated to one specific mission folder she'd read while lacquering them.

Dragon Lair. Poenari Castle. Vlad Dracul.

Everything rounded back to that bloodthirsty tyrant. What was she missing? She flipped forward in her mental files. Past Poenari. Past Jack's fall. Through the decade hunting Order members. Past finding Jack and the burning of Talon in DC. Past Virginia and the destruction of their house and the invitation that returned them to Talon. That took them to Paris.

Her mind slowed when she reached the Père Lachaise Cemetery, drifting over the tombstones to the secret monument entrance. The stairs descending into the ground. Torches flickered at the edges of her memory, lighting a corridor of crypts with names chiseled into the squares cut along both walls.

Brașov. Constantinople. Austerlitz.

"Here, history buff. Maybe something you can interpret." Beatrix tossed a map over her shoulder. It landed behind Ivy.

She dusted cocoa powder from her fingers, then picked up the map and read its title. Symbols of the Ancient World. It marked cities and locations of great import and near-mythological standing. Rome with a Christian cross for its symbol. The Isle of Ithaca with a longbow symbol. England and Stonehenge. Burgundy and a bolt of cloth. Târgoviște and a crescent moon.

A corridor of crypts with names chiseled into the squares cut along both walls. Brașov. Constantinople. Austerlitz.

"Târgoviște!" she gasped.

Washington frowned at her. "What?"

"Târgoviște. A city in what was then known as the Principality of Wallachia." With shaking fingers, Ivy smoothed out the map on the desk and pointed to the town in Romania with the symbol of a crescent moon curved around it.

"I saw it inscribed on one of the crypts in Père Lachaise. In 1457 the townsfolk were punished by Vlad Dracul for their involvement in the assassination of his brother. The elite were impaled and placed around the city as a warning to all who would cross him. The rest of the townsfolk were enslaved and forced to build Poenari Castle. Afterward they, too, were placed on the spike."

"I dare not doubt your encyclopedic memory, Mrs. Vale"—Victor tapped the side of his head—"but how does an entire impaled town connect to Dragavei?"

"Because it's surrounded by mountains, and look"—Beatrix pointed to another map that showed topography, rivers, and bodies of water—"a waterfall. *Cascada Gaura de Apa.*"

"'Water hole of the waterfall,'" Ivy translated.

"*Cascada Gaura de Apa.*" Vajda crossed himself. "The locals call that place *Striga*, meaning 'to scream.'"

A chill raced down Ivy's spine. "*Strigoi* in Romanian mythology are troubled spirits arisen from the grave who feed on the blood of their victims." If that didn't describe the tormented place of a Riser, nothing did.

Vajda rose from his chair and walked to the door. "You will need agents going there. And weapons. I would guide you myself, but the Parliament assassinations require immediate attention. Come. I'll show you the arsenal."

Being of no use with a broken ankle, Beatrix remained with the maps while Victor, Washington, and Ivy followed Vajda to the basement where the weapons were stored.

At the bottom of the stairs, Ivy slipped in front of Washington, blocking him from entering the arsenal. A single lightbulb bobbed overheard, casting eerie half shadows on his face.

"Did you swear to kill Jack if he was captured?"

"Of course. What kind of leader would I be if I could not allow a man his dignity?"

"And what kind of wife would I be if I didn't kill you if I saw you following through on said dignified promise?"

A smile tipped his lips. "A rather bad one in my estimation." The smile thinned. "He could not become the monster again. He made me swear. For you. I am a man of my word, but when the moment came . . . I could not."

"You're still a man of honor." She glanced over her shoulder at the shelves loaded with guns, bullets, and explosives. "Where we're going, it's a trap."

"Without a doubt." Washington smoothly pulled the pistol from the back of his waistband and checked the clip. "Shall we?"

THIRTY-ONE

Transylvanian Alps, Romania

Oily light spread across the cave's slimy walls. Foul water dripped from the stalactites and splattered onto the rocky floor.

Splat. Splat.

The grogginess from being drugged slowly cleared from Jack's head. He arched against his chair, hating the familiar curve of the planks at his back. The worn seat beneath him with its lip cutting into the back of his thighs. The missing chunks in the armrests where his fingernails had gouged out the wood in spasms of pain. This chair had stood witness to ten years of torment and now insulted him further with reinforced bands to restrain him. Jack could not gain an inch of relief from its cruel embrace.

Nor could he escape the hypnotic stare of the Silver One as it bored unblinking into his soul. How he had tried to scrub her from his mind, but her blackness stained too deep. In her presence it once more oozed to the surface.

Dragavei slowly circled the chamber, taking her time examining him from every angle. Her long skirts dragged behind her over the wet rocky floor like a dead carcass.

"I am pleased to see you again, my Riser." Her voice scraped over his nerves.

Even his head was strapped to the chair by a leather band. Only his eyes could follow her.

"I will *never* become a Riser again. I will put a bullet in my heart first."

Something twitched in her eyes. Surprise. But the she-devil was surprised by nothing. Her fangs were sunk too deep in the marrow of happenings for her to miss the telltale vibrations of coming change.

Unless her Riser defected. He was a weapon and weapons did not speak, did not disagree, and most certainly did not take action without her command.

"What's wrong, you old toad?" Jack smirked. "Don't like it when your weapon talks back? Your lackeys should have Dusted me in the car instead of using a mere sedative, but then, you prefer to watch the humanity drain from my eyes."

The twitch of surprise sharpened. As if to cut through his flesh, muscle, and bone and shred his soul from existence.

"Your present condition is most disconcerting. That will be remedied in time." She resumed her circling. "Odd that you should choose heart over head. Was it that wife who made you feel as if you possessed one again? An organ to pump precious blood, warming you all over, making you feel alive against the oblivion that would otherwise crowd your mind. Is *she* what now flows through your veins to give you hope? Is it *she* who controls the thumping of your heart? Will it take a bullet to silence her siren spell?"

His smirk vanished. "Do not speak of her. You do not deserve to whisper even of her existence with your foul tongue."

"Shall I tell you a secret?" Dragavei leaned close. The smell of decay flooded Jack's nostrils. "She can never fully love you. Do not trick yourself into believing that she could love a monster like you."

The demons inside crowed, pricking him with their lies.

"Shut up, hag."

Her bloated face was inches away. A horror he could not escape as she prodded the fears rooted deep inside him.

"I see the riots within you. The desire to be the man you were before, but there is no going back, no matter the poison *she* drips into your ear to give you hope. Hope is dead."

He tried to twist away, but the leather band cut into his forehead.

"How I have missed you, my Riser. Now that you have returned home, we can finish our work. You will be the blade to cut down all who oppose us."

"You call this a home? This is a place of torture built of nothing more than rocks and dug into the side of a mountain. How great is your cause when you must slither about in hiding, conjuring old prejudices of a sadistic dictator who's been festering in the ground for over four centuries? Do you have nothing better to do with your time, or have the mushrooms addled your witless brain enough that you think you might actually succeed in this endeavor? Wake up, you moldering crone! Your Order is a lost cause."

Straightening, she took a step back. "The duty of the Order of the Rising Moon is too righteous to be lost. *We* are the catalyst to the reformation of decadent civilizations. Our sacred commission is to take a civilization that has reached the pinnacle of depravity and restore the balance by purges."

Her face angled upward as if the glorious purpose were etched on the cave's roof.

"I, as the Order's glorious leader and the only remaining descendant of Vlad Dracul's chosen ones, shall lead the world into a new dawn uncorrupted by man's greed."

"I almost crave the Dust if only to block out your tedious droning, witch." His tone dripped with acid. "You've gotten grayer since I last saw you. Not that you were ever much to look at."

She clutched at the frayed black shawl, tugging it tighter over her frizzing hair. "The nothingness will come in time as it is fated for you, my Riser, but the hour is not yet upon us."

"Waiting for the perfect moment to turn me into your executioner?"

"So you understand. Good." Her eyes glittered. "In a few days' time I will give word to the Order, and on that day my followers will overthrow those in seats of power and bring them to me. You, my Riser, will be at my side, my symbol of power, proof that I control all, including life and the ability to end it. You will execute them one by one on my command. The photographers and newspapers loyal to us will spread the truth, and the world will see once and for all the strength of the Order. No one will dare try to stop me with my Riser at my side. *You* are here. All that remains is for me to give the command, and the purging will begin."

She motioned to someone behind him.

A man in a white lab coat stepped from behind the chair and slipped a leather muzzle around Jack's face, immobilizing his jaw. He heaved against the shackles on his wrists and ankles. The cold metal bit into his skin as the straps held tight.

A needle pricked his arm. He tried to scream.

"There." Dragavei grabbed Jack's hands. Her thick fingers dug between the tiny bones.

"Let it become a part of you once more. Let it bring you within reach of who you are truly meant to be."

The thickness surged in his veins, its heat scorching his blood as it pulsed around the precious memories he had painstakingly gathered.

The day he was sworn into Talon. Fishing in the Potomac River. Slipping a grenade pin on Ivy's finger.

Ivy. The way she rested her head on his shoulder as they danced. He held tight against the pain as the Dust threatened to burn him out. He remembered Ivy laughing from the back of a snow bike. Her hair shining reddish gold across his pillow in dawn's light.

The heat receded, forming rings around the pieces of himself he could not lose. In the shadows the nothingness ebbed like a black tide, waiting to devour him.

"A few more drops and all will be well."

Jack gritted his teeth.

"To give you fully to the Riser now would be most satisfactory, but there is exquisite pleasure in patience. I want them to bear witness to your agony. I want them to see the sacrifices that must be made to correct the world they have helped corrupt."

Unblinking, her colorless eyes stabbed into him in search of a tender spot she could claw. "Will you not ask who our honored guests are to be?"

He refused to give her the satisfaction of an answer.

Deep in his gut, he knew. Ivy would never stop hunting until she found him again. While it was an attribute he most admired about her, it would likely get them all killed. She was walking into a trap where he was the bait.

Dragavei did not smile—the evil in her would not allow such a positive expression—but the hanging folds of skin around her mouth and chin wobbled.

"Your wife is clever and a zealot for lost causes. No doubt she wishes to be reunited with the one who delivered you to me. He is most anxious to see you again." She pulled her hands away.

"Do you remember him?"

Jack remembered the boy he took off the streets and trained to fight. He remembered his ally as they had stood side by side and back to back to take on all opposition. The brother who had guarded his weaknesses, then turned them against him.

The lies might have been forgiven. The broken trust mended in time. But the betrayal had cracked him wide open, carving out the good man he might have been to a hollow shell that refilled with only bitterness and hatred.

The brotherhood was no more.

No amount of begging for forgiveness, for understanding from Ivy would change that. She had no right to ask it of him. Why did she not rally for revenge against the serpent who had lain in wait to strike? Why did she leave him standing alone in retribution for the life they might have known together? For the child they would never hold?

The black tide of nothingness surged forward, eager to blot out the pain. With a mighty effort Jack held it back. He wanted to feel the hatred rushing through him.

"Philip is the reason I have blood on my hands. The reason I never hesitated to pull a trigger. The reason I am damned to a lifetime of nightmares."

"Hold on to that, my Riser. Know him for the *slăbănog* he is." She withdrew a small object from the folds of her shawl and placed it on the table next to his pistol.

A bullet. *His* bullet. The one he had carved Philip's name into.

Jack tore his eyes from it and pinned them on Dragavei.

"You call him weak, yet you still use him."

"To get to you. From the moment I saw you at Dobryzov Castle I knew you to be my Riser, but I knew also that you would not come willingly. So I took what was already in that boy's mind—the fears, the selfishness, the jealousies—and amplified them against you. Until *you* became the evil lurking in his nightmares, and *you* needed to be destroyed for him to live free. I commanded the paranoia that led him to shoot you off that ledge, and you fell into the river that washed you to my feet at the shore."

She gazed at him like a starved hound before the feast. "I was right all along. You are my most magnificent weapon. Together we are fated for terrible and glorious deeds for our Order."

"My fate is to kill Philip, but I'll come for you next. Make no mistake about that." He had not told Ivy the entire truth back on the ship.

It was a burden that might have collapsed her with the hideous strain of its weight, and he would not force that upon her. Philip would face the consequences of his actions, but not those set by Talon. Jack had his own version of justice to be served with a single bullet.

The river rushed over their heads, its pulsing current pounding against the cave's rocky ceiling, drops trickling through the cracks.

Splat. Splat.

Dragavei circled around him. The hem of her skirt dragged wet streaks across the toes of his shoes. Stopping in front of him, her hands lashed out, latching onto his skull. She dug her fingers into the sides of his head and pressed her thumbs to the corners of his eyes.

"You are fated as I tell you, Riser." She released her hold and moved behind him. "Not too much Dust. I want him to believe there's a chance of escape. Then I'll snatch it away while she watches."

Before Jack could tense, the needle pierced his arm once more. A scream ripped from his throat. The thick, white pain flooded his veins, and the nothingness consumed him.

★★★

"Those buffoons circled the wrong location on the map. The city of Târgoviște is not on a mountain," Washington shouted over the rush of water dropping from the mountainside. The spray from the foaming cascade speckled his bald head. "And now I'm completely soaked."

Victor stared up at the majestic falls, impervious to the noise and wetness. "If you were an evil villainess, would you make it easy for hikers to wander into your secret lair?"

Ivy wiped the mist from her face. "Dragavei would know that Jack tried to fill us in on as many details as possible about where to find her. We're lucky he was able to remember a waterfall and cave, because there was no chance of us finding this lair ambling around the Transylvanian Alps without a clue."

"Yes, well, he failed to mention that the secret entrance to this secret lair is hidden behind a waterfall," Washington grumbled.

They'd arrived in Târgoviște a mere two hours ago, spotted the mountains in the distance, and immediately set about finding transportation. Only one local had been willing to give them a ride on the back of his wagon, and he'd forced them off before they came too close. He'd crossed himself then whipped his horse into a frenzy and sped away the moment they were all off.

After trekking the rest of the way and halfway up the indicated mountain, they found the place. The waterfall itself was at least forty meters high, dropping off a ledge straight down into what looked like a shallow pool that spilled over into another drop that landed in a rocky river that cut a path through the woods. Behind the second drop they'd found an opening carved out of the rock, at least twelve feet high and across. Dragavei's entrance.

Standing before it now, Ivy felt a chill race along her spine as she imagined hearing Jack's screams from within.

"You men"—Washington pointed to two of the five agents Vajda had assigned to assist them—"Stay here and keep watch. You three, with us." He glanced down at Ivy and Victor. "Are you ready?"

"I've been ready for ten years." She pulled out her pistol. Inside it awaited the bullet she had carved Dragavei's name into. "Let's go hunting."

No sentries appeared to challenge them as they skirted behind the rushing water. Traps didn't require guards. They would have deterred the very thing Dragavei wanted.

Careful not to slip on the slimy rocks, they found a cleft in the stone with steps chiseled from the mountain itself leading up. The water seemed to roar all around as they climbed. A gunshot would be lost in the noise.

The stairway must have carried them nearly to the top of the mountain where a narrow passage was carved out. Water seeped between cracks in the rocky earth overhead and puddled at their feet, while patches of red rust and green mold streaked the corridor's stone walls, which were lined with kerosene lamps. Cold dampness closed in all around them.

"Love what she's done with the place," Victor muttered.

Washington crept ahead, gun at the ready. "Plotting world domination leaves one time for little else."

Ahead, the pathway split in two. The dank walls seemed to shrink, drawing them deeper into the trap with little hope of escape. Despite the lack of guards, Ivy knew beyond a doubt Dragavei controlled each step the Talon team took. Like a spider yet to reveal herself to the prey trembling on her web.

Brushing her fingers over the handle of her hidden blade, Ivy drew a steadying breath. The trap, the web, not even the spider mattered at that moment. She needed to find Jack.

Washington stopped when they reached the diverging paths. The left continued along another lamp-guided passage, while the right ended a dozen steps ahead at a door.

"Should we flip a coin?"

Ivy moved to the door. "A closed door is used to keep people from seeing something you'd rather they not."

"Or to keep something valuable locked in." Washington pointed at two of the Hungarian agents. "Search the other corridor."

As they scrambled off, Ivy tested the door's handle. Locked. She almost smiled. At least Dragavei had made the effort to provide one obstacle. Ivy pressed her ear to the door. *Splat. Splat.* Drops of water hitting the floor.

A sound echoed from within. A moan.

Jack.

With no lock to pick, she shot off the door handle and pushed inside as the blast echoed, announcing to one and all—if there had been any doubt—that the rescue party had arrived.

The chamber was round, roughly hewn from the mountain's innards. A long table and shelves lined with gleaming metal instruments and containers filled with all manner of liquids and powders took up one side. A tray of spent syringes lay precisely in the middle of the table. More kerosene lamps burned along the walls, clouding the ceiling with smoke that twisted around the jagged stalactites like serpents and casting yellow light against streaks of wet rust, turning them to hues of blood.

Jack was strapped to a chair in the center of the room.

Ivy rushed to him and touched his cheek. Red indentations marred his face as if a muzzle had been strapped on him. She bit back a cry.

"Jack? It's all right. I'm here now."

His head lolled toward her. He was drained of color and warmth with a feverish light glowing in his eyes. A sheen of sweat soaked his hair and shirt. He blinked once. Twice. The clouded fever dissipated as recognition set in.

"Ivy!" He bucked against his restraints. "Get out of here! Now."

"And leave you? Hardly." She unbuckled the strap over his throat.

He heaved in a lungful of air through cracked lips. "It isn't safe."

"You don't say."

"Fool woman!" His gaze skittered to Washington, who knelt to unbuckle the ankle straps while the Hungarian agent stood guard at the door. Victor patrolled the perimeter. "It's a trap. Take her and get out of here before it's too late."

"We know very well it's a trap," Washington replied calmly as if nothing could be more natural.

Except there was nothing natural about it. Her husband was chained like an animal and pumped with an amount of drugs she couldn't fathom, and meanwhile their archvillainess awaited them somewhere in the bowels of this godforsaken place ready to annihilate them. Well, if they were going down, it would be together in a blaze so magnificent it would shame the tedium of a peaceful death.

She undid the straps holding his arms, then raised his hand to her lips. His fingers were ice cold. Any scrap of fear clinging to her shriveled. All that remained was glorious rage.

"We end this today." She put her hand under his elbow. "Can you stand?"

"I'll crawl if I need to." He pushed out of the chair, swayed for a moment, then stood solidly on his own two feet. "Did you come with a plan?"

"We came with weapons and explosives." Washington patted the grenades strapped to his belt. "I thought improvision would be best suited to this situation."

"Weapons aren't difficult to come by here." Jack briefly closed his eyes and squeezed his temples as a flash of pain struck his expression. "Dragavei has an arsenal that would put the Allied army to shame. It's her favored place to hold court. We'll most likely find her there. Waiting."

"This belong to anyone?" Victor pinched a single bullet between his fingers. "Someone took the trouble of carving Philip's name into it."

Jack snatched the bullet from Victor's hand and shoved it in his pocket before grabbing his pistol. He moved toward a door she hadn't noticed. It stood half hidden behind crates serving as shelves lined with bottles of glittering liquid.

"This way."

Ivy caught his elbow. "Jack." She eyed the empty syringes. "How much Dust did they give you?"

He glanced at the syringes. "Too much, but not enough." His shoulders sagged for a second before straightening with purpose.

"She awaits the opportune moment to summon her Riser. A moment that will never come."

After examining the shelves, Victor rammed his shoulder into them. They tipped and crashed, bottles smashing on the ground.

"Whoops."

Jack led them through the second door and along a twisting tunnel howling with wind that bit straight through clothing to the skin. No wonder the creature-woman was murderous. There was no sun here, no warmth, no comfort of any kind. Only rock and smoking lamps and cold.

A hazy light appeared just ahead, bobbing in and out of focus until Ivy realized what it was. Daylight. Or rather, an overcast sky. As she emerged from the tunnel, she shielded her eyes to adjust to the bright gray light and quickly examined their surroundings.

The mountain range curved around them to form a bowl, as if a giant from lore had pressed his thumb into the soaring crags and left an indentation nearly a quarter of a mile long. A small lake pooled at the far end where it seemed to flow out through a crack in the mountain.

Ivy shifted her gaze and gasped. A castle had been built partially into the mountainside. Or what remained of a castle with gaping holes in its walls and roofs caved in. They stood in what was once one of three watchtowers posted at each corner of the ruins. The stones were cut from white limestone, but centuries of age and weather had rotted them gray and black.

She stepped forward, peering over the crumbling edge to the two-hundred-foot drop below. "What is this place?"

"If evil had a name, I was never given a proper introduction." Jack surveyed the ruins through hooded eyes. "I only knew it as Draco."

The uniquely accented word tingled through Ivy's encyclopedic brain. "Dacian for dragon."

Nodding, he pointed to the heart of the castle where a great square structure still held its walls and roof. "The arsenal." He started down a flight of steps that hardly looked capable of holding any amount of weight. "They'll have seen us by now from wherever she has lookouts hidden."

"We shouldn't make it too easy for guards to keep track of us," Washington said.

"I remember . . ." Jack's brow creased in concentration as he scanned the crumbling walls. "I remember a back way. The footing was—*is*—treacherous, but it leads to the back entrance of the arsenal. With any luck, she'll have fewer guards posted there, and we might be able to stage a surprise attack."

It wasn't the worst plan they had concocted off the cuff, but it certainly wasn't the best. Then again, how could they gain the element of surprise in a trap set well in advance? By spontaneity.

Washington turned to Victor. "Victor, take Igor here—"

"Andor, *úr*," the Hungarian agent corrected, expression absent of insult.

"Yes, you then. Find the other Talon agents. Start picking off guards and circle around the arsenal. We'll need eyes on the target should this go south. You have the extra explosives?"

Victor patted the pack strapped to his back. "Never leave home without them."

Victor and Andor split off, and Ivy, Jack, and Washington spiraled down the tower's steps, veering off on the second floor and creeping past chambers that were little more than shells. Jack turned into the last room and motioned them through a crack in the wall to a narrower corridor with a low-hanging ceiling. Gray light filtered through chinks and missing stone.

"Servants' passage," Jack explained as he proceeded. "Watch your step. Most of the floor has fallen through." Gun in one hand, he reached for Ivy's hand with his other. Washington followed at a halting pace as he squinted to make out the next foothold.

Ice crept over her skin as she gripped Jack's hand. How many times had he traversed this path to know the safe stones from those about to give way? Had he gone this way in hopes of escape, only to be dragged back to that awful chair? The questions came like an avalanche, but she could not give them voice. They would have time enough later for her to break down over what her husband had endured. Crying did not serve well while hunting.

Jack paused at the end of the corridor and stretched out his hand. "I think there was a door here." He pressed against the solid darkness. "Aha." A rotting door creaked open. He peered inside before stepping through to another chamber with a pile of dead grass and sticks in the corner that looked like some critter's nest. Hopefully said critter wasn't currently at home. They crossed the room into another main hallway with slitted windows for archers lining one wall.

Washington ran his hand over the chipped stone around the window. "This castle must be well over three hundred years old. These marks are from swords and arrowheads." He fairly jittered with historical delight.

Jack didn't spare a glance as he turned right and kept walking. "Dragavei mentioned the ghosts of her ancestors stalking these halls. How they managed to escape the fiery pit of the next life to come here must surely have been a feat."

Keeping away from the windows lest their shadows be spotted, they moved swiftly down the hall and into a circular corner tower that broke the corridor into another wing. A staircase spiraled up and down.

"I remember these. The tread isn't wide enough for a man's foot—when there are steps—and my heels hung. Odd how the little things return to my memory when I see them again."

"It's known as recognition memory retrieval," Washington said. "The ability to identify something only after seeing it again. In Germany scientists have done a fascinating study on mice and cheese—"

"Astounding, but perhaps another time," Ivy said. "We need to save the free world first."

"Quite right. Lead on, Jack."

Jack started up but stopped suddenly, hand to his head as if in pain. Ivy grasped his elbow. "Are you all right?"

Shaking off his upset, the lingering effects of Dust no doubt, he offered her a brief reassuring smile before climbing once more. "Watch your footing."

An understatement that had Ivy's short legs throbbing as she jumped over missing pieces and nearly cracked her toe when she landed too close to the wall. Jack was there with his hand outstretched to catch her. It was the most natural thing in the world, sliding her hand into his, stalking toward their common target, but this mission filled her with apprehension. What lay at the end of this path was the destruction of the madwoman who had twisted their nightmares for far too long. But also, Philip. And he was where her path diverged from Jack's. She dreaded that confrontation.

Reaching the top of the stairs, Jack pushed on a trapdoor overhead that swung up into the tower's uppermost room. Gun before him, he crept up the last three steps into the space.

Ivy started after him but fell back as the door slammed shut over her head.

But not before she saw Philip's face looking down at her.

"Jack!" She pounded on the door over her head. Locked. "Philip!" She shot at the wood.

Washington grabbed her arm. "Save your bullets. The door has been reinforced with metal. We can't shoot our way through."

"Then we'll find another way."

They scrambled back down the curved stairway to the floor below.

"This corridor should take us to the next corner tower. There should be another staircase we can take up to the next floor and come at Jack from the opposite direction." Washington sprinted ahead of her. "With any luck—"

Crack!

The floor caved, sucking Washington straight down with it.

Ivy threw herself at the edge of the hole and peered down. Debris choked her lungs as she squinted into the darkness below where her mentor lay strewn haphazardly on top of the crumbled stone.

No. No, please, no. "Washington!"

He didn't move.

A dry, rasping sound moved behind her. Like a snake slithering over its shed skin. Ivy spun around, gun ready in one hand, blade in the other.

Dragavei herself stood there quietly. No expression lined her face, yet all the hatred of the world was carved there.

Ivy squeezed the trigger.

Hands clamped around her wrists, jerking them down. The bullet hit the ground, followed by her clattering knife.

"I knew you would come for him." The faintest light glimmered in Dragavei's dead eyes as she looked at the two guards holding Ivy and the four others crowding behind her—all dressed in black with a red dragon encircling a crown stitched on their chests. "Take her."

THIRTY-TWO

COLD RAN THROUGH JACK'S BLOOD AS HE FACED OFF WITH HIS BEST FRIEND turned enemy.

Ivy's shouts were muffled through the trapdoor as her fists pounded uselessly against the reinforced metal. She might try to shoot her way through, but it would be to no success, and she would go look for another way to reach him. It would take time. Good.

Jack needed this moment alone with Philip. No witnesses, no listening ears, no one else's opinions to stand in judgment. Only two broken brothers with confessions to spill. Once the accusations were out, Jack would kill his betrayer.

The tower's circular walls crowded around them. There were only three possible means of escape: the trapdoor, over which Philip stood, and two arched doorways, one leading to the eastern patrol path, built atop the defensive walls, and the other to the northern path. Jack had no need of them. There was no escaping until his target was terminated.

He calmly reached into his pocket and pulled out the smooth cylinder a bit smaller than his thumb. A .45 rimless, straight-walled cartridge with 230 grains that could travel 830 feet per second. A veritable man-killer.

"Do you know what this is?" Jack held his words tight, clipping them at the ends lest his roiling emotions cause them to waver. He pinched the bullet between his forefinger and thumb and held it out for inspection. The copper casing gleamed beautifully.

Gun hanging loosely in his hand, Philip had not moved a muscle since he'd slammed the door shut. He stood as a deer with the scent of blood in its nostrils, muscles tensed for action, breathing in short bursts. His eyes told the truest story. Dark and sharp as arrows ready to pierce Jack's heart. They narrowed, never leaving Jack's face as he answered.

"The bullet you think to end me with, if I had to guess."

The corner of Jack's mouth ticked. "I carved your name into it." He'd done it after Paris, then stitched the cartridge into the back of his collar as a reminder that Philip had stabbed him in the back. Jack had drawn strength from the metal pressed against his neck.

Unfazed, Philip flicked his narrowed gaze to the bullet then back to Jack. "How thoroughly specific of you. As if there was any doubt of revenge."

"Doubt of revenge, no. That's an absolute certainty, but there was plenty of doubt about where to aim my retribution. Or rather, at whom. You saw to that when my veins were poisoned with Dust. Funny thing about being drugged—it not only snatches your life away but also wipes your memories clean. The ones that are left are scrambled until you can no longer piece them into cohesion. It's maddening. To the point you crave death, but death won't come, and you're forced to carry on with the bloody mission. I have one final mission."

He slid Undertaker's magazine and replaced the top bullet with Philip's. He ran his thumb over the crudely carved name, just once, then snapped the magazine back into the gun.

"It is my duty to kill you and incidentally my pleasure. And you know I never miss."

A sneer twisted Philip's face. "Still reeking of arrogance. Perfect

Jack Vale. The excellent marksman. Top agent. Go-to leader. Never met a brick wall he couldn't charm. You always had all the luck in the world."

"The only things I wanted were a home, a woman I loved, and good friends. You took them all from me. Including the good man I might have been. Handed me over like everything between us meant nothing."

The air hung heavy like a weight pressing in on all sides, squeezing out the possibilities of what might have been.

"You think I didn't want those things? That I didn't want to be a good man? That I didn't want to be the hero just once?" The gun shook at Philip's side. The weapon seemed an afterthought, as if his primary need was to get his pent-up words out in the open.

"Heroes don't betray their friends."

"Nor do they abandon them on a frozen lake to be taken by the enemy!" His teeth snapped with ferocity as he took a step forward. "Ten months Balaur Tsar tortured me. Over and over again with the Dust and the pain. I wasn't even good enough for their torture. They wanted you all along. The perfect man to become the perfect weapon. That was when I understood. You were never truly the hero. You're dangerous to everyone around you, and you needed to be stopped. By me."

"Yet it seems like you can't make up your mind about which way to stop me. Death or Dust."

"You're right. Death is the simplest way to get rid of you, only you turned out to be difficult to kill. Not to mention your death at my hand risks the Silver One's wrath. Stopping you with Dust certainly has its appeal, since you'll live out a miserable life." Digging the heel of his hand into his forehead, Philip growled as if fighting against a gnawing pain. "If I hand you over to the Silver One, she'll turn you into the Riser and order you to kill all those world leaders. The rest of the world will know exactly who you are. They'll come for you, demanding your death. Either way, your story will not end happily."

"So you betrayed me out of jealousy, is that it? Your hatred for me must burn deep."

"Because they burned everything good out of me!" Torment blazed in his eyes. Hot as coals from a pain that scorched deep and red. The kind that shredded a man's soul. Jack knew that pain. Had felt it blistering his insides until he turned numb, until bullets and blades meant nothing as they carved his skin. Nothing could break through such unrelenting numbness.

The blackness that lurked among the shadows of his mind hissed in annoyance as it circled around a memory. A memory that refused to be extinguished.

"Ivy doesn't believe that's true," Jack said. "She thinks Dragavei has corroded your mind, that you truly couldn't have meant to do such a despicable thing as lie to her for ten years and let her believe my 'death' was an accident. She believes something worth redeeming can be found in you." His wife had always been more of an optimist than a realist. "I'm inclined to side with you. You're burned out, nothing more than the shell of a pathetic boy who deserves to be put out of his misery."

Philip's grip on his gun tightened. "Leave her out of this."

"I cannot. She is in everything I do. I fight for her. I would die for her again and again and again." Anything required, he would do for her.

"Of course you would. It's the Achilles' heel between the two of you. Unable to leave the other to the detriment of all else." The coals burning in his eyes sizzled under a wet sheen. "Including turning yourself into the monster again. So go ahead and do it. Pull the trigger. Prove what you've become. Be the monster and slay me where I stand, the shadow beast you helped to create. Because that's who you are. Not the hero. The killer."

Killer. The word hit Jack as if he'd fired the bullet into his own chest, creating tremors through his entire body. He clenched his teeth to fend off the tremble threatening his voice.

"I am the beast because I had no choice. Before, I tried to live my life as an honorable man. I killed hundreds to save innocent thousands and loved only one woman. What I am now was through no choosing of my own."

Philip slammed his fist against his chest. "I loved you too! I was your brother, and you weren't there for me. You left me. After you said you would always take care of me." A tear broke free and streaked down his cheek.

"I waited for you. Day after day in that rank cell. Just one more day, I would tell myself, hold on one more day and he'll come. Jack will never leave you here. But you never came, and then one day I stopped telling myself you would." With a ragged breath, he swiped away another tear and leveled his gun at Jack. "Then you came after all, and now here we are."

Jack's finger hovered over the trigger. He had the shot, yet the anger that had poured through him was not quite heavy enough for him to press the trigger. Hatred, malice, spite. These were not the true creators of a murderous beast. Fear was. Fear had broken their brotherhood. Fear would never allow him to be the good man. His finger slid away from the trigger.

Boom!

An explosion ripped the floor out from under them, hurling Jack backward. He slammed onto stone. Noise roared in his ears and his vision spun like a disorienting top. He squeezed his eyes shut and reopened them. His vision leveled out to quickly assess the damage.

The tower's entire floor and the one below had been blown way. Had Ivy and Washington set off a bomb? Coughing from the cloud of dust, he peered over the edge, but there was no sign of them. He pulled himself to his feet and stood from where he had been blown through the eastern doorway.

Across the chasm Philip pushed rocks from his legs and stood, grasping at the wall for support. Red trickled down his arm from a gash.

"Philip!" Jack called.

Hand trembling, Philip raised his gun at Jack. His finger curled around the trigger.

Jack's gun was lost somewhere in the rubble. He braced for the bullet. Philip's hand shook. Clenching his jaw, he bared his teeth and growled with primal rage, then turned and fled down the northern patrol path.

"Philip!" Jack clawed through the debris to find his gun busted beneath a stone. Snapping open the chamber, he pulled out Philip's bullet and took off after him.

Cold hit his face as he entered the part of the castle carved from volcanic rock. Cold and darkness. He brushed his fingertips along the wall as he raced on. Having trod these passageways many times before, he required only the barest light seeping through the arrow-slit windows. Not that daylight lingered long over this place. It was night-time when this hell came alive under the moon's watchful beams.

Feeling for the next turn, Jack sprinted left down a winding stair-case that opened into a small courtyard. His gaze sliced to the square bailey squatting dead center like a throned toad.

The arsenal. He hesitated in the wall's shadow. Mold slicked the stones all around like rotted teeth. Vines slithered through windows. Rancid water trickled somewhere deep in the corridors' bowels.

Yet there was not a single living soul to be seen. The hair prickled along his arms. He could not see them, but they were most definitely watching him. Dust pulsed in his head. He gritted his teeth against it and willed his mind to focus.

Where were Ivy and Washington?

Long past the use of invisibility, he peeled off the wall and ran across the courtyard to the bailey. Black grime filled its cracks as the ancient structure groped three stories high in futile hopes of scaling its surroundings. Here it hunkered in decay and wasted purpose. The doors, splintered with age and sagging on metal hinges, pulled open with one tug. No lock. Any care for stealth disappeared.

"Philip?" he bellowed, marching into the cool hall. "Witch! Where are you?"

Lights flickered on. Not sconces of flaming torches, but electric lights that had been strung from wall to wall with modern efficiency. They buzzed and crackled, throwing their sickly yellow light against the impenetrable stone walls and into the cracks of the flagstone floor. Gone were the great pikes, swords, and shields of yore. In their places stood racks and shelves lined with guns of all makes and sizes, grenades, explosives, mortars, flamethrowers, gas canisters, and every other imaginable weapon man had designed.

In the center of it all was the Square. A chalked-off twenty-by-twenty-foot area on the floor. Nothing touched it and no one walked upon it but for one purpose. Battle. Weapons were forged in a pit buried beneath the bailey, then carried up a wooden staircase to this area to be tested. Two men would be chosen. Only one was allowed to leave alive. Whichever weapon held out the longest earned a spot on the rack. If both men were killed, both weapons were kept.

Jack walked to the chalk line. His toes brushed against the white powder. Even now without the Dust in control, he could not bring himself to cross over. Not again. Not when the stones were stained dark with the blood he had spilled here.

"*Bine ai venit acasa*, my Riser." Slithering up from the pit, Dragavei stood across the Square from him.

"This is not my home." Jack's hand flew to his gun. Or where his gun should have been instead of buried in rubble. He moved to a gun rack.

Dragavei shook a finger at him. "Turn your hand from the weapons."

"You prefer I strangle you with my bare hands? Fine by me."

"Your bravery has always been commendable, but it is overmuch in these circumstances." Waving two fingers over her shoulder, she fastened her eyes on him like hooks as footsteps thudded up the wooden staircase from the pit below. She cackled with glee when her captive emerged.

Ivy. Hands bound and surrounded by four guards.

"Jack!" his wife cried. The guards tightened around her.

Jack instinctually moved toward her, but Dragavei raised her sparse eyebrows in rebuke. "*Nu*, Riser. Have you forgotten so easily the rules of my kingdom?" She flicked a glance to the Square. "None may cross without battle."

"Keep your games. I'm no longer playing." Vengeance burned in his blood. He stepped across the line.

Hissing, Dragavei jerked her head at the guards. Three of them marched forward while the fourth pushed Ivy to her knees and yanked a knife to her throat. She didn't whimper or plead. Her eyes flashed too violently for such weak theatrics. *Let your demons run.*

It was all the encouragement Jack needed.

He charged the attackers, knocking down the middle one with a single punch. He rounded on the next who came at him with a knife. No guns. That would be too quick and unsporting for Dragavei.

Jack ducked, blocking the downward blade with his arm before kicking at the man's kneecap. He dropped. Jack drove his knee upward into the attacker's nose. Blood spurted.

The man cried out and grabbed Jack's foot, slashing at his thigh. The knife came higher, aiming for Jack's stomach. He grabbed the man's hand and twisted until there was a loud pop and the fingers went slack.

Jack snatched the knife and stabbed the attacker's neck. He fell over dead.

The third one was the largest of the bunch. Jack remembered him. He drew pleasure from pain. Even now, a grin smeared across his scarred face in anticipation of drawing blood.

He charged like a bull, hooves flying and horns down with a blade gleaming. Jack sidestepped at the last second and drew his own blade across the bull's side. With surprising agility that belied his size, the bull turned and rammed his shoulder into Jack, throwing him off his feet.

He crashed hard and the bull pounced on his chest, heaving the air from Jack's lungs. Jack drove his knife into the bull's leg. The man roared and reared back, giving Jack enough space to lunge, roll him over, and straddle his chest.

The bull drove his knife between them, but Jack grabbed the handle and forced it around, piercing his opponent's throat.

Dragavei clapped, her fleshy palms slapping together again and again. "As one who claims to deny his killing instinct, you have not lost your touch, Riser." Now standing beside his wife, the creature dropped one hand on top of Ivy's head, twirling a bloated finger through her hair.

"It is dangerous, is it not, to see how far the two of you will go for each other? Dangerous and beautiful."

Ivy tried to jerk away, but the guard's knife held her in place.

Blood, hot and furious, pounded in Jack's ears.

"It's me you want. Let her go."

"She is not innocent. Are you, *Maiden*? *Da*, I know how you have hunted my followers." She hissed in Ivy's ear. "You have both sinned against me. Her torment is the price you must pay for your reckless abandonment. You will never disobey me in that manner again, Riser."

With a vicious yank that snapped Ivy's head back, Dragavei raised her bulbous gaze upward where guards had crowded the catwalk that ran along the second-story perimeter. Her stare fixated on one familiar face.

Philip. "Do you not agree, boy?"

Color drained from Philip's face, making him little more than a pale smear against the backdrop of moldy stone and ring of black uniforms.

"Philip!" Ivy's shout was hoarse from the bent angle of her neck, but her eyes pleaded far louder than her voice ever could. "Help us!"

Jack climbed off the man gurgling to death in his own blood and pinned his attention on Philip.

"Is this not what you wanted?" He spread his arms wide. Blood dripped from the knife in his hand and trickled down his wrist. "Like a coward you distracted me so your cronies could kidnap my wife! The woman you called a sister! You make me sick to the very marrow of my bones. Come down and fight me. Let us end this once and for all. Fight me!"

Philip had the audacity to look dumbfounded by the events unraveling before him, his mouth flopped open with stupidity.

"I would never—Ivy isn't supposed to—" Mining for some sort of latent accountability, he hardened his limp jaw. "Dragavei! You promised she would not be touched if I gave you the Riser."

Ruthless delight glittered in the creature's eyes. She was like a vulture cornering its maimed prey, counting the erratic breaths until she could sink her beak into succulent flesh.

"I changed my mind. Fate binds them together. Where one goes, so, too, does the other. They are each other's heartbeat. Take them apart and the heart ceases to beat." The delight froze to pure ice.

"As my own ceased the day you plunged my beloved Yuri over the cliff at Poenari Castle. I found his body washed up on the rocky river shore below, ice clinging to his skin, his impending mark on the glory of mankind frozen against the tide."

"Should have known you'd fall for a madman like Balaur Tsar. It was pure pleasure watching him fall to his death." A knot bobbed in Ivy's throat as her neck muscles strained against the backward tilt of her head. "If a heart does exist within you, I'll carve out its rottenness with a dull blade."

"Let her go!" Philip rushed down from the catwalk straight toward Dragavei. With a flick of her fingers, two guards snatched Philip and dropped him to his knees next to Ivy. "She wasn't part of the deal."

"You are not a deal worth honoring. Your body is weak and your mind a sieve through which I poured my own truths and purposes. Do not trust your mind, boy, for it belongs to me." Oiled malice seeped through her every word. "I entered the vines of your mind with Dust running through your veins and sheared away the pitiful bond of brotherhood you once held so dear. In its place I planted thorns of hate and revenge, feeding them with the jealousy already rotting in a dark corner."

Philip clutched his head with trembling hands. "No."

"Yes," Dragavei said. "And as I have used you for my purpose, so, too, will I use her as I see fit."

"I'll have your head on a spike before you get the chance," Ivy said.

Under different circumstances Jack would have swelled with pride at her unflinching arrogance. As it was, the only thing that filled him now was seething rage. A rage so hot it burned cold in his veins. He stepped toward Dragavei, making a circling motion with the tip of his blade. Ruby-red droplets fell from the tip and plopped to the floor, then oozed between the cracks.

"You should appreciate the neatness of a circle come fully around with that ending, impalement being the sport of choice for your tyrannical founder."

Dragavei's lip curled. "Tyrannical. The unworthy call him so."

"Tell that to the townsfolk of Târgoviște. Vlad impaled them all in revenge because they murdered his brother, though I'm certain he had it coming."

"Falsehoods from the mouths of those who would vilify us."

"You do a good enough job of vilification on your own. The Order of the Rising Moon is nothing more than a gang of murderers led around by a lunatic draping herself in righteous purpose."

Dragavei laughed then. It was only the second time he'd heard such a screech. The first had been in the halls of Dobryzov Castle right after he shot out Balaur's eye. He didn't care for it the second time around either, with its dry tone pitched to scratch the fine bones of one's inner ear.

"Oh, my Riser. What has this *frumos* deceiver been filling your ear with?" She curled her bloated fingers through Ivy's hair, clawing out hairpins with callous abandon.

"Human sacrifices? Blood drinking? Dragons that breathe smoke? The purpose of our Order was made clear long ago. We wish to purge the world of corruption, an undertaking that began in the town of Târgoviște. That much is true, but Vlad Dracul came not because of his brother's assassination. He came to make an example of them, his own Gomorrah, a stain on the greatness he intended to build in Wallachia before enrobing the entire world under his standard.

"He threw the townsfolk upon sharpened pine stakes, all but two as proof of his mercy. These two became the founding members of the Order, and I am the last living descendant. My ancestors built this very castle within which we now stand. Here we have gathered over the centuries, growing and expanding across time and continents with roots stretching ever deeper into the soil from which we have sprung. We have waited in the shadows as the world waded further into malfeasance, ready to spring forth and temper its evil. Famine, plague, war. All tools of necessity we have used to draw closer to our goal."

Jack took another step forward. The knife molded to his hand, ready for service. "You use catastrophes as smoke screens. Men were cut down like stalks of wheat in bloody no-man's-land during the Great War, while you hosted bidding wars on weapons that could annihilate country borders."

"That war should have ushered in a new era for our Order. While countries and kings squabbled over scraps of land, we were to cleanse the entire world with White Wolves and an army of Risers and begin again with only our brotherhood. Until you came along and destroyed everything we had worked toward."

Dragavei yanked Ivy's hair. Strands of reddish gold dangled from her fingers.

"Like any good leader, I was forced to adjust. Instead of an army, I fashioned you into a single killer striking to inflict the most damage and allow Order members to slip into the newly vacated seats of power. Now they await my order for the final act. When the stars align tomorrow night, world leaders will be dragged before me and executed by you, my symbol of ultimate power. My Riser."

Jack started forward, the knife an extension of his arm. "I'll see you in hell first."

"Not if I take her first." Feral triumph gleamed in the hag's eyes as she raked her fingers over Ivy's head and down her face to curl around her neck, pushing the guard's knife away from her throat. Her other hand brought out a milky white syringe from her skirts.

The needle's tip gleamed a dull silver. "Shall we see what Dust does to her? Turn her into the thing she hated most of all while hunting down my followers as the Maiden? If she survives at all. Or perhaps it should be the one you once called friend." She moved the needle to Philip's neck. "Take revenge for what he did to you. Make *him* the Riser, hmm? Make your choice."

Memories of ice flashed. It was Lake Baikal all over again. He had made a choice then, and it had cost him everything—had cost all three of them everything. Only the heartless coldness of a Riser could doom anyone to such a fate, and Jack swore he would never be that again.

Looking into Philip's eyes, he saw the same fear that had been present the day Jack found him on the street as a kid. A scrawny orphan who had looked up to him and grown to be closer than a brother through late-night sparring lessons. The brother who had Jack's back in every back-alley fight and stood as his best man. The reckless brother who had risked his life to save Jack and Ivy when they were nearly blown up in Crimea. Philip had no thought of safety for himself in that moment. The true Philip had been selfless.

Now Jack had a choice: be the good man he desperately wanted to be, the man Philip had once looked up to, or bind himself into the monster.

Ivy's eyes bulged with panic. She knew him well enough to know what he would do before he said it.

"Don't do it, Jack! Leave now! Do not let her take hold of you again."

Jack's eyes softened as he looked at his wife. Anything required of him . . .

"As if I could leave you." He tossed the blade away and looked at Philip. "I vowed never to become the monster again, but I can't allow someone else to become the killer in my place."

"Stubborn man. Always having to be the hero." Ivy swung her leg sideways and knocked the guard off his feet, then thrust upward, aiming her head for Dragavei's chin. She missed, clipping Dragavei's cheek instead.

Seizing the miscalculation, Dragavei snatched the shawl from her head and flung it around Ivy's throat, yanking the ends tight as she pressed the tip of the needle to Ivy's neck.

"No, wait!" Philip struggled to his feet, his eyes focused on Dragavei. "Take me instead. Only spare her."

"I do not want you. Your weakness is a blight to everything I am striving to achieve. And the woman will die as punishment for every Order member she has executed." A smile pulled at Dragavei's lips. "But this choice I give to you: she can die excruciatingly at my hand, or you can take the needle and administer a swift death to her yourself."

Philip's eyes widened in shock as his eyes darted to Ivy. A strangled noise escaped his lips.

"As if there is a choice. We both know you will do anything to keep her from pain." Dragavei yanked on the scarf, exposing the throbbing vein in Ivy's neck, then held out the syringe to Philip. "Release him."

The guards stepped away from him. He approached and took the syringe in his shaking hand. He stared at the needle for a long moment as his free hand curled into a claw, digging into the side of his head.

"Good memories erased and human weakness twisted to evil for your use." His free hand dropped as he turned to look at Jack. Something flickered there. The shadow of a bond shared long ago. "I've done many things wrong in my life, but I don't consider this one of them."

He swung around and stabbed Dragavei in the neck.

"Run, Ivy!"

Ivy scrambled to her feet. Jack sprinted toward her.

Boom!

The north wall exploded. Flying stone slammed into racks of weapons, scattering them into broken pieces across the floor.

Jack lunged over fallen rocks from the wall. Ivy stumbled as guards lurched after her.

Boom!

A second explosion tore through the eastern wall, splitting the fortress open to the darkening sky. Guards were flung from the catwalk, their bodies crunched beneath the spewing stone. Those remaining fled, not bothering to help their comrades who clung to the broken rails by their bleeding fingertips.

Dragavei was on her back, her feet tangled in rocks, wriggling to free herself. Ivy crawled to the dead guard and grasped his knife between her palms, sawing it through her bindings. Jack reached her and took the knife, making short work of slicing the ropes.

Boom!

Chunks of the western wall imploded. Jack threw himself on Ivy as a large chunk of stone flew over their heads, missing them by mere inches, and smashed into the floor. Smoke and fire poured in through the holes in the walls.

"Don't let them get away!" Dragavei screeched as she yanked the needle from her neck. Eyes gone wild, she was a demon possessed as she clawed at the rubble covering her feet.

"Guards!"

Fleeing guards swerved back to Ivy and Jack at her command. Jack pulled Ivy's arm, but she ground in her heels with frantic desperation and pointed to where Philip lay trapped beneath a pile of bricks close to Dragavei.

"We have to help him."

Survival and justice battled within Jack's moral compass, one he'd thought long since broken. In that moment it pushed aside everything and ticked again, propelling him toward Philip.

The ceiling crackled.

Jack's terrified eyes met Philip's.

"Get out of here!" Philip waved him away as Dragavei pushed out of the rocks and swayed over Philip.

"Not without you."

"Always the hero." Grunting in pain, Philip reached as far as his trapped body would allow and grabbed Dragavei's ankle. From his shirt pocket he took out a grenade. He pulled the pin.

"I always wanted to go out with a bang. Forgive me, brother."

Dragavei screamed, but Philip held tight.

The ceiling cracked with a mighty roar.

Jack sprinted to Ivy, slung her over his shoulder, and raced toward the door as the ceiling gave way.

A second later, another explosion.

"Philip!" Ivy's scream reverberated in Jack's ear as he raced on.

Smoke choked the air, writhing through the rubble like a serpent and flicking its scorching tongue to the sky. It burned Jack's eyes as he struggled to keep Ivy upright. Fire roared behind them, greedily licking splintered shelves.

A familiar figure crouched low in what was left of the bailey's doorway. The wall around it had been blown to piles of dust and ash.

"Jack! Ivy! This way!" Washington. Blood trickled from a gash on his forehead as he motioned them onward.

"Where have you been?" Ivy swiped ash from her face, leaving gray tear streaks on her cheeks. "I thought you were dead when the tower floor gave way."

"And leave you to fend for yourselves? You still have a thing or two to learn from me, Agent Vale."

They raced out of the collapsing bailey and across the courtyard. All around them Order guards scattered like ants with their nest on fire.

"Victor and the Hungarians have set more explosives around the perimeter. They should be waiting for us outside," Washington said as they ran. "We have four minutes at most before this entire place goes up. I saw an escape route when setting up the explosives."

Veering away from the tower that would take them back to the cave, Washington led them to a drainage gate built along the bottom half of the northern defense wall. He kicked at the rusted metal until it gave way.

They fled the castle ruins to the lake where Victor waited by a single boat. Besides the cave, it was the only way out of the mountain stronghold.

"Hurry up, you lot," Victor said, untethering the boat. "I sent the other agents to wait down the mountain."

They piled in and Jack and Washington grabbed the oars while Ivy and Victor squeezed between them as they paddled for dear life. Behind them, stone and earth rumbled, then roared as the castle erupted into an inferno that torched the night sky.

THIRTY-THREE

IVY HAD NEVER CONSIDERED IT POSSIBLE FOR THE SAME HEART TO BREAK yet again in a million different pieces. For those pieces, already shattered from loss long ago, to shudder once more with each sob and drown beneath a flood of tears. For those pieces, so carefully stitched back together, to rip apart again without care for the old scars.

She would have thought those pieces would collapse into a heap of pain so unbearable that they would never again stir to life enough to rebreak. But pain had a life force all its own. It gathered that agonizing pile of memories, laughter, and love and jammed a searing blade into its gut, forcing out a single cry.

Philip.

Tears coursed down her cheeks, rolling off her chin and plopping onto her knees, drawn up to her chest, her arms clutching them tight. He had been her brother, her friend, her shelter, her home. He had shared her smiles and tears. He had been part of her, and he had betrayed her. Had betrayed them all. Yet in the end, he had saved them.

Philip had been woven with flaws and goodness—who wasn't? Perhaps one day she would summon the strength to understand why he allowed darkness to set his path. But today it was too much.

"I'd forgotten how badly head wounds bleed." Washington

lowered himself to the grass next to her. He touched the gash on his forehead. In the haze of moonlight, the dried blood shone a dull brown.

They sat on a hill at the edge of a forest with the river they had escaped on rustling softly over rocks behind them. All around them the furtive sounds of evening emerged. A chilled breeze through the trees. The flap of owl wings. The cold sigh of the earth as it turned away from the warming sun.

Farther back through the thick trees loomed the Transylvanian Alps, their rugged peaks stark as teeth against the fire burning in their cratered middle. Through a sheen of tears Ivy had watched the fire's shadows gnawing against the rocky sides as the castle burned like the mouth of hell while they paddled away. She had no desire to witness it again and kept her gaze on Târgoviște glowing sleepily on the nighttime horizon.

"We need to find a first aid kit or you'll be sporting a humdinger of a scar," she said.

"It shall only add a bit of danger to my otherwise mysteriously erudite appearance." He stretched out his legs with a groan. "I fear I also have a few broken ribs that insist upon clacking together with each breath I take. Quite annoying really. I may have a fractured wrist as well. Are you all right?"

She shrugged. "Overall soreness and some nasty bruises. Nothing I haven't managed before."

"That is not what I meant," he said softly.

She discreetly rubbed a leaked tear against her shoulder but failed to control the accompanying sniff. "I know."

They sat quietly as a breeze tugged leaves from their branches and frosted the air with coming winter. Cold shifted up from the ground, leaching through her clothes to chill her skin. She didn't bother moving; she rather welcomed the numbing sensation that cinched around her body and constrained the chaos ringing inside.

Washington shifted next to her, grunting as he tried to find a comfortable position. "Over the past few weeks, I've been giving serious consideration to the future. Though you may protest, I do believe my years have been catching up to me." He waited a beat for her to disagree, but she only offered the flicker of a smile. "Ahem. This mission has been the jolt I needed to know that my sentence is complete, and retirement beckons."

Suddenly the air froze around her. "Retirement? You can't."

"Whyever not?"

"Because . . . because you're Washington!" She sputtered as if he'd suggested the White House was to be axed apart and used for firewood. The moon to career from its orbit or the tide to flow sideways. It simply wasn't done. "You are Talon."

"My dear, Talon has been, is, and will continue to be. Many captains have steadied her helm, and it is time that I step aside and allow fresh blood to steer the course. Someone's hands into which I can place her with confidence, knowing she will be well guided." His gazed fixed firmly on her, waiting, studying, calculating. As if adding up the pros and cons that tipped a person's true character on the scales.

Long ago she had found that stare nearly unbearable, always wondering if she could ever measure up. Then she had learned to meet his eye and dare him to find the faults. There had been many, certainly, but he never made her feel as though she was less because of her shortcomings. He offered her the opportunities to repair them.

She gazed back at him, bold as brass, not in challenge but in respectful understanding. Slowly, she shook her head. "I am deeply honored, but no."

"Talon would do well under your leadership. After all, I mentored you."

"Talon has been my home and family and it always will be, but my heart isn't there anymore." Her gaze drifted to a lone figure standing on the tip of the hill about twenty yards away. Jack was little more than a black outline against the darkening sky, but in him her entire world centered.

"Beatrix could certainly whip new agents into shape."

"If I could drag her and Victor apart long enough." Washington shifted again and sighed. "Perhaps I'll entice her to delay their wedding to hunt down Order members. Dragavei may be gone and world leaders safe enough from a doomsday execution, but her followers remain. They'll need to be eliminated. Care to join us in the hunt?"

Jack turned so his face was in profile. Still dark in the dimming light, but she could trace the smoothness of his forehead, the straight nose, full lips. Images she had called to the surface of her memory all those nights she'd lain awake and alone in her cold bed. He had felt so near she could almost sense him next to her. She would smile against the pillow, a rush of warmth and peace stealing her away to better times. Before she had become the Maiden. A name forged in heartbreak and revenge, splotched with blood and reeking of death. It deserved to be forever buried.

Smiling, she shook her head again. "I think not, but I wish you the best of luck." She stood and offered him her hand.

Washington rose and took her hand, turned it palm down, and bowed over it in a courtly manner. "As I wish you the best of luck, Mrs. Vale." Releasing her, he stepped back and squinted down the hill. "I do believe Victor and those Hungarian fellows are taking their time in locating a wagon to transport us. I'll go see what the holdup is."

Ivy frowned at the way he cradled his middle as if to hold in the broken bones. "Should you be moving so much?"

"I require a hot bath, food, and a physician. None of which are to be found standing here."

She knew his leave-taking was as much for his own comfort as to give her and Jack privacy. Seizing the opportunity, she moved over to where he stood and slipped her arms around him from behind. Comfort washed through her as she pressed her cheek to his back and felt the rise and fall of each breath he took. He smelled of blood and death. Gunpowder flowed in his veins and fire burned in his eyes, but she would take it all. He was her star, burning her, guiding her, and without him her world knew only darkness.

"I would stand here sometimes." His quiet, deep tone rumbled. "Not all my memories have returned, but I do remember that. Standing here with snow piled a foot high around my legs, watching the stars rise over the horizon. It was so cold some nights, but I didn't seem to feel it. I would just stand here watching as lights pricked the sky, shining brighter and brighter until they seemed the only life pulsing against the blackness. I can't say it gave me a sort of peace—too much Dust was filling me for that kind of sentiment—yet it meant something to me. To a part of me that wasn't dead."

Ivy linked her hands over his flat stomach, squeezing tight. Had she not done the same? Staring up into the night, feeling a pull that ached to her core?

"I never wanted to feel that deadness again, but then when we met Philip in Paris and I knew him. I remembered Baikal—" Jack swallowed hard. "I would have welcomed the nothingness then. Anything to cut off the pain of betrayal striking my very soul. Then you said he could not be blamed for his actions because his mind had been manipulated, and I felt—Death would have been a sweeter torment than your absolution of his deeds."

The anguish in his voice cut straight to the guilt blistering inside her, lancing through her excuses and flaying open the rawness. "Jack, I was wrong to—"

He spun around with such speed it nearly knocked her off her feet. Grabbing her hands, he pressed them hard to his chest.

"I need you to listen." His fingers dug into the delicate bones of her hands as his eyes bored into hers, silencing her with desperation.

"I hated him. I wanted to rip the bones from his body, burn them to ash, and spit on them. I wanted to riddle his carcass with bullets. I wanted to flood his veins with Dust until he drowned in it. I wanted him to feel my pain because only pure hatred could have driven him to such evil. But why? How could the man I called brother have allowed a devil like Dragavei to feed on his insecurities and hurts?"

His lips pressed tightly together into a bloodless seam as his throat muscles convulsed. The night had grown dark with the barest wisp of moonlight peeking out from behind clouds, but it was enough for Ivy to see his tears gathering.

"I understood today." The tears spilled, racing down his cheeks in surrender. "I betrayed him first."

"No, Jack. You would never—"

"Lake Baikal. I left him there! He waited for my rescue until he gave up. He lost faith in me and was forced to place it elsewhere. All because he was scared." Another tear careened down his face, a silver bullet streaking through the ash and filth covering his skin. It shot off his chin and struck their hands locked against his chest.

Tears clouded Ivy's eyes as her blistering guilt boiled up, exposing her need to be purged of the poison trapped within. "He wasn't the only one scared. I made excuses for him because I didn't want to face the truth of his betrayal. Because then I could no longer live under the illusion of a happy family, which is all I have ever wanted."

"All *we* have ever wanted."

She nodded as the tears fell, hot and greedy with pain. "Our cobbled-together family broken apart—it was my greatest fear come to life, and I was desperate to keep it from happening. Even to the point of hurting you. Will you forgive me?"

"Only if you forgive me for putting you in danger because of my own vindictiveness."

"Our pasts have a lot to beg forgiveness for. I only wish Philip were here. I didn't get a chance to tell him everything I wanted to."

There was no stopping the purge of poison now. It boiled out fast and hard, blinding her with tears of anguish.

Jack pulled her close, tucking her head under his chin and circling his arms around her like a protective wall that held in her brokenness.

"Neither did I." Ragged emotion crippled his voice. "He died saving us, and that says more than all the pain, lies, treachery, and tears we've endured, and for now, that's enough."

They stood holding each other for countless minutes, hours, or lifetimes. Who bothered to count? And in that sure, steady moment, they simply were.

Too soon his arms loosened and he took a half step back, leaving Ivy with the inexorable desire to follow.

"There's something else." He pulled a dented bullet from his pocket and held it in his open palm. *Philip* gleamed dully up at them. "He deserves to be put to rest."

Ivy's own bullet carved with Dragavei's name was buried somewhere in the rubble of the fortress after her gun had been confiscated when the guards captured her. She hadn't shot it into that monster's head, but her evil had been stopped all the same.

Kneeling in silence, they scraped away handfuls of dirt in the cold ground and gently placed the bullet in the hole. Together, they covered it with earth.

A tear slipped down Ivy's nose and plopped onto the disturbed earth. Her necklace of interlinking circles slipped free from the confines of her blouse as she leaned forward to rake over the tear-splotched dirt before she stood.

Jack stood, blinking back wetness from his own eyes, and stroked a finger down the necklace chain to where the rings rested over her heart. With great reverence, he gently cupped the silver circles in his palm. Like a sinner cradling his alms before an altar. With his other hand he gently drew her blouse away from her throat and moved to slip the necklace beneath the material.

Ivy closed her hand around his, their mingled fingers bruised and stained to clash against the silver chain. She lowered the rings to rest outside her blouse.

"Here. For all the world to see." Cradling his face between her hands, she drew him down to rest his forehead against hers. "We're free, Jack. No more hiding."

Eyes briefly closing, he put his arms around her and drew her close into his harbor of safety. When they opened again, the blueness was dark and steady.

"No more hiding."

His kissed her then. Slow and deep, and a thousand pinpricks of light exploded behind her closed eyelids.

"Will you do something for me?" she asked moments later when they stood quietly together collecting their breath. Why she asked was beyond her reckoning—perhaps it was the need to share words with him, to voice out loud desires that had simmered inside her for so long. Inquiring was a mere formality. If asked, he would kill for her, but she would never ask for that because he instinctively moved to protect without her needing to say anything. As she did for him. As they would always do for each other.

"Anything." He kissed her cheek.

She smiled as the warmth lingered and spread. As it always did and always would.

"Take me home."

EPILOGUE

JACK CHECKED THE EMPTY CHAMBER OF HIS PISTOL BEFORE SETTLING IT into the holster strapped to his suspenders. He picked up two small knives and flicked his thumb across the blades to test for sharpness before slipping one into his waistband and the other into the top of his boot. All these months later and his hand longed for the reassuring weight of his familiar gun, Undertaker, but it was buried beneath smoked rubble in Romania. Along with his old blades. He now had the severe misfortune of adjusting himself to new weapons.

Not that he needed weapons at the picture show, but old habits died hard. Despite no further rumblings of the Order or a new leader hoping to take up the mantle, he couldn't shake the urge to look over his shoulder whenever the odd shadow fell across his path.

The possibility of catching the newest Charlie Chaplin picture was looking less and less likely if his wife didn't hurry. She'd gone into town for groceries nearly two hours ago. Most likely she'd been cornered by the mayor's wife, who had taken it upon herself to recruit Ivy into the local sewing bee. A mission bound for failure.

He checked his reflection in the mirror above the bedroom

bureau. Clean shirt, pressed trousers, hair neatly trimmed and combed to the side, necktie slung around his neck to be secured at the last possible minute. No hat. The thought of having anything closing over his head still made him break out in a cold sweat all over his body. It was a deeply rooted reaction he doubted he would ever overcome.

He spread his hands over the bureau's wooden top, his grenade pin wedding ring shining a dull silver against the smooth dark grain. This was what helped keep the demons at bay—furniture he made with his own hands.

Pale yellow curtains had been hung over the window by his wife. Pictures of the two of them in silver frames lined a shelf. A postcard from Jamaica where Beatrix and Victor were honeymooning rested on the bedside table. Ivy had declared it the perfect location for their own revised honeymoon, the first one being entirely too brief, freezing, and not private in the least. He patted the front of his shirt pocket where two boat tickets bound for the Bahamas awaited. He would surprise her with them after the movie.

A cool, enticing breeze shuffled through the open window and beckoned him closer. Leaning his hands on the sill, he stuck his head outside and inhaled the scents of changing leaves and crisp earth that wafted over the backyard and settled across his shoulders like returning friends. Heralds of autumn across the threshold of the home he and Ivy had built together.

He had wanted to rebuild on his great-aunt's property, but Ivy convinced him otherwise. They sold that land with its terrible memories and bought a place all their own farther down the river, tucked among the trees and sheltered in the shadows of the Shenandoah Mountains. It wasn't quite finished, but there was a roof and walls, doors and windows, and each day Ivy added another touch of paint or curtains to make it a home.

Their home.

It would have been easy to use the money Jefferson had willed to him, but Jack couldn't stomach it. Instead he sought atonement by donating the inheritance in full to Talon. A new headquarters was well under way at their old address on Massachusetts Avenue. Washington had invited them to the completion day celebration come the new year when Beatrix—who had chosen the sobriquet Jackson but denied it had anything to do with his volatile temper—stepped into her role as Talon Master Agent incumbent, but Jack wasn't certain about attending. Many agents believed him a murderous traitor. Perhaps those bloodstains would never wash clean from his hands, certainly not from his soul, but he was slowly coming to reconciliation with his past, if not peace.

"*You're a good man,*" Ivy had said to him the other night as they lay entangled in the cozy quietness of their bed.

He knew better. The memories of horror would forever haunt him as penitence.

"*I'm not,*" he had whispered as he softly stroked her hair in the starlit darkness enfolding them. "*But I love you for thinking it's possible.*"

The sound of an old Ford's tires churned into the dirt drive out front. Jack grinned. Ivy was home. The kitchen's screen door screeched open as he hurried down the stairs.

"I was about to send out a patrol," he said, rounding into the kitchen while wrangling the ends of his flapping tie. "Mind giving me a hand with this? You're at perfect eye level to keep the knot from going sideways."

She stood at the sink with her back turned. A pile of mail littered the floor at her feet.

He stopped and frowned. "What's wrong?"

"Absolutely nothing." She turned to him with a dazed expression. Late-afternoon sunlight gleamed over her resized grenade pin wedding ring as her fingers shook, holding an open envelope and piece of paper.

"It's from the Richmond orphanage. They have a brother and sister no one will take. They want to know if we will."

Jack's jaw could have plunged to the newly sanded floorboards. "The orphanage."

They had written to the Richmond Orphanage for Lost Children months ago, and each day Ivy returned dejected from gathering the mail. Until today.

"Couples go in looking for babies. No one wants the older children. Especially not a pair. This pair is four and five." She drew out each syllable as if testing their validity.

"Not much younger than we were as orphans."

"Yes." A smile curved her lips. "What shall I tell the orphanage?"

"We won't tell them anything. We'll leave first thing in the morning and bring our children home tomorrow." Tie forgotten, he grabbed his wife around the waist and twirled her high in the air.

Ivy laughed as joy bloomed across her face. It sank deep into him, loosening the knots of fear and doubt that tried to snarl him. For all the wrongs he had committed, for all the heartache they had endured, here was the chance to begin anew. To find the happiness they had sought for so long.

"A family, Jack." Tears glistened along her lower lashes.

He carefully lowered her feet to the floor and kissed her forehead. "I know, love." Gathering her in his arms, he began to rock them back and forth to a familiar tune.

"All that I ask of you is love."

"A long time ago, when Dragavei first filled me with Dust, she asked me to describe home. It was a form of torture to see how much of the injection was required before such memories were wiped clear." He took her right hand in his and threaded their fingers. Delicate and pale against calloused and scarred.

"I started describing the strands of gold in your hair, the color of your eyes in the rain, the sweet rose scent of your skin, until I realized she had expected me to talk about a place."

Ivy lifted her head. Rays from the setting sun mingled with radiant life in the brilliant green of her eyes. "Do you feel like you're home now?"

He nodded. "You?"

Pressing her lips to his, she joined his humming.

"Without you, life is incomplete. I'm yours beyond recall."

"With you, always."

The End

AUTHOR'S NOTE

THIS WAS A HEAVY BOOK TO WRITE. MUCH OF THE SUBJECT MATTER (TRAGedy, death, and breaking hearts) forced me to dig deep and pull out the ugliest and most broken emotions a human being can experience. However, I firmly believe that in order to appreciate the light, one must walk through the darkness.

While I do my utmost best to represent history in truth, please keep in mind that this is fiction. A real man named Vlad the Impaler did exist. Did he form a secret society that carried on for centuries in a crumbling castle buried in the Romanian mountainside . . . eh, I doubt it. That's why writing fiction is fun. I can take the cool bits of history and ask the all-powerful question, *What if?* But just to set the record straight, I've included a few facts for your consideration.

PTSD

In 1927, the term *shell shock* was used to describe the suffering of soldiers who fought during the Great War. Nightmares, flashes of violence, depression, confusion, and fatigue are but a sampling of the symptoms. Today we have a better understanding of this condition, known as post-traumatic stress disorder, which is triggered by experiencing or witnessing a terrifying event and is not relegated to soldiers. Many characters in *To Free the Stars* deal with trauma of some kind. Ivy lost her husband and child. Jack was forced to become a brain-washed assassin. Philip was tortured and haunted by betrayal and then his own guilt.

I tried to show different aspects of the condition and ways individuals deal with their own trauma, some trying to move past it while others are so steeped in the pain that they don't see a way out. In no way could I have covered the vast and varying degrees of symptoms experienced by those affected, so I chose what made sense for each character and how their particular personality would handle the pain burning within. Ivy chose to funnel her fury into becoming the Maiden. Jack could not abide having anything near his face after being muzzled for so long. And Philip chose to feed his anger by lashing out in revenge.

PTSD is not a condition that will simply go away after a few kind words and hugs. It is a condition that latches on deeply to its victim's conscious and subconscious. Time, patience, and therapy are all ways to help alleviate parts of the trauma, but it is not one easily rooted out. If ever.

My aim is never to make light of such suffering, and perhaps this story will encourage anyone feeling overwhelmed or hurt from a past trauma to seek the help they need. Throwing peas across the dinner table is never the answer!

Josephine Baker

An American-born dancer, singer, and actress, Josephine Baker dominated the entertainment scene of the 1920s. Dubbed the Black Venus and Black Pearl, she was the first black woman to star in a major motion picture, but she was not welcome on her home soil and quickly found acceptance in Paris with the Folies Bergère, performing in a short skirt of bananas and a beaded necklace that became an iconic image for the carefree Jazz Age.

During World War II, Josephine aided the French Resistance by gathering intelligence at parties and night clubs and writing the information in invisible ink on her sheet music. She also hid Resistance fighters and supporters in her French château and supplied them with visas. After the war she was awarded the Croix de Guerre for her brave contributions and named Chevalier of the Légion d'Honneur by General Charles de Gaulle. She then went on to tour America as a performer but was often denied acknowledgment as a star because of racial discrimination. The hatred pained her deeply, and she soon became an advocate for civil rights, refusing to perform for segregated crowds and attending the 1963 March on Washington as the only official female speaker alongside Martin Luther King Jr.

Josephine truly did own a cheetah named Chiquita whom she bonded with while performing a night club act together. They became inseparable friends, strolling about Paris together, Chiquita on a diamond leash, traveling the world, attending the movie theater, and even sharing the same bed.

This woman led an incredible, often scandalous, but always brave life. Sadly enough, today she is mostly remembered for her banana skirt.

Helena Dragavei

The Silver One is a fictional villainess who was inspired by the real-life Helena Blavatsky, a Russian mystic who was the nineteenth century's most famous occultist and godmother of the New Age movement. Fascinated by all things religion, philosophy, and science, she cofounded the Theosophical Society in 1875, which proclaimed it was reviving an "Ancient Wisdom" as an underlay to all world religions.

Madame Blavatsky and her cofounders traveled to India, where they learned much about Hinduism and Buddhism, and afterward traveled to the United States and England spreading the influence of Eastern religions to Western cultures. Capitalizing on the era's obsession with spiritualism, she wrote a number of books explaining her philosophies while also partaking in seances, earning praise as a sage from her champions and condemnation as a charlatan from critics.

Père Lachaise Cemetery

I remember watching one of the Fantastic Beasts movies and being struck by the scene of Grindelwald's followers meeting in a cemetery with a hidden amphitheater. Johnny Depp gave this rousing speech about purebloods and blue fire was all around. Of course, I immediately looked up the details to see where this scene was filmed and knew without a doubt I had to include it somehow in my story. While neither Johnny Depp nor a fire dragon make an appearance in *To Free the Stars*, Père Lachaise Cemetery serves as the setting for the Silver One's gathering with her followers, which the Talon team is only too happy to break up.

This necropolis is the largest in Paris and most visited by people from all over the world. Established as a cemetery by Napoleon when other burial sites were filled or closed, he declared, "every citizen has the right to be buried regardless of race or religion." However, as the cemetery was outside the city boundaries and not blessed by the Roman Catholic Church, many refused to be buried there. It wasn't until the remains of Jean de La Fontaine and Moliere were transferred to the cemetery that its popularity began to grow, and people clamored to be buried next to the famous citizens, which now include Jim Morrison of The Doors, the French singer Ediaf Piaf, the dancer Isadora Duncan, the writer Oscar Wilde, and composer Frederic Chopin.

The grounds have been expanded several times and now include a columbarium for cremations and several monuments for those killed during war, victims of concentration camps, and victims of the Paris working class uprising. Burials still take place at Père Lachaise Cemetery, but there is a waiting list, and it has strict rules: the person wishing to be buried must have lived or died in Paris.

A Few Other Fun Facts:

- Lady Caroline Lamb did live at Dover House and had a notorious love affair with Romantic poet Lord Byron. However, I doubt she used a secret elevator to canoodle with him.
- The Gaslight Club was a real speakeasy located in the historic Gaslight Club building at 1020 16th Street NW. Entry was gained on the third floor through the men's restroom by turning a faucet. Today, it's simply an unassuming office building.
- The citizens of Târgoviște were indeed punished by Vlad III for their involvement in the assassination of his brother. The elite were killed, and the young were sent as slaves to build Poenari Castle, which was featured in *The Brilliance of Stars*.
- I taste-tested a few 1920s drinks for research purposes and the gin rickey, which Ivy orders, is a lovely and refreshing choice for a hot summer day.
- Gadsby's Tavern has been operating since 1785 and hosted many notable guests who helped shape America, such as

George and Martha Washington, John Adams, Thomas Jefferson, and Marquis de Lafayette. Sadly, I could not find evidence that a secret agency named Talon was headquartered here.

ACKNOWLEDGMENTS

TWO VERY LONG YEARS—THAT'S WHAT IT HAS TAKEN FOR THIS STORY TO percolate, find its way, backtrack, then find its way again as I rewrote, struggled, laughed, and cried all the way to the finish line. Honestly, it's starting to feel a little long in the tooth. It has seen a changeover in editors, three book releases, depression, return to stay-at-home mom, homeschooling, breakdowns, relocating my office to the basement just to get away, and more than a few extra pounds I wasn't sporting two years ago. Most of this can be attributed to COVID-19, the dreaded plague that turned the world upside down and nearly broke my sanity. Thankfully, as I sit here writing this, it appears that the worst days are behind us, and we can start planning for the future again instead of resigning ourselves to life as shut-ins.

I know I mentioned in notes of the previous book—gee, I think I did. It's been so long since I wrote it—that this story idea came because I was watching too many Marvel movies, particularly the Captain America ones that left me wondering what would happen if the Winter Soldier fell in love. I set out to answer precisely that. The first half of Jack and Ivy's story is the foundation of how they met and fell in love. It's filled with lovey-dovey goodness, and that's fantastic, but it's really this second half that drew me to answering that question in the first place. What happens when the person you love most in the world goes off the deep end? What lengths will you go to in order to bring them back? I wanted to explore what that love looks like after ten years apart and becoming different people. Can it resemble what it once was, or must it become something new entirely? Jack and Ivy's relationship is put through the wringer of guilt, trauma, loss, and tragedy. Each turn seems insurmountable, but they forge ahead and learn to accept each other all over again for who they are and not simply because of who they were. It is only with that acceptance that hope begins to bloom for them.

Dear reader, I hope you are able to laugh, cry, smile, and rage with them. Most importantly, I hope you love them as much as I do.

P.S. It helps when you imagine Sebastian Stan as Jack. Just sayin' :)

Linda, thank you for your unwavering support and for always championing great stories!

To my fearless editors, I am indebted to you for sticking with me for so long and through the ongoing growing pains of this story. Jocelyn, for first believing in Jack and Ivy when I pitched them to you over breakfast at the American Library Association conference way back in 2020 (I still think it would make a great trilogy). Laura, for coming onboard halfway through with a fresh enthusiasm I really needed to keep going. And Jodi, somehow you have slogged through my line edits and yet still want to work with me. You ladies are the best!

To the incredible team at Thomas Nelson who make me look awesome and never quit trying to reach as many readers as possible. I'm so grateful you've got my back!

Rachel McMillan and Aimie K. Runyan, not only are you amazing storytellers, you're pretty great human beings too. Y'all kept me sane during lockdown as we plotted our novella collection and tried not to go crazy together. And no matter what you say, termites are not as exciting as fire, Aimie.

Kim, my sparkly unicorn. You're always there with a willing ear as I go on and on about Buck Winter. And you're hands down the best plotter ever, especially with a glass of wine or two. Kristen, do you remember cobbling together ideas on our trip to Roanoke? The story may look a little different from when we first discussed it, but man, did we have a blast.

To Benjin's Asian Bistro. How I missed your delicious combination fried rice, and it was you who we ordered from first after lockdown was lifted. I will always crave your amazingness!

Bryan and Miss S, I know you've put up with a lot from me over the past two years as I tried to write this thing. Through days of shutting myself in the basement and tears of frustration because my creativity had dried up, you never stopped believing in me and encouraging me to keep going. I would not be here without you.

DISCUSSION QUESTIONS

Includes spoilers!

1. Over the course of ten years after losing her husband, Ivy Vale transformed herself into a ruthless assassin in an effort to smother her heartache. With all her suffering, do you see this as a natural progression of her character?
2. At first Jack finds it impossible to forgive Philip for what he considered a betrayal of the worst kind. Ivy, on the other hand, still saw Philip as the lost orphan boy and wanted their relationship to return to how it once was—when the three of them were a family. Who do you believe was right?
3. Loyalty plays a strong role in *To Free the Stars*. Do the characters have a similar definition of loyalty, or does it differ from one to another? How are their loyalties tested through each of their unique trials?
4. Ivy and Jack were reunited after a decade of separation. How did those lost years affect the dynamic of their relationship?

5. How does Talon, the secret agency, function as a character in the story? How does it dictate the characters' actions and, in some instances, spur them to rebellion?

6. Philip was once Jack and Ivy's greatest friend and brother, but his abandonment on Lake Baikal changed something in him. Ultimately, do you feel sorry for Philip or hate him for his retaliation and lies?

7. Ivy never gave up believing Jack could be rescued from his torment. Do you find her devotion admirable or delusional?

8. After everything they endured, do you think Jack and Ivy should have stayed within the safety and familiarity of Talon, or were they right to seek happiness on their own terms?

9. Do you think Jack truly tamed his demons, or is there a threat of them resurfacing?

10. How far would you go to save a loved one?

ABOUT THE AUTHOR

Photo by Bryan Ciesielski

A BESTSELLING AUTHOR WITH A PASSION FOR HEART-STOPPING ADVEN-ture and sweeping love stories, J'nell Ciesielski weaves fresh takes into romances of times gone by. When not creating dashing heroes and daring heroines, she can be found dreaming of Scotland, indulging in chocolate of any kind, or watching old black-and-white movies. She is a Florida native who now lives in Virginia with her husband, daughter, and lazy beagle.

★★★

jnellciesielski.com
Instagram: @jnellciesielski
Pinterest: @jnellciesielski